W9-BPJ-031

For Georgia and John, and for the old town

Stealing Fatima

FRANK X. GASPAR

Stealing Fatima

— a novel —

COUNTERPOINT
BERKELEY

Copyright © 2009 by Frank X. Gaspar. All rights reserved under International and Pan-American Copyright Conventions.

This is a work of fiction. Names, characters, places, and incidents are the product of the author's imagination or are used fictitiously. Any resemblance to actual persons, living or dead, is entirely coincidental.

Library of Congress Cataloging-in-Publication Data

Gaspar, Frank, 1946–
Stealing Fatima : a novel / Frank Gaspar.
p. cm.
ISBN 978-1-58243-516-9
1. Clergy—Fiction. 2. Life change events—Fiction. 3. City and town life—Massachusetts—Fiction. 4. Redemption—Fiction. 5. Cape Cod (Mass.)—Fiction. I. Title.

PS3557.A8448S74 2009
813'.54—dc22

2009029152

Cover design by Natalya Balnova
Interior design by Megan Jones Design
Printed in the United States of America

COUNTERPOINT
2117 Fourth Street
Suite D
Berkeley, CA 94710

www.counterpointpress.com

Distributed by Publishers Group West

10 9 8 7 6 5 4 3 2 1

Speak more clearly, said Jesus. It's impossible, said God, human words are like shadows, and shadows cannot explain light, and between shadow and light stands the opaque body from which words are born.

—JOSE SARAMAGO

Virginity, like all monstrosities, has its peculiar richness, its absorbing grandeur. When chaste people have occasion to exert their bodies or their minds, when they are required to act, or think, they have muscles of steel; their intelligence is reinforced by intuitive knowledge—diabolical energy, or the black magic of the will. In this respect the Virgin Mary—regarding her for the moment only as a symbol—eclipses in her greatness all the Hindu, Greek or Egyptian archetypes. Virginity, mother of great things, magna parens rerum, holds in her fair white hands the key to higher worlds.

—HONORE DE BALZAC

"Our parson has gone mad!" cried Goodman Gray, *following him across the threshold.*

—NATHANIEL HAWTHORNE

one

A HIGH WIND, A GRAND WIND, BLEW IN FROM THE CHOPPY SEA ON the night Sarafino Pomba returned from the dead. Father Manuel Furtado would mention the wind in his ledgers, which he kept faithfully and obsessively, writing in them upstairs in the spare cell of his study during the late, black hours, when all the houses on the lane were dark and the church locked and the rectory silent save for the small ticks and creaking of the building's ancient wood. Early that evening the priest finished his supper in the little kitchen, cleaned his dishes and put them away in the cupboard, tidied the room, and went out to the parlor to sit in the wooden rocker before the window. He opened the window a crack just to feel the fresh air on his face, and he kept the room in darkness, the better to see outside. He was pleased at what he observed. Small strings and clusters of town kids roamed along Church Street. Today was the Vigil of Saints—All Hallows Eve—and the children were trick-or-treating their way up to the Halloween party in the parish hall, behind the church.

The center of town would be starting to bustle already along Front Street, a great carnival for the tourists and other People from Away—elaborate costumes and parties, shows in the noisy bars and bright cabarets, stunning drag queens parading in faultless riots of color—but here, just a few lanes back from the waterfront, a different town moved among smaller, quieter streets. The clear stars of fall had risen, and the gusting wind brought with it a mild chill and a brisk dampness from the ocean. The old teardropped streetlamps cast their grainy light along the hedges and fences, and the windows of the narrow houses shone white and yellow, and the porches and steps were lit, some with carved pumpkins whose candles flickered madly behind their slitted eyes and lipless grins with each flurry of the freshening wind. Father Furtado saw one or two skeletons or ghosts among the smaller children, but most of the costumes now seemed to come from popular movies or video games. The priest watched a random parade of serial killers with claw hands and ruined faces, outer-space creatures, galactic warriors, sometimes a fancy pirate, once in a while a ray-gun princess. A few preteens walked along with just a dollop of grease paint on their faces—more likely some mother's makeup—and wearing that new, safe, reflective clothing as they rapped on doors carrying pillowcases for sacks, or orange-and-black store-bought bags and plastic jack-o'-lantern buckets. But no one knocked at the rectory. Everyone knew that was not to be done and that there would be treats and gifts in the parish hall.

The priest looked on until the little street slowly cleared of travelers, and then he waited about thirty minutes before walking out the rectory's back door and crossing the parking lot to the party. It was merely an appearance. The priest was not expected to linger at such parties. But he circulated and spoke to everyone, kids and parents. Not as many were there as in the old days, when he himself was a child here in the town, but there were fewer families now, and he was pleased at the turnout. Indeed, since he had come back to take over the Parish of Our Lady of Fatima, attendance at everything was up and the town seemed to be pulling together again. It was what he had been sent to do. And now that Idalina Horta had left town—fled, the priest might say—Mariah Grey had stepped in and organized a splendid party. It was the first such *festa* in his memory that either Mrs. Horta or his own mother did not personally direct.

He took things in quickly. He did not want to appear to be supervising. Mariah and her party committee had hung the hall with orange and black crepe and decorated the walls and tables with bouquets of helium balloons and string-and-cotton spiderwebs. Suspended from the center of the hall's ceiling was an enormous piñata, a papier-mâché jack-o'-lantern head with a goofy grin and cartoon Band-Aids patched all over the sides of its face. It was one of Winslow's creations—the priest had no doubt about this. Its eyes were crossed—one had a black half-circle under it—and sticking out from the head, on thin, transparent wires, were little spirals and comic-book stars. The effect was that the head was already punch-drunk from being whacked with the piñata stick and was seeing these loopy things. But Winslow, clearly enacting a prank cooked up by the committee, had used her artistic touch to shape the eyes, the nose, the long mouth—even the hint of an ecclesiastical collar—so that the paper pumpkin head was unmistakably meant to resemble Father Manny himself. He could only wonder at what sort of prizes Winslow had stuffed inside the thing. But he would not hang around to see himself split open.

Beneath the piñata stood long bright tables—they would have to be moved later when the game began—and on them sat bowls of punch and beside them homemade congo bars stacked on paper plates, and trays of *trutas*, *suspiros*, and *malasadas* from Lucia Braga's Portuguese Bakery. Furtado had hoped to see his sister at the *festa*. She worked at Braga's bakery. She was going to bring the trays of sweets up to the hall, but she had called him earlier that afternoon to tell him that Tommy was in from fishing and she wouldn't be there. She said someone else on the committee—it was either Maureen Avellar or Joanna Nunes—would stop by the bakery and pick everything up. There was an off-putting tone in her voice, something pinched and short—breathless, almost. He didn't ask about it. He didn't want to open up any kind of discussion of her woes and troubles at that moment. And anyway, there was nothing unusual about Tom coming in early. All the boats would have motored in that afternoon ahead of the blow that was building up.

He took another circuit around the hall. He strolled, he joked with some of the kids. He noticed that Mariah also had seen to it that the younger ones got a bag of candies and finger-rosaries and little blue plastic miraculous medals with silver-looking chains. Older kids received small, abbreviated missals, all of which Mariah had bought on the Internet at half the price they would have cost through the nearest Catholic-supply outlet, all the way off the Cape, up in Calumet. Furtado watched her now, how she stayed in the background, how she was letting the mothers and grandmothers carry things forward, as they had always done for Mrs. Horta. A very few of the mothers were not taking well to Mariah, but most were warm and sociable, laughing with her, even hugging. When she'd first joined the church and then begun to volunteer so much time and energy, the priest hadn't had a complete picture of what she was capable of. He hadn't understood her right away. But it didn't take long before he saw that she was someone he needed, that she was just the sort of person to help him with his plans for the parish. She quickly became more and more important in the daily business of running the church. And as he looked back on it, it was inevitable that she and Mrs. Horta would clash. Perhaps if he had paid more attention, if he had been able to pull out of his own mind for a while, he might have done something. He might have seen what was coming and found a way to cut short—even avoid—all the unpleasantness. It was absurd that so much had to come from something as seemingly trivial as the squirrels.

Idalina Horta had worked for the parish since Furtado was a small boy. She seemed to live beyond time. Furtado could not even picture her anymore as a younger woman, as though she had always been gray and short and somewhat hunched, even when she had been Father Santos's parish secretary back when Furtado was growing up. For as long as she had worked for the parish, her husband, Louis, had been caretaker of the grounds and general handyman at the church. In his spare time he built and sold elaborate bird feeders in all manner of design. Some were like little cottages with glass walls so a person could see the level of birdseed inside, and others were fancy cylinders or miniature fishing boats. One was even a model of the Pilgrim's Tower, that commanding granite megalith that rose incongruously, nearly three hundred feet in the air, from the town's highest hill and that commemorated the town as the first landing place of the Pilgrims, though they'd found the land rough and bare and inhospitable and had not stayed and settled there. Louis Horta, with his narrow, expressionless face and long, thin hands, would walk the church grounds and make certain that the sparrows, finches, starlings, jays, catbirds, and robins were all fed through their seasons. But also the squirrels came. He didn't mind. He built more feeders and fed the squirrels, too.

This is what Mrs. Horta and Mariah had their final words about. Of course, with Mariah volunteering so much at the rectory office, Mrs. Horta had already been feeling pushed out. Furtado should have seen it. He did see it. This was what he chastised himself for. He saw it but it did not register, and it did not register because, underneath it all, his will was working in a way he did not wish to acknowledge. He needed new, energetic people to help with his plan for the parish, and he had a sense of having to carry the Hortas, who came with the church as a kind of legacy. They must have seen how he had been giving more and more of the important work to Mariah Grey and less to Mrs. Horta, who after all could not cope with the computer in the office, and who could offer him no real thinking about the directions he wanted to take the church in. He hadn't witnessed himself as being callous, but of course he should have moved far more gently. When he looked back on those days he saw all the small tensions, the little reverberations, between the two women. He saw them clearly now, but at the time they were occurring they passed over him with no touch whatsoever.

The argument—if that is what it was—started with apparent innocence. Mariah, who knew about such things, suggested that the Hortas were doing something harmful with the feeders. She talked about how the coyotes were already raiding the town for food, and she said that the feeders were pulling the squirrels from the woods, too, turning them into pests. "They need to stay wild," she had told them. But the Hortas were townspeople whose families had lived there since coming from the Azores in the 1880s, and Mariah was one of the New People from Away, and they did not appreciate what they felt was her superior attitude. Mariah at first thought their reaction to her had come from their disapproval of her living with Winslow, but the priest made it clear. The Hortas minded their own business about such things, as most of the townspeople had for generations. But they felt they were being bossed by an outsider, and that could be a problem. It was a delicate thing. He and Mariah talked about it, and then Mariah decided she would ease things by trying to apologize.

Furtado was not present for the final quarrel, so he did not witness its escalation. He could not imagine what either of them ended up saying to the other, but he knew that Mrs. Horta had become so agitated that she had to go home and lie down. "I tried to make it okay, Father Manny," Mariah had told him. "I truly did." She was shaken by the whole thing. And he had been clumsy when he called Idalina and tried to arbitrate. Finally, she'd accused him of taking Mariah's part. "I know all about you, Manny Furtado," she had said. "Don't think people in this town don't remember what you were like. Your father was a good man, God rest his soul, but you were always full of secrets and up to no good. Now you're with the outsiders." She sounded unhinged. The priest realized for the first time how much she disliked him. How it must be that she had always disliked him, and he, so foolish, thought he moved in nothing but her goodwill and affection. It was said that Mrs. Horta and his mother—those pillars of the church—competed for everything and were rivals for his father's hand when they were girls. They remained rivals and, losing out on Pai Furtado, Idalina prevailed at the church, becoming Father Santos's mainstay back in the day. Furtado noticed that in her screed, she did not mention his mother. Finally, he could do nothing with the old woman. She would not return to the church.

It was when Mrs. Horta lapsed into silence that she did her damage, for the priest did not hear from her again for weeks, during which she and Louis, with great dispatch, had sold their family house—grandly, he figured—into the booming real-estate market, and she began calling the diocese in Calumet with her complaints and stories. This was the worst time. Something had given way in her. Not a snapping, but a crumbling. Giving out like a kind of death. Such fear and confusion. She recanted later, after Father John Sweet had been sent from the archdiocese and an inquiry had begun. Sweet was a professional fixer, discreet and intense—an odd man—but not given to hasty judgments. Furtado would give him that much. Sweet had kept everything from the parish council except the barest generalities, which he and Furtado presented together, in case there was any talk going about. Furtado knew immediately who it had been when Father Sweet first came to tell him of the unidentified caller who had made troubling allegations about the diocese: the voice of an older woman.

The Hortas were already living off the Cape by then, but she was truly ashamed when confronted, and she explained the pressures. The New People. The town being unlivable. And Manny Furtado giving over to them. Opening the church to them. Pushing her aside. Belittling her in the town's eyes. So she made the calls and told about the priest's drinking and hoarding drugs. She had spied. She had snooped. The other part, the part she had made up, had been not just wrath or imagination, but something that had seized her as pure truth. Something that had been pointed to with hints and signs. Something that clicked into place like one of those exotic puzzle boxes, carved from dark wood, with sliding pieces and hidden latches. She believed it all utterly while she was saying it. She was not well. She had told them that the priest was interfering with young boys. *Interfering* was the word she had used.

Furtado was stunned by all this. He could only think that she had made something out of his affection—what else to call it?—for two of his Mass servers, two boys from among the few newer families that had immigrated to town from the Azores. Jose and Fernando. Joey and Freddie. He would spend time with them going over English—not just vocabulary, but getting them to pronounce with more of the American crispness. They were already lacing their language with the town's own variation of the New England accent. And they would spend a lot of time kicking the soccer ball around. This was something Furtado could do a little but not well, which they loved, for the priest, though barely into his fifties, must have seemed ancient to the boys, and they were keen with the ball, dribbling it up on their knees, showing him up and laughing. Still, soccer was something he could play at without aggravating the old injuries to his neck and shoulder, which had been flaring for some months, and he liked the exercise. He wanted to be kind to the boys. He knew it must be hard for them, coming here like this. Both of their fathers worked on fishing boats. One of them sailed out of New Bedford and was not home a lot. The mothers did not speak much English but clung to the church and were taken in by the women there.

Furtado's innocent affection was what Idalina saw. He understood extreme states of mind, and of course there were all those scandalous revelations rocking the Catholic Church everywhere—much to feed a wild imagination—but still, he could not comprehend the shadow that had moved over her.

Yet certain damage had been done. Regardless of the awful things that she had conjured in her mind, she had been accurate about the many bottles of liquor and the cache of medications she had found up in his study, and this was not the first time in Furtado's life that this problem had come up, as the diocese was well aware. It would keep an eye on him. So Father John Sweet and Father Manny Furtado had been brought together, toward whatever end, soul to soul.

It was according to the wishes of Father Sweet that Furtado sat at his desk and wrote in his ledgers every night. The writing was part of Sweet's prescription for him. It was not a penance but a form of therapy, for John Sweet, in his role as a fixer, was among all else a doctor of psychology, and he believed its methods were useful in his very difficult work. Sweet now came to meet with Furtado once a week to help with his sobriety, and they talked together and they prayed. Sweet could not have suspected what he was setting loose when he told Furtado to open himself, without holding anything back, in these private pages. Sweet referred to the pages as *journaling* but after a while—maybe surprised at how much time Furtado spent on them, maybe attempting irony because of how often Furtado mentioned references to Augustine in the beginning—called them his *Confessions*. Father Sweet never read from the voluminous entries, which Furtado kept up with a zeal that might have unnerved the other man, but he would use them as a starting place for conversation. He always asked how they were coming, if any discoveries had been made. Sometimes he suggested topics or pieces of scripture to begin from. They would in the end become important, for among their prosaic details, their threads and fragments and pieces, as well as his wild flights and long passages of narrative, would lie the only firsthand record of the events that were to unfold, but of course there were no intimations of that in the early going.

Furtado had found the blank ledgers—these particular, unwieldily proportioned books—in the attic of the rectory, back in August, when he'd finally become annoyed at the racket that the squirrels were making up there. His sister, Alzaida, had taken to feeding the animals after the Hortas had left, and now they scurried, leapt, crawled, and clambered in half-wild abundance through the churchyard's many tall trees and all around the grounds and buildings. Mariah Grey prudently said nothing further about them. It happened on a Saturday, the feast of Saint Maximilian Kolbe, martyr, Knight of the Immaculata, and it was the day before the Sunday of the feast of the Assumption of the Blessed Virgin Mary into heaven. It was exactly the afternoon after John Sweet and Furtado had finished their first official session and Sweet had finally left and driven up the long Cape back to Calumet.

Along with the directive to write his mind daily, Sweet had left Father Furtado with a good many things to think about. He had even given him a glossy notebook filled with printed handouts and numbered exercises, and with various pamphlets stuffed inside its slender vinyl pockets. Sweet called it literature. But Furtado had wanted only to put all that out of his mind for the time being. He had not yet figured out how much he would give up to Sweet and how much he would not. He wanted, at least for the moment, to purify his head of this strange priest and of the idea that he would be stuck with him now until who knew when. He decided on a physical task. He decided to have a look at what the pests were doing in the attic. He had a good hour before he needed to go over to the church to start the four o'clock confessions, so he found a flashlight and set up a stepladder in the tight hallway at the top of the stairs, pushed on the wooden hatch in the low ceiling, and crawled up under the angles of that ancient roof.

He had not been up there before. The space was gloomy and cramped, and the heat of the summer day had gathered and increased there, and now it struck him in the face. Slender bars of light canted in through the screened vents under the eaves, but he still needed the flashlight in order to see. Above him, the wooden sheathing of the roof was stained with age and punctuated in repeating patterns with the rust-dark and oddly blunt tips of shingling nails. The headroom was so low that he had to half walk, half squat over the uneven planks of the flooring. Everything was covered with dust and also with a fine grit, grainy and unpleasant to lay hands on.

He stopped and knelt, and he shined the light in sweeping arcs from side to side. He found droppings everywhere, and the remains of many nests, small heaps of trash and leaves and desiccated twigs, and more spoor. It must have been years since Louis Horta had come up to check. Old Louis Horta. Maybe it had been beyond him, getting up there. The priest himself felt the strain of being bent over in the cramped space. His neck and shoulder had already begun to nag him with their dreary ache.

As he rested a moment, he regarded the attic. It would all have to be cleaned out. It was a fire hazard, if nothing else. The space must have been used for storage at some time, for there were three or four boxes pushed against the east eave, just as it joined the wall. They were furred with dust and grime. He made his way to them. One contained a tangle of strings of primordial Christmas lights, the braided insulation on the wires brittle and flaking, the bulbs strangely large—fist-size, and faded to smoky and vague suggestions of color. Another held a huge old typewriter, as thick as some primitive engine block, with rows of teeth and all its inner rods and cams showing. Next to this was a long corrugated carton filled with bolts and odds and ends of cloth, crisped and soiled beyond any possible value. The remaining box was wooden and nailed closed, not very big, maybe a foot by a foot and a half, but heavy. He held the beam of the flashlight over the top, and he could make out that it was a shipping crate. He wiped away the dust and spall with the heel of his hand and read the darkened label, the name and address in faded blue ink, a sprawling and slanted but carefully ornate longhand: *To Fr. Teofilo Braga.*

The priest dragged the box along the planking. He banged his head then against a rough joist and felt a stab of anger. In that instant he blamed

Louis Horta for all this mess, for his having to crawl up there, for whacking his head. If Louis had been younger, had been more on top of things—but then he caught himself and tried to bid the uncharitable thoughts from his breast, even as his forehead dripped its small tear of blood, even as he felt the knot rising over his eye.

Blank ledgers. Long and heavy and green, and lightly lined in pale green ink, with two narrow columns in red at the left and right of each page. Twenty-four books. Hundreds and hundreds of pages' worth, all told. This is what he discovered when he came down the ladder and took a clawhammer and pried the nailed top from the little crate. The books had been sent to Father Braga from a company in Brockton, Massachusetts. The invoice was dated April 12, 1929, and the cost had been $28.

Father Braga had been the pastor in town for nearly thirty years. Furtado had never known him, but he had a memory of stories about him from his mother and father. He seemed eternally old in those tales, a severe cleric who had ruled the parish with an iron hand. Braga, as a young man, perhaps a seminarian, still living in the Old Country, had been at Cova da Iria in Fatima on that rainy Friday the thirteenth in October 1917, when the Virgin Mary appeared and cast aside the dark clouds and made the disk of the sun spin in the sky in front of a hundred thousand people.

But Furtado knew a secret about Braga, told to him by the old priest's niece, Lucia. It was a story that had been kept only in the family, except for telling Father Santos, God rest his soul. The priest from Away who had come after Father Santos had passed on, Father Kinzie, had not been told—he had been from the outside, and such a thing could not be trusted to him. But Lucy felt that because Manny was from town and now the parish priest, he should know. And that he could be trusted with the secret. Father Braga believed utterly and entirely and had devoted his life to Our Lady of Fatima. It was held as special that he been among the crowds at the great apparition. But the truth was that he had seen nothing. And he never forgave himself for whatever the imperfection was that did not allow him to see. For he was there in the rain. And furious. Others seemed to see something, but not he. He never forgot that day. He never forgot his being denied. Lucy believed it was what drove the old priest—The Terror, as he was known—to push for the name change of the parish. By the sheer force of his will, he had persuaded the diocese to rededicate the old church, formerly Our Lady of the Sea, as Our Lady of Fatima, something more fitting, since the parish in those days was nearly 100 percent Portuguese. It was the fact that Braga had *not* seen that drove his vocation. But Furtado was sworn never to tell this to anyone, which, it can be said, he technically never did.

Furtado was careful not to make too much of finding the ledgers on the very day on which Father Sweet had enjoined him to pour out his thoughts and feelings. At one time he had believed all coincidence was the result of a divine hand, but he was much more guarded about such things these days, and wary of how such ideas could take on unseemly proportions. He knew they could be like a doorway that opens just a crack, just enough for a splinter of light or draft of air to pass through, and pretty soon, if you're not careful, you think you can actually hear the heavenly hosts.

It was sometime after midnight on All Hallows Eve when Furtado finally climbed the narrow stairs to his study. The Halloween party was long over and Church Street was again dark and quiet, save for the wind in the heavy limbs of the trees. He did not draw the window shade but went through his nightly routine of kneeling in his own manner of prayer at the old *prie-deux*, then sitting at the little desk to take up the ledgers. The several pain pills that he had taken had already begun to work on him, their familiar luxury crowning through his body, and he drank deeply from the iced tumbler of gin that he had set on the desk before kneeling to prayer. That he had stayed with his gin and his pills even while going through his sessions with Sweet was a matter he considered his alone, and he saw no reason to tell his visitor from the diocese that this was the case. No, there would be many things that would be kept away from Father Sweet.

Furtado wrote in the ledger. From his old yellowed copy of Augustine, which lay open now on the desk next to the goosenecked lamp, he copied this: *Lord, since eternity is yours, can you be ignorant of what I say to you? Or do you see what happens in time only at the moment it is happening? Why then do I put before you the story of so many things?* He sipped some more gin. The ice clacked in the long glass and the warmth and euphoria continued to spread. Any scraps of pain or discomfort from his neck and shoulder were tucked now in some soft closet where they would be quiet for a while, and whatever was heavy about him—his bones, his flesh, his muscle—rose and became light and pleasing. He had become another self now, different in important ways from his daylight person. His mind roamed old, peaceful boulevards. He wrote in broad script using a fountain pen, which he liked because of its heavy line and also because it had to be held in a certain aspect to keep the golden nib at the right angle, or it would not work. It was a small discipline. He did not remember how he came by it. He used anything at all to write with down in the office.

He was never mindful of time when he was up here. He would write out long conversations with Saint Augustine about time. He would recall Heidegger's idea that time has no measure at all, that we can only gauge one process against another. Arbitrary. But his processes were beyond measure here. His body lifted. He shuddered with pleasure.

Outside, the wind shooed and moaned. It gusted and blasted and retreated. It was grand wind. Full of the ocean. High in the trees. There was a comfort in such a wind. And then he heard the noise. Sudden. A crash or a thump. It was already in his memory, the instant it happened. He tried to bring it back, to examine it. What was it? He thought of a tree down. Church Street and its old, lofty trees. The town had been canopied once with great elms, and now, through disease and storms, there were only seven left. But two of them were on Church Street, and one in the church-yard itself. And there were oaks and chestnuts and maples. The wind roved in the bare limbs, and the priest thought he could even hear it groaning up in the stone arches and loopholes of the Pilgrim's Tower on its dark hill just east of the church.

Then there came another bang. Perhaps something loose. A door pounding. Perhaps it was only a car. He couldn't tell. Furtado sat in his lethargy taking small breaths, and then he willed himself to rise. He felt as though he might continue to rise right off the floor, so light was his body now. He tried to sense the direction of the noises, but a small chime rang deep in his inner ears and suddenly he could not hear above it. He stood uncertainly until it faded and then abruptly stopped. Then he could hear the wind singing again against the glass of the window. He moved as though through water. That kind of languor. He closed the ledger and made his way down the narrow stairs. He did not float yet. Not exactly. He would not call it floating. But there was a buoyancy. There was that kind of gesture toward the suspension of certain laws.

The parlor was lit dimly downstairs, and he crossed it carefully to the rectory office and then slipped out its side door and into the breezeway that led to the church. He did not turn on the lights in the breezeway but followed the narrow passage in the soft glow that spilled from the office door behind him. He walked softly. Mariah Grey was supposed to have locked up after the party, but perhaps she had left one of the doors open in the church and the wind had gotten behind it. Or maybe someone was there. He could feel the wind pushing now against the flimsy walls of the breezeway. He could hear that sirenlike rush.

When he reached the door to the sacristy, he took his key ring out of his cassock pocket, found the heavy key, and felt for the lock's groove. He found it and lost it several times, brushing his fingers over the notch in the cold brass medallion, but the fumbling did not bother him, and finally he managed to slip the key in, slowly and quietly. When he leaned on the sacristy door, it opened slowly and soundlessly, and he traversed the darkened chamber to the open threshold that looked out onto the sanctuary. From inside the church wafted the muddled perfume of beeswax, flowers, traces of incense, the mellow lemon polish and oil soap from the rubbed wooden pews. All a sweetness. And the sanctuary lamp burned next to the tabernacle, blood red in its gilded enclosure. An amazing light in the honeyed gloom of the church, where the only other radiance came from the little swarms of votive candles racked in the iron stands just inside the lateral doors. It was like a sky-glow or a gloaming. The priest swayed there for a minute before he pulled himself back into his body. His cheeks tingled. His lips were numb.

He backed quietly into the sacristy and moved to the electrical pane and tripped two switches, altar left and altar right. The effect was to bloom the statues in the alcoves, Our Lady of Fatima on the west side of the altar, and the Sacred Heart of Jesus on the east. Molded fiberglass, both of them. The new materials. A great advance over the old methods. Considerable savings. And who knows, with their polymers and pigments, they might last forever, they might survive with the cockroaches into any number of afterlives. How his thoughts entertained him.

The chime sounded again in his ears, a hum now, really, not unpleasant. He thought it might be a legitimate musical note. He wondered if a note could be assigned to every sound in the world. So much he didn't know. He could hear above the tone this time. Now he regarded the statues. His mind moved with comfort on how things could be measured in order forms and inventories, contracts and vouchers. Dollars and cents. How the parish ran. How *he* ran it. And there was Mary, Mother of God, serene, all-giving, that perfect pose, her hands along her outer thighs, palms out. You could make of it what you would. Her blue robe, Her crown of stars. And opposite her, Christ, His heart exposed in his open chest, red, almost burgundy, in this light, under the resins, the red picked up again in a nice rolling line around the hem of the robes. Savage in a way. What to think of that look on his face—*I offer you infinite love—refuse me and I will let you suffer for all eternity*?

But Furtado had come here because of that noise. He steered his mind. It swept wide, like a ship. It took its time coming around. He thought that someone might have broken in, trying to get at the poor-box again. Though now he didn't keep anything in it after dark, since it had been robbed twice that summer. Each night he would empty the contents, never too much, into a coin sack, and he or Mariah Grey would lock it in the strongbox in the rectory office, where someone from the counting committee would take it up, run it through the counting machine, and bank it, and then Mariah would enter the sum into one of the spreadsheets she had created for the parish. No, there was no money to be had in the church at this hour, but that meant nothing. Someone was here. Furtado could smell him. Or her. But no, surely him, surely a man's smell. Sweat. Urine. Tobacco, maybe, or just the rankness of body. Maybe he was feeling a presence now the way a beast detects danger or prey. He believed something within him lifted with each slow breath, readying him.

He stepped back and flipped two more switches and opened the lights at the rear of the church. The building became a great cave suddenly. A chamber in a great cave. He flowed like water along the center aisle. Sumptuous in his movements. The gin. The pills. Pleasure in his flesh. There could be no menace here. "Hello," he said. "Hello. Can I help you? I'm afraid the church is closed at this time." His voice sounded reedy against the humming in his head. He called again. "Can I help you?"

Then someone moved in a pew all the way back by the confessional. The old wood creaked. Something scuffed. *Yes*, he thought, *someone has broken in to sleep in the church. Someone is lying down in a pew.* Not unheard of, but this sort of thing happened mostly in summer, when the town was full of tourists and visitors of all sorts. Vagabonds sometimes, if there was such a thing anymore. Probably not. Probably something else. Another word. He couldn't think of one. Where did all the tramps and hoboes go? Where were the vagrants? Had they morphed, all of them, into the great sea of the *homeless*?

The numbness in his lips. The little bell far off in his ears. Another sheet of wind swooshed out in the night. He could hear the sound of the high, heavy tree limbs. It was like they were speaking. Mariah Grey must not have locked the doors. He should have checked. "This is Father Furtado, the pastor here," he said, still walking slowly toward the back pew.

There came a shuffle and a groan. Then a figure rose. Unsteadily. Maybe painfully. Maybe drunk. It was like a ghost rising—and after all, it was Halloween night, or now the wee hours after. All Souls. The dead coming up.

"I'm Father Furtado. I'm the pastor here," he said again. He floated slightly now. Not unpleasant. The man's face seemed to float, too, above his body, disconnected. The priest could see that it had been laid to waste. "You're not well," he said. This man was not a thief. Then what? Why here? Something passed between them in the stillness of the church. The candles. The man's ripeness. The other smells.

The stranger took a breath, with difficulty, it seemed. "This is the house of God," he said. The voice was weak, something caught in the chest, wet or dry, Furtado couldn't tell.

"Yes," said the priest. "The church is the house of God. But I can't let you stay here. It isn't permitted. I will help you, though."

"Just don't renege on me."

"Sir," Furtado said. "Sir, if you need help . . ."

The man had been looking away from Furtado, looking off to his side, as if he didn't want their eyes to meet, but now he turned his head and fixed on the priest. His eyes were the color of coffee. Nothing white in them. Hair gray and stringy. Filthy. Bald on top. A long face, pale as soap in this light. All Hallows Eve. The wee hours after. He did not look like a ghost. Neither like something buried in the earth for a long time. But the truth was much worse than that. The priest could see that this was a living man, and something unspeakable had happened to him.

"Manny," the man said. A rasp, hardly above a whisper. He forced the words out. "Manny, look at you. You are actually a priest. It's unbelievable."

"Who are you?" Furtado said. He wasn't floating anymore. Or a part of him floated, then a part of him was anchored.

"Take a look, Manny. Can't you tell?" He turned his head slightly from side to side.

Underneath everything, Furtado was suddenly annoyed. He didn't care for this game. The man talked like a townie, making his sounds back in his head somewhere. The sharpness of the long vowels. The way words rose in the middle of a phrase. And *cahn't*. Not Boston. Not pretty speech. It was town. West End. It was how the priest himself had once spoken. "I don't recognize you," he said.

"I came back, Manny. You and me. Brothers. Always together."

"You aren't making sense. I only have one sister."

"Yes. I know. Allie."

"What?" Furtado stared hard at him.

"It's me. Sarafino," said the man.

"Sarafino?"

"Sarafino Pomba. You probably thought I was dead. But I came back. I'm here now."

Then a small wave swept under Furtado's feet, almost to carry him off. The wind gusted again outside. Wind up off the harbor, up from where the fishing boats lay to at their moorings. Up from the dark wharves and along the little streets. Over the canted rooftops. The whole church tipped lightly from it, a schooner heeling to lee. A little fist of nausea clenched in his stomach. But that face. And then from that face slowly emerged another, from beneath its ruin. Something the priest could almost recognize. The flare of the nose, the heavy lower lip, the sag or tilt to the mouth. Yes, he could see it all there. Yes, this could be Sarafino Pomba. Yes, it was him, indeed. Some shadow of him. The wind combed the world outside, riding the trees. A broad wind. A grand wind. The old timbers of the church sighed and groaned. Everything was in motion. Sarafino's ghastly face spun in a slow reel. Then it didn't spin. The priest's lips were numb. "Sarafino," he managed to say. He hadn't put him all together yet. "Sarafino, it's been so long."

"I know there was that story. Me being dead."

"Yes," said the priest. "There was something. It was a while ago. Nobody really knew anything."

"Manny. I should call you Father. Look at you. A priest." He steadied himself with both hands on the carved back of the pew. His wrists were like broomsticks. Laths. "I'm not doing so hot," he said.

"You are ill."

"Things happened. I never meant for anything bad to happen."

"Sarafino Pomba."

"You and me, Manny. What stuff we did."

"A long time ago," said the priest.

"I came all the way here. Right to the church."

"Sarafino," said the priest, "I'm going to take you into the rectory. I want to give you a place to lie down and rest. Can you eat?" He looked like he had not eaten in a long time. Something very serious. How little choice there was in some things. No choice now. None. A script we are handed. The painkillers buzzing in him. Lifting him. They were very potent. There might have been three of them with the gin. His lips numb and that sweet tone in his ear.

"I came back because of you," Sarafino said.

"Come with me," said the priest. "We can talk later."

"But I came to the church, Manny. I came in through that window. Through the little room behind the altar. Like we did that one time."

The priest did not rise to this. He let the words flutter away. He narrowed everything to this one physical task. All his attention now. "Let me help you." He guided Sarafino from the pew and into the aisle. He heard the little bell in his ear. He pressed his lips together to feel them and he tasted the residue of the sharp botanicals, the bitter compounds. A good taste. Mariah Grey, then, had not forgotten to lock anything. Good woman. A ragged duffel bag sat on the pew, and the priest took that up also. Sarafino felt so light and fragile. So he had broken into the church once again. There would be something to this. But not now. Not now. Here they walked slowly down the aisle together, Sarafino's small weight on the priest's shoulder and the duffel in his other hand. They walked carefully through the sacristy and then the breezeway and then into the rectory together. It was All Hallows Eve. The Vigil of Saints. Sarafino so flimsy and brittle, like a dry leaf, with the wind raking the world outside.

two

SARAFINO SLEPT ON THE LONG OVERSTUFFED SOFA IN THE RECTORY'S parlor. A shallow, fitful sleep. Two pillows, one upon the other, and the top pillow cradling his head in its shallow crease. The priest had unfolded a patchwork quilt over him, an old, warm, cotton-stuffed bed-cover that one of the town ladies had pieced together years ago, when people did such things as a matter of course. It was sewn from a panoply of yellow, blue, red, and green squares of cloth, all salvaged from worn-out garments and scraps, each small, hand-size section topped with a knot of green yarn. It was one of a half dozen or so that lay in trunks or closets in the rectory, gifts to the priests over the years. They had been passed along to Furtado with the rectory and its furnishings when he returned to town, and he had no notion of who had assembled them or when, but his sister, who could herself sew by hand, had rehabilitated several of the more worn covers. This was one of those. She had sewn in new patches where the cloth had tattered to nothing and padded them with bats of cotton wool. All the knots were new, done by Alzaida.

The quilt, supple and yielding, had settled over the ridges and angles of Sarafino's body the way a tarp might repose over a bundle of sticks. The priest watched as Sarafino lay on his back. His eyes were closed but they rolled continuously in some violent perturbation beneath the thin, sealed lids, and his skin shone luteous and waxy in the morning light. Outside the windows, bright shoulders of cumulus lofted above the roofs, and the wind still swept the trees and hedgerows, but the pale sun kept breaking through in places. The priest watched the high shadows come and go, a brightening, then a dimming, then a brightening again over the churchyard and its narrow street.

Furtado had not slept more than an hour or two that morning, but that was not unusual during this time. He woke with many questions, but his mind felt clear. The day would have its demands. But he would walk upright and steady. Capable. He had just come back to the rectory after saying the Morning Mass of All Saints. He had read from the *Missal, ordinary time, Revelation 7, 2–4 and 9–14.* Apocalypse. *I John saw another angel come up from the East, holding the seal of the living God.* Lately the readings were difficult for him to get through. Difficult to keep running those words through his body, yet that morning he had found a breath in himself. He had struck a tone. His voice had been full. There were twelve, maybe fifteen people in the church. It was not bad for an early morning, not a Sunday. Nothing like the old days, but that was part of what he was working on. Gathering. Rebuilding. He rose each day to such work. The work was always good. If there was any gift that remained in him, that was it, that capability. He believed it was the one thing left that saved him from being a complete mystery to himself, and he understood that a man who is his own mystery is a disaster. It was for God to be a mystery. God and the lives of others.

It was still early. Furtado walked quietly out of the parlor and started a kettle of water on the white enamel range in the rectory's kitchen. Then he slipped back to the parlor to look at Sarafino again. Furtado had no intention of waking him, but Sarafino heard his step. He groaned. He opened his sunken eyes.

"Sarafino," the priest said quietly.

Sarafino began to come to himself at this. He didn't sit up or otherwise move. He just stared at the priest. "Oh," he said after a moment. "Oh, that's right. It's Manny. It's Father Furtado." He drew several small quick breaths. "I thought I was dreaming." That townie accent. The knifelike edge of the *i*. The always-dropped *g*'s. *Was* like *whuz*. That, more than anything, brought Sarafino back into the world for the priest. It *sounded* like him. It sounded like the boy Furtado had once known when he himself was a boy. And before that. Their mothers would tell them about nursing the both of them together at the kitchen table, pushing them in big-wheeled strollers when they were babies together and the women would take them to the wharves in summer to watch the men coming home in the boats riding low in the water, with their huge catches of cod and haddock, and the men at the packinghouses icing and dragging the heavy pine boxes of fish into the semi trailers bound for New York and Boston. The mothers had taken snapshots, black-and-white Kodaks with scalloped edges. Snapshots, too, of them all together on the narrow beach behind the North Atlantic Cold Storage, both boys skinny and dark, swimming in drooping bathing suits, and all the mothers, maybe a dozen of them, huddled under beach umbrellas against the Cold Storage's wooden seawall, and Alzaida scowling and squinting in the summer sun. Allie still kept those old photos now, in a big black book with dry crumbling pages, always saying she was going to get new, vinyl albums someday but never getting around to it. When had he and Sarafino not known one another?

"Not dreaming," said Furtado. "Not dreaming now." He studied Sarafino's face. How had he come to this? He regarded the little body under the quilt. The sunlight blossoming suddenly, booming into the windows as clouds blew past, the quilt's colors flaring. Sarafino drawing his eyes back painfully from the brightness. "I am heating some water for tea," the priest said.

Sarafino was silent. Then a grunt. Almost like a cough. His legs kicked under the quilt. A little spasm shook through him. Then he spoke. "I am not feeling so hot, Manny. I have got to tell you that."

"I know you are sick," said the priest, still standing over him. Outside the clouds still scudding. Sun fading behind them then returning. Striking Sarafino. The skin on his face like a drumhead. The priest stepped to the near window and drew the shade just enough to keep the direct light off the sofa. "I am going to help you get cleaned up, and then I'm going to call a doctor for you."

Sarafino licked his lips slowly. Dry, cracked. His tongue white. "No. You can't do that. That's all over, that part."

"I'm trying to understand all this," Furtado said. The small rocking chair sat opposite the sofa, and the priest pulled it over by Sarafino and settled stiffly on the edge of it. "I don't know anything that's going on with you."

"I know, Manny. It's been a long time. You never left my head, though."

The teakettle stuttered for a moment in the other room, then built quickly to a full whistle. The shrilling filled the parlor. "Wait," said Furtado. He went to the kitchen. In a few minutes he returned with a tray. A teapot, cups, a plate of plain toast. A spotted banana. A plastic bottle of water. "Can you try this?" he asked. "Can you take a little something?" Sarafino had refused—or had been unable—to eat when the priest had brought him into the rectory the night before. They'd gotten no farther than the sofa, which Furtado made as comfortable as he could for him, and Sarafino, exhausted, had swooned on it, clothes and all.

Now Sarafino pulled himself up and rested his back against the pillows. The priest slid a small glass-topped table within Sarafino's reach and poured him some tea with sugar, and set a plate with the toast and the banana on it. The light from the street flowed warmly into the room now, steadily, but the priest watched the tremor, the black veins in Sarafino's hands. He tried to assess his condition. "Can you eat solid food?" he asked.

"Sometimes," said Sarafino. "But mostly it's over. That part." Neither moved or spoke until Sarafino pulled his knees up and cradled the cup and small plate. He nibbled some toast. He sipped some tea. A hummingbird's worth. A moistening of his lips.

"I think you are very sick," the priest said.

Sarafino did not seem to hear. He shifted his stale-coffee eyes and cocked his head, like a cat sensing something in the far corner of the room. A spider's scuttle over dust, or the *swish* of a field mouse that had come slinking out of the hedge to winter in the luxury of the rectory's plastered walls. The weather was turning around. A new season bearing down. Furtado tried to see the boy Sarafino again, summer-tanned and wiry. But the man on the couch blinked slowly. Those eyes. Reptilian. His presence so strange here in the priest's home. So difficult to comprehend. Sarafino blinked again. Then, looking around quickly, as though he had just arrived at the scene of a terrible accident, he asked, "Where's Allie?"

The priest pushed back into his chair. He let it rock for a beat. "Allie doesn't live here," he said. He stared into Sarafino's face. "Do you know where you are now?" he asked.

"Allie married Tommy da Silva," said Sarafino. "I know that much."

"Yes. Tommy runs my father's old boat. The *Ilha do Pico*. It's a lot of trouble, but it's still afloat, still fishing. Allie works at Braga's bakery, just like before. They had a little boy, but he died when he was about one."

"I slept but my heart was awake," said Sarafino. He shook his head. "Did you think I was dead?"

"I heard it. From someplace. I don't remember. People just heard it."

They were quiet again for a while. Then Sarafino spoke slowly and carefully. "You are trying to figure out if I'm crazy or not," he said. "I am making you uncomfortable."

"This is all very sudden," said the priest. "It's been so long. And I can see you're not well."

"I admit it, Manny. I'll tell you straight out. My head sometimes, it goes sideways. I was on some medicine. Now I'm not. I see things very clear. You won't have to worry."

Something left over from last night touched Furtado then. Something bitter and chemical on his tongue. He took some hot tea. He swallowed against the taste in his mouth. The noise in his ear came back. His right ear. A tiny plastic whistle this time. Almost not there at all. A ripple of lightheadedness passed over him, like someone running a comb through his hair. He drank more tea. Hot going down. Then everything settled. "I need to know what's going on with you," he said to Sarafino. "I need to know what we can do here."

"You can't tell?"

"No."

"I have to finish something."

"Oh," said Furtado.

"Except some things got wrong. Confused, I mean."

"Are you confused now?" said the priest. "Is your head sideways now?"

"Yes and no. I'm tired out. I get better than this. But you know what? I remember things like they were right in front of me, right now. It's always been that way. Like Braga's. Allie worked there when we were kids."

"Sure."

"And we'd come knocking on the back window before the sun came up. After an all-nighter or something. Before they were open. When Old Man What's-His-Name would be baking the bread, and she'd pass the hot loaves out to us and we'd go eat them down on the beach. Right?"

"Yes. That's right. I haven't thought about it in a long time."

"Me either." Sarafino drank more tea. He nibbled the toast. Furtado reached over and peeled the banana for him and laid it back down on the plate.

"Go slow," said the priest. "Take some water, too."

"I want to thank you, Manny. A priest. I understand that. In a way."

"You need to rest. Then we need to talk about everything."

"I came back, Manny. I came back for you."

"Now I'm losing you, Sarafino. I don't follow that."

"First I have to tell you: You can't tell anybody I'm here. You can't tell anybody that you've seen me. I know how this sounds. I'm aware of that." A change came over Sarafino's complexion. He went green, then the color of rose petals, then violet, then white again. But it was a trick of light. A beam of sun had struck the crystal prism hanging from the window shade, and colors splayed in the room. They moved over Sarafino's skin and the hardwood floor and the thick rug. The dark furniture. The old piano. Pure. Attached to nothing. Outside now the sun was gleaming, but a drizzle of sweat appeared on Sarafino's face. "I pray the Rosary," he said, brushing his mouth with the back of his hand.

Furtado didn't say anything. The colors of the prism were still arrayed on the wall beneath the mahogany crucifix that hung near the hall doorway, Christ's hip cocked to the left, his body caught in the sway of death. There were things to do. He was thinking about how he would have to rearrange his day.

"I pray the Rosary, and I wear a Brown Scapular from the Carmelites. Just so you know. I'm aware I could give you the wrong idea."

"I don't have any kind of idea, Sarafino. I am still trying to catch up to one thing. That you are here. That it's you. It's strange. So sudden."

"Yes." He chewed the banana with a deliberate rhythm. Like he was counting. He took some tea. His hand unsteady. The cup and saucer clicking. "I may as well tell you the rest straight off."

"It's all right. You mean about where you've been and what happened to you?"

"I wasn't dead. Actually. I mean, I was, in a way of looking at it. I'm sorry. Something happened, and I did and said certain things. So people would just think I was dead. I thought people might care about the other thing. I know better now. But here's what I mean to say. What's important, the Virgin Mary appeared to me."

"Sarafino." The priest shook his head.

"More than once. She still comes. She told me things."

Furtado's mind ranged over the possibilities of what he could do.

"It's true. You think it's because I'm sick, but She told me to come back here. She told me to come here and that you would take me in. It's because of that night we broke into the church. We took the Virgin."

Furtado sighed. "Where are you going with this? That was all so long ago."

"I cursed Old Man Coelho," Sarafino said solemnly. "However you look at it, it was on me. And we took the Virgin. And that's why I came back."

"Maybe that's why you stayed away."

"That and other things. Everything got mixed up."

"You didn't harm anyone, Sarafino. That's the truth."

"I know what I know. The Virgin came to me. She chose me. It was that night she chose me, but I never knew it then. It wasn't until later." Sarafino's eyes feverish now. Smoldering. He pushed the tray away from him. His body atremble. "Manny, Manny. I'm sorry, Manny, I'm going to be sick. Please."

Furtado leapt to his feet, and the rocking chair slid backward on the rug, nearly tipping. "Come," he said. "I've got you." Sarafino stood, the quilt dropping, and the priest took him under the arms. A smell rose from him. Still in his clothes. Filthy tube socks, two baggy flannel shirts, one buttoned over the other. Brown corduroy pants hanging from his hipbones.

"So hard, Manny. All these years. And being chosen like that."

"It's all right, Sarafino. Right down the hall with me. Right into the bathroom." Furtado walked him as briskly as he could. A straw man. He shambled along but he talked now with even more urgency, panting between words.

"Manny, She has told me. Some very important things. She is going to send me a sign, Manny."

"Right in here, Sarafino, Right in here," said the priest. His mind squalled over a hundred things. Everything he was going to do today. And now Sarafino Pomba, after all this time. He would have to be careful and not be disrupted. Sarafino must be dealt with. That much was clear. He had come back to be taken care of. Furtado would have to find some facility for him. He would have to make some calls. He was thinking about whom he could call. "Right inside, Sarafino," said the priest, holding him, moving him along. Then he felt him giving out. He wrapped his arms around him and lifted him over the threshold and into the bathroom. "It's all right, Sarafino," he said. "You are not well. You can let all that go now. Right here. We are going to get you fixed up."

But Sarafino began shivering harder. "One of the things, Manny. One of the things the Virgin told me. She has a sign for you, too."

three

THE PRIEST SAT AT THE BIG DESK IN THE RECTORY OFFICE, MAKING some notes and rearranging his day. He called and postponed a few meetings and visits, but he did not put off his meeting with Mariah Grey, for they had a deadline whose effect reached eventually all the way to the diocese. He had not been working long when he heard the familiar racket at the kitchen door. It was the way Allie always summoned him when her hands were full. He walked out of the office and through the parlor into the kitchen. He saw her through the glass pane of the aluminum storm door just as she knocked again, with her elbow against the edge of the door so that it rattled in its frame. He let her in. She carried a brown paper grocery bag in each arm. The day outside had become blue and luminous. A river of cool air rolled in behind her.

"Let me," said Furtado. He took the two bags from her and set them down by the sink. He had by then already moved Sarafino from the parlor into the spare bedroom at the far end of the rectory, the bedroom that had been used in former times when there were two priests in the parish. That morning, in the bathroom, Sarafino had vomited the little food he had taken and then gone into a shivering fit and a terrible loss of control, which had left him soiled and unable to stand on his own. The priest had taken care of him. He removed the fouled clothes and put Sarafino on a stool in the shower, and, taking off his own shirt, he leaned into the shower and helped him with the washcloth and scented soap. He shampooed him. He shaved the grizzle from his chin and cheeks. He noticed the hollow of the cheeks and then saw how many teeth were missing. Those left were stained and stubbed. He was gentle on the flaccid skin. Easy on the flesh that barely covered the bones. There was so little to him. Even sitting on the stool, Sarafino's buttocks seemed nothing but two curved bones. And Furtado saw the lesions. Purple. Blotchy. He wasn't certain, but he had a pretty good idea by then.

Through all this, Sarafino had been silent. Perhaps too weak to talk. He'd stared off at some invisible thing. It was strange to touch him. What the boy had become. It was strange for the priest to consider what he was doing. Once Sarafino was clean, Furtado had dried him and given him some water to sip, put him in a pair of clean sweat clothes from his own closet shelf, and fed him a little bit of chicken broth that he heated from a can. Then he laid him in the bed in the small room and placed two quilts over him, and put a tumbler of water and orange juice, mixed half and half, within reach on the nightstand. Now Sarafino was sleeping—or resting, at any rate. He was warm now. He was clean. Now Furtado would have to tell Allie all about this. This sudden stranger, who was not a stranger. But who was a stranger nevertheless.

"I've got a big, heavy sack of birdseed in the trunk of the car," Alzaida said. "I've been driving around with it forever. Maybe you can help me put it out in the storeroom." She went over to the linoleum-topped counter and began pulling things out of the grocery sacks. "Here's the olive oil you paid me for," she said. She pulled a slender golden bottle out of one of the paper bags. "The Halloween party go okay?"

"Okay," said the priest. "I'm sure they missed you."

"Sure they did. I heard about the piñata. Very funny. So everything went okay, though? How did Mariah do?"

"She's wonderful."

"Some big wind last night." Allie didn't turn around to talk to him. She fidgeted with her back to him.

"Here's two loaves of *massa sovada*. You can freeze one or give one to Mariah."

"Let's give it to Mariah. She's coming to do some things in a little while.3"

"Okay, well, and here's some *queijo* Sao Jorge."

"Allie."

"I didn't just *take* the stuff, Manny. Well, I took the bread. But it was going to go stale. Things will slow down now that the holiday is over. But the cheese is from Lucia. She's just taking care of her priest. Like everybody did in the old days. You have to let her."

"She has a good heart."

"She can be a pain in the ass, too." Allie reached under the sink and brought out a can of cleanser and a sponge and began scrubbing the countertop, even though the priest had cleaned up the kitchen earlier, after he had put Sarafino to bed. Her body twitched and her heels bounced in whatever anxiety had her unsettled now. He was the same with his own disquiet, worse when he was young, always jiggling or vibrating. Habits they had formed in their house as kids, caught in the pulls between their mother and Pai.

Allie wore baggy jeans and a long, green woolen workshirt that covered her hips. She was getting heavy. Clumps of errant gray hair had begun to sprout among her dark, wild curls. She looked like their mother now more than ever. Furtado supposed he favored their father, though he had kept all his hair so far, still thick and dark. He cut it weekly himself with an electric trimmer, shorter than a crew cut, the same shortness all around.

"What is it, Allie?"

"I don't know. Just a mood. Is it that obvious? I'm sorry." She turned around and faced him. "It's always something with me. That's what you want to say."

"You seem jumpy."

"Well." She shrugged. "I don't know. If you want any news, Tommy got written up again. Him and Frankie. *Fishing out of area.* He's always so pissed at everything." She leaned her back against the sink and with her forearm brushed an imaginary strand of hair from her brow. She still held the blue sponge in one hand and the can of cleanser in the other.

There was so much to do. The priest did not want to go too far with any of this. It was daylight. He was his daylight self. His head was still clear, but there were so many things to think about. "It's always been hard," he said. It was too dismissive, and he was sorry immediately. "Even when it was good in Papa's time," he added. "It was hard. Hard work."

"They barely get any days offshore anymore, and Tommy has to call the government guys at three in the morning to find out what they can do and how much and all that. He calls them the college boys. He says when they actually ever do go out on a boat, once a year or whatever, they throw up."

Furtado moved to the table. A twinge in his shoulder now. A little nag in his neck bones. The refrigerator kicked on and began to hum. It was old and loud. He gestured with his head. "Everything is clean, Allie. Everything is put away. Stop fussing and sit down. Do you want some coffee? Some tea?"

She pressed her lips together, whitening them. Then she put the can and the sponge away and took a seat across from him at the little table, her back to the door. She gazed blankly past Furtado into the hallway. The afternoon light pressing through the storm door backlit her and shadowed the small lines in her face, the little crow's feet, the crescent at each side of her tight mouth. Not laugh lines, but the slow creases from the grimace she so often wore. It was what her face did now. Furtado thought she should use some makeup. Something. But she was fierce about her plainness. She obliged you to take it in. It made him think of his own vanity, the little black dumbbells on the floor by his bed, his sit-ups. Nostrums for his chronic aches, he told himself. Then the priest settled. He must do something about Sarafino. Sarafino Pomba had come back. He started to tell Alzaida about Sarafino, but in her nervousness she jumped into the moment's silence.

"They've been having trouble with something on the boat, too," she said. "Some part. A manifold, maybe? They took the truck up to Chatham the other day. They went up to see some guy about getting it fixed. So they said."

"Tom and Frankie."

"Yes, Tom and Frankie. Who else? But you know what he did? He actually talked to the guy up there about selling the boat. About getting rid of it. The thing is, nobody will buy it, even with the license. He tells me about this. He says, 'Oh, it just came up.' Like it wasn't in his head to begin with." The citation was new, but everything else was an old story. Yet Allie put a tone into the room. Something played on her nerves. Not just the usual anger. Furtado let it run. He had too much on his own plate.

"It's not his boat, I told him. It's both of ours. It was my father's, not his father's. And the house is gone. That was *his* big idea: sell the house and get out of town because all the rich gays from away were buying up everything. So we had Papa's house, but now I'm stuck living over in the Village. I may as well be in the woods. I have to drive back into town anytime I want to see someone or do something. Now it's Papa's boat he wants to get rid of." She looked at him, waiting for him to say something. He could feel her leg pumping under the table.

"It's a nice house" was all he was willing to say.

"It's not where I'm supposed to be living. I should be living here in town. I let him talk me into selling Papa's house, and we didn't even get a good price for it. It was before the big run-up. Now the old place is worth a zillion dollars and I'm living in the sticks. If I don't screw everything up myself, I let Tommy do it."

Alzaida wanted him to say something, one way or the other. But again he wouldn't take the bait. He wouldn't defend Tom or blame him. His neck hurt. His ear pinged—or maybe it was the refrigerator. Some weird harmonic. He got up and moved to the stove and filled the kettle and lit the burner beneath it. A poof. A ring of blue flame, yellow dancing at its upper edges. "I wish you and him would get along better," she said as he was sitting back down. But she looked away from him as she said it.

With his weight in the chair now, Furtado felt a small flourish of last night's sensations pass through him. Perhaps it was merely the desire to be lifted again. To float above his own body and all its imperatives. It overtook him and then faded. Two or three heartbeats. He tried to focus. He thought then, suddenly, surprising himself, about how much he loved his sister. This fisherman's wife. This unhappy woman. In this moment there was no doubt in his mind about loving her. That was one thing that he knew for certain right now, though he was puzzled by it, too. Just how it was supposed to play out in the world. Exactly what he could do for her.

Even though she and Tom had come into the house and boat free of any liens or encumbrances, the priest knew there had been some money problems. They had taken money out of the sale of the family house, and then later a loan against the new house. And then a credit line. Allie had said nothing about these things, but Furtado had been told in confidence by George Campos, an old school friend, now an officer of the Mariners' Savings Bank and a member of the parish planning committee. All this must weigh on them. He knew they fought about it. And there had been the baby's death so early on. That had left a mark on her. On Tommy, too. That was twenty years ago now, and they'd never had another child. It had been an accident, but Allie blamed herself. A terrible thing. She had set down a mug of coffee on the edge of an end table, and little Jaime, just beginning to walk, had reached up and pulled it down on himself, aspirating some of the hot coffee. The rescue squad came and eventually took him up the Cape to the hospital, but he died there the next morning. They were still living in the old Furtado home in the West End then. They hadn't moved yet.

Furtado was not living in town at the time, but he'd come home for the funeral. A Mass of the Angels, because little Jaime da Silva had been baptized and cleansed of Original Sin but had not reached the age of reason, so, according to the Church, he was taken into heaven and transformed into an angel. But dark stories had been going around already: Tommy into all kinds of things. Bringing bales of marijuana in on the boat. Bringing in cocaine and heroin. But when had the town not been like this? Since its beginnings, there had been lawlessness out here. The end of the line. As far as one could go. Gun runners in the Revolutionary War. Whalers and Grand Bank fishermen with their wild days ashore. Women. Witches, some believed. Moon-cussers with their false lights, luring boats ashore. Wreckers. Castaways. Bootlegging fishermen during Prohibition. No excuses there, of course.

Then Furtado had heard about Tom and Allie being stoned all the time. Alcohol. Cocaine. Why the baby died. Careless. Neglectful. Wacked out of their minds. He did not believe that part of it. He refused to countenance it. He understood how stories could get started. But whatever the truth, a sadness had fallen over them.

The priest did not want to love Alzaida merely for her sadness. He found himself attracted to it, and he wanted to be better than that. But that was the thing that reached out to him now. It was the part of her that he felt in his own breast. "Tommy and I get along," he said, wanting to give her something. At least that. "I admit we have butted heads."

"You are prideful and he is stubborn," Alzaida said.

"We're fine," he said. Across the table, she shook, almost invisibly. Of course things would generally be easier if he and Tom were somehow closer, but what was she aiming at specifically now? For there would always be one thing or another that Alzaida would be driving at, pointing to. *Something always in the wind with that one*, their mother would say. The last blowup he and Tom had had was that summer, just before the Portuguese Festival. But they had come past that now. Allie had been hurt by it, though. It had been a mistake on his part as much as Tom's. Allie had desired a big *festa* as much as anyone else. It was what Bishop Mayhew wanted. It was what Monsignor Rego wanted. It was a way of showing that the Church was a central force in the town again. Rebuild. Restore community. The businesses, the motels, the restaurants—they all wanted it, too. And why not? It was a good thing. Tourist revenue. Good for the whole town.

In Furtado's own childhood—in his father's day as a fishing captain—the festival had centered on the Church's blessing of all the town's working craft. Big trawlers and small draggers, long-liners, scallopers and trap boats. The fleet was near to eighty boats then, and all the captains and crews would clean and paint and decorate the craft with pennants and buntings, and motor in a long queue past the end of the town's main wharf, where the bishop, having come all the way from Calumet for the occasion, would bless each boat with holy water as it cruised past a platform erected for him at the outermost tip of the wharf. There was a special Mass and a great parade with Portuguese marching organizations and bands from all over, and members of civic halls and social leagues from as far away as Providence and Boston would caravan down the Cape in cars and buses to take part in the *festa*. A statue of Our Lady was carried through the town on the shoulders of the fishermen, and there were games and contests and dancing in the streets for several days before and after the Blessing.

But in recent years the waters had become fished out, the government had come in with its strict regulations, and the fleet had dwindled—Furtado could count no more than a dozen working boats, almost half of them as old as the *Ilha do Pico*. So even though there would be a small blessing, the festival had moved its focus more ashore. Now there would be more games and picnics, a great outdoor feast, bands and street dancing. A taste of the old, but without the great fleet, just a taste.

Well, you couldn't really go back to the glory days. That's what the priest told everyone. Not to lower their hopes, but to get them to think along new lines. He understood things. What they *could* do. He took charge of the festival committee. He sent for *fado* singers from Lisbon, Brazilian drummers. A poet from the Azores would read from her books. He set everyone to work. He went to every shop on Front Street. Every rooming house. Every eatery. He talked to parishioners. He talked to People from Away. He stepped aboard every fishing boat. He offered everyone something to gain. He offered everyone a part to play.

And he got Tom to do the street flags and bunting.

The mistake was pride. Allie was right. He'd walked outside that afternoon, a week before the festival, to admire his handiwork. It was the only time he had ever left the rectory after the gin and the pills. The last time he had taken them together during the daylight hours. This was not more than a few weeks before the difficulty with Mrs. Horta. He strolled in the sunshine along Front Street, crowded already, barely a car wide, teeming with bicycles and scooters and visitors in shorts and sandals and sunglasses and ball caps, choking any possibility of moving traffic. All the shops were open and busy, and all the brilliant flags streamed in the breeze, hung from their dark, bellied wires, crisscrossing the street. Furtado walked in slacks and shirt, no clerical collar. He could feel the floating beginning, the pain in his shoulder and neck being shunted off to a place where it did not matter. Beyond that, the pleasure rising in his blood. The little ringing in the ears. The numbness in the lips. Basking. The breeze. The antiseptic light. The alkaloid bite of the pills still in his mouth, but the sweetness of life, its flurry and hum, all around him, the wasp of the motor scooter and the cry of the gull. How the day's warmth soaked into him.

But the flags.

The flags were not merely decorations, of course. They were real signal flags. They had meanings and uses. They made an alphabet from A to Z, each with its own phonetic name, and each with its own signal worth as well. The *Bravo* flag, for instance. Solid red. *B*. But also *Fueling*. Or the *Oscar* flag. Red over yellow diagonal. O. But also *Man Overboard*. Oh, yes, he was Pai Furtado's boy, and he knew the flags, though he doubted any of the brightly dressed tourists would know or think about this. Maybe some fishermen from Gloucester or New Bedford would notice. It was such a small thing.

After this was all over, he would go through it in his mind. Why would he have stopped? Because of the double letters, which caught his eye on that lovely, dazzling sunlit day. Why would Tom have had his crew put two of the same flags next to each other if they were for decorations? It caught at some aesthetic burr in Furtado. Some little tilt from how things should be. Just enough to stop. And read. And then he resumed walking, and read, here and there, a wire of flags. Read them. All the blues and whites and reds, the bars and chevrons. Two *Sierra* flags side by side in front of the Wheelhouse bar. Two *Echo* flags. A *Foxtrot*. A *Romeo*. Finally, *Free Pussy*. In front of a gentrified guest house, *Lots a Queers*. Entering the town square, at the foot of the main wharf, *Fuck the Whales*. It went on in similar fashion as far as he looked down the narrow street, but he changed direction right there. His body became radiant. In the square, the breeze was lustrous and briny, and all aslant with the smells of onions from the hot dog stands, and of chocolate fudge and roasting peanuts from the candy store. Light everywhere. Rising from the asphalt, the clapboards. Luminous bodies. The sea glinting beyond. A bowl of rhinestones. His eyes felt absurdly widened, hyperopen, as if the lids were being blown back by the gusts of light. He headed straight down the wharf to the *Ilha do Pico*.

Poor Allie. He wished more for her. That was what Furtado thought as he watched her now at the table, and that was what he'd thought then, when he saw Tommy sitting on the weather-beaten hatch of the *Ilha*, a can of beer in his hand. He simply wished more for her. Something went off. There were three or four boats tied up at the wharf. None were decorated yet. They were still working. Tommy looked up at him from the deck. His face was dark from the sun and the wind. He looked younger than he was. Always that look. Thick curls. No gray in them yet. Furtado could lay the trouble to anything. The pills and the liquor, of course. Wanting something better for Allie. Maybe it would have happened differently if Frankie had been there. Whatever. But what came out of him was a bark. "Take them down," he said. "You take those flags down."

Tom just kept looking up at him. He took another pull from the beer can.

"Get off this boat right now and fix those flags right. You know what I'm talking about."

Tommy regarded him, then shook his head. "It's just joking around, Manny. Something amongst ourselves. It doesn't mean anything."

"It means something because *I* know what they mean. Don't you get that? Get rid of that stuff."

Tom got up now and walked to the gunnel. He was still slightly beneath Furtado because of the tide. He drew himself and squared his shoulders. They each stood like that for a moment. Absurd. Locked up. Furtado did not understand his own actions. Something pounded in his head. Finally Tom shrugged. "I'll take care of it," he said.

When Furtado went back downtown later to check, around suppertime, the flags were gone. All the flags. All the wires. Tom had taken the whole street down. The next day Allie called to say he was taking the boat out of the Blessing, and that is exactly what he did. He kept it tied up to the wharf with all the festivities going on all around it. The only boat in the fleet. It was intended to hurt the festival, but it meant little. The bishop noticed the boat but made nothing of it. Of course Furtado had had to round up another crew to get the flags and put them back up correctly, but that wasn't difficult. No, who was hurt was Allie. She cursed. She raged. And she wept. She had had plans of her own. Like the old days when Papa had the boat and there was always a big party onboard, offshore. She had looked forward to old school friends, a big propane grill forward of the mast with hot dogs and broiled *linguiça* and *chouriço*, and tubs of iced beer. Someone always jumped overboard, and if the water was warm, then everyone did. They'd anchor off Long Point and party into the night. But it was not to be. And of course she worried about the town people talking. How screwed up they all were. It was shame as well as anything else. Tommy was Tommy, and Furtado understood that he himself had overstepped. But there were apologies later. Tommy even sent some fish up to the rectory.

The priest understood how such things had long half-lives. Yet there was no room for any of that in this moment. And there was more to this mood of Allie's, anyway. Always something in the wind. That much, he could judge. He didn't care now. Now he wanted his sister to sit up. He needed her attention. Mariah Grey was coming and he needed to meet with her. He would need Alzaida's help. Sarafino Pomba had come back now, and he, Furtado, must do something for him. Yes, he needed help. And so his sister's dolor irritated him now. Enough. How she could weary him. All this in a moment. How long does a feeling take to pass through all the gates and circuits of the body?

"Alzaida," he said, "I have to tell you about something. All this other business, whatever it is, let's put it aside for now."

"What, Manny?"

"Something incredible has happened. Let me tell you."

Allie narrowed her eyes and looked into his face. He could not tell what she was thinking, but he knew she was frightened, and she tensed herself up as though she were trying to figure something out. As though he might have a clue to some puzzle that might save her life. Then she sat back and gazed past him, over his shoulder. She just froze that way. When the priest was to reflect on that moment, it would seem to him to have lasted a very long time. It was like something from a movie. He would write this in the ledgers. How he watched her face change and change again. As though they had sat at the table going through this, over and over. And all the while his own mind moving around, racing ahead, slowing down, speeding up again, trying to intersect with her.

But before it came to him to turn around and look behind him, or to do anything at all, she said quietly, barely moving her lips, "Oh my God. Sarafino."

four

SARAFINO LEANED IN THE DOORWAY, PROPPED AGAINST THE FRAME for support. The rummage-sale shirt, the rummage-sale pants, hung from him like a stage disguise—a tramp from the silent films, or a circus clown. But the clothes at least were clean. He was cleaned up now. Furtado had done well by him, though his thin bowl of hair stuck up in places like the ruffled feathers of some wild bird. The bright daylight in the kitchen favored him at this moment, and you could see yet more of the young Sarafino beneath the layers of damage and age. Allie knew him quickly. She wasn't puzzled. But she looked at him hard, and then her eyes welled up with tears. They rimmed and glistened in the light, but they did not run over onto her pale cheeks. "Sarafino," said the priest. "Come. Come sit with Allie and me." He rose and put his arm around Sarafino's shoulder and walked him the few steps to the little table.

Sarafino slumped in the chair. "Well," he said, "here we are."

Allie looked him up and down. Nothing changed in her face. She just said, "Sarafino." She repeated his name several times.

"What I wanted to say," said Furtado. "Sarafino has come back to us. He came last night. To the church."

"I wasn't feeling too hot this morning, but Manny here fixed me up. Father Furtado."

Alzaida studied the two of them. She bit her lip and sighed, then pushed back from the table abruptly, as though she might turn and run out the door, but she simply held herself there, staring.

There was a moment of uncomfortable silence, and then the priest finally spoke to Sarafino. "I want you to try some more soup," he said. "Something to drink. All right?"

"Maybe in a little while," Sarafino said.

And to Allie, Furtado said, "Sarafino and I haven't had much chance to talk yet."

She turned to Sarafino. "It's been a long time."

"Well, I'm not dead. It's good I'm here. Right?"

"Yes," said Allie. "Of course. You look so tired, though."

"I'm tired, all right. But Manny here, he fixed me up."

"A little bit," said the priest. "We have to take some time and figure some things out. But you don't look comfortable in that chair. Let's go into the parlor. You could sit on the sofa. You could lie down there."

"All right," Sarafino said.

The priest moved to offer Sarafino his shoulder, but Sarafino stood and sidestepped this gesture. He walked slowly and stiffly between the priest and his sister, and the three settled in the next room. Sarafino took the sofa but did not recline. He reached to one of the small decorative pillows and sat holding it to himself as though it were a heating pad or a stuffed animal. "I slept, but my heart was awake," he said to Allie. "I am like a green olive tree in the house of God."

Alzaida turned and looked at her brother.

"Psalms," Furtado said.

"You'd be surprised," said Sarafino.

The priest sat in the rocker again, and Allie sat loose-limbed in the big easy chair by the window. The sun was by now on the afternoon side of the building, and the rectory itself cast a long shadow out on the churchyard. The light that flowed inward was soft and languid. It suited the room, which was where the priest sat with parishioners in counseling or held small meetings, and where he sometimes took his sessions with Father John Sweet when he came to town. The brass lamps on the end tables recalled the oil lights of sailing ships, and a brass barometer and tide clock hung on the wall. The floor was of the original wide planking that was found in so many of the ancient houses and was painted with gray deck enamel and covered with thick area rugs. Allie had sewn the gossamer curtains and the little arm-protectors on the sofa and easy chair, and had fashioned the cushions on the oaken rocker.

There was an upright piano against one wall, but no one could remember anyone ever living there who could play it. On its top, a vase and a bowl held cut flowers. The rectory office and adjoining parlor were treated halfway as public spaces, and Mrs. Horta had kept them up fastidiously. Now Mariah helped. And Allie would sometimes come and clean, though that was not her forte. Another thing he hadn't yet ticked off on the endless lists: a housekeeper.

The light and the undemanding comfort of the room eased something among the three of them. Not that Sarafino suddenly fit in. Still, to Furtado, the world seemed less oddly tipped. Maybe also because Allie sat with them now. For if she was present, then Sarafino could not be the priest's apparition alone. There had to be some sensible course of action for him to take. He would have to find it.

Furtado could not bring himself to pass a casual remark, and Allie and Sarafino watched each other—gazed or stared (the priest would later write both words in the ledger before lining each one out again). "Tell us something, Sarafino," he said after a while. "There's so much we don't know. Where have you been living?"

"What do you mean?" Sarafino asked. He spoke slowly, pausing to take several breaths before going on. "Do you mean all the places since I left town?"

"Are you homeless?" Furtado asked.

"I think so," he said in that same halting manner. "I think you could say so. In a way."

"What do you mean, you think so? What do you mean, 'in a way'?" Furtado's ear buzzed. The ear closest to Sarafino. Buzzed and popped. Such a great deal in his head. It occurred to him that he had not eaten anything all day. Some coffee. Some tea. It was too early to take any pills, but the dull beginnings of something stirred in the low bones beneath his collar.

"Maybe you don't need to cross-examine him," Allie said.

"If we had some information," said the priest. He turned back to Sarafino. "You see what I mean?"

"Absolutely," said Sarafino. "I am making you nervous again."

"Are you cold?" Allie said. "Is that why you're hugging that pillow? I'm going to cover you up." She rose and fetched the quilt, which was lying folded on the top of the piano bench. She stood over Sarafino and shook it open, then leaned and tucked it around him. "I think you might have a little fever," she said.

"Sometimes," said Sarafino. He took hold of the quilt and lay back against the pillows. A field of color and then his weary face, his coppery eyes.

And then there came a tapping at the office door. Furtado looked at his watch. "It's Mariah," he said.

"Who's that?" said Sarafino.

"Someone I work with," said the priest. "We were supposed to do some parish work this afternoon." He saw now how all this had to be taken care of quickly, this disruption from Sarafino's coming back. There was too much to be done. He hadn't worked anything out yet, and it disturbed him that he hadn't. But Allie was here now. Yes, he needed her help. Then he reflected on the troubles of that morning. The sickness. The mess. He didn't wish to leave her to something like that if it came around again. But Alzaida saw him hesitate.

"It's okay, Manny," she said. "You guys do what you have to. Sarafino and I are good here. This is so amazing. We can talk. We'll stay out of the way."

"Allie can fill me in," Sarafino said. He seemed to be speaking to himself.

"We could go out back to the hall," the priest said. "We're on a deadline, and Mariah made this time just to go over some papers with me. Otherwise, I would put it off."

Mariah tapped again.

"Go ahead," said Allie.

Furtado looked at Sarafino, then back at his sister. "Come get me if you need me," he said.

On his way to the door, the priest swept by his desk in the office and gathered up two stacks of thick manila file folders. Mariah stood in the breezeway, wearing a green L.L.Bean ball cap and a light down vest over a turtleneck. Furtado unlocked the door and stepped out. It was not cold outside, but the air in the narrow corridor was fresh and brisk, touched with the woods and ocean, laced with the brash, sweet odors of fall. Mariah had a scent about her, too—maybe it was just the occult smell of the new season's clothes having been taken out of storage. Cedar, Furtado thought. Or maybe naphtha.

"My sister is doing some work in the parlor," he said. "We'll be better out back in the parish hall. What made you knock?"

"Winslow dropped me off. She's got my keys. I didn't think of it until she drove away." Mariah carried three hefty black binders. She was a handsome woman. She wore many small looped earrings in the top part of her ear. Furtado remembered thinking that there must be a word for that part of the ear, but he could not come up with it. She wore a tiny post in the lobe of each ear as well. An open, bright face. A boy's haircut. She was perhaps going on forty, but she was one of those people who would look twenty-five for most of her life, even as her short blond hair was giving over to a mild shade of pewter, even as years out of doors had begun to freckle and line her light skin. But youthful. Yes, and she had stepped right up when old Mrs. Horta left. She had been ready to. He was glad of it. And she was making changes, and they were for the good.

Mariah Grey understood things. She understood what Furtado needed—sometimes even before he could articulate it. She was agile and fluid on the computer, reaching everywhere in seemingly endless reticulations of functions and programs, websites, graphics, graphs, statistics. She built a web page for the parish, and she moved nearly all of their purchasing to online vendors, buying vigil candles, cruets, tapers, altar bread, altar candles, candle followers, books, and pamphlets, allowing Furtado to transfer the savings—there were bargains everywhere in that wild electronic sphere—to other line items in the budget. She took charge of the *Beacon*, the parish newsletter, and put everything on templates in the word-processing program, a new look, sleek and easy to read, with photos and illustrations scanned into them. She came each day and sat at her own desk at the rear of the office, tabulating offerings, tallying charities, updating lists, making agendas, setting calendars. And now she carried the binders with all the material in them that would be selected and arranged and placed into the proposal to be voted on by the Parish Planning Committee and then sent to the Diocese Council. This was Furtado's proposal, a keystone of his overall strategy for lifting Fatima from its present circumstances. Not God's work, exactly. But God's work, inexactly. Or several times removed. It was the Church's work, at any rate.

For the moment, he could turn his head toward figures and projections, debits and credits. All intangibles, written as they were in ink and pencil or printed from the computer, but for all that, they moved people and objects and caused important things to happen in the world of matter. The work would be an anchor for him for a few hours. It would settle his head. It was all about forgiveness, this proposal—forgiveness of monetary debt, which could be measured and weighed, added and subtracted. And the Church of Our Lady of Fatima would rise to solvency. He would see to that.

He and Mariah Grey walked together through the breezeway and out the other end, not into the sacristy of the church, but out another small open doorway to the right, which let onto the narrow, oiled parking lot between the church and the parish hall. The day was still bright, even though the fall sun was lowering now. Above them the sky was moving in long gauzy streaks, as if being drawn off to the west by the great invisible gales of the stratosphere, but around them a mild breeze blew out of the far woods, rising and falling, bringing the tang of bark and fallen leaves with it. The land fell off sharply on the western edge of the church property into a steep hollow where the shingled roofs of old small houses peaked under the gnarled bare limbs of broadleaf. You could see off to some distance. More houses and then more treetops, mostly oak, clumping off in the direction of Caldeira's pond, what was left of the closer woodlands.

Between the church and that far pond were still some scrubby patches where small potholes of lead-colored water collected among the thinned trees. None of these was large enough to be called a pond or have a proper name of its own. They were just rife-smelling little fens choked with cat-o'-nine-tails and alive with tadpoles and screaming frogs in summer—and in winter, crucibles of gray ice that you could slide over with just a good running start and the soles of your shoes frozen slick. Sarafino and Furtado had crossed them in childhood, coming home from school or from church sometimes, calling the route a shortcut, but of course it was not. And they'd had to shoo Allie away from following them and getting into trouble.

Yes, there was Sarafino again—the priest remembering despite himself. This and that. Odd little things. When their bones were still soft and their flesh was light and not fully formed, and they understood nothing. Just kids roaming. There were not so many of the little pond-holes left now. More buildings. The town just growing like that. Money from away. People from Away buying and building. Board by board and shingle by shingle, all the construction was something that spawned some heated talk among committees and at town meetings, but in the end no one was standing on the brakes too hard. No one's hand was on the gearshift, looking for reverse.

"What we have going on in the rectory," Furtado said, surprising himself that it would just come out of him this way, "is that I've taken in a homeless man"—that word again—"someone I grew up with, actually. It's only for a day or so."

Mariah Grey nodded. Her eyes glinted blue-green. Mineral. The color you might see in a smooth wet stone being tossed in the shorebreak out on the back beaches. Her eyes were quick, and when they settled on you their intensity made you feel that you were being physically touched—pushed or pulled.

"He's been away for most of his life, and now he's come back," Furtado continued. "He's in very bad shape."

He watched her as she registered this. She nodded. "I see," she said.

They reached the back door of the parish hall, and the priest pulled his ring of keys from his pocket. Even on such a bright day, the kitchen's north-facing windows were not enough to cut the gloom—or perhaps their eyes were slow in adjusting after the fall sunlight. Furtado held the door open behind him while Mariah tripped the switches for the fluorescent lights above them, and the silvery air breathed into the damp, metallic smells of the broad kitchen and its storeroom. A silence hung for a bit. Then they laid out the work on the stainless steel table and pulled up two metal stools.

They had been working on this plan, in one fashion or another, for months. It was the material accompaniment to the other works—spiritual, civic, social—that the priest had accepted. He had formed a strong assumption of how far the diocese was willing to go, and he knew that part of the bargain was that Fatima would get real fiscal help in return for the renewal in spirit that Furtado was to bring about. You weren't going to get the one without the other. Furtado had pressed his advantage. Yes, he would take this on, but the parish would become more inclusive. He would reach out to everyone. All the diverse communities in the town. He gently and firmly pointed out that the diocese had made mistakes. That was implicit. And now Monsignor Rego and Bishop Mayhew—without admitting as much—moved to redress these errors. It was all unspoken in their many talks, both before and after Furtado took the parish. The assessments had been outsized. The parish had languished, was taken for granted, and when it started to wither, no one had noticed quickly enough. But Rego was a new man, diocese liaison to the Portuguese communities, and he understood that because of its history the town was a unique place, and a specific kind of attention was needed.

"We have insular tendencies," he had told Furtado, his tone conveying that this was to be a given and not something to be debated. "You are a native son. You will be welcomed and trusted." Rego was a small man with a gentle face. His hands were delicate and he used them for emphasis when he talked. Furtado's predecessor was not mentioned much by name in these conversations, but he was a certain Father Kinzie, who never quite connected with the townspeople and seemed ineffective at managing things fiscally. "We will shore up things out there. And this gives you a chance to get yourself back into the life of a secular priest. It's where your heart is." Furtado felt, in those moments, that, yes, that was where his heart was, the secular priesthood. Yes, a parish. Yes, he could run things. It was his strength, was it not? That is what people told him.

There were voices in the chancery and at the diocese that must have put him forward for this posting—so he surmised. Even while he was held in abeyance for two years—it seemed like an abeyance to him, despite the care and brotherhood—while he had prayed and worked and meditated and rehabilitated into sobriety in the far landlocked, rolling fields and orchards of the retreat facility of Mount Perousia, these mysterious voices must have spoken up for him. How else could he have been summoned back to Calumet to be given a parish on his own again so soon? It might have come from Rego and Mayhew themselves, but it did not seem possible. He invented scenarios, invented these avuncular unknown men who would have looked over the situation down at Fatima and said, *Furtado. He would be right for this. Let's give him his chance.*

With the help of the parish planning committee, he and Mariah had gathered documents and figures, looked back over the years at the flow of money, the upkeep of the infrastructure, the demographics, the assessments and loans. Now they were ready to assemble their own documents. Furtado had drawn up a rough diagram with boxes, lines, and labels. Mariah riffed through the binders, and they inserted real numbers into their proper places in the schema. Furtado's drawing was in felt marker and pencil on several sheets of printer paper, taped together, but once they finished, Mariah would transform all of this into color charts, circle graphs, explanations, all those mysteries of ones and zeros in the electronic traffic of the computer's neurons—or whatever stood for neurons.

It went smoothly. Parish income: a little over $3,000 a month, with the summer months holding up the winter months in this average. They would include a description of additional outreach and fundraising activities, and after some debate, Furtado prevailed in not attaching any hard figures to projections in that area, lest they be held to them. They also omitted projected parking lot revenue for the time being. That would have to be refigured once the lot had been refinished and lined so that the parish could charge for tourist parking in the summer. The debt to the diocese was $57,624. A box for that. That did not include the yearly nut—the yearly assessments—a tax to the diocese. They held that out. They would box that later. But it was clear that without the diocese forgiving, or at least buying down, the debt, it would be hard to recover. The indebtedness could be perpetual.

There were other figures that had to be line-itemed—outreach activities, catechism classes, the newsletter. But those were nothing compared with the infrastructure needs. There was almost nothing that didn't require repair or renovation. And once something was opened or touched, all the new construction codes must be met—new codes set in place by the building boom. The parish hall was newer and needed very little except plumbing and septic upgrades, but the rectory and the church hadn't had significant work in decades. There would have to be money for new roofs, and a new furnace for the church. These projects would require specific bids that would come only later, after the diocese had acted upon the proposal in some way, but for now they could use rough estimates. In a sense, the proposal remained a kind of argument.

The priest had composed, actually, two plans. The first: Diocese forgives everything. Zero out the debt, give the Parish of Fatima a two-year payment skip on the regular assessments, and then start over again, clean. Loans for infrastructure to be negotiated. The second plan: Reduce the assessment and give the parish a dollar's forgiveness for each dollar paid on the debt. Debt to be frozen at current level, with no new interest added. Loans to be negotiated. The plans were simple. The documentation that they were now assembling would be convincing. By Furtado's calculations, the diocese would reject the first plan and accept the second. And the second would be a very good deal for the Church of Our Lady of Fatima.

They worked together seriously, small-talking, a diminutive joke here and there. Good work. Some part of Furtado forgot—or rather, laid aside—the memory of the nighttime raptures and desponds. The gin. The painkillers. Only his shoulder reminded him, but it was easily moderated, that little nag against the happiness of the work. Yet behind all was a dispiriting eschatological presence. Every small happiness seemed always a suspension over a gorge or an abyss. Always fraught with plummeting. And the plummeting always came. There were chemical changes in his brain. He had read about such things. They discussed such things at Perousia: dependence, addiction. And other, particular problems of the priesthood. How could one combat his own cellular mutations? What could be hiding among them?

"I can get started on a mock-up draft of this tomorrow," Mariah told him, when there was no more to be done there at the steel table. "If the office is okay to use. The homeless man," she said. "Your old friend. I don't want to get in the way."

Yes, that. The homeless man. Enough now to tip him over. For despite the years, and despite his dire condition, Sarafino came with baggage. And so the priest drifted down. It must have shown in his countenance. Yes, down he came, and she watched him. There was an opaqueness about her. Her eyes were not windows that one could see into. Everything streamed outward. A scrutiny. A presence. He knew more than a few things about her. She lived in a condominium, one of the new buildings, a disgraceful scarring edifice over by the big pond, with her partner, Winslow, a large and quiet woman who had lived in the town for decades, and who, the priest understood, had some significant reputation as an artist. Mariah possessed a doctorate in biological science and wrote papers and books on the lives of wild things. Before she came to the town, she had worked for the state of Minnesota, flying an old tail dragger of an airplane—an old Piper Cub that she had bought from a farmer in Galesburg, Illinois. She had fixed it with big pontoons then. She would fly to remote lake islands or lakeshores and live alone for weeks at a time counting waterfowl. She often flew with her golden Labrador, Darwin, a puppy then, as her only companion. She had since written papers on geese migration and flyway patterns on the Cape, and now she was studying something called regime shifts in the kettle ponds: one species multiplying out of proportion and thus altering and taking over the micro-environment. She was interested in sunfish and horned pout. Or perhaps it was bluegills.

Mariah had flown the Piper to town, intending to sell it if she decided to stay. But she crashed it. She came in on her approach to the town's little airport, out by the dunes and the back beach, but she dropped just short of the beach road, just short of the runway, missing the edge of the stunted pine trees that lined the road there, but coming down with no power onto the soft hillocks of sand dune. The plane flipped. Darwin was fine, but Mariah sustained a broken jaw and collarbone. "So that's how I came here, Father Manny. Slammed right into the town. I ran out of gas," she would tell with half a smile. "The wire got stuck." She would explain that the old Piper's fuel gauge was simply a wire that rose and fell on a float in the gas tank. A cork in a beer bottle. But Winslow would say that Mariah fell out of the sky to be with her. "Right out of the sky," she would say. "Like a gift. You ought to be able to appreciate that, Manuel." She meant because of his being a priest, which Winslow always treated with some degree of irony. He did not think it was a remark directed at his own plane crash, deep in the past, which he rarely talked about, and which Winslow probably would not have heard about. But hearing Mariah's story when she first started coming around to the church attracted him. It shone a light on her, so when she first asked about doing some volunteer work, he was inclined to pay attention.

Winslow drew and took photographs but was mostly a sculptor. She fashioned objects out of materials she found in the town's old middens and abandoned dumps, or that she salvaged from the flotsam along the beaches. Furtado found her compositions difficult to figure out. Sometimes they were twisted and airy, sometimes dense and hulking. One exhibit of hers that the priest did understand was a series of large color photographs, starting with the recovery of an enormous, elongated, irregular boulder of wine-colored rust and moving by stages to the object that had lain within it, an antiquated eight-foot kedge anchor. She had discovered the anchor out at the very edge of the flats at the west end of the harbor. It had been an extremely low tide, and she had been walking along with her Garrett metal detector, looking for the odd coin or tool that she sometimes turned up. The machine buzzed something very large under the sandbar, and she had to come back with some men at low tide the next day to dig around the massive object. Once they saw what they had, they fastened a cable to it, and then a painter with a float. She prevailed on one of the fishing-boat skippers to ease over the water—shallow there even at high tide—and winch it up. The photos showed the stages of Winslow's process and hung on a wall behind the reclaimed anchor itself, which sat in a boarded bed of white sand—black, scarred iron, shank, flukes, and mostly withered stock—in a gallery of the town's Heritage Society.

Winslow herself seemed as much the subject of the photos as the anchor. In the pictures, as in life, one got a sense of her imposing presence, her powerful body. She was perhaps a decade older than Furtado, in her early sixties, but her skin was smooth and her features still held to a vital relief. Heavy, yes, but she carried her weight as a kind of strength. Her hair was an almost fluorescent silver, and thick, and she wore it usually in a dense braid that fell down between her shoulder blades. "She is the most beautiful woman I have ever known," Mariah had told him once, but, of course, Mariah was in love with her.

In that same conversation, early on, when Mariah had first begun to come around the church, she'd told the priest something about her journey.

"I saw myself alone, Father Manny. I mean, as I was then. Alone. And I had made peace with that. That's part of what drew me out here. Not just the Cape, but the very outermost stretch of it. Land's end. The farthest reach. The last resort. It all sounded like a conclusion. I'd read all about it, and I knew there was a good deal of work I could do on the ecology here. But short of an island somewhere, this seemed right. It seemed like my life. There were complications. I suppose you hear such things all the time. But it was the loneliness. Not lonely for God. I don't mean that. I mean for another life. *Another's* life, I guess I should say. I wanted to be with someone. I fell in love with someone at the last of it. Someone unavailable. Very unavailable. Someone from the church I had been attending at the time, married and with two little kids, and not inclined to reciprocate, to put it euphemistically. She lived in another world. I made a terrible, terrible fool of myself. Horrible. It was true heartache, as dumb as I know that can sound. I had gotten to the point where I believed that a relationship—let me just say it, *love*—was never going to be possible for me. So I resigned myself. I would come here to this far place and live alone with Darwin and I would—I don't know—write my books and papers and live quietly by myself and grow old. It seemed even pleasant sometimes to think about it. But then Winslow was here. What a wonder. After I had become so complacent about not having hope."

"But you weren't that old," the priest had protested. And he wanted to hear more. "Why such despair?"

"I was so tired of trying to find someone and it always being the dead-wrong person. It seemed all my fault. I don't know," she had said. "But when I saw Winslow for the first time—it was at a gallery, but she wasn't the one exhibiting. Somebody else was opening. I don't even remember who. But when I saw her, the moment I saw her, I was frightened, Father. Oh, not of her in particular. But of what I felt inside me—and after I thought I had laid all that to rest. After I had banked the fire. I felt that rise up in my breast. It was just in that one moment, and I hated it because I felt so stupid. I didn't know what to do. There was wine there. You know, kind of warm white wine in those little plastic cups, and food, and so I took a cup and a paper plate, and I stood back and decided I would watch her. I didn't know anything about her, of course, if she was married or with someone or whatever. I couldn't believe what I was already starting to put myself through.

"And then she must have seen me watching her or something, because she looked right at me and something moved in her face—that great face of hers—not a smile or a frown. Nothing you could put a name to. But then she walked right over to me, and do you know what she said? She said, 'So, who's the new girl?' You could have knocked me over. Well, that's it, Father. I came here so much at the end of my rope. My wits' end. And then Winslow walked right into me. So I believe God wants me here. I believe I have been guided. If that doesn't sound presumptuous."

He hadn't taken her up on whether or not she thought she was being guided when she was lonely and despairing. But she had presented herself to him, and she was youthful and fresh and electric, and he saw that this was someone who would be very useful. He had been thinking mostly of community building then, reaching out to her particular community, but she'd quickly shown him much more than that. She'd worked to make herself indispensable. He knew about that himself. He knew what that was like. He knew she was planting a flag for herself in the Church. She was proving something, no doubt. It didn't matter. He considered his own needs. He had accepted it all.

Winslow did not attend church—the priest had invited her a few times, then made it a point not to press her on it—but she occasionally came along with Mariah and helped her with small chores. There was clearly something significant between them, a kind of devotion, that was palpable, and on a given day it could set the priest to wondering about the exact lineaments of worldly happiness, and this could leave him feeling stranded. So much of his calling entailed opening himself only to the woes and laments of others.

Furtado felt something—his pulse, most likely—beating softly but sorely along the fissures of the old injury in his neck. Then his ear went dead for a few seconds, against the long beep from inside his head. He realized that Mariah Grey was simply staring at him, as he stared at her. The priest tried to recover. "The homeless man," he repeated.

Mariah waited for him to finish. Not moving her gaze. Her attentive face.

"He's very ill," said Furtado. "I will have to do something for him."

"Can you tell me?" asked Mariah.

She asked, and so he told her. That was how he brought her into it. It was the only thing to do. There would be no turning back after that. She would become part and party to everything now, to all that was to come. He told her everything he knew about Sarafino Pomba.

When they had finished, Mariah and the priest carried their materials out of the building and into the flattening light of the late afternoon. The world was quiet. They did not speak until they reached the office door, and then Mariah handed him the binders and told him she would be back in the morning. She would walk home along the small lanes and side streets that led to the condominiums out by the big pond. When he entered the rectory, he found Allie sitting in the easy chair in a globe of yellow lamplight. At her feet was the round wicker sewing basket that she kept at the rectory, and next to it lay a small stack of folded clothing. Pants. Shirts. In her lap, another pair of pants. Sweats. She was hemming them up.

"How is he?" Furtado asked. It struck a nerve that Sarafino was not in the parlor with her.

"He's in bed. Did you two get your work done?"

"Yes," said the priest. Then he added, "Thank you."

"I got these from the rummage sale bin," she said, though he could see that for himself. "The pants just need to be shortened. The shirts, I can't do much, but I moved the buttons so they close up better and won't hang off him. He won't look so bad like that."

"Good," Furtado said. "He was okay, then? You didn't have any trouble? I didn't think we'd be so long."

"He ate. We talked a lot. I kind of wore him down, I guess. But he really wanted to talk, Manny. It's been so long. It's so strange, seeing him."

"Yes."

"He was, like, one of us. Family. I mean, a brother. I guess Papa never liked him much, though."

"He called me 'brother' when I found him in the church. Did he say how he came here?"

"Some guy gave him a ride from Boston, he said."

"He's got to go to a clinic," said the priest. "I have to find a place for him. I'm going to make a couple of calls. Mariah is, too. I can't help him here."

"He doesn't want anybody to know he's here, Manny."

"Well, Mariah's here all the time. She needed to know."

Alzaida shook her head. "I'm talking about this clinic stuff. You can't do that."

Furtado looked at her. She leaned toward him over the sewing in her lap. She had not issued an order. It was an appeal, the way her voice tracked upward through its three or four notes.

"All that stuff about being dead. He was in jail, Manny. Prison. That's when he started the rumor that he was dead. He couldn't bear it. Like anybody back here would know or care after all those years. Except us."

Furtado just nodded.

"He's mixed up sometimes. But here's how it went: He was in prison for a while for armed robbery. A place called Souza-Baranowski? It's here in the state someplace. He had been in trouble in New York, too. He wasn't too clear on that, but I think some jail. Drugs. But then he got out on parole."

"He's an ex-convict, then," Furtado said.

"He's sick is what he is, Manny. He says he's going to die."

"Alzaida."

"Don't, please, Manny. I know you're going to get all . . . however you get. This is Sarafino we're talking about."

"Who we haven't seen or heard from for most of our adult lives," Furtado said.

He could see his sister's face begin to crumble, and he could see her efforts not to let it. She glared at him finally. "He says the Virgin Mary appears to him."

"That much he told me," said the priest. He suddenly felt worn out. He moved to the couch and sat down. He looked at his sister's face. A scowl. "What is it, Allie? What else?"

"Manny, he got into trouble again." She hesitated. She regarded the blue sweatpants in her lap as though they were an open book. Then she looked up. "Why you can't say he's here—there's a warrant out for him. The police are looking for him. He says he doesn't have too long to live. He wants us to help him. To save him. Otherwise they'll put him back in prison, and he'll die there." Her voice rose to a bare plea now. "He came back to us, Manny. We can't just turn him out someplace. We have to help him."

"A warrant," Furtado said. "What for?"

Alzaida bit her lip and sighed. "Armed robbery," she said.

five

HE DID NOT BELIEVE THAT JESUS WAS DIVINE OR THE SON OF GOD, nor did he believe that God impregnated a young girl through the Holy Spirit (which reminded him now of Zeus and all of his disguised copulations with humans). So he did not believe that Our Lady appeared to Sarafino Pomba or ever to anyone else. He did not believe in the Resurrection. He did not believe that God would sacrifice a son to be tortured to death in order to redeem a race of beings He Himself created imperfectly. The idea seemed barbaric and disgusting to him. Degenerate. He had believed these things utterly at one time and then lost the belief one time before, regained it, and now had lost it again. He knew this was not extraordinary. He and Father John Sweet talked about such things, though in roundabout ways—Furtado was always circumspect in the company of the other priest. It was discussed at Mount Perousia, too. It was no mystery. And it had even been a subject at seminary. There was a great deal of literature on it. There were retreats and seminars. A vocation had its arcs and stages. The skeptical priest, so-called, was more a way station than an aberration. He was more common than the laity might expect. This was something one passed through, worked through, this loss of faith. So it was said. But it was a trouble nonetheless. Folly to say it was not a trouble.

None of this much changed the way Furtado's daily work at the parish evolved. Aside from the very real business of keeping the physical operations viable and solvent, the pastor, after all, was there to save the flock. It was not a matter of eternity for him, this salvation, but a matter of lifting the quotidian despairs and depressions, the wounds and griefs. And of pointing out the small happinesses. The generosities of spirit that bloomed ephemerally in the world. The sinful world, he might say, but what was sin but humanness? And anyway, he was not bereft of God. God was real and present in his life and everywhere else. Exactly how was a huge conundrum. There were just too many bad ideas about Him. He understood all the skeptical rhetorics, so-called—Maimonides, Hume, Kant, Schleiermacher—they nested in his bookshelves along with others. This was one more thing he wrestled with. Were there *only* bad ideas about Him? That seemed part of humanness, too. And so when he prayed, his prayers took many forms. Sometimes he appeared to pray directly into his ledgers in gouts of language. He came from wildly different positions. He never knew where he would be standing. He saw no contradictions. There were no balancing acts. There was just a kind of fluidity where everything coexisted. His own dark shifts of mind. His own doubts. There was light, too. Sometimes it was impossible to tell the difference. It was impossible to tell, for instance, what seemed to be rushing toward him (and there was a real sense of that, of something bearing down on him) or what the conclusion of anything might be.

When Sarafino arose later that night, the priest tended to him. He fed him from groceries that Alzaida had run out and purchased for him before she drove back home. Safe food. Banana, boiled rice, some toast, watered apple juice. Together they had gone through his grimy duffel and pulled out a few things that Sarafino wanted: a blue glass rosary, an old missal with a fat elastic around it, holding its pages in, and a small, powder-blue, plastic statue of a guardian angel, chubby-faced, hands clasped in prayer. Sarafino had no wallet. There were some thick, worn manila envelopes at the bottom of the bag, but they left those alone. The priest left the few items of clothing alone, too. He took some clean socks and underwear from his own drawers and laid them in the small dresser in the spare room, and he added the pants and shirts that Allie had altered. Sarafino did not speak much. He was warm to the touch. The priest tried to take his temperature, but Sarafino refused. He washed at the bathroom sink and used the toothbrush that Allie had brought along with the groceries. And together they went back to the bedroom and Furtado got him settled in the bed. Sarafino asked for a candle, and the priest brought in a little votive glass and a plaster statue of the Virgin, and he set them on the bureau next to the angel and lit the candle. Sarafino asked to pray a Rosary together, but then he was too tired to speak, so the priest said the Our Fathers and Hail Marys aloud, and Sarafino moved the beads accordingly through his fingers, his eyes closed. The priest sat in the semidarkness of the candlelit room until Sarafino became lost in that noisy breathing, the edgy collapse that was, for him, sleep.

Furtado left Sarafino's door open, and he gathered his tall glass tumbler from the kitchen and filled it with ice and quietly climbed the little stairway to his study. He kept the door to his study open as well, so he would be able to hear Sarafino if some urgency arose in the night. It was late when he finally knelt at the wooden *prie-deux* that sat beside his desk. This piece of furniture, too, had come to him with the rectory, and he had kept it where he found it, there in the room with the scarred desk, the rough, plank bookcases, and a step stool that he'd found he could use to reach the higher shelves when his shoulder would not cooperate. The *prie-deux* was not comfortable. It was not meant to be. He had added a quilt to it, folded across the hard kneeler as a pad to lessen the stress on his knees, but that was its only modification. He knelt and he prayed with the practiced discipline of a priest. He prayed to the great mystery that perplexed him. He addressed the silence with his own voice from deep inside his head, and then he listened to the silence. The long silence that came back to him. He asked for nothing.

When the pain increased so that it began to radiate into his head and spine and he could no longer kneel in that position, he moved to the desk and took from the top drawer one of the fat, copper-colored plastic vials and dropped several of its long tablets into his palm. He put them into his mouth and bit through them, tasting their bitterness, and held them on his tongue while he took the bottle of Gordon's from the taller, lower drawer and poured the bright, transparent gin into the tumbler. The ice had melted some while he prayed, and a small bit of water had pooled in the bottom of the glass, but it was nothing so clear as the gin that he topped the glass with. Nothing like that metallic shine in the desk's halogen lamplight. Or those deep, peaceful odors of botanicals and spirits.

His own spirit was far from quiet. The good work of the day, the facts and figures of the parish debt proposal, was far behind him. No, not far behind him—it was gone entirely. Absent to exist in an alternate world. A place he no longer inhabited. Now the great circle of Sarafino's return encompassed him. There were things not quite right about it, of course. Things that didn't add up. But to come back to the church, and then to bring up Old Man Coelho. Out of nowhere. After decades. He wrote the events of the day while he ruminated on this. Then the gin and the pills began taking hold. The pain, while it didn't actually recede yet, turned in another direction. It became irrelevant. And better was the sense of leaving behind the weight of his body. That lifting. He allowed himself to lapse into that comfort. It spread like grace among his cells. He swallowed from the cold, clear tumbler. He lifted himself from the world of matter. He wrote from Augustine: *Great is the power of memory! It is something terrifying, my God, a profound and infinite multiplicity, and this thing is the mind, and this thing is myself. What then am I, my God?*

To which there was no answer. But in the deep quiet of the night, the gin and the pills and one small lamp on his desk, the pen strokes leaning and streaming across the pages of the ledger, he went back after Sarafino. He went back after himself.

He made several beginnings. He could not find where to begin. He lined things out. Great emotion-filled strokes, slashes of ink, embossed there with the wild force of the pen. And then winter. Early winter. That seemed to be a key. And the war. The war had been distant trouble. It had meant nothing in the town, as far as the boys could tell, except for the draft, which had hung over him and Sarafino like an iron hammer. It kept their heads bowed. It and the townspeople, the old Portuguese. No fancy deferments here. No one had ever heard of draft counseling. No one thought of running to Canada. That all happened in other places. For other classes of people. Both he and Sarafino had already been called to Boston for their preliminary physicals. Now they simply waited for the final letter.

They waited.

The summer came and went. They were finished with high school. There was no fishing for either of them. Furtado had always refused to fish with his father—a privileged summer job for captains' sons. That great soreness between Pai Furtado and his son Manny. So now, in fall, there was no work. Not the remotest idea of college, nothing for them to do. No inclination to go anywhere. Then Sarafino received his induction letter. Sarafino first. This time, no coming back to wait. He would report to Boston and be transported to Fort Dix, New Jersey. So they drank and did whatever drugs they could get hold of. Beautiful Sarafino. Dark and lovely, like the angel he was named for. And himself, Manny Furtado. They believed they would die for one another in those days.

They were not good boys. They had done inhalers that night. Maybe it was two nights in a row. The priest saw how difficult this was. How could he be certain what was memory and what was not? What he constructed out of the pieces and fragments? He reflected on Augustine again, his optimism. Augustine, who believed that God was logical, that God thought with the same logic that humans used. That the pieces would lead to the whole. The priest himself was not so certain, but a thread unwound with momentum and he took it up.

Inhalers: Furtado had bought them at Parson's Pharmacy, and they'd taken them to Sarafino's house, where no one was home. These were the green plastic tubes, like lipstick tubes, that you sniffed to unblock a stuffy nose. They unscrewed the casings and took out the cotton inserts that were saturated with Benzedrine—in those days, no one cared about such a thing—and then they steeped the cotton in hot water, as though they were making tea, and drank the clear infusion. Bitter as gall.

And somehow it became day again. The day was utterly clear in recall now. The two of them. High. Cranked. Wired. Like two paper birds skidding around in the sky of some crazy diorama. And then he held the rifle and had Sarafino pinned down behind what was left of the cement foundation of the old icehouse out at Caldeira's pond. The pond in those days—one of those places, the mild wilderness of something abandoned to slide back into the original land. Here was wild grass and brush, briar and thorn, scrub oak, alder and poplar.

The dirt road leading in was once a wagon road, the ruts carved from iron-tired tumbrels and drays. There was only one house along that road then. Or two. Back where the oiled tar road faded into the packed dirt. The edge of town then. The house, or houses—he thought there must have been two—gray-shingled, small, with uncertain brick chimneys up through the center of the roofs. Choked with brush. Paint long since weathered away. And the wagon ruts coming out on the level adjacent to the pond.

Still one building standing, a two-storied shed or barn of some kind, close to disintegration. The pond itself here was wide-bellied, its water black and ruffed in the wind. No ice yet. Or perhaps a little collar, glasslike, a tissue beginning to pucker along its shallow edges. The black water spread out to the east, and through a waterway smaller than a footpath, it joined another pond. To the west it narrowed into long, creeklike arms and fingers, a mile or more among impossible marshy tangles until it gave out at the edge of dunes. But here, the remnants of the ice works. A bridge still rose partially from its collapse in the dark water, its gray-white timbers like the fossil bones of some antediluvian creature, and in the ground sank the deep, wood-lined pits where the ice, harvested in winter by men with long-handled saws, would be buried and packed in straw to last well into the summer months, preserving fish on the long trips to market.

A gray day, the grayness of everything, but then the black pond and at its most distant edge, the profound green of the scrub pines, gleaming like kings on the crowns of the far sand hills.

Furtado emptied a clip at the top of the wall of the old foundation, and the bullets cracked off over the water in staccato ricochet. They did not whine like in the movies. Just a flat *crack-crack-crack* multiplying itself in echo over the cold black surface of the pond. Once Furtado burned through the clip, Sarafino got up and ran, heading for another piece of low wall about twenty yards away. Furtado slapped another clip in and pointed the rifle—a long, slender .22 with a blond stock, his father's gun—just behind Sarafino's heels, *crack-crack-crack*, and Sarafino leapt, dived headfirst behind the foundation, and Furtado peppered the old concrete just above where he knew Sarafino would be crawling.

Furtado spent a whole box of shells that way, and then they switched places, Furtado behind the walls under this playful fire, Sarafino at the trigger. The Benzedrine heartbeat. The lightning thoughts and reactions. The jagged perfection of movement. This was it. This was the world into which they were being conscripted. They were making a game of it. It was breathtaking.

The priest swallowed some more gin. The pills, deep in his system now, gave up a pungent, alkaloid taste in the back of his throat. So agreeable. His lips numbed. A small wave of contentment passed through his nerves. His thick, heavy handwriting filled the lined pages. The gin was cold, but it warmed its way down into his depths. It lit small fires. There he was, walking that old dirt road then. The stock of the .22 over his shoulder, his hand on the barrel, balancing it there. The dusk coming on. The illusion of it rising from the tenebrous mist among the wild brambles, the trash woodlands that crowded the wagon ruts. A place in memory now. Opening to him.

How they came to the church. How they decided on the church. Not so clear. But it was hours later. Furtado thought it could have been ten o'clock or so. It was more of a calculation than a recollection. A drizzle falling. Half rain, half fog. A veil. Cold, not quite ready to snow, but the streets were deserted. The town had retired or receded from itself so that there were only dark streets and darker buildings. They would remain high for hours still. The beauty of doing that kind of inhaler. Sarafino going off to the Army in the morning. He would still be high.

They were laughing when they reached the church. Their bodies became laughter. All of this was to them, after all, too funny. Furtado could not remember where the dolly had come from. That could mean Sarafino had brought it. Or maybe they had stolen it together on their way.

Now Sarafino was pushing the dolly—a perfect dolly. Heavy. Industrial. With web straps and pneumatic wheels. They could have been invisible if they'd wished. Perhaps they were. Such was the frenzied thinking. For weeks they had been hiking out to the state road with a roofer's hammer and smashing the hood-eyed, yellow blinking light where the road divided near the state beach, at the bathhouse and parking lot. What townies would never stop calling the *new road* and the *new beach*, though other names would be given. Each time the light was repaired, they would go out and smash it again. They were sure that Chief Matta and the other town police must have watched, trying to discover who these vandals were, but how could they be caught at anything? They could disrupt. They could run or crawl through any darkness. They could make the world pay for its slights and injustices. They were beyond any insipid laws. Above any foolish ideas of order. Yes, such was the thinking.

The priest put down the pen and rested his hand. He rose slowly from the desk and stood in the doorway. He listened to the house. He thought he might hear Sarafino's breathing from downstairs, but there was only silence. If he strained he could hear the ticking of the tide clock in the parlor. His own ears were quiet within, the ringing and beeping having gone off someplace. There was no pain. Just a kind of marker where the pain had been. Where it would return. He went back to the desk. He finished the small inch of gin and melted ice at the bottom of the tumbler.

And the boys crept along the street. More trees then on Church Street. Wet bark. Trunks crowding. Limbs disappearing up into the drizzle and darkness. Smell of elm. Smell of decaying leaves. Wan halos in the gloom around the ineffectual streetlights. The windows of the houses, black. The windows of the rectory, black. Sarafino and Manny, then. Up to the far side of the church, and then around to the back. Not much there in those days. The parking lot. The hill beyond where the new elementary school sat, but all that was a table-land of blackness. Their aim was the small window at the back of the church. It was not locked and they knew this, though the priest now could not remember how they had learned it. It was not locked because it could not be locked. The pin was broken. It could be shut tight, yes, but not locked. If you pulled hard, outward, on the upper casing, it would slip, and then you could pull again, downward, opening the top half of the window. They pulled. It gave. It slid. Yes, they had broken in that way before. They had robbed the poor-box at the back of the church—$7.75. Mostly quarters. Some half-dollars. A couple of bills. No one seemed to have noticed.

Furtado lifted the window and wiggled through. He came down heels over head into the blackness of the shallow room behind the sanctuary. Once inside he turned and, feeling the casing, closed the window carefully so that no one could see that it had ever been opened. Then he walked from behind the altar, and in the light of the sanctuary lamp and the glow of the votive candles, he made his way to the west side door of the church—the door that faced away from the street and the rectory, faced only that same embankment that was there today, the crepuscular hollow, its heavy-limbed trees, its blind houses. He opened the wide, heavy door, where Sarafino was waiting with the dolly, and let him into the building.

The church was cold inside. It seemed barnlike in the stillness and gloom that the breathy light of the candles did so little to dispel. They had brought a small flashlight with them, and they used it then, pointing it downward at their shoes to keep the beam from scattering through the ruby, purple, yellow, green, and blue stained glass in the Gothic-arched windows, each window showing a scene from the gospels, each embossed with the name of the fishing boat whose captain and crew had made the donations that purchased it. One of the windows was from the Furtado boat, the name there under Christ as He leaned back from the apostles' little craft and calmed the sea: *Ilha do Pico.*

They understood, somehow, that none of their stealth was necessary. No one from town would be abroad on such a night. No one to ever see a random beam of pale light strike the colors of a stained-glass window—if such a light would even show through the weather and gloom. And if someone did see, nothing would be made of it. Old Father Santos, they knew, slept off in the rectory on the far side of the church. If he were to come, they would hear him. They would vanish. They had come to steal the church's new treasure, the marvelous statue of Our Lady of Fatima. They would not be discovered.

The statue. It stood about five and a half feet high and was carved from heartwood—this was a detail the priest would not remember, the name of the wood, the name of the tree—and finished and painted and lacquered in layers and layers to a beatific shine. Her garment was porcelain white and trimmed with gold piping. Something—perhaps even gold dust—embedded deep in the finish gave a starlike sparkle to her refined curves. Her face was pink, her eyes dark and set in such a way that one could read in them a compassion that was so heightened that such an expression would never be found in life. And yet you recognized it. Her lips were a muted red. Her mouth was inscrutable—a smile, yes, but with such sadness behind it. A smile that encompassed everything. And on her head a golden crown. She gleamed, when the light struck her, like fine china or glazed crystal.

It was a triumph for the parish, for Father Santos had been leading efforts to commission and procure such a work of art for years. It had become the old priest's particular mission. It was said that Father Braga himself had such a thing in mind—something to stand in the church that he had campaigned so hard to rename in the honor of Portugal's own dearest Lady—but he never had the time to complete the project. So Father Santos, coming after him, had led special collections, fundraising fish fries on Fridays, and rummage sales, extra collections, even penny drives at the weekly catechism classes, all to bring to the parish—all of the communicants Portuguese or Azorean then, of course—the most lovely image possible of the Holy Mother as She appeared in the Portuguese Miracle.

It had taken years, but the donations had kept coming in steadily, and from time to time Father Santos would announce the progress from the pulpit at Sunday Mass. And then there was Manny Furtado's father. His enormous father. Like all of the other captains, he laid down serious money in the name of the boat whenever he could. For the luck. For the blessing and grace. And, the priest would write, for the vanity. Finally, when the measure was close, it was Pai Furtado himself—Pai Furtado and the *Ilha do Pico*—putting the fund over the top with a great sharing of wealth after swapping out their otter trawl for a scalloping chain and grinding home each night loaded down to the gunnels. They might as well have struck gold. It was as though Pai had wrought the statue with his own huge arms, so great was his claim on it.

And so it came to pass. The statue was ordered. Or statues. The three children would be represented, too. The carvings would be done in Portugal. The very special and resilient wood from Portugal—or had it been Brazil? No, it would not come to the priest as he wrote—the name of that hard wood. All he could think of was cork, Portugal's major export, the only thing he ever remembered being said about Portugal in school. Even then, that oddness. As though they, the Portuguese in town, were real only to themselves. None of their teachers ever even told them that Magellan was Portuguese. Or Vasco da Gama. But now this wonderful statue would be a piece of the Old Country to stand in the church. This would remind them. This must have been Braga's original notion. They must not hold themselves back. The Virgin had performed the greatest miracle of the modern world on Portuguese soil.

The parish had held a dedication at the end of summer. A special Mass and benediction. The church had never been so full. The Knights of Columbus marched in full regalia—the capes, the plumed hats, the gleaming silver swords. The Holy Rosary Sodality Choir sang "Tantum Ergo Sacramentum" and a beautiful "Ave Maria," Mae Furtado's sweet voice the favorite of all then. She could bring God right into your heart with that voice, was what the town said of her.

Yes, his mother sang, and the air bellied with the strident perfumes of incense and altar blossoms. It was a great moment for the town. And so what better devilment than to take the statue and hide Her? And then, after a few days, after the right amount of time for just the right effect, put her to be found in some crazy place. One of the freezers in the West End

Cold Storage, say. Or a classroom at the high school. Or the boys' showers. Well, that would be Manny's job—Sarafino would be off at boot camp. But all the better. It would be a mystery. Something to set the town afire with gossip. Too, too funny. They could think of nothing else in the world so funny.

They sat there for a while in the silence of the church, but it took great effort to remain still. The body wanted to move. The mind raced. The dolly now lay at the feet of Our Lady, between Lucia—the oldest of the three children—and the little kneeling Francisco Marta, who died only months after the visions. His sister Jacinta died not long after him. But Manny and Sarafino were not interested in these children, except that their images might be bolted to the floor, and might have to be unbolted—at least one of them—if the large statue of the Virgin was to be lowered onto the dolly. They waited. They listened for one unbearable moment longer. They heard nothing. No car's motor. No priest's footsteps in the breezeway. So they began.

Furtado opened his windbreaker and from beneath it pulled out a bulky rectangle of heavy blue plastic tarp. He took a thick spool of ganjon twine from his pocket. Sarafino produced a small chrome crescent wrench. They both wore the cheap white-canvas work gloves that the wharf laborers wore. That Sarafino's father wore. They laid the flashlight on the floor, flat, so that the light only scattered and bounced enough for them to see their work. The white gloves and black jackets made them seem like actors in a play. It was hard to keep from laughing. Then it was hard to keep from shouting for their good luck: the statues in the alcove were not bolted down at all. Manny rocked Francisco, then slid him out of the way. The small figure was much heavier than it looked. The children had clearly been carved to rest on a stable base formed by their knees and garments. Lining the bottom was a flat steel plate held by a large single bolt, recessed, extending up into the wood. They approached the Virgin. In the tableau She was positioned so that She gazed down at the children but also seemed to look out over the world. There was the calm certainty of one who is so close to God. One who understands great secrets. The sacred Mother, who knows that despite all the trials and disasters of humankind, all will be well.

They rocked Her. Her base was flanged—again using the garment to allow an opening-out to the wide steel platform, a footing on which the image rested in perfect stability. They slid the lip of the dolly beneath Her and then tipped Her, laying Her down, the dolly beneath Her. They were surprised to see that the crown, which appeared to have been placed separately on the Virgin's head, was actually carved from the same great piece of wood, an intricacy, yet solid upon Her. And touching Her was like touching glass, all the layers of clear resins over Her painted colors. They maneuvered Her so as to wrap the tarp around Her several times, folding and tucking the folds of vinyl at top and bottom to seal Her, and then wrapping Her from head to base tightly with the ganjon twine. When this was done they passed the webbed holding straps of the dolly around Her and levered them tight. She was theirs now. She would go with them.

Her weight was something they had not figured. Yet the dolly balanced Her perfectly on the fulcrum of its wheels. The rails fit their hands with a solid correctness. They put Francisco back in his place, made sure they left nothing behind, and then they wheeled the shrouded Virgin Mother down the center aisle and then along the transverse aisle to the side double doors where they had entered. They halted there for a minute and listened. Then Furtado cracked the door and passed through. The drizzle still fell, close to freezing. So light that it almost fell upward. The side yard of the church was dark and glistening. The hedge was a black loaf in the murky night. Nothing moved. Nothing saw.

They rolled the dolly out onto the walk and let the door lock silently and carefully behind them. Then they turned and wheeled Our Lady of Fatima across the back parking lot, hugging the toe and shadow of the hill behind them. Up the banking at the side of the high school. Under the shadow of the Pilgrim's Tower and its wooded hill. Up Cemetery Road. Nothing around them. Past houses now. A field on their right. Then the graveyard itself—or graveyards. Another town, it seemed, behind the town. Hills and valleys of graves. Hundreds of years' worth. They were dazzled by their own brilliance, for what places are more deserted at night than graveyards? And the asphalt path that wound and crossed the rolling hills of the cemetery came out near the highway at the edge of town. And across the highway lay the woods, and they knew by heart every path in them.

The blackness of the graveyard was nearly absolute. The priest, in remembering, in that trancelike otherworldliness of re-creating, believed that his sense of that blackness must be mistaken. Something added now by his mind. Perhaps a transference of some other blackness—that one other blackness, also from a time long past, that sometimes came to him, dreamlike too, but always unbidden. He refused to stray. He stretched at the desk. He touched the knobs of his spine where his neck rose from his collar. He kneaded the soft tissue—still some good muscle there along his shoulder. The little dumbbells. He shook his hand limply so that the fingers made a plopping sound as they flagged into one another. Then he took up the pen again. *The blackness of the graveyard was nearly absolute.*

It was almost impossible to find their way, except that the gravestones rose as less-dark shadows than the sodden rolling earth beneath and around them. That and the boys bent close to the ground, following the wet, even darker, asphalt path among the plots. The drizzle, cold and drifting. The quiet was broken only by the faint metallic clanking of what at first sounded eerily like a chain, but which they quickly realized was a metal turnbuckle tapping the iron flagpole at the top of the rounded knoll that rose to the east. They heaved the Queen of Heaven before them, taking turns at the dolly. They followed that narrow strip of pavement that was the hearse road. The caretaker's way. They were close enough now to see, through the scatter of the falling mist, the dulled and blurred lights of the last building in town, the VFW Hall.

Such a happiness came over them. So safe among the tombstones. So smug to think of a route where no one would ever venture. Where no cruising police car would ever idly stumble on them. Where the chance of a passerby or a face in a window was impossible. Who could have thought, then, that a body would rise from a grave?

But that is exactly what happened.

Such was the appearance. Someone lifted up—or walked out from, or materialized in front of . . . Furtado could not be sure precisely how it happened. But suddenly, right before them, there stood a man. They screamed. They jumped. The Benzedrine. Blood pounded. Furtado dropped the dolly and the upper rail barked his shin before the whole thing clanged to the ground. Then the body in front of them shouted something. Their hearts must have ratcheted. Sour chemicals must have sputtered in their veins. And then the apparition spoke. "Jesus fucking H. Christ. You goddamned hoodlums!"

What then? Confusion. A thousand small lights—sparks—scratching the back of Furtado's eyes. All in an increment of time so small, there could not possibly be a name for it. The Benzedrine surged. His heart might have burst. His body lurched and began to run. The thought, fully formed: *the darkness*. No one had seen his face yet. But then he did not run. He did not move. There was something about that voice. Familiar somehow. The lilt and gallop of Portuguese riding under the man's speech. For he *was* a man and not some thing come up out of the grave. And they knew one another, in that way in which the very old can know people's kids, their families. It was Old Man Coelho, the guy with all the beagle hounds who lived back around the corner. Near the Cold Storage. By the Carvalhos' house. They all stood uncertainly. The drizzle rose and fell like a curtain on a breath of wind. Black and silver. They were little more than shapes molded out of the solid night. Perhaps they measured each other, but it was not likely—Furtado and Sarafino were cranked beyond the safety of any rational thought. Yet they could see—Furtado saw it clearly. Divined it, perhaps, through his heightened senses. The old man tottered. Swayed and weaved. He was drunk. He roared at them again. "You goddamned fucking hooligans out here fucking with these gravestones! I'll kill you, you sons of bitches!"

"You're drunk," Furtado said. "You're a grave-robber." He did not know what prompted him to say that, but it *was* like a movie, the three of them, the blowing drizzle, the graveyard, the mist. One of those old black-and-white films you watched on Boston Movietime at one in the afternoon on winter days when you skipped school or just stayed home sick. But that did not mean he knew what to say next. What came next. The old man did not seem to have noticed the dolly and its bound cargo. It could have been a water heater or a big propane tank. No one would know. But still. Furtado's heart beat in his throat. The speed, the adrenaline. He fought to catch his own breath. Then he saw Sarafino. Sarafino was bent over, holding himself around the middle. Furtado's first thought was that he had been hurt, that the old man had struck him. Cut him, even. Then he thought maybe he was sick. The speed. But neither. Sarafino began to hoot. Out of control. Shaking and hooting with laughter. Laughing so hard and hysterically that he could not stand up straight.

"You think it's funny?" said Old Man Coelho. "You think it's funny, huh?" Furtado could make out the man's silhouette, his short flared coat, his narrow-brimmed fedora. He always dressed the same. He had always looked the same. He had always been ancient, gray, grizzled, his face like a yam. One of the *velhos*, the old ones.

Furtado began to speak. "We were just . . ." But then Sarafino shouted suddenly: "*Maldição*!" He was still laughing. Still hooting. A lunatic sound. An addled sound. He jumped in front of the old man and then dropped to a crouch. He gnarled his white-gloved fingers and waved them over Mr. Coehlo. "*Maldicao*!" I have the ability to curse you. I put you under the evil eye. I place a curse on you."

"I know who you are, you son of a bitch. I'll get you. *Você é um criminoso*!"

Sarafino laughed. That insane laugh.

"*Corisco*!" said the old man. "*Cagao*!"

"*Uma maldição*!" cried Sarafino. "*Uma maldição o das sepulturas*! I have the power of the evil eye! I curse you from the graves!"

"I'll take care of you, you little shit," said the old man. But he was too drunk. He stumbled out onto the wet ground and walked around the boys. A wide berth. Then he weaved back onto the path, behind them now. Heading back into town. His form was swallowed immediately into the gloom, but he continued shouting and cursing back at them until he either stopped or moved beyond their hearing.

"What was that? Where did all that come from?" Furtado asked after they had stood in the quiet for a while. His pulse still raced. His thoughts were a jumble of short-circuitry.

Sarafino looked away through the mist to the bottom of the hill. To the little blurred squares of yellow light that were the windows of the Veterans' Hall. "Drinking at the Vets'. He *lives* there." Sarafino catching his breath. His shadow heaving. "He was drunk. He was taking a shortcut. He didn't see anything. He won't remember anything."

They were cold and wet now. They gathered themselves. They picked up the dolly and pulled their way closer to the edge of the cemetery and watched the Vets' parking lot. Two or three cars. Nothing moving. When they were certain, they wheeled the statue down the hill and cut quickly east along the state road and then onto an all-but-invisible path that led into the woods. They used the little flashlight then, stabbing at the edges of the path with it as they made their way deeper into the thickets. When they had gone far enough, they pulled the Virgin off the path, up over a banking, and down behind a small rise. They laid her down in the high brush, where she would not be seen by anyone.

What came next was a lacuna. Blank space. Dead air. A plan of some kind. Surely there was that, but he could not call it up. They separated. That much was clear. That much he could say for certain. Sarafino leaving for the Army in the morning. Final things. Things he simply could not remember. Maybe a pledge to see him off at the bus station. It would make sense. But no image came to the priest now, except walking alone along the highway, west, then up Cemetery Road and into the town, the mist falling like snow, though it was not snow, the streets constricted and slick, lampless windows, and dark doorways. Streetlights muted in the gauzy drizzle. And then slipping into the house, and the house asleep or empty, he could not tell. He crept to his bed and lay upon it under a curtain of visions, Benzedrine lightning striking small fires along the ridges of his brain. At one point he was looking through the dark, his gaze moving over the objects in his room—the little three-drawer bureau, the straight-backed wooden chair with its days-deep pile of rumpled clothes, the black-and-silver crucifix by the door. And then he realized that his eyes were closed and he was seeing everything through the suddenly transparent skin of his sealed eyelids. When he opened them, the room collapsed into utter darkness.

But when he rose in the morning, it was already too late to meet Sarafino. The bus had left. One, maybe two hours ago. He did not wake, exactly, for the speed did not allow sleep. Yet there was something, some other order of consciousness. A wrack of dreams and half dreams, rolling cascades of thoughts and half thoughts, things he couldn't name. The Benzedrine was still working in him. Jitters. The precipice of coming down, the awfulness of the descent beginning to loom. His clothes were still wet and stuck to him, body-warmed in places, cold in others. Clammy. The day outside was gray. He walked downstairs to the kitchen. The house still empty. Or empty again. On the table some dirty dishes, a stale ashtray. His father's coffee mug, half-full of milked coffee, cold and congealed. Down at the boat, no doubt. He didn't think they would have gone out fishing that morning, but you never knew about Pai Furtado. The *Ilha do Pico* made money because his father and the crew worked hard. His mother would be at the church at prayer or doing some service or another. They would have discovered the statue missing by now. Soon the town would know.

He opened the refrigerator out of habit, then closed it again quickly. Eating was impossible. It would be a day or more before he could eat again behind this speed. He was about to go back upstairs and change into some fresh clothes when the telephone rang. The call was for his father. It was how the news began to circulate through the West End. But it was not news about the statue. "Tell Pai that Old Man Coelho is dead." It was how the story unfolded and then passed from house to house and repeated up and down the streets of the neighborhood. Mister Coelho had died in the night, keeled over in his walkway, and had lain in the foul weather until somebody from the Carvalho house went over there to see what all of the old man's dogs were barking about, all the beagles in the pen, baying and crying, and Old Man Coelho, stiff and dead on his own sidewalk, just a few feet from his door.

six

"WHAT IS THIS PLACE, MANNY? IS THIS WHERE YOU WRITE YOUR sermons?"

The priest jumped. Sarafino stood in the narrow doorway of the study. His words broke on the room like a board falling. Sarafino. The dark landing and stairs behind him. Furtado rose from his chair and felt the rush of blood from his head. He thought he might go right down to the floor, for everything swam for a second or two. And then that other world where he had traced the lost boys through the long crawl of his memory, so real and alive, faded, vanished, dissolved like smoke around his shoulders. And *this* Sarafino, here in front of him so suddenly, taking the place of the young man with the jet-black curls and flashing eyes. The boy in the story, the boy in the dream. Everything gone off now, Old Man Coelho, the baying hounds, the dreary gray of that long-past morning. He thought to grab at the dream with his hands, and he remembered the gin and the pills, and then he thought, *I must be very careful.*

"Manny," said Sarafino. He stepped uncertainly into the little room. The only light came from the tensor lamp on the desk, but it seemed as bright as a moon now, shining down over the ledger, onto the scarred wood. Furtado was aware that the tumbler sat amid the many dark rings on the desktop, rings from his coffee cups and tumblers, and rings from years in the old desk's history that he knew nothing about—cigarette burns, too, and an odd gouge that ran diagonally off one corner. The gin glass was empty, but he would need to be cautious.

Sarafino had been sleeping in the dark blue sweats that Allie had hemmed for him. They looked wrong somehow—the priest believed they were on backwards—Sarafino, gray, sallow, sunken. He was an affront to any memory of him, and Furtado tasted a mild disgust. He was reminded, too, that he himself was no longer young. That whatever might be called truly good in his life might lie in the past, and if he had to reckon or justify his time on Earth (which he did not believe to be the case, even though he often visited this hypothetically, a perverse way of keeping himself off balance), he would not be satisfied with any of his own answers. He steadied himself. If he were to close his eyes, he might pitch into some sinking reverie. He drew a breath. "What is it? What are you doing here?" The words sagged with reproach. "I didn't hear you come up the stairs," he added, as mildly as he could.

"It was slow," Sarafino said.

"You shouldn't do that," Furtado said. "You shouldn't be up walking around if you're sick." And then, he couldn't help himself, "You shouldn't be wandering in and out of rooms."

"I saw the light up here. I didn't mean anything by it." Sarafino leaned on the *prie-deux* and steadied himself. The movement seemed theatrical. After all, he had climbed the stairs. But he was ill. Yes, he was ill, and even the little lamp with its sharp light bouncing off the desk showed that clearly enough. The eyes shone yellow now. The tremor in Sarafino's torso was not an illusion.

"Sit," said the priest. He closed the ledger and moved it off to the side of the desk, along with Augustine and some papers and his pen. He imagined this flurry of movement would disguise his also sweeping up the empty tumbler and setting it on the edge of one of the lower shelves in the bookcase. He turned the oaken chair toward Sarafino. "Just sit down here," he said.

Sarafino let himself down into the chair and leaned back. The chair barely tilted from his weight. The ancient springs under the seat squeaked softly. "My mind works sometimes at night and I don't rest," he said. "You get so tired, but something else kicks in. You get wired up, like."

His right ear. A stunned silence from without, and within a metallic beep, sustained, an agreeable pitch. But the situation now was most disagreeable. It was because Sarafino had walked up the stairs. It was because he was in this room with him. It was because of the time of night. He let the tinning in his ear run its course, and then his hearing returned. Like a switch being thrown. He heard himself speaking. "Some things are not right, Sarafino."

Sarafino nodded slowly, as though he were in accord with some carefully drawn algorithm. Or a blueprint for a bank heist. The movies again. But his eyes were vacant behind their brutish stain.

"Which is to say, some things are wrong," the priest said. When Sarafino did not answer, the priest continued. He had not meant to continue, but some part of him was on the wing now. As he spoke he wished for his pen and his lined pages, for he would argue with Aquinas this time. Aquinas, who came into his head now. While the words formed in his mouth, while they took their shapes in the air. *When we profess that the Holy Spirit is God, we imply that all things are ordained to the end of divine goodness.* Goodness as the end. Aristotle, of course, but Aquinas arc-welding the Greeks to the Creed. What good did they cruise toward now? What good would come of this? Now, as he said to this stricken man, "You come here. You come here, and there's too much that comes with you. You hold things back. You don't talk straight."

The beeping again, suddenly. Floating, too. His lips numb. The room went soft around him. He moved over to the wall and pressed his back against it. He spread his hands to his sides and steadied himself against the cool uneven plaster of the wall. And now he was ashamed of his speech. He wondered, too, could Sarafino divine his state, the gin, the pills?

"I hold things back for safety," Sarafino said quietly. Quiet, too, the rattle in his voice. Like a second voice beneath the first, fluttering.

"I need to be clear about you," said Furtado. He came back to himself a little. He settled. He found the paint-scarred, plaster-spotted stool by the bookcase, and slid it around the desk and turned it so that he could sit on it with his back against the wall. His head was now slightly lower than Sarafino's, showing him at a different aspect, half of his face in deep shadow. It hid the ravage. Or transformed it. It made him look like a black-and-white portrait photograph, a study of a face whose bones were still good, bones that gave up a surface to work with the light, to deepen with the shadow. Sarafino, then, had grown to be a handsome man before all his troubles befell him. Such was the evidence in that small room, in that fortunate accident of outline and silhouette, planes and surfaces. "You have to tell me now how you came here," said the priest, gazing at the sculpted face. At the illusion.

"I was given a sign by the Virgin. That I should come back here to the town," Sarafino said calmly.

"Physically, I mean," Furtado said. "Let's begin there. Who brought you here?"

"I paid a guy for the ride," Sarafino said, speaking more to the room than to Furtado. "I paid this guy $200 to drive me. And I bought the gas."

"And the church?" said Furtado. He would not ask now about the money or where it came from. "Climbing in the back window? That's not correct."

"It was a thing to say to you. A connection, like. The guy that drove, he helped me jimmy the side door. Well, *he* did it. He had a little kit of tools. He wanted to take things, too, Manny. He thought he could just take a few things. I put the kibosh on that. I want you to know that. I locked the door after. I slept in churches before. I figured you'd find me come morning, or I would maybe go to the rectory and knock. I hadn't figured that far. The church, though, I had to go back to it."

The priest leaned forward, elbows on the tops of his thighs. No pain. Sarafino seemed lucid now, and Furtado was floating again slightly, ready to take in whatever he could. He said gently, "You spoke to Allie about some things. Prison. And an armed robbery. And a warrant. She told me about them."

"I would have told you, too, Manny."

Furtado understood that telling Alzaida was the same as telling him. "It's all right," he said. "But this man who drove you. What about him? Is he still here in town?"

"He's gone. He went back to the city. He couldn't stay around here. He's a city guy. He's just a guy I kind of knew." Sarafino caught his breath and raked his hand back over his forehead, as though a lock of hair might have fallen and he were brushing it out of his eyes. But there was no hair. Nothing but his skin and shadows. "About this last thing I got into," he said. "I never knew it was going to be like that. It wasn't my gun. I didn't know there was a gun. I will swear this on the Virgin." He paused and just breathed for a while, and Furtado watched him. He didn't think Sarafino would be here if he had someplace else to go, regardless of what he said about coming back. Or about the Virgin Mary.

Sarafino went on now. Slow. His mouth was dry and his lips and tongue clicked when he spoke. "This one guy—I didn't know him all that much, but we had started hanging out a little. One thing leads to another. So then we thought—it was one night—we just thought we could boost some bottles from this liquor store. Just a little thing like that. Something to drink, and then maybe one to sell. Something upscale. Scotch or like that. He had been to this store before. A little place." Sarafino stopped again to breathe. The priest kept quiet and waited for him to continue. "It was supposed to be a distraction thing. I was wearing this sort of raincoat. I was supposed to grab the bottles and stuff them under that. I mean, this was a small thing, Manny. Two bottles, maybe. It wasn't like a big heist or something. This other guy, Alphonso—I don't guess his name means too much now—he was supposed to get in an argument with the clerk. Just some kid behind the counter. I didn't know Alphonso had the gun. That's the God's honest truth."

"You were sick and you were stealing liquor? And you were on parole? I'm just trying to understand this," said Furtado. "I'm just trying to follow you."

"I know how that sounds. We were high on meth. I'm not going to lie to you. We weren't thinking straight, I guess you might say. Anyway, I'm in the back, and then, I don't know. I don't know what happened, but I was thinking, *This is all ass-backwards. The good stuff is up front behind the counter*. I'm back by the beer cooler. You know. And then I hear Alphonso and the kid yelling at each other. Next thing I know, a gun goes off." Sarafino paused, taking some breaths, puffing his cheeks when he blew out. But the priest could tell he was caught up in telling his story. He just waited.

"This proves it, in a way. That I didn't know Alphonso had the gun. It was a little double-deuce. Not anything big. You couldn't tell he had a gun, Manny. You see, I thought the kid had shot Alphonso. I go running up there because I didn't know Alphonso had the gun. So then I see he's got the kid backed into a corner and he's got the cash drawer open. I think I started yelling or something. Alphonso, he just flips out and shoots up the place. It was a nine-shot. One of those little revolvers. But he emptied it. It sounded like the Fourth of July. He shot up the bottles and stuff behind the counter." Sarafino shifted in the chair, pushed with his feet, and rolled it a bit. The light left the contours of his face. Now the shadows did not favor him. "We were on a camera the whole time, you know," he said.

"And so this is why the police are after you?"

"I guess that would be right. I was known, you might say. They call it "in the system," which you probably know about. I'm opening my heart here, Manny. I am telling you everything. You might think I'm nothing but dirt, but I've made peace with all this. I have Our Lady to guide and keep me."

Furtado—the priest now—saw that Sarafino needed to be contradicted. To be brought back into the fold. "I don't think you are dirt. It's all right," he said. Adding, "my old friend." Genuinely. It just came forth. But it seemed too much, all the same. It called his own attention to how he didn't know this man. The boy, he knew. But this man in his chair, he did not.

He had had enough, but something kept him going. He found he couldn't back off just yet. He felt he could rise and pace back and forth now, but the room was far too small for that. "There's this other matter, too, Sarafino," he said. "I understand that the Virgin comforts you. But you say she comes to you. She appears. I want to say that I will help you, and you don't need to say that about Her to convince me. I will help you no matter what."

"Will you?" Sarafino asked.

"Yes," said the priest.

"I can't go back," Sarafino said.

"I don't know yet what kind of help I can give you, but I will do whatever I can."

"She *does* come to me," Sarafino said.

The priest searched out Sarafino's eyes now. Met them. Yellow eyes in yellow light. Yellow eyes in shadow. Furtado had hoped this would be easier. He tasted his own lips, still bitter. What could he possibly read in those eyes? But there was something there. It was fight. Fight in that look.

He knew that look. How little choice there really is with all this choosing we do. Little scripts we are handed. Then the floating. They were both just balloons in the wind now. Like those government weather balloons, loose and invisible, high up in the cold, immoderate air. "Apparitions are very serious," he said. "The Church has rules about how to approach them." He softened his tone. "Sarafino, not all visits from the Virgin are real. Not always actual. In fact, most aren't. So the Church has certain tests."

Sarafino thought for a minute. "Why?" he said. "I don't have any news for the Pope or the Church. Just for me. And for you. What does the Church care?"

Furtado felt himself nodding. All right, he would let it go. Jesus was not divine, and God did not go around impregnating young girls as the Holy Spirit, and there was no virgin birth and no Holy Virgin. But there was God, still, and it was clear that He loved us, in some mysterious way. When we cared for one another, for instance. Wasn't that also the love of God? Hospices. Nursing homes. Hospitals. Yes, and churches, too, with all the odds stacked against them. *Something* was possible. It was what kept him at his work. He let it go.

"I suppose it doesn't matter what the Church cares," said the priest. "But they approve of visions, too," he said, just to even things out.

"You don't believe me," said Sarafino. "They never believed those kids at Fatima, either."

"True enough," Furtado said.

"You know I've got the virus. That's a fact. I've got the papers on that." Sarafino was speaking with some effort now. He was tiring again. His burst of energy, whatever it was, was wearing off.

"It's all right, Sarafino," said the priest. "I figured that. Don't wear yourself down now. We don't have to finish this now."

"She *does* come to me," he said. "It's not the virus in my head. She came to me before I got sick. That's a fact." He swept his forehead again, and Furtado saw now that he was not batting at imaginary hair but wiping a thin film of sweat.

"You are better now than when you showed up in the church. The rest and the nourishment are doing you good," said the priest. "You can get better still."

"No, I cannot," said Sarafino. "You have to promise me that you won't start that shit up with me. No disrespect. But I know what I know."

"Let's go downstairs. Let's not wear you out. I'm tired, too."

Sarafino did not seem to hear him. He began speaking. Halting. Taking breaths. He was talking to Furtado, but he also seemed to address the desk and the ceiling and the bookcase. He spoke to the shadows in the corners. Or just to hear something he might have carried in his mind but had never let out into the air of the world before. "My best time," he said, "in my life, my best time was here. Walking the woods. Fishing in the harbor. Taking a boat out to Long Point. Camping out in the dunes. And then that campsite we built. No matter what kind of shit was going down, there was always that campsite we made. A place to go. Then everything got crazy. Not just me. The whole world. That's what I think. But you know the Virgin chose me. She chose to be in my life on that night we stole Her from the church. I didn't know it then. I didn't know it right away, but that's what happened.

"The last thing I remember about the town. After we robbed the church. It was early in the morning. We were supposed to hook up, but the wires got crossed. This was whenever the bus was supposed to leave for Boston. I was standing outside the chamber of commerce building. You know. You remember those old green buses. And then somebody, maybe one of the old ladies that worked inside, was talking about Mr. Coelho. You know how fast things got around town. That he died that night. Then I got on that bus. The next thing I know, I'm in old North Station in Boston. And I was still high. I was so high. I was still speeding."

Sarafino coughed. It was a cough that the priest understood. He had heard enough of such a cough in hospice homes and hospital rooms. He was pretty sure he understood the cough. It took a moment for Sarafino to gather his breath. Furtado's nerves spilled out into the room, a splendid sensation, for even though some part of him inside was darkened by Sarafino's being in his study, his sanctum, he could spread out beyond his own unseemly limits. He could smell Sarafino now. Not the odor of filth, as on the first night, but an odd smell. Oddly pleasant, though on the edge of being too much, at the edge of something fulsome. Like heavy yeast. Or vegetables a few days in the bin. He thought about smell. He'd read about that, too. How when you smell, you truly take the molecules of the thing into your own body. In with the air. So Sarafino entered him in this way. Furtado waited on the rest of the story—true or false, he wanted more of it now.

Sarafino shrugged and shook his head. He cleared his throat. "I remember taking another physical. It was just a quick one, but then we waited there all day. I'm pretty sure it was all day. Part of the night, too. Just waited. I was going crazy. I said to this one guy—a sergeant or a doctor or something—I said, 'Look, let me go. I'm high on dope. I'm high on dope right this minute,' and he just laughs and tells me to sit down. You know what it was like. All these freaked-out guys from all over. The Cape, New Bedford, Calumet, Fall River, Fairhaven, Boston. All of a sudden we're all looking at one another, and you could feel everybody getting this at the same time—that we were all losers. We were going off to this fucked-up war. We were going to get blown away, maybe. Like we had no say in it. They just came and got you and that was that. We ate that cold shit off of tin trays and everybody yelled at us constantly, like they were all pissed at us for something. Everybody was scared, really. Everybody was, like, trying to make jokes about it.

"But all of that, Manny, and all I could think about was the statue and the old man. They herded us on a bus. It was dark. It was night. And I was so whacked on the speed that I just kept thinking that I had special powers.

You know, I cursed a guy and he died. Like that. It wasn't even a real curse. It was just goofing. But I know I caused his death in some way. Then boot camp. There was other stuff to think about then. And everything else."

"What else? What did you do? You went over there, right?"

"Yes, I did, Manny. But it doesn't mean nothing to me now. That was all a long time ago. I didn't enjoy it. A lot of people got hurt in very bad ways. It was a long time ago. I mostly guarded a fence, which you would think would be easy. Fuck all that. End of story."

Sarafino stopped suddenly and looked at Furtado, just remembering something. Furtado could see it come into his head. "You got shot," he said. "I heard you got shot down in a plane or something like that."

The priest felt the smile on his face. "No, I was never shot," he said. "I was in an accident. I was in a plane."

"You weren't shot."

"I broke my neck," the priest said. "Technically."

"That doesn't sound so good."

"I just broke it a little bit." Furtado gave up a little laugh in spite of himself.

"Our Lady was watching over you, too," Sarafino said. "You know, Manny, I knew some priests, but I only knew them for priests. Do you see? But you, I knew you from the start. So you're a priest, but you're also a person. So I get to see both sides, like. I never thought about that before."

"What did you think?"

Sarafino shrugged. "I don't know."

"Well, priests are people, all right," Furtado said.

Sarafino ran his hand over his face. "I'm sorry I busted in on you," he said. His eyes caught the tumbler on the bookshelf, but then he looked away. "I interrupted your work."

"One thing," said the priest. "One thing, Sarafino, while we are talking here. While our heads are back there in that time. The Virgin. The statue. I looked for it after you left town. I didn't go off for another whole month after you. You know my father and I got into a big fight. He didn't want me to go in the draft, so I joined the Navy. That's how come the airplane. So I signed the papers and I had about another month after you left. The statue wasn't where we left it. I looked and looked. I used to take the rifle and pretend to be hunting, but I just looked all around where we left it.

"It was a scandal, you know. The whole town was crazy about it. It made the papers all the way up to Boston. The police couldn't figure anything out. The *velhas* were all making a connection between Old Man Coelho and the Virgin, too. Like She carried him off or something. But nobody ever mentioned you. Or me. There were prayer vigils. The Knights of Columbus raised money for a reward. Other stuff, too. I guess my father was furious. He thought some fishermen had taken it. You know, a rival boat. He got into a fight with someone up at Juney's Tap over it. That was after I had already left for the Navy.

"But the state troopers had come in, and they came up with the idea that it was People from Away who stole it and that it was probably long gone off the Cape, right from the get-go. It was a big deal. But I looked for it before I left town. I even knew right where we hid it, and I couldn't find it. There was some talk, I think, a while after, about starting up a drive to replace it, but I guess it never got anywhere. I believe the archdiocese asked Father Santos to sell the little statues, the kids, to some parish up around Boston, and he did. I think he was just too old by then to care. Somebody found Her, though. Somebody found that statue of Her and kept it."

Now Sarafino drew himself up in the chair. The priest would write it, would describe it as Sarafino pulling himself together for one last push in this conversation, for he was looking small again and his speech was slowing. Yet he spoke. He coughed into his hand and leaned to Furtado and told him, "Nobody found Her. That's a fact. She's there in the woods. I need you to help me get Her back. She has signs for me and for you. I can't do it by myself now."

"Sarafino," said the priest, "I don't think that's right. You might not be so clear on that."

"She's in the woods," Sarafino said.

"There's been a lot of changes here, Sarafino," said the priest, growing truly weary now and thinking about Sarafino's health, of course. "All those years. I was away, too. It was always hard for me to take it all in whenever I came back here. The National Park Service, for one thing. They took over the whole woods and the dunes. They have changed everything. Bike paths, trails. They have rules. People would have found Her."

"You ever hear about one of those National Park people finding the Mother of God? Anybody?"

"No," Furtado admitted.

Sarafino took a series of small breaths. He narrowed his yellow eyes, glazed and on fire in the dim room. "That night. Right after we split up. I took the East End way into town. As soon as I crossed the highway and started walking up the street, I saw this shovel. I swear. Leaning up against a house. Right near the door. Under the outdoor light. You know, when your head is all jacked up like that. *Zing, zing*. And this shovel is in the outdoor light against the side of a house. It was like a whole idea in itself. This was just a few minutes after we split."

"You went back with the shovel," said the priest.

"I buried Her," Sarafino said.

seven

IT WAS JUST AFTER NINE-THIRTY. A CLEAN MORNING LIGHT STREAMED into the rectory through every window and glassed doorway. The sun was high enough now to illuminate the roofs of the houses across the street, falling at a soft incline and warming the subdued colors, the flat, brickish red of the composition shingle, the gray-going-to-brown-and-moss of the cedar shake, the crystal glint from the black, old-fashioned asphalt—a muted patchwork of crests and angles. Above the roofs rose the burly limbs of the tallest trees, scarred and ancient, bold now against the pale sky. Out in the churchyard an occasional squirrel would take an astounding leap—close to flight—and it would float for a moment, and then it would plummet to a lower branch, land deftly, and spring into the air again. There were still feeders hanging on most of the church's trees—Luis Horta's creations, all—and drab birds flitted among the hedges and along the grounds and rose to some, while the squirrels descended upon others. Mariah Grey and the priest sat beside one another on the parlor's sofa, stared absently out the windows, and waited. Neither one spoke.

The doctor's name was Peter Khyber. He was an old friend of Mariah's and Winslow's, and as Mariah told it, he was a man who understood the disease, professionally and personally. He lived and practiced a few towns higher up on the Cape. Mariah had told him the important details about Sarafino, and he had agreed to come. He was someone to trust. When he finally emerged from Sarafino's room—it had become "his" room now, that quickly—the two of them rose to their feet and turned to face him, but still neither spoke. Peter was a compact, small-framed man. Middle-aged, well exercised. Someone who clearly took care of himself. His skin was creamy black, smooth and tight over the small bones of his face. He kept his head shaved to a mere shadow, and he wore small, silver-rimmed eyeglasses. He had been with Sarafino for about a half hour and he came to them now, little leather satchel in one hand, stethoscope over the shoulder of his flannel shirt. In his other hand he carried one of Sarafino's big manila envelopes. "He didn't want to come back out here with me," Peter said. "He's pretty tired."

The priest gestured for him to sit. "Please," he said.

Peter took a seat on the sofa beside Mariah, and Furtado slid over to the rocker. "It's not good," Peter announced quietly.

"He keeps saying he's done. Finished," said the priest.

"He is terminal. That's correct, according to what I have here." Peter tapped the manila envelope. "It's stage IV small-cell carcinoma of the lungs."

"Not AIDS, then," Mariah said.

"Oh, yes. He has AIDS. Full-blown. That's the infuriating part. Ten years ago, I would have greeted this differently. But now there's so much more treatment available. He didn't have to get himself into this fix. He was seen in New York. He's had the active virus for a while. Those lesions are indeed Kaposi's. He's had PCP. His CD4 count has been under 130. The lung cancer was found in Boston. That was, let's see, nine, ten months after

New York. It's all here. There's a radiology report, bloodwork. They were going to do chemo for the lungs, but they evaluated him and decided he wasn't a candidate for that. It's all meth now, you know. That's what we're seeing. You can see an increase in infections and these kinds of complications. These guys get so that nothing matters. They don't take care of themselves. They don't get treatment. Or they do, and then they go right back to destroying themselves again. They drift into . . ." He shook his head, a word not coming to him—or one he did not care to use.

"And he won't go into a hospital? Or some care facility? Something?"

"He's pretty clear about that."

"*Is* he clear?" Furtado asked. "Did he seem clear-minded to you?"

Peter frowned. "If you are asking is he competent, then yes, he is. I would say he's competent enough to know what he wants. He has an odd conversation at moments. I think there's some hypoxia involved. Just a gross check, but neurologically I didn't see any flags. Nothing in those charts. I don't think there's anything that signifies ignoring his wishes. I know that he has some legal problems, too."

"Trouble with the *law*, Peter. We all know the difference," said Mariah.

"I guess technically he violated parole just by being out of state. I wouldn't know a lot about that kind of thing. After this workup in New York, he was given some treatment, some meds, but he never followed up, as far as I can tell. He just hit the street and started killing himself all over again. He admitted to meth and heroin."

"He's had a hard life," Furtado said, though he didn't know a great deal about it. Something in him wanted to defend Sarafino, although Peter's tone was even. It wasn't an accusation. Just the facts, as they say. "He doesn't want to die in jail. He wants—he wants essentially palliative care. He came home to die. I'm sure you know that."

"Would he die if he got treatment?" Mariah asked.

Peter looked over at the priest, and then looked around the rectory's parlor, taking it in quickly, as if he had just noticed where he was, though he had passed through the room when he came in. His eyes stopped on the crucifix for a fraction of a second, then he said, "Yes. He's very ill." Peter hesitated. He had a soft, deep voice, authority in it. Assurance. He was easy to listen to. The priest could tell he was used to being listened to. "The best option is to make him comfortable. That's what he wants. I think there are definitely some things we can do in that area." He looked around again. "Will he stay here?"

"It's awkward right now," Furtado said. "But there might be some alternatives."

"I'll get you a few things. Something for pain. For fever. I'm going to write a scrip for oxygen, too. That will help. Has he done any drugs since he's been here?"

"He had some old medicine bottles in his duffel bag."

"Heroin. Speed. Like that?"

"No. I'm sure not."

"He's very religious," Peter said. He stated it like another fact. Another symptom, perhaps.

"He told you that?" Mariah asked.

"It came through," said Peter. "There's a few more things I want to check. I drew some blood. I'll have some panels run. And I'll have to bring a few things with me when I come back." He tapped the manila folder but did not open it. "He's had some serious addictions. You know, there's a belief that street drugs further compromise the immune system. No real data that I've seen yet, but who's to argue?"

They talked for a while longer, maybe a half hour. The priest did not check the time, but the light out over the roofs changed, the sunlight in the parlor changed. Sarafino did not come out to join them, and no one had gone yet to look in on him. The situation had altered now, and there were new places to stand, different vantages to get used to. Now that Peter Khyber had come.

And finally he rose to go. “I should leave now,” he said plainly, when there were no more questions, no more suggestions. “Father Furtado, will you walk out to my car with me?”

“It’s Manny, please,” Furtado said.

Mariah stood up. “It’s time to go check on my new friend,” she said.

The priest led Peter out the rectory office door and out the breezeway to where his car was parked. A white Jeep wagon. Shining. Peter stopped before he opened the car door. He looked at the priest. He squinted a bit in the sunlight. “I loved someone,” he said. “My partner for many years. A wonderful man named Yusef. He died. He did all the things he was supposed to. Not like your friend. Yusef took his meds. He went for his checkups. He took care of himself. And when it came to it, *I* took care of him. Diet, rest, everything. But he died anyway. I cared for him right up until the end, in our home. It was the right thing for us. It was where he wanted to be. And it was where I wanted him.”

“I understand,” said Furtado.

“What I’m saying is that this might not be right for you. If you decide to keep him with you.”

“Yes,” said the priest. “That’s what I understand. There are other considerations, too.” He looked back at the church and the rectory.

“All right,” said Peter. “Well, I will call again. I’ll have some results from the blood. I’ll be in touch with Winslow and Mariah. They are good friends. And Mariah respects you very much. She will handle things. She’ll give you my number, so you’ll be able to call, too, but let’s just see if we can work through her. It will be discreet. Nothing official.” He gave a tight-lipped smile, the only smile, or gesture toward one, that the priest had seen from this man. “No bills. No paperwork,” he said.

“This is very generous of you,” Furtado said. “Thank you again.”

"Mariah says you've known this man for a long time."

"Yes and no," Furtado said. "We grew up together."

"And have you seen him since?"

"No," said the priest. "I'm sorry. I thought Mariah might have told you the story."

"A bit. But I'm asking you if you have been tested recently. Is there any reason to? I can take care of it for you."

"No," said Furtado. Then he added, "There's no reason to."

Peter Khyber reflected on this. "All right," he said, after a pause. "And this man? Sarafino? Did you love him?"

It was not a question he expected. "We were very close as boys. Growing up here in town, there is a kind of closeness." The priest let the sun and the chill breeze break over him. No noise in the ears. No floating. The sparse hedges here in the back of the church looked grim in their winter brown. Like they would never come into green again, though he knew that wasn't the truth. When Peter Khyber drove off in his white Jeep, the two men waved at one another.

FURTADO WAS LATE LEAVING THE RECTORY. WINSLOW HAD COME BY and picked up Mariah, dropping off a small television with rabbit ears and earphones, and they'd all fussed with it a bit, hooking it up for Sarafino, who'd watched it for a few minutes and fallen asleep. It must have been nearly two before Allie showed up. She had said she'd be there around lunchtime, but, well, that was Allie. Furtado loved her, but he knew her ways. He wouldn't leave without someone there.

While he waited, he turned his thoughts from Sarafino for a while. He allowed himself the fiction that because Peter Khyber had come and spoken, things would somehow be guided. Clearer lines to follow, at least. He had to digest it all, but now he gave himself a respite by turning back to some parish work. It was a tonic. He sat in the office and fiddled with some numbers and considered what to do about maintenance, which he had left hanging for too long. Louis Horta had not been the greatest man on the job, but he at least had been on the job. The grounds volunteers came and did their small chores, to be sure, but Furtado needed to bring someone in to oversee the upkeep. Both the Hortas were paid, and their pay was still on the books. Their absence had accumulated a small sum. He considered whom he might bring in, who might be available, who might be agile and handy enough. But now, of course, that was not enough. Now he would have to be careful, vigilant about whom he let near the rectory if Sarafino were to remain there. It would require finesse.

Once Allie arrived, he explained about Sarafino and the doctor. "It's just what Sarafino told us," she said. She looked in on him, still asleep, and then took out her sewing things. "I'll fix him some more clothes." She avoided talking about Sarafino, but soon she was grumbling again about Tommy, about the boat, about the idle winter months that were coming. Furtado gave her his sympathies, but he couldn't linger, really, he told her. He had several parish visits to make and errands to do. He told her blandly that they would work it all out, these difficulties. But he had his own problems on his mind. By the time he left the rectory, he had already formed an idea.

He drove off in his little Toyota, the sun still bright, a breeze freshening. The town was quiet, the weekenders and Summer People mostly gone, their finicky gardens gone brown and shriveled behind their fences. Here and there, some of the houses still flew flags—rainbow, Portuguese, American. The festival atmosphere of the town had subsided now, though the true quiet would not come until full winter. Furtado drove by the harbor. It was busier now, with couples here and there moving along the narrow sidewalk and cars parked up and down the street. A few more flags shrugged in the breeze on guesthouses and storefronts.

He had already begun to ache. The shoulder, the neck—just a little. But also a sludgy, shadowy ache in his thighs and calves, the lateral spaces of his back. Nothing of consequence. His errands would carry him through it. When he turned down the main wharf, the true force of the day hit him. The sun bored into the windshield and throbbed in his eyes. He reached wharf's end and turned the car so that the light came in over his shoulder, and he looked out at the water. The sea gleaming. A mottled blue, deep blue, stern and bold under that rinsing light. The wind blew from the west-southwest, and out here, away from the shelter of buildings and streets, he could see that it was fresh and strong, blowing maybe fifteen knots. Small lines of pale froth had begun to show on the darker bellying tide, which ran full high now. A number of boats were tied off to the wharf on the east side of the packinghouse, tall on the water, and along with their masts and rigging, Furtado could see their wheelhouses rising above the concrete surface of the wharf. He swung around completely and pulled into a narrow parking space just behind Tom and Frankie's new truck. It was a white Ford, one of those sporty models, and it had the extra seats behind the driver's cab. They had bought it and registered it to the boat, out of the boat's share of profits. A legitimate idea, since Tom and Frankie both used it equally to get around town, and they hauled gear back and forth from the boat with it. It sat there now, as Furtado knew, with the doors unlocked and the keys in the ignition. It was how things worked out on the wharf. Everybody knew Tom and Frankie, and if any of the fishermen needed to move the truck to get it out of the way to load their own boat—or just to borrow the truck for something, for that matter—all they had to do was get in and drive it.

The *Ilha do Pico* lay tethered just outboard of the *Minha Prada*, Dickie Avellar's trawler, a highliner, western-rigged, the wheelhouse sleek and faired, set well forward of the center line, all white with green trim. Even with the fishing in such uncertain times, this boat was a killer. When it sailed, it killed fish. That's what Tom said. And fish was still money.

The wind slapped against the priest's face, vigorous and astringent on his cheeks when he stepped out of the car. He turned and shaded his eyes and looked south, past Long Point, past the mouth of the harbor and out toward the far hills of the bent wrist of the Cape. Dark and high in the glittering distance. So much easy wind, so much sun. Everything gleaming. The air not wintry so far. Salty and fish-smelling. The herring gulls screaming. The season was changing, though. Winter would be early this year. The true cold had not arrived yet, but it was showing its knives, and Furtado had prepared, dressing in a wool watch cap and heavy sweater.

He walked to the edge of the wharf and put a leg over and climbed onto the solid, well-scrubbed deck of the *Minha Prada*. Now, *here* was something. Dicky Avellar had used his head. He had kept the family house in town, and when the value had risen several hundred thousand dollars—and this on a house that, like so many others, had been framed with unshivered timbers and quit-claimed into his family for payment of some long-ago small debt—he had used a piece of the equity to finance this high-tech fishing machine. Dicky's was a face—ruddy, bearded, round—that the priest always counted on seeing at Sunday Mass, when he wasn't out on the water or dealing with the boat in some other way. His wife, Maureen, always came to Mass with him, and his younger daughter, Katherine, was an altar server. He was a strong voice on the parish council, a younger man than the priest—too young to have known him in school. The *Prada* had been the first boat to pass by the end of the wharf for last summer's Blessing of the Fleet, a place of honor that no other captain contested. As he motored by, his decks crowded with family, friends, and other townies, the big engine thrumming—a lovely sound, as Furtado thought of it, that power, that spectral smell of diesel, too, floating on the briny air—Dicky, in ball cap and designer sunglasses, flashed a V for victory sign from the wheelhouse. He had worked hard on the committee for the Blessing festival. But it had been a strange moment for Furtado as Bishop Mayhew, gray-haired and many-chinned, standing next to him on the raised platform at the wharf's edge, shook his aspergillum and sprinkled holy water over the bow of the

Minha Prada. It was the first time ever, as far as Furtado knew, that his father's boat had not been blessed, by either priest or bishop, and though it was never said between them, he believed Dicky had been giving him the high sign, just to show that everything had come off all right, even though Tom had caused the Blessing some problems.

Furtado had stood in the wheelhouse of the *Prada* a few times. Everything in there was modern, state-of-the-art. Equipment that his own father could never have imagined: satellite-positioning navigation, a sonar fish-finder, a computer with programs that read out weather and depth, the screen showing the boat's position with such accuracy that you could see the ship's head against the wharf, precisely angled.

And there, tied off to the bigger boat, the *Ilha do Pic*o nudged and shouldered in its lee and shadow. The *Ilha* was a little smaller, at forty-eight feet, and sat lower in the water. It was an old, originally eastern-rigged dragger, built in New Bedford in 1939, though Pai Furtado had bought it from its first owner in the '40s, after the war. Its wheelhouse sat in the aft of the boat. On its deck, forward, lay a strictly ordered litter of stacked plastic tubs, steel baskets, coils of line, and other gear, all secured neatly in the spaces around the mast and the winch and the main hatch. Tom and Frankie sat on boxes amidships, bent to their work. Frankie spotted Furtado before he had a chance to call out to them. "Hey, Father Manny! You going to come down and mend some net?" He thrust his arm forward, stabbing at the air with his mending platen. "Fill up that *agulha*!"

Tom looked up just as the priest was hopping down to the deck from the *Minha Prada.* "Sure he is," Tom said. "We can just go home now."

"Nobody's as good as you," the priest said, "but don't think I couldn't."

"Come have a beer," Tom said. He didn't miss a beat with the flat Norwegian needle, flicking the twine over, under, around, back up, pulling the mesh together. A cigarette burned short between his lips, and a sixteen-ounce can of Budweiser sat by his foot. He was wearing heavy sneakers, high-tops. The wind ruffed the curls of his thick hair. "I can put the beer in a thermos, Manny, if you want one."

"Sure," said Furtado, though he did not want one. But he was mindful of his errand. Then he thought of Father John Sweet and considered the thermos. "I'm okay with a can," he said finally. He spotted the bucket of beer and pulled a can out for himself. He popped the top and took a drink. His fingers cold around the iced can. The beer cold. All wrong for the day. But still, here they all were. "Allie told me you guys would be down here," he said.

"You haven't been around much," Frankie said.

"No, not so much," said the priest. "I'm going by your house to see your ma in a little while, though. How is she?"

"Same-o, same-o," Frankie said. He was a few years younger than Tom, a thin wiry man who lived in his Red Sox baseball cap. He was fair-complexioned for a townie, and the sun and ocean had laid a permanent scorch on the skin of his face—deep weathering with long wrinkles that fanned back from the corners of his narrow eyes. He grinned his snaggle-toothed grin. "You're doing God's work, Manny."

"Yes," said Furtado. "I am." He drank from the can again. A beer, a single beer during the day, meant nothing to him. An insinuation. But it was always easier to be around Tom with a beer in your hand. The deck nodded slightly under his feet. A sweet little shimmy. A roll. The decking itself was straked and cambered and worn. You could witness all the years in it. Sometimes Furtado could see the boat abstracted from its purpose, an object, a thing of muscular beauty. Its lines and curves, the piebald colors of its clutter, its latent mass. Even the rocking underfoot, the way it settled in the sea, part of it, but not part of it. This had been his father's kingdom, his father's life and glory—and his cross, too. Then to Allie and, by marriage, to Tom. There was no substitute cosmos that Furtado could imagine in which the boat would have been his own, would have come to him.

In his father's day, owning a dragger made you a prince in the world, and you could swagger into any of the fishermen's bars along Front Street and be hailed from a dozen tables by the other men. His father, Pai Furtado to everyone in town, was foremost among them, but there were the others, too. Tough characters. Hard as nails. And they were not simple men, either. They understood their place in the town. They knew where they—or their families before them—had come from, and they understood that they *were* characters, and because they lived publicly, they wanted largeness in their lives. They wanted people to know about their labors on the sea. They wanted people to hear their footsteps on the earth. So they called his father Pai—Papa—but others were called Blackbeard, Barrabas, Flash Gordon, Captain Blood, Charlie Foo, Mongo, Geronimo, Johnny Switchblade—more than Furtado could remember. All of them with the quieter names underneath, of course. Pires, Freitas, Alves, Correiro, Santos, Cabral. None of them were left now. No one still on the water from that generation. And most of the boats gone, too. But here was Pai's. Tommy's. The *Ilha do Pico*, which Pai had named for his birthplace back in the Azores, though he'd left so young he could not remember it—only the stories of it from his own father and mother—and wish as he might to go back and visit, he died before he ever did.

Furtado found himself staring again, off to the east, watching the chop on the water fall way in the distance, a continuous motion in the fabric of the water, hypnotic. Some whitecaps beginning to show. The tide turning now, running blue and peaked under the breeze. The wind and the sea, great forces, with no mind in them. You couldn't reason with a gale. Job tried. The mind of God, then, was what? Tommy gauged his silence. Finally he said, "What's up, Manny?"

"Well, I had an idea. I've come to ask your help with something. You too, Frankie."

Tom laughed expertly, a short plosive from the corner of his mouth that was opposite his cigarette. The cigarette jiggled. A puff of smoke. His hands never stopped passing the needle. A rhythm like a dancer's or a drummer's. "Because it worked out so good last time?" he said.

Furtado shrugged. The breeze delicious on his cheeks. "Old Louis Horta," he said. "He's been gone a while and I need help up at the church. I'm thinking fishing is slowing down. Winter is coming. I have some money in the budget. I'm thinking you guys could help me out of a jam. Even just until spring."

"A job?" Tommy asked.

"More like helping me out," said the priest. He shouldn't have mentioned the money so soon. There was nothing he could do about that now. "I'm hoping for some construction, maybe by the summer, but I need some upkeep until then, at least."

Tom looked over at Frankie. He put his needle and twine down. He was quiet for a minute, then said, "Did you and Allie talk about this?"

"No," said Furtado. "But I was going over some budget things when she came by the rectory, and then it came to me that you might be interested. It's just a little something." He didn't bring up Louis Horta again. "I really need someone."

"No flags, at least," Tommy said.

"That's what I figure," said the priest.

Tom let out his small laugh again. "Did Allie tell you I talked to somebody about selling the boat?"

"She did," Furtado said. "She didn't make a big deal out of it. This isn't about that."

"Well, she did make a big deal out of it, Manny. To me she did. All I did was mention it to this broker. It didn't go anywhere. The boat's in really bad shape. I couldn't sell it if I wanted to. And if I could, I'd talk to you first."

"You know it has nothing to do with me either way, Tom." The priest took a long tug on his cold beer.

"Well, it does and it doesn't, Manny. I mean, everybody knows this was your father's boat. I respect that. I know it's mine and Allie's, but he was your father, too. I would have said something to you if I was serious. That's all I'm saying. But this boat. It's like a stone around my neck sometimes. It's not even that it needs work. It needs a whole new boat. That's what I was saying to Allie. She gets upset when I talk about it. We get into it sometimes."

"There's a lot of pressure," said the priest. It was a practiced thing to say. It meant nothing, but it was all he was willing to offer at this point. Tom did look tired. He had risen to his feet, and Furtado saw the tightness in the cords of his neck, the dark puff under his eyes—not unlike the darkness beneath Alzaida's eyes. What did the nights hold for these two? The priest had talked through enough marriages, counseled enough couples, to have some general idea. Neither Tom nor Allie could be called an easygoing person.

The priest had grown up with Allie's tantrums and piques, of course. She was like their father in that regard—she jabbed and pushed at the world with her feelings. Her life was a flail. And Tommy possessed his own dark humors, as well Furtado knew, though Alzaida claimed that he had toned way down in the last few years. He used to get into bar fights from time to time—probably no more than a lot of the town guys, but the worst trouble seemed to have happened a few summers before Furtado came back to the parish.

From all the versions he'd heard, it started when a Summer Person knocked Allie off the sidewalk, right in front of Parson's Pharmacy, and she stumbled into the street and skinned her knee. It was an accident, of course, but Allie said something, and then the man who bumped her said something. There was a little back-and-forth, and then the man sneered at her townie accent or at something she said, or how she said it—something disrespectful. Then Tom said something. Then the man said something.

And then Tom nearly tore him apart. They were both lucky—the tourist that he wasn't killed or permanently injured, and Tom for the same reasons. Tom went to court over that, but eventually the case was dropped. He grew quieter afterward, Allie said. And she told Furtado that since then, she'd never let him come into town at night at all, from June to October.

Now Tom stepped over to where Furtado leaned at the gunwale. He took the end of the cigarette from his lips and flicked it with thumb and forefinger in a way that spun it up into the breeze. It carried off to lee. "Allie is attached to the boat," he said. "It's like an idea for her. It's something in her head. She doesn't have to work on the engine or mend the nets, or try to hold the damn thing together from day to day. It's old, Manny. That's all I'm saying. I swear if I could swing it, I would buy something new. It wouldn't be a trawler, either. I'd get into the whale watching. The cruising. I'd take the whale huggers out. That's the future, if you want to call it that."

Furtado had heard this before. This and more like it. But Tom couldn't swing it, so it was mostly just talk. In the glare from the ocean, Tom's eyes looked red and wet. The boat moved under them, nudging and compressing the white-foam fender buoys between the *Ilha* and the *Minha*. The shadows thrown from the packinghouse and the larger boat had grown longer, and the wind now carried a true chill with it. Furtado pulled his watch cap down tighter on his head. "So what do you say?" he asked. "Help me out for a few months."

If they would do the work, then he would have two men who knew how to keep their mouths shut. They could be brought into this business with Sarafino Pomba, and his presence would be secure. He didn't want just any town guy working up there if Sarafino were to stay there for whatever time he had left. Yes, and he could use their help with Sarafino, though in what form he was not sure. He couldn't see ahead that far. He said nothing of this. He said nothing of Sarafino. He did not know what Allie might have told Tom, but he would wait and see what their answer was before he took them into confidence.

Tom looked over at Frankie Boia. So did the priest. Frankie, with that weather-slapped face, that wire-hard body, where there was nothing extra, no waste, just muscle and his thin bones, and that snaggletooth. He pulled out his case knife and snicked it open. The short, flat blade flashed from sun to shadow as he cut the end of the heavy-gauge twine. "What do you think, Pard?" Tom said.

Frankie shrugged and smiled. "Whatever," he said.

"The church," Tom said to Furtado.

"The church," Furtado said.

"Let me and Frankie think about it. We'll talk about it among ourselves."

The priest looked at the two of them, and then he looked around the old boat again and squinted off to the east once more—the chop running high, moving in ragged lines, just the tops showing white now and then. "All right," he said.

He drove the Toyota back up the wharf and down along Front Street toward the West End. He was thinking he would have to shorten his visit with Mrs. Boia. He was debating whether he would stay and take the cup of tea and plate of sweet bread that he knew she would offer. He would say a Rosary with her, and then he would beg off—more errands and visits. He would see her soon. She was a shut-in not so much because of health—more by choice. The priest always included her in his weekly round of visits with the Eucharist, but he visited her additionally as well.

Biggy and Pai had been close, and Furtado remembered Mrs. Boia from when he was growing up in the West End, Frankie a little kid then—too little to be noticed by Manny and Sarafino and their friends. Her husband, Biggy, had been one of the old captains of the glory days, and he had retired and sold his boat while Frankie was still a small boy—too young to run it. Furtado could not remember when Biggy died—but Frankie had stayed at the old house with his mother, in her eighties now, and never left. He had crewed on a number of the town's draggers before he teamed up with Tommy. Although Tommy was a few years older, they had grown up together, and they had been together on the boat now for years. The story you would get about Frankie Boia always depended on whom you talked to, or even in what mood the very same person might be—what day of the week or what weather. Such was the town. Either he was a good boy looking after his *mae*, giving of himself to help her along—or he was shiftless, no ambition, a grown man and still fouled up in his mother's apron strings.

Furtado checked the clock in the dashboard. The taste of the icy beer still lay on his tongue, and his face tingled agreeably yet from the wind off the ocean. His ear chimed, went dead, came back to life, all in an instant. In his shoulder, in his neck, the slow pull toward full aching. Yes, he would need to shorten his time with Mrs. Boia, for he had other errands to run. In truth, there were no other parishioners he had intended to visit today. That was all a blind. Today was his day to drive up the Cape, to the several different small pharmacies in the several different towns, which held his many falsely duplicated prescriptions for the pills, and he was running late after his trip to the wharf, which he hadn't planned. He wanted to harvest all the medications in their abundance, not have to drive up and make the rounds again on another day. Too much going on now for that—Sarafino not the least of it. He would stop at a few markets and package stores on the way back home, too, and bring in a store of the Gordon's gin. He drove along now as quickly as the narrow street would allow. The sun was already well to the west, oddly white, the sky whitening. Yes, he would decline the cup of tea. Just a Rosary. He would come back another day. There was so much going on. There was so much to be done.

eight

"YOU HAVE NO IDEA, MANNY. I SEE INTO THE DARKNESS OF SO many hearts. The torture there. That's right, anguish and torture. Torture of the self. It looks like something else from the outside, something that is usually judged vile and obscene. Or merely foolish. But it's pain, Manny. All this black sin. All this iniquity. You would have no idea of the ache that is in the hearts of some of these men." Father John Sweet's eyes shone. They swelled in his head whenever he was carrying on like this. Brown eyes, heavy lidded. The two men sat in the parlor, the hall door closed, and he had Sweet with his back to the door, at any rate. Sweet was not to know about Sarafino Pomba. Furtado had even thought of the bathroom: It was not working. Waiting for the plumber to come. They could use the one in the parish hall if they needed. Just a temporary thing, he hoped. A sheepish smile, a palm half raised—these little annoyances, you treat them with humor. He had made tea and brought out a plate of *doces* from Braga's bakery. What manner of self-absorption would make Sweet think that he, Furtado, would have no idea about those bleak and pain-wracked hearts of others? Yet it was a boon that he thought this.

Furtado made no gesture to protest. He sat quietly and nodded. The more Sweet talked, the more he himself did not have to, and he had been going on for a long time now.

"It's a measure of the woes of the Church. All these priests. All this terrible business coming out. And, Manny, I'm there to pick up the pieces. It's what I'm called to do. And I do it gladly. There's grace in my heart, if I may say so. If I dare say such a thing. But I gather the scars in my own way. You don't remain untouched by such goings-on." He paused. He looked wild and at the same time resembled some overgrown boy, rangy, long-faced, and horse-toothed, his hair parted to one side, a bit of a cowlick, a little flip-wave at the front. Five o'clock shadow, though. And he wore his tatty sport shirt buttoned up to the neck. Never the white collar and black shirt. He was younger than Furtado by at least a decade, maybe more. He would have been cast as the storefront Baptist minister in any film about the clergy. Furtado made it a point to dress in a cassock each time they met.

"John," he said, "you have done something important with these men." He let the implication sit there: *These men. That's what you should be doing now. Them. Not me*. But he did not let himself say it. He understood that of late his own impulses ran to extravagance, but it wasn't enough to merely understand this—he had to be continually mindful of it, and certainly in Sweet's company. Sweet, too, he had come to see, exercised an extravagant soul. It occurred to him that this fixer might be madder than some of his charges. Maybe the work was indeed too much. Maybe you did not remain untouched by it. Maybe you contracted madness by proximity, like a contact high or a head cold.

Sweet gesticulated. He shuffled his feet. There was something wrong with one of his feet. The left foot. The shiny black shoe on the left foot was built up underneath, blocky, thick. Corrective of something. Sweet had mentioned it once, only once, catching Furtado's eye on it. "A little gift from God," he had said. "Now I am an inspired walker." His thighs showed muscular and heavy beneath his trousers. Yes, he rolled a little when he walked. But now he waved his arms and rocked his body. He might have been sitting behind a drum kit. "It's the aftermath, Manny. That, too. Coming in behind, going into the parish, taking stock of the damage." He caught himself here, though, and brought himself back down a bit. Furtado could see the dash light come on. "But we are here for *you*, Manny, and you are nothing like that, thanks be to God. Your difficulty is something we can manage. Something you are managing. And your lovely parish. Eden. Oh, I know, I know, the difficulties, the diversity of the communities here, not just the Portuguese. The work you are doing here. The challenges. Rego talks to me. Mayhew, too. They think highly of you. They understand your, uh, liberal interpretations, and they are letting all that alone for now. They praise your abilities. When a man is spoken about like that and he is not present—a wonderful thing, Manny. Now, I'm not trying to diminish your own situation. But in comparison . . ." Here he raised his hands and shook his head. "I just thank God it is what it is, and not something else. We can take this as a blessing. The Lord is moving us both."

"Yes," said Furtado, "He may very well be."

"How many drinks did you have this week?" Sweet asked suddenly.

Furtado was ready for him. The air in the room was almost visible between them, and he could read it. Auroras sparking in the ether. He admired how Sweet had let him know that he was discussed by the powers, and that Sweet was party to those discussions. Another boon for him. It didn't put him off balance. It kept him alert and on his toes. "Two," he said. "I drank a beer down on my brother-in-law's fishing boat."

"Tell me about it," said Sweet, the psychologist now.

"One beer. Solidarity. It's part of my work here."

"And the other drink?"

"Come to think of it, there was only one."

Sweet scowled thoughtfully, retreating into a deeper appraisal. Sweet's focus was the drinking. After he'd learned that Furtado's old injuries flared now and again, he understood that the Horta woman had simply exaggerated his store of pills. Father Manny needed strong medicine from time to time. He was a veteran, after all. He was seeing a doctor. Sweet had discussed prudence with Furtado, and he was reassured. And Furtado's functioning—his work here—didn't that count for evidence? You couldn't pull off a major addiction and still do all the things that Manny Furtado did. No, he looked at the drinking, and Furtado gave him that much. It was a bobble. It was a slip-up. A bit of confusion, quite over now. That's how he wanted it to stand. Sweet shifted in his chair. "So that one beer," he said. "On your brother-in-law's boat. Did you enjoy it?"

"Truth be told, I didn't."

"Truth be told," said Sweet. "Yes, the truth be told. The truth is always told in one way or another. Didn't enjoy it because it wasn't six? Or eight? I have been there, Manny."

"I didn't enjoy it because it was too cold, John."

"Do you know what I never get from you, Manny?" Sweet said, leaning into him now, eyes on him in their fullness, long lashes, the long curved lashes of a young girl.

Furtado waited him out.

"Despair," said Sweet. "Despite whatever your trial is, there is no despair. This is why I know you are fundamentally sound. You are not damaged in the deep structures. There are angels everywhere," he said, and he rolled his long head and regarded the parlor, as if to find someone settled in a corner, taking notes. "The Holy Spirit recruits. This sad business with your former assistant. The poor woman had her problems, but she delivered you, in a sense. And I am glad to be here, to have met you. There are things I can learn from you. I will have a parish one day. When this part of my work is done. No more roaming. And I hope I can be like you. Someone who understands his flock, someone who knows how to care for them. So this is good, Manny. And I hope I am being helpful to you as well." He paused. "You've thought about the meetings some more?"

"I have," said Furtado. Now it was his turn to lean in. There was something he liked about Sweet, despite himself. They sat now in the postures of earnest engagement. He could smell Sweet's aftershave. Old Spice. "I am all right without them. They might even work against me. I don't"—he hesitated—"I don't think being around all that is the right thing for me. There's work here, and that's where my focus is. And I am all right now." Sweet had suggested AA meetings. There was a group for clergy up the Cape. Sweet had also mentioned, very deliberately as a passing remark, he thought, that a return visit to Mount Perousia would have been available to him, should things have spiraled out of hand. Sweet understood that the logistics weren't ideal right now, though. And Furtado had figured this out quickly. Neither Bishop Mayhew nor Monsignor Rego wanted any disruptions down there. They wanted the parish resuscitated. They understood they could lose it. Other small parishes had gone under. So now that everyone was satisfied that he, Furtado, was not part of the recently notorious larger troubles that were at this moment rocking not only the diocese but also the archdiocese—even the archbishop himself—they would give him plenty of leeway to do his work. As far as anyone knew, he didn't really have a drinking problem anymore.

And now there was Sweet to keep an eye on him, just in case. An illustration that the Church was exercising due diligence. No disrespect to Father Manuel Furtado—it was just that things had changed greatly for the Church in these last few years. An epidemic of accusations and outings. Mistakes had been made. Now there must be attentiveness, scrutiny. Everything, no matter how small, was treated as a serious matter. They just had to dot all the *i*'s and cross the *t*'s. Even though details of Sweet's sessions with him were supposed to be unreservedly confidential, Furtado was fairly certain that the fixer carried back reports.

Of course, Sweet could mandate the AA meetings. But he didn't. He gave a single confirmatory nod. He was thinking. You could watch him think, a faraway look, a minute parting of the lips. Sweet knew the complete story—Furtado's earlier bout with drinking, his being relieved of his parish and furloughed to Mount Perousia. Perhaps he was ruminating on the emergence of a pattern. Furtado had considered such a thing himself. He had also thought of himself as possibly, simply, moving through a series of impersonations, this thing that was his life, his calling, his vocation. There was nothing inauthentic about this, for behind it all there was the will of God. But how far behind it? And what of his own will? Now, a script we are handed. Illusions of choice. How he wished that Sweet would rise and go. Sarafino Pomba—did he sleep beyond the door? Mariah Grey was with him, but what did that guarantee?

Before his two-year furlough at Mount Perousia, Furtado had been pastor at Saint Severus, in Mashtook, a onetime textile town near Fall River. The Portuguese had settled there in the late 1800s to work in the mills, as they had in so many other towns, and after the mills closed, they stayed. The families established themselves, and the children, some of them, ascended to the middle class. Mashtook had gone through its depressions, like so many factory towns in the state, but it had come again to life starting back in the '70s, with light manufacturing. A number of small plants moving onto the sites that the cloth mills had once occupied, the most prescient of them a few small factories that sliced up silicon wafers. Nothing terribly high-tech. Just another step in the refinement of this odd commodity. Each wafer—the cutting evidently needed special equipment, some kind of precision machinery—yielded an octet of silicon chips, which were shipped to companies all over the country, which would then transform the raw element into . . . into something Furtado didn't quite understand, though you found them in everything nowadays, from the computer in the office to his Toyota's engine. Once the demand for chips, and thus the wafers, took off—who could have seen this coming?—Mashtook ascended with it.

Saint Severus was a good parish, but it needed to grow into the needs of the rejuvenating town. The church building itself required refurbishing, and the number of communicants was far too low for the population. It was poorer, by the Church's books, than it ever needed to be.

Furtado oversaw the growth, the building. It took only a few years. He nearly doubled the number of families attending Mass, and with more funds coming in, with local help, with help from the diocese, he brought Mashtook into its new age. A remodeled church, a new school, and a gymnasium—which he leased out to community functions as another source of revenue. People spoke Portuguese at the parish hall suppers, and indeed there had been newcomers from Portugal, a new wave—though most of them were from the mainland. But they livened the flock. Furtado's own language skills improved. He coached boys in basketball. He started a soccer league. He was popular, shooting pool with the men at the Knights of Columbus hall, presiding over *festas* at the Portuguese American Civic League, entertaining the women with long, exaggerated stories about his own family, about his mother's wonderful Old Country cooking. He was liked by everyone.

Then he began drinking. It wasn't some failing or malignancy. It simply started. Or *he* did. If you asked him, he would be unable to say when or how, but it had something to do with sameness. Not the same as boredom. But the sameness of being. The sameness of self. So that when he drank—and now he always drank—there was this pushing or knocking at the edge of who he was. It seemed to open up new ways of thinking for him, variations from his own mind. It was almost as though he could be someone completely *other* for long periods of time. Alcohol was not a splendid drug—by itself it was dulling and stupefying, but he didn't reach out for anything more in those days. Whatever its limitations, it was enough for the job.

He drank hard for two years, and then, when he simply became sick from it, he went to the diocese with the problem. By himself. Of his own accord. And he was indeed very sick from it. And that got him his furlough.

Mount Perousia was a haven of retreat for priests in need of special attention. A place for rest, contemplation, simple work, and recovery. For rehabilitation. It had been a farm once, orchards and pastures in the Berkshire Hills, out in the western part of the state, deeded to the Church early in the 1900s. The extant buildings had been expanded and refurbished—in the case of the great barn, completely restructured to contain a chapel—and a number of small cottages were constructed over the years, the work all done by the brothers and priests of the Order of Saint Matthew of the Mount. Any diocese could apply for a space there for one of its priests.

Some of the men were alcoholics, there for *rehab*, in the modern parlance. Others suffered various troubles and would stay for extended periods, depressed, disillusioned, chosen by God to undergo these special trials. Christ's words from the Sermon on the Mount, as written by Saint Matthew, were the foundation of Mount Perousia's activities, and the grieving and the poor in spirit—all the wretched and afflicted—were understood to be Blessed. The chapel and the refectory, the library, were all places of community, but Christ's injunction to *pray in the closet* was also taken very seriously, and thus the small cottages allowed each man his privacy to live and pray alone. Everyone worked to his abilities to serve the community, but the Brothers carried out most of the real tasks under the direction of Father Robert, the chief administrator.

Furtado, sober and clearheaded among the ancient oaks and fiery maples, the rolling hills, the wild apple orchards, discovered two things while at Mount Perousia. The first was that he did not appreciate being away from the running of his own parish. It seemed to him that that was his best self. Holding things together in the material world was important, and he was of greatest use in that role. He did not like that Perousia was administered by others. He did not humbly accept the quotidian chores of laundry or kitchen work when he knew his head was filled with ideas of how he could improve the way things ran.

The second thing was that amid all the study and contemplation and private prayer, he abandoned the Creed. It was there that some scaffold within him collapsed, and with it went the Resurrection, the divinity of Christ, the miracles of the New Testament, the Nativity, all of it. All of it. Only the mysterious Creator God remained for him. He was horrified at first, for this meant, if nothing more profound, that his entire adult life had been thrown away. As much he loved running a parish, he actually thought he might have to leave the Church now. It was a shattering notion in its own right. He often thought of Saint Paul in those days—*this birth of mine was monstrous*!—and Paul had uttered that at the moment of belief. What was Furtado to say of his own transformation, the utter collapse of belief? That the Church was founded on rumor and superstition, the polemics of a few fanatic old men? He didn't eat for days at a time. He barely slept. He remembered the revulsion he felt at just the sight of the crucifix. What kind of people would hang such a disgusting image—the instrument of unspeakable torture—in their places of worship? What could be more demeaning to the Creator of the Universe than to say he would sacrifice a son whom he loved, to die nailed to such a thing? That image alone conveyed to the priest all that was wrong with humanity.

When he was to reflect on his transformation, it would seem as though it had come upon him in an instant. A moment. More likely it had been a slower process. It was not unusual. Several of the men at Perousia were wrestling with similar woes. As one of the Brothers liked to say, "Around here, it's either the DTs or the DDs." *Deist drift*. No one much abandoned God, just the irrationality of the Son. Just the orthodoxy of the Church. And so God became a distant concept and not a blood redeemer. Such was the place Furtado found himself in. God loved him. He loved God. That somehow was true, though impossible to completely understand. But the rest he could not abide. He recovered his orthodoxy for a time, but then he found it lifting from him again, like a fog burning off the ocean under a bright sunlight, lifting and drifting until it was gone. The absence persisted even until now, though he did not let this enter into his time with Father John Sweet. John Sweet the shrinker of heads, the fixer of problems. The comforter of madmen in his parlor.

Sweet, that odd man. What could he divine in Furtado's heart? He seemed to be contemplating deeply, with that otherworldly gaze in his eyes. How did Sweet see him? As a bland pastor, just easing into middle age, going through the not-so-extraordinary difficulties of the priesthood? A man whose impressionable housekeeper had betrayed him over nothing? When he finally spoke again to Furtado, he simply asked, "How are the exercises going, then?"

Here, Furtado did not need to dissemble. "Every night," he said. And then, like a good student, he reached for one of the filled ledgers, which he had placed on the side table for just this moment. He held it up to Sweet and riffed the pages, showing the fullness, the completeness, every page filled with the bold pen strokes. "It's very helpful."

Sweet nodded and smiled.

"I like the intimacy, the privacy, of it," Furtado added.

The great eyes widened. So Furtado was not about to offer a sample. "That's the key for you, then," Sweet said. "No censors. Your hand to God."

"Yes."

"I'm glad that it's more efficient for you than the chairs," Sweet said.

"I never disliked the chairs," Furtado said. "I concede, I thought they were silly at first." The chairs were another way Sweet and Furtado did their work together. Sweet always called it work. Furtado would place a chair next to his own and address it as though a person he needed to talk to were actually sitting in it. Sweet would nudge him into talking to Allie and Tom, sometimes his mother, too. But Pai Furtado interested him the most. He had been the drinking father. Sweet thought this was important. After Furtado addressed the person in the chair, Sweet would have him get up and switch places. He would have him become that other person. Inhabit him. Speak from him. Furtado had done this a number of times—anything to placate the fixer. Pai Furtado was difficult, he had to admit. Always a rush of confusion and then a closing up. He was supposed to do the chair exercise on his own, too, but he let it lapse. And yet his ledgers, his *confessions*, comprised, among all else, scattered forays into the unresolved heart of his father.

Furtado thought he heard a noise from beyond the hall door. His shoulders tensed. His ear hummed—so silent for so long and now it hummed, out of nowhere again. He glanced at his wristwatch. They had been talking for over two and a half hours. Sweet caught this motion and looked up at the handsome wall clock, an artifact, the white face yellowing like ivory, the delicate Roman numerals, the filigreed hands. "One day at a time," he said. "Should we pray?"

On his way out, Sweet said again, "If you could know, Manny, the things I see, the things I have to deal with. And you, here, so blessed with this lovely parish. If you only knew."

"I am pale by comparison," Furtado said. "So I would hope." Yes, let the Church's great difficulties, then, diminish his own. Let him scurry unharmed in those long shadows.

"I will carry the message back," Manny said. "I will carry back the optimistic news."

He walked Sweet to his car, Sweet with his rolling stride, that high shoe. The rectory would have been available for him to spend the night, but because of their work—thank God—Sweet did not feel it appropriate to lodge there. With a per diem from the diocese, he often stayed in town at one of the guesthouses. Sometimes he drove directly back to Calumet. Furtado did not ask where he was going this afternoon.

MARIAH GREY SAT BY SARAFINO. SHE HAD PULLED THE STRAIGHT-backed chair close to the bed, where Sarafino sat propped against a nest of pillows. The afternoon light sieved through the gauzy window curtains and lit Mariah in a way that deepened the attentive set of her face. They had spread out a number of papers on the bed, across the quilt that covered Sarafino's lap, and they appeared to be studying them when the priest tapped and entered. "Father Sweet has left the building," he said.

Sarafino wore a fresh sweatshirt. His scant hair was washed and combed over the crown of his head, and he was clean shaven. A plastic basin of soapy water sat on the bureau, away from the Virgin and the candle. Several amber vials of capsules and tablets had been set there also. "We have said two Rosaries," Mariah told him, "and then I have learned all manner of things." She saw Furtado glance at the array of pill bottles. "I have all the instructions written down: when, if, how much." She didn't mention Peter's name.

"How do you feel?" Furtado asked. He tapped Sarafino's foot where it stuck up under the quilt. He watched the quick, small efforts of his narrow chest. "How is your breathing?"

"I still remember how to do it," Sarafino said.

"There's oxygen coming today," said Mariah. "Winslow is picking it up."

"I'm tired," said Sarafino. "I could close my eyes."

"I've worn you out," Mariah said. "I'll fix your pillows so you can rest."

"Do you hurt?" asked Furtado.

"I exult in tribulation," Sarafino said.

"Do you want your beads?"

"Yes."

Mariah gathered up the sheets of paper from the bed and took the big aquamarine rosary from the folding tray beside her and placed it in his hands.

"The unclean spirit seeks rest and does not find it," Sarafino said. And then, "Ha. That's not me, though." He looked up at Mariah, who stood over him now, adjusting his bedcovers. When she laid her hand on his forehead, he said, "Maybe you are the sign I'm supposed to get."

"I'm not a sign," she told him. "Do you need to walk down to the bathroom?"

"If I do, I will."

She gathered up the scattered papers and lifted the basin from the bureau top, and when she did, Furtado came after and took up all the pills, and together they left the bedroom, closing the door behind them but for a crack.

Mariah and the priest settled in the kitchen. There was still some coffee in the Pyrex warmer, and he poured them each a cup. "Thank you so much," he said. "I thought Father Sweet would never leave. Thank you for staying with him like that. I don't want to take advantage."

"Not for a minute," Mariah said. "Really. I like him. There's something about him. The way he believes in his signs. The Virgin Mary."

"He's not an innocent," Furtado said. "He's been around."

"So have you, to hear him say," she said, smiling. "And I know he's a hustler. It's all right. He gets these spurts, though. He gets these fits of energy. He talked a blue streak. I'm afraid of grinding him down."

"I'm going to have to find a better solution for him. A better situation."

Mariah took this in. Two faint marks, little vertical grooves, appeared in the clear skin of her forehead. Then she picked out one of the pieces of paper she and Sarafino had been looking at, and she slid it across the table to Furtado. "Look at this. Look at what we came up with."

"I don't get it."

"It's a diagram. A map, actually. He says it's where you kids buried the statue of the Virgin."

"He told you about that?" Then, "I wasn't there. I didn't bury anything."

"Well, *he* buried it, then. I know this place, more or less. Check me out on it. See? We talked our way through it. See this? It's a pond. And this? And the next one?" She pointed to two wobbly circles. "And the road goes up this way. And that's the highway, way over there. See that? And in between the two ponds, nothing but thicket. And then the third, here, totally hidden. I know the ponds. I've done work on them. This one here, bass and snapping turtles. They dominate." She traced among the marks with her finger, slender and red-knuckled, he noticed. The nail clear and short. Buffed smooth. A band of dull silver on the third finger of the same hand. "He says he put the statue off in there. Off that end of the pond. It should be more of a little oval here. This end faces the dunes."

"Let me see," Furtado said. He peered at the paper. Without an explanation it would have looked like scribbling or doodling. But the priest knew what it represented. He knew very well just where this was. "That poor man," he said.

"Because this haunts him so much, you mean."

"Yes."

"He's sick, but his head is working. We drew this up together."

The priest stared at the drawing. "It's a real place, all right. We used to have a camp there. We hunted and fished. You know. Kids. Everything was secret. There was no path in, though. Just brambles and bushes. And trees.

Pines. Completely hidden. He told me that, too. That She was out there. I don't know how he could have gotten Her out there. I think he might be confused. You know, because we spent so much time there. This is all a bit much."

Mariah took a sip of coffee, and then he took a sip of coffee. It was stale and bitter.

"Tell me one thing I should do, Manny."

His ear was ringing. His mind was slowing. Too much John Sweet for a day. And now Sarafino. He wasn't quite sure he heard her correctly. He didn't want to ask her to repeat herself. "Perhaps that oxygen," was all he could think to say.

nine

MARIAH GREY RETURNED, AS SHE HAD PROMISED, JUST AROUND suppertime with an apparatus for the oxygen. Winslow came with her. Together they set everything up in the little bedroom. A large, elongated green tank with a flowmeter and a regulator dial attached to its nozzle. A stand with a handle and rubber wheels. A hose of plastic tubing ending in a cannula, which would fit under the chin, over the ears, and into the nostrils. "I have all the instructions here," Mariah said, and indicated a folder. "It's not for continual use. Just when he needs it. Okay to ease sleep. If it comes to it, we will get a converter for steady state, but this is what we need to use for now." Again, she left Peter's name unspoken.

"I'm going off now, dear," Winslow said to Mariah after everything was in place. "I'll come get you in a little while."

"I've got you figured out," said Sarafino.

"What's that?" Winslow asked. She cocked her head and regarded Sarafino, her lips pressed in an easy smile, her eyes bright.

"You're a Protestant."

"Sweetie, I haven't protested anything in years," she said.

"Don't worry," Sarafino said. "Everybody gets saved."

"Yes," said Winslow. "I know."

After Winslow left, Mariah tried to get Sarafino breathing with the cannula. Sarafino did not like the setup at all. He was in a jumpy, darkened mood. He twitched. He complained. First, there was the candle to the Virgin.

"I want that!" he said to Mariah as she blew it out, sending a squib of blue smoke into the air. "I never negotiated that away!"

"You can't have it," Mariah said. She fixed him with her eyes. That mineral shine. "You can't have the flame around the oxygen."

"Then I don't want the oxygen," he said.

"Sarafino, be reasonable," said the priest.

"You think you know about it?"

"Know about what?" Mariah said.

"I possess the Brown Scapula," Sarafino said. "From the Carmelites."

"Yes, I saw it," she said.

Sarafino twitched some more and fussed with his covers. "Where's Allie? She was supposed to be here. Why isn't Allie here?"

She had said she was coming up to the rectory after work, it was true, but she hadn't shown. Furtado didn't know where she was. Mariah looked to him. He didn't say anything.

"Well, don't take that candle," Sarafino said finally.

"It stays," said Mariah.

"That's what I'm talking about," he said.

"We just won't light it."

He turned and looked hard at her. His yellow eyes narrowed. "Is your heart pure?"

"No," she said.

He looked at Furtado. "This is the same old shit," he said.

"What now, Sarafino? This will make you feel so much better," Furtado said. "You wear this. These little tubes go into your nose."

"You think so? You think I don't know about all this?"

The priest reached down and put the tube and cannula in place.

"You know what I never noticed when were kids, Manny?" Sarafino's nostrils widened. He fiddled with the clear tubing. Furtado thought he might take it off, but he left it. He took some breaths. "You kind of look like your father. You resemble him. You favor him. That big Portagee head. You are just like your old man. Your old man was a son of a bitch. He was a prick. Did you know that?"

"Yes, I know that," said the priest. "He was a hard man to live with. You were around him enough. You were around Allie and me enough. You know we all knew the score." He turned to the oxygen tank. "You're going to feel better with this. It will be a little while. You'll see."

"Then let us no more pass judgment on one another," Sarafino said, "but rather decide never to put a stumbling block in the way of a brother."

"Just breathe. Like regular," Mariah said. "Nice and easy. Just relax."

"You think I don't know about it?" he said. Then he glared at the priest. "My old man worked on the wharves, hauling fish boxes, and he got laid off every winter. And the wharf never paid anything to begin with. My ma would fight with him all the time to ask the great Pai Furtado for a berth on the *Ilha do Pico*. To crew. And he would ask. He would always humble himself and ask. And then he'd come back and tell my mother he asked. And he never got on. Years, Manny. And your old man took other guys, but never my father. We didn't have a pot to piss in. You know that. Why didn't your old man ever let my father work with him? There was good money then. We never had nothing in that house. Not like you. Most of the time we never had hot running water, and my mother had to live like that, and all your old man had to do was let my father work on the boat." Sarafino snuffed at the oxygen, his nostrils flaring. "I bet you never thought of that, Manny."

"No, Sarafino. I didn't know about that." The truth was, he didn't remember if he'd known then or not. It was a void, a blackness. He thought to say to Sarafino that maybe his father had never really asked, out of pride, and had only told his mother he had asked. But he held that back. It would do no good here.

"Maybe it just didn't mean anything to you."

"You just breathe naturally," Mariah said. She leaned over Sarafino and stroked his forehead. She smoothed his hair.

"You a nurse?" he aked.

"You know I'm not. I'm a biologist."

"I should never have buried Our Lady," he said. "That was a mistake. She was too beautiful. She was like you. She didn't belong buried. It was disrespectful. I would go and unbury her. I should have done that while I still could. She shouldn't have gone in the ground. You know that sometimes people dug up a saint's body and there would be nothing wrong with it. It wouldn't be all rotten or bones or anything. It would be perfect. That's how you could tell it was a saint. It was a sign. You think maybe the Virgin would be like that? All beautiful and like that. I thought about it. I should have dug her up. It could be the sign."

"A sign of what?" asked the priest. "What is it you want?"

Sarafino was silent for a minute. Then he said, "Not all that much." He looked at Furtado and pointed to Mariah. "She knows," he said. "The church, the Virgin. Mr. Coelho. The whole thing."

"I know she knows," said the priest.

Mariah continued to stroke his brow and head. She had given him some of his meds before they'd started the oxygen, and perhaps they were beginning to work to some effect. He began to settle. He leaned back on the pillows again. Then they sat and said a Rosary, Mariah and the priest intoning the prayers and Sarafino working the blue glass beads in his hands.

"I'm sorry I said that about your father," Sarafino said when they were finished. "But he could have made our lives so good. Just that job. For my old man. I never understood that. I thought you knew."

"I never knew that about *your* father," Furtado said. "I don't think Pai ever talked about that around me. He was a difficult man. I never understood him."

He finished his prayers, he sat at the desk, he sipped some gin, he swallowed some pills. Downstairs, Sarafino slept, eased by his own medications and his oxygen. By the time the priest moved to the desk, a bar of pain sat across his shoulders like a yoke. Glass in his neck. But he opened the ledger and wrote the events of the day, the records of conversation, the workings of his mind. After a time, the familiar tides began to rise in him. He sat over the open book. Its vistas were without limit. The smell of the gin. Like something you could apply to a wound. The long white tablets, so pleasingly bitter. He thought of Job, calling out to God, and God answering with his withering sarcasm. And when did that ever stop any man or woman from crying to Him, calling Him out, asking for His accountability? *Where shall wisdom be found? And where is the place of understanding?* What man or woman would be content with fearing God and turning their face from evil? Better to send them to the mines, into the bowels of the earth, to bring up the precious gold and lapis lazuli. Better yet to send them into the ocean with hooks against leviathan.

And as he wrote and the chemicals traversed his nerves, his aches lifted as he knew they would, but now something different entered the room. Something lingering from the afternoon, perhaps, from Sarafino's remarks. For in that chamber now, his father slipped through the clapboards as if he rode on a current of air. Beyond the priest's own will. Not the direction he had set for himself. And the heavy script seemed to struggle a moment on the page—*send him with hooks against leviathan*—and then it followed him off, and then the priest was writing Pai Furtado. Yes, a cold draft from the street, under the sash of the black window. Pai in familiar places. Pai in memory. Pai sitting at the kitchen table with his head in his hands, just watching the tabletop, after his mother had gone to bed and he thought no one watched him. Or leaning over his bar stool at Juney's Tap and shouting and swearing with the other West End fishermen, when Furtado would creep through the heavy front door and ask for a dollar in the middle of all that cigarette smoke and bluster. Pai's black skipper's hat on the back of his big round head, and his eyes heavy from drinking.

His poor father. Yes, he could say that now. He could feel a kind of compassion for him, a tenderness almost, that had been impossible while he was alive. So bitter and strange, that man. Pai Furtado had been just a boy himself when he came to town from the Azores with his family. He grew up in the town, but he seemed always more from that other, older world than from this new one. A sadness haunted him. More than *saudades*, that untranslatable sweet yearning that connoted a sense of both belonging and displacement, a tender lamentation, an almost joyful sorrow. No, there was some deep trouble in his breast. He was two different men, two difficult men. In the town, he could walk into any room and be the center of it, provided a crowd of men was present. But at home he was always off somewhere behind those gloomy, deep-set eyes, or else he sat around seething, uttering screeds against anyone or anything that seemed to cross his mind.

Mae spent most of her time up at the church. She taught catechism. She was on all the committees. She had sung in the choir since she was a young girl—the Sodality had a much bigger group in those days, and they would sing from the organ loft at the back of the church, an elite space then, and Furtado could remember her voice rising so high, and her solo

"Ave Maria" bringing tears to the eyes of the *velhas*. Furtado knew a great part of her involvement was the way it kept her out of the house and away from Pai's vinegary moods, but it was also true that she loved the church for itself, and she taught him that it was a place of peace and refuge through her own actions, as well as her instruction to him.

Sometimes Furtado would see his mother shake her head at Pai and with affectionate humor call him her ignorant Portagee, and he would simply grunt and let it pass. But other times, when they truly fought—when he was drunk, especially—she would use those same words like a leather strap on him. She had been born in the town, but her grandparents had come over from the island of Flores. That was the surname that had been entered in the documents for them in this country. She sometimes spoke of another name—Cota—but it never appeared in the town registry nor in the church's archives, which were kept in a safe in the rectory office, and which showed the Furtados' marriage, as well as the dates now of their deaths, in the scratchy black inkings of a steel nib. So Flores was her maiden name, and his father would hurl that at her now and then during one of his eruptions—raging, but of course now, seen from this distance, perhaps just flummoxed, overwhelmed—"Flores, a little goddamned flower. There's nothing I can do that's good enough for you!"

But the battles never stopped quickly—the two stayed at it, blades drawn, until Pai eventually ground her down, for, like the king in the myth, his well was connected to the sea, and so his source of anger was inexhaustible. Invectives would pour from him in great tidal cascades, and no one was spared. When his mother finally withdrew in silence, his father would continue, railing at her, at Furtado, at Allie, and then he would move to the other captains, neighbors, women friends of Mae, and even Father Santos and the Church itself. It would begin the same way—at supper or after supper—and drag on until he fell asleep in the chair in the parlor. It didn't seem to matter how much he drank, but he drank every night. On good nights he would leave and walk up to Juney's Tap, but even those nights carried their own curse, for there would nearly always be a fight about his going, Mae objecting to the money he would spend there, and when he came home, he would be full of the same bitterness, roaring his disgust with everyone.

When Furtado reached high school, he got Mae to sign a note for him giving him permission to go up to the poolroom. In those days there was a five-lane candlepin bowling alley on the land side of Front Street, east of the town hall. It was cramped and ramshackle, and above it was the poolroom, six tables, five of them old and scarred with deadened rails, and one, the so-called money table, somewhat preserved and level and clean. The walls were dark wood, unadorned with decoration save for the long racks of wooden cues. The floor was gritty hardwood, oily, black, sagging in spots, and overhead, naked bulbs hung from black cords and glared down on the ancient green felt of the tables.

This smoky, profane hall became Furtado's home every night of the week that Pai Furtado spent ashore. He had promised his mother that he would do his homework directly after school in return for the note, which anyone under eighteen had to have, and at first he did, but when she never checked, he let it go entirely. Every night he would slip out right after taking out the garbage and helping Mae and Alzaida with the dishes. If the timing was wrong, he would have to fight with Pai about leaving. Although Pai might have been able to physically stop him then, he always turned away in disgust after a few minutes, choosing instead to begin listing his son's worthlessness and weaknesses to Mae and Allie. And that's when Furtado would slide off into the night.

He became good at shooting pool, of course. He was there all the time. He started out as everybody did: with eight-ball, fifteen cents a game. And then he moved to nine-ball, betting nickels on the five, dimes on the nine. When he got good enough, he asked Boozy Corea if he could play on the money table. Boozy, an old, hunched man who always held a wet cigar stub in his mouth, ran the poolroom for his nephew Leno, who owned the building and ran the bowling downstairs. Boozy had been keeping an eye on Furtado. You had to be good to play on the money table—it was one of the ways Boozy kept the table from getting torn up. No drunks, no kids assholing around on it. Most of the players there were out of high school already, longhaired sullen guys. They weren't the fishermen. They worked here and there. Nothing much. They gambled on their skills up at Boozy's in a bored way. Boozy kept the best cues separate for the players at the money table, and if you wanted, you could pick one out and rent it as your own for a dollar a week. Soon Furtado was making money, and Sarafino was right behind him.

Sarafino was never as good, but Furtado watched out for him. He kept Sarafino out of the tense straight-pool games, but when there was a crowd at nine-ball and Sarafino drew behind him, he would watch his leaves and let Sarafino clean them. No one caught on—it wasn't all the time. Just enough. He made sure Sarafino, always short of money, came home with a few dollars. They'd stay until Boozy closed up—no special time, just when the tables got empty. During the week it could be pretty early, sometimes as early as nine. If it closed early they would find a place to hang out—sometimes just a doorway, where they'd smoke and loiter with other guys who didn't want to be home. When Furtado figured Pai had finally fallen asleep, he and Sarafino would trudge on back to the West End, hands in pockets, collars turned up, not talking too much.

There would always be a mystery for him: why his mother and father remained locked in that mortal struggle. He laid it to Pai, of course. The easy answer—always the wrong one, he had become certain of that—was drinking. But drinking was nothing but drinking. The true darkness hunkered below that. Other mortal struggles, invisible mostly. Pai should have been happy—as much as anyone. He had a good living, a house, a family, a boat. He had respect. But there was something corrosive lying deep.

It could have been something from the Old Country. It could have been simply that Pai was baffled by America—even the off-kilter America of the town, which had been described in early days as the tenth island—the farthest-flung headland of the Azorean archipelago, lushly European and superstitiously Catholic. Yet at its center stood that towering monument, fittingly gray and flinty, to the Protestant English and their tightly wrapped covenants. And then there were wild summer crowds, People from Away with money and lives of a scale that no townperson could conjure in even the most immoderate flights of imagination. They beckoned with a bigger world, and it was one in which anyone or anything in the town became insignificant. Yes, this was a peculiar and insular place.

But these thoughts led him nowhere. They rolled away like smoke. Nothing would lead him to his father's secret heart, and anyway, what he had resented most about him when he was growing up was that other Pai. This was the man who loved a joke, who surrounded himself with laughter and camaraderie, even among the men he would rip and tear during his kitchen and parlor tirades. So he would sully the air in his own house, poison Mae's small gestures toward happiness, sour his children, but out and about he was the great man, the top captain, the high roller full of the best wishes and spirits. Everything was a posture for him, and the statue of Our Lady of Fatima was no different.

Manny was wise enough by then to see it all for what it was. Pai thought of it as his personal triumph. He worked hard to raise money for it, but he worked harder to attach his name to everything that had to do with bringing Her here. So stealing Her from the church was not exactly a whim for Furtado. It was not, maybe, a conscious premeditation, but when it occurred to him on that night long ago, it rose up fully formed as an idea, fit together in the dark cellar of his own spite. He struck out at his father, and he struck hard and secretly in a way that would hit him in his most public guise. All this was easy to understand now that he let his mind run to it. This was what Sarafino had brought home to him now. All of this, all tangled up in something that Furtado believed he had laid to rest long ago. But here it all was again, and he hated it.

He interrupted himself now. He lifted himself from the desk. In the room, the precarious sweetness of intoxication. He drifted. He wished for another word, something that would do justice to this state, which was like a chamber that led to another chamber, and then another and another. A public hall of dark oak and marble, where different laws and axioms pertained. You could see the antique robes of the magistrates suspended quaint and limp from their elaborate clothes hooks, their powdered wigs hanging above them. The judgment of common reason didn't enter here. He forgot the clamorous engines of the body for a while. What would he trade for this world? What would anyone?

There was a small taste of death involved. He would concede this tariff. In AA meetings you heard the terrible stories, the heartbreak, the ruin. But there was little talk of the dividends. Not the equal of prayer or meditation, but not their opposite, either. Always, though, the awareness of great debts being piled up. His flesh reveled in itself, waves of pleasure, pain banished. Whatever the mind was, whatever the spirit, profoundly touched and shaken loose. What wouldn't anyone trade for this? He rose and glided to the bookshelf and took something down: Meister Eckhart, *The Sermons*. With no sense of searching, he found the passage and copied it out, underlined it. *For the Now in which God created human beings, and the Now in which the last member of the human race will pass away, and the Now in which I am presently speaking to you, are all the same in God and are nothing other than a single Now.*

What Augustine spoke of as well. But then Furtado sat down in the chair again. At the desk. At the ledger. It would be impossible to describe the interval of time that had just passed, but now his father was here again, too, and only because of his son. Furtado's own mind, his own spirit, in the single *Now*. Let himself be the spirit who haunted the old man. He, Manny, could percolate down into the yard behind the old family house, lush in summer with ambrosial hedge and long-spined hollyhock and the morning glory and hydrangea—the hydrangea that covered the old islands, pink and purple, deep blue, here all over the West End, *the tenth island*. Then the priest could settle in the sun on the plain black dirt in front of his father's gear shed. And he could be small again. Or reach that place where he had never ceased to be that child—small, yes, small enough to creep unnoticed and without significance among the citizens and effects of the world.

There were people in the house. Not neighbors. Not Summer People. But a man and a woman he had never seen before. They were sitting with his father and mother in a room, and he was sitting in another room, after only the shortest glimpse of them. Listening. "We were in Red Rock, Colorado," said the woman.

"Red Rock, Colorado," the man said. His voice was thick, and he spoke with an authority that was different from Pai's. A register of speech Furtado had not heard before.

Then the woman spoke. "And there were two mountains, and they were red, with these big red boulders on the top of each one."

"We went to the top, and the air, you could feel it, it was thin and cold."

"And you could hear music," the woman said. "There was music up in the air. Everywhere."

This wonder. This marvelous thing.

"We were way up there," said the man.

"We were up in the radio waves," said the woman. "We were up so high we were in the radio waves, and you could hear the music traveling along in that high air. It was all mixed together. The most beautiful music in the world. It was just so beautiful."

"Well," said his mother, "maybe it was God's angels you heard. You never know."

"It was quite a place," the man said. "I never seen anything like it."

"The sky was full of stars, and you could hear all the music in the radio waves," the woman said again. She talked some more. They all did. Long into the night they talked, back and forth, and Furtado was lulled asleep by the cantillation of their voices.

In the morning no one said anything to him about the visitors. He went outside into the backyard, into the white sunlight, and he could not forget that story. He sat before his father's shed. His mother had planted a small garden by its side, and the yard was filled with the smells of mint and anise. Behind them, the tang of the sea air. Bees rummaged through every open blossom. At the front of the shed he pulled and scooped at the black dirt with the wedged tip of an old shingle until he had formed two dark cones. Then he found two smooth, egg-size rocks, and he peaked each mound with one of them.

When he was satisfied with his mountains, he opened the plank door to his father's shed and went inside. Light fell through the open door and through a small, dusty, square window at one end of the narrow shack. The air inside was warm and still and thick with the smells of net tar and turpentine and bottom paint. He crept deeper inside and reached into a row of paint cans and found a gallon of red lead. Its weight surprised him, and the wire handle of the can pressed a bright groove into his palms as he lugged it from the shed. He went back inside for a screwdriver, and after a long struggle he was able to pry the top of the can loose. Then he mixed the heavy lead paint with a stick and dribbled it all over his twin mountains.

Red. Red Rock, Colorado. Where you could hear music in the sky.

He sat in the yard and he thought about that far place where such a thing was possible. He thought about the world and the wonderful things waiting in it. And after a while his father came striding through the gate in his rolled-down rubber boots and his fishing clothes. "What?" he said. "What is this?"

"Red Rock, Colorado," Manny told him.

This was the first time he would remember really seeing his father's face, seeing into it. That look. He could not name it, but it was something hard and yet something crumbling at the same time. And then Furtado felt something begin to sink inside himself. He could not comprehend what was happening.

His father gazed at the dirt for a while, that look on his face. Then he said, "Stay out of the shed. Stay away from that paint."

Furtado came back outside later that day, and the mounds of dirt, the paint, the rocks, were gone. And that little part of the yard had been returned to its own appointed limits. Smoothed and tamped down, he understood, by his father's heel.

Then the boy wept. A child's keening, outsized and self-regarding. He cried for those celestial harmonies. It was as though he had been locked out in the cold and everyone's attention had been turned elsewhere because he was nothing and his fate in the world would never be considered. His weeping filled his ears, and now it filled the small study under the eaves of the rectory, drifting into the room, a breathless sort of moaning, as if carried forth on its own spectral currents.

But of course it was not Furtado who cried. He did not weep and he did not hear that boy in the yard weeping. It was Sarafino Pomba in the downstairs bedroom, and something had happened to him.

Now the room twisted a little. It spun for just a second. A low beep peaked in one ear and then faded. He stood up from the chair, and the movement wrenched something in the vessels of his head. He came to the ungainly weight of his body again. Sudden ballast. As though he had put on some type of cumbersome equipment—a fireman's heavy coat and helmet, or an armored vest. He willed himself carefully down the stairs. There, in the dim radiance of the bedroom's nightlight, he found Sarafino down on his hands and knees. He moaned in that same indistinct voice that the priest had heard up in his study. He stepped and reached for the wall and found the switch and struck it, and the room burst into glaring relief under the ceiling lamp. Everything rushed upon him at once. He swayed. He put his hand out to the wall to steady himself. He saw that Sarafino's bed was completely torn up—blanket, sheet, quilt. The pillows lay scattered about the floor. The oxygen tank sat massively against the wall, green and dull, but Sarafino had pulled the tubing from his nose—or perhaps it had ripped loose when he fell or threw himself from the bed, jumped or kicked his way out of it. He was breathing rapidly, like a runner. But not deeply. Like he was about to say a single word but could not call it up, and so he took that same word's breath over and over. A kind of pleading. He didn't move from his posture on the floor, but he raised his eyes and looked at Furtado.

"Sarafino," said the priest. The numbness in his lips no longer pleasing. An impediment now. His voice a disturbance. A vulgar noise. An issue from this carapace of body. He made himself speak again. A worthless articulation: "Sarafino, what? What?"

There was a long moment when nothing happened. Neither movement nor sound, and the priest half considered that perhaps he was still up at the desk, deep in those chambers of imagination and memory, and that none of this before him could be touched in the crude world. Then Sarafino said, "She was here."

The words were enough at least to summon an action from the priest. "Let me help you," he said. He straightened the bed as quickly as his body would work, and then, moving very carefully, he knelt on the floor and lifted Sarafino until he had his legs under him. Once he had a firm hold of him, he swiveled him back onto the bed, laying him back against the pillows. Then he spread the sheet and blanket and quilt over him, and tucked their edges under the mattress on either side. "Keep this on," he said, as he slipped the oxygen tube over Sarafino's ears. The priest himself remained dazed, but he asked, "Did you fall?"

"The Virgin was here, Manny."

"You were on the floor. Did you hurt yourself?"

"She was here. It's not the hour of my death. It's not the hour of my death."

"No, it isn't, Sarafino."

"Where's Allie? Why isn't Allie here?"

"Allie is home. Mariah is home, too. I'm here with you."

"The Virgin will send a sign. She was here. I am paralyzed, Manny. It's too much. You can smell the perfume of Her. Like roses. You can feel Her in all the parts of your body. I never should have put Her in the ground. I should go get Her, but it's too late. I don't have the power. She wants to come back out of the ground. She wants to rise."

"Okay," said the priest. "All right. But now you need to calm down. You need to get your breath."

"She is this huge force, Manny. All my heat is gone."

Furtado put his hand on Sarafino's shoulder. He could feel the tremor through the quilt. "You are having a chill."

"In my bones. I can't stop shivering. Our Lady appeared."

"Let me warm you," Furtado said. His voice came out in barely a whisper. If he ever flew, he was stooping back to ground now, like a maple leaf, spinning. *And where is the place of understanding*? He lifted the tucked covers and slid into the bed. Sarafino rolled himself slightly away to make room, and Furtado pulled himself against his back and draped his arm over him. Sarafino did not feel cold through the sweat clothes, but he shivered nonetheless, every inch of him. Furtado held him closer. Their bodies curved together like fishbones, Sarafino so thin, so small, he seemed hardly there but for the scraps of flesh and knobs and protrusions of bone under his waxy skin. The priest felt him, what there was of him, and this time he didn't think of Sarafino as he had been as a boy, wiry with muscle and sinew, alive and darkly bright. Now he simply held the shivering man. He willed his own heat into him.

ten

THE PRIEST BEGAN VESTING HIMSELF. HIS SINGLE ALTAR SERVER for the morning had already come into the sacristy and was dressed in his alb and cincture. His name was Gerald, a man in his forties who had been an altar boy in his youth, when they were still called altar boys. He was from away—Pottstown, in Pennsylvania—and had lived in the town for nearly twenty years. He was stout and pleasant, with a full head of russet hair and light eyes. A broad, happy face. He had already rinsed and dried the cruets and then filled them, one with wine and the other with water. Likewise, he had readied the chalice and paten and laid out the pall and the corporal and purificator. He greeted the priest but kept to his preparations, finally walking out into the sanctuary and lighting the altar candles with a long taper. Father Furtado dressed, putting on his own alb and cincture, and then the stole. He picked out the white chasuble from the vestry and put it on over the alb and the stole. Gerald joined him back in the sacristy, and then the two of them walked in procession out to the sanctuary to begin the Mass.

And where was Allie?

The priest had arranged for her to come the rectory early in the morning, before he had to say Mass and before she had to be at work at the bakery. When she did not show, he called the house. He reached her message machine and spoke into it, but no one picked up. He would not have been so concerned about leaving Sarafino unattended for the forty-five minutes or so that the Mass would take, but because he had tumbled from the bed, because he had had his unsettling episode the night before, Furtado did not want to take any chances. When he couldn't wait any longer, he telephoned Mariah Grey. He told her what had happened and why he needed her. "He's sleeping now," he said. He told her about Sarafino's seeing the Virgin and falling from the bed. Mariah had just come in from the beach with Winslow and the dog. It was ten minutes to seven.

"I'll be right up, Manny," she said.

So the situation had been rescued. But Furtado was off balance. Sarafino occupied his mind, much in the same way he now occupied the rectory. Sudden and then ongoing. Factual. A presence.

The Mass was a special memorial Mass. Alma Dutra, a *velha*, one of the last of one of the oldest families, the East End Dutras, had requested it for her husband, Richard, as she had done once a year every year since his death. Furtado saw at a glance that she was present, along with her daughter and four other town women. A bearded man and a heavy, gray-haired lady he had never seen before sat together in one of the back pews, and Walter, Gerald's partner, sat in the back on the opposite side. Walter did not have any connection to the Dutras, but he attended Mass on Sundays, and he came to every Mass that Gerald served, no matter what the occasion. That was it—nine souls.

The priest moved through the Order of the Mass. He gave himself over to the details. To the ritual. What he himself believed or did not believe counted for nothing now. This was his calling, too. The point of the Mass—the awareness, the presence, of the sacred—was up to him. It was what he would now do, even if Sarafino Pomba hovered about him, demanding something of him. Some corner of his mind, at the very least. No ordinary distraction. A mild, soft tone arose in his ear just between the Kyrie and the Gloria. It should have been a marvelous moment. Angels should have hovered. They might have, in some sense. Once you allowed a single symbol, the universe expanded and kept on going. You had to draw your own lines after that. Or consult a map.

He tried to see the altar and himself as Alma Dutra did. He prepared the altar. The bread. The wine. He moved through the Washing of Hands. He approached the Eucharistic prayer. Did Alma Dutra believe that the Man-God Christ was being called into literal presence now? He brushed past her quickly with his eyes. She wore a black coat. Her thin hair was dyed black. A black like nothing on this Earth. She sat and knelt and stood with an unchanging expression on her face, unchanged also the slumping curve to her shoulders, the slightly bowed head.

He felt his fatigue then. The long night. Little rest. The chemical letdown, too—let him be accurate about that. But he found his voice and led the Lord's Prayer. He broke the bread. He held communion. He was deliberate, and still Sarafino Pomba was there, an immanence. John Sweet, too. And Alzaida. His annoyance with her kept her near to him, as though it were something physical of hers—a scarf, or a cup she had drunk from. His disappointment, too—though after all these years he should be at peace with who she was. Tom called her a free spirit, but there was nothing free about her spirit at all. She just had trouble keeping up with the world.

They all assembled now, in him, around him. As far away as he could hold them. But they were there nonetheless, all present and accounted for. The effort of concentrating brought a shiver and a rush to his skin. He felt himself sweat.

Yet he Blessed. And he Dismissed. What he said to Alma Dutra after the Mass was a blur, but he took her hands into his own. He remembered her hands. Living hands. Spotted and strangely muscular. Big hands, big-veined. And warm. He did not expect such warmth. They were warm and dry, and he realized that she must be feeling his own, cold and wet. He had been steady, though, with his own hands. He recalled how he had not trembled.

When he finally returned to the rectory, Mariah Grey was there. She had made fresh coffee and tidied up the kitchen and was sitting at the table with Sarafino, who looked up at the priest but beyond that gesture did not acknowledge him. He was dressed in a different set of the hand-me-down sweats that Allie had altered for him, gray on the top, and he slumped and withdrew into the worn plush of their folds. Like a whelk, it seemed to the priest, pulling back in the tide from some dimly sensed fisher of whelks.

"Did my sister call?" Furtado asked.

"No. Nothing," Mariah said. There was a slight flush on her face, and there still hung about her an intimation of the beach—maybe it was a smell or a bit of dampness sleeping yet in her baggy woolen sweater and heavy jeans. He pictured her and Winslow out on the far sandbars, low tide, running the gray-muzzled Darwin among the eelgrass and clam-pocked flats. That was it—a lacing of salt air and under it something sweeter—almost, but not quite, fulsome. Methane from the wrack and seaweed. Her brass-and-silver hair was unruly, and this and her ruddy cheeks made her appear even younger than usual. Elfin and hoydenish.

He saw that Sarafino had eaten something from the now cleaned plate before him on the table. He sat with his hands folded around a half-full mug of tea. Mariah had already risen from her chair and was at the counter, pouring coffee for the priest. "You really look all in, Manny," she said. "I'll toast you some bread. I'll shuffle around some appointments, too. Give you a chance to rest up."

"There's a lot to do," Furtado said vaguely. He was indeed tired. He pressed his eyes hard with his knuckles, as if this might lift him, but it only unleashed a shower of yellow sparks in the blackness of his head. No pain yet. His ear quiet. Just that feeling of being draped with a heavy cowl.

Mariah came back to the table and set the cup and a plate of hot bread and butter in front of him, but she did not sit down. "Sarafino and I have been talking about last night. About his vision. About Our Lady of Fatima being in the ground."

Sarafino looked up at her, but his face was expressionless. The priest did not speak. Mariah's eyes flicked from one man to the other. She pressed her lips together, and two tiny lines bracketed the corners of her mouth. "Hold on a second, please," she said. She left the kitchen and returned in an instant with her fat black daybook, which she opened now and began tapping with a wind-chapped finger. "Oil delivery today," she said. "I'll call Joe Zora later and I'll take the check down to the office. The bank, I'll push over to tomorrow. There's the Parish Council meeting tonight—I'll move it. And that will be good for me, too. I'll have another day, at least, to get all the stuff collated. I'll call everybody. Knights of Columbus fish-fry tickets— she paused, tossed her head once. "Manny, there's nothing here I can't move or take care of."

The priest looked up, looked across the table at Sarafino, who was still off somewhere inside himself. Before he could say anything, Mariah said, "I'm going to wait for Alzaida, and you can take a rest. The day is clear for you."

Out of reflex, more than anything, he started to protest. But, so strange to him, when he spoke, he simply said. "All right. Thank you, Mariah. I will lie down for an hour."

He lay in his own bed and slept. Sometimes he half slept. Sometimes he dreamed—uncomfortable, garbled, kaleidoscopic dreams that faded as quickly as a breath when he floated uneasily back up toward consciousness. Sometimes some part of him was aware of himself lying there, though he couldn't move a limb. Mostly he felt like he was anchored just under the surface of some vast, rolling body of water, dark and foreboding. Whenever he would gesture or rise toward waking, he would form the thought of getting out of the bed, now dank with his own sour perspiration, but nothing came of it and he would fade back down into the murk.

What finally roused him was Alzaida's voice, and when he rose to it, all the dissimilar aches of the day immediately began to settle into their familiar places. "Manny," she was saying, "things are not working out." Her face was delicately swollen and her eyes were shot with red. He could not see clearly beyond his impression of her features. He sat up and rubbed his own eyes.

"A minute," he said, groggy, aggravated. "Just give me a minute." He squinted at the digital clock on the nightstand. He had been in bed for a little over five hours.

Allie retreated from the doorway, and he dressed and went into the bathroom, splashed water on his face, and neatened himself. He did not greet Sarafino when he passed the open door of his bedroom, but he looked in and saw him lying against the pillows, moving his rosary beads along with a gentle spurring of his fingers. The oxygen cannula was in place, the earphones over his ears. The little television, silent, cast a varied rhythm of staccato blue flashes over the room, but Sarafino's eyes were closed.

He caught up with Alzaida in the kitchen. He could see through the glass door that Mariah's truck was gone. "I got here hours ago," she said. "You had just fallen asleep. It was so decent of Mariah to stay with Sarafino like that. I apologized to her. I'm so sorry, Manny. I made sure Sarafino was okay before I woke you up. He's been resting okay. I have been with him. I have been making sure."

"He had a rough night," the priest said.

Alzaida nodded. "It's the virus. I know. This shouldn't have to fall on you." She stood by the door, just to one side of it, the dry dusty light of afternoon not flattering her. Her curls were limp and matted, her face pale, her features cast in deep and troubled relief. She had put on her carpet-lined barn coat, and she drew close to him. She spoke in a dramatically low voice. "Let's go outside," she said. "I don't want him to hear."

Furtado grabbed his jacket off the hook. It would be futile to remind Allie that Sarafino was wearing earphones down the hall, and anyway he desired the outdoors now. They walked together out behind the rectory. The breeze carried down from the north now, sharp and cool and clean smelling. They walked over to his car, where it stood parked next to the backyard hedge. The fenders had warmed just a little in the sunlight, and they settled back against the steel, the way kids used to lean against the fenders of cars in front of the town hall, smoking cigarettes and joking, watching one another and relishing being watched themselves on late-fall Saturday afternoons, when all of creation extended merely for a few significant blocks—the only space that counted—starting at Parson's Pharmacy and reaching across the town hall and its hierarchy of weathered benches, and ending at the Bowlaway, with its three pinball machines and five narrow lanes, and, of course, Boozy's poolroom.

"Tommy and me fought all night," Alzaida said, after a short, freighted silence.

Furtado crossed his arms and then his feet at the ankles. He closed his eyes, and the sun made a scarlet dance beneath his quavering eyelids. He waited for more.

"I made a big mistake," she said. She folded her arms, too, and looked down at the weather-beaten tarmac of the parking lot. "He left me," she said.

"Alzaida!"

"Maybe I threw him out. I don't know. I don't know exactly how it went. What does it matter? He left. He's gone. It's all my fault."

"He's blowing off steam," Furtado said. "You know Tommy better than anybody. He's just blowing off steam."

"This is different," Allie insisted. She gestured toward the back door with a tilt of her head. "See, this all goes back to Sarafino." The priest considered this but did not try to make sense of it. There was a plaintive edge in her voice—but a weary hollow, too, in the shape of her words. Furtado didn't move or say anything. He took in the clean woodsy air, the light off the changing sky. He squinted to the west. Crows were swooping over shimmering roofs, over the reaching bare limbs of scattered oak trees in the middle distance. "It seemed not so hard at first. Tommy's got a good heart. I thought if I could explain the whole thing . . ." She wavered. "The thing I had to do was take him in. To our house out in the Village. There's room, it's out of the way. You can't have him here at the church. What if somebody finds him?"

Furtado turned to her and started to reply, but she jumped in again. "And your work, Manny. It's too much for you. It's an unfair burden. But, I don't know, it went all wrong. I told Tommy about Sarafino coming back and being sick, and how serious it was, and then he flips and says he doesn't want that in his house. The virus. No way, he says. *His* house. That's what he said. So I'm going, Tommy, it's Sarafino Pomba, from when we were kids, but you know Tommy didn't really know him the same way we did, and I'm saying he was like *family* to us. But Tommy wouldn't listen to anything. He turns everything around so it's about him. What *he* thinks or what *he* wants. He's worse than Papa was. That puffed-up Portagee thing. Full of opinions and he doesn't know shit."

There was little to be done with this. The priest decided he would at least try not to feed it. "You've been all wound up since Sarafino appeared," he said. "I'm the first to admit he's put a strain on all of us. Very sudden. Very unexpected. But I'll see this through. You settle things with Tom. I think that's what's important now."

"I told Tommy to get off it," she said. "All his crap. I told him that if it wasn't for Papa's house and Papa's boat and me, he wouldn't have two nickels to rub together. *His* house! Like he's the boss. I told him that without me, he'd be living with his mother, like Frankie does."

"You lost your temper," Furtado said.

"Well, I'm not going to go through the whole thing. I'm not going to go into the crazy part." She stopped and shook her head. "I feel horrible. That's what I feel."

"I didn't help with this," Furtado offered. Despite the fresh breeze, he felt a wave of heat move over him. "I'm going to keep him here. It will be all right. You're helping, and Mariah will help. We have the doctor. We will take care of him here." As he had known they would for some time.

Alzaida's protest seemed real, though. "You can't do that, Manny. Not here, in the middle of everything."

"You have to think of him, too, Allie. You wouldn't want him in between you and Tom right now. That wouldn't work. And we have already set him up here. Just don't fight about it anymore. Just let it go. We'll do it this way."

"Oh, Manny," she said. Then she turned suddenly and put her hands on Furtado's shoulders and pulled her head to his chest. "I don't think right," she said. "Maybe I don't pray enough. You got all that part. You got it from Mae. I don't know."

He felt himself stiffen and start to pull back, but then he put his arms around her limply. He held her. And then he relaxed and held her firmly. He pulled her weight easily to him. He had held her like that only one other time that he could remember. It was right after his father's funeral, when Allie still lived in the old house on Front Street, and Furtado had flown back from the seminary in California. They were going through some of their father's things. He remembered digging in the bedroom closet with her, throwing clothes in piles to be taken up to the church, and he pulled out Pai's long, gray dress-wool overcoat, which he had bought at Jordan Marsh, in Boston, and which he wore only to Mass in the winter and nowhere else, and suddenly Alzaida broke up and took hold of him and buried her face in him, crying while he held her tight against himself.

Furtado never wept for their father. There was by then too much distance between them—and even physically, the girth of a continent was not mere accident. He wondered, looking back at that moment, what had brought so much emotion to Allie, for even though she was the one who had watched Pai through those swift final days after the stroke—and even though she had stayed in town, more or less in her mother's stead, at his beck and call for years, he was never that kind to her. He never even spoke well of her. What manner of resentment could he have held against his only daughter? There was not much left of him after Mae's death. It was too unexpected and cruel for him, she the younger and full of vigor. It scared him, no doubt. For despite their difficulties, whatever they had together, it was binding. He and Allie both saw that. Who wouldn't have expected Mae to go on forever, to finally take her place among the *velhas* of the town, at least. It was Pai who had found her, lying on the floor by the kitchen counter. There had been vegetables on the counter, and pork chops on the wooden cutting board. The faucet had still been running. Just like that.

Maybe Pai expected, after all, to be forgiven for all his meanness, his gruffness, his stubbornness. He expected others to see these only as a show and to divine somehow his abiding kindness or goodness underneath. And it was true—he was generous publicly. He got people's attention. But early on, Furtado had come to believe that his fundamental kindness did not really exist, except in some deep and deeply incorrect version that Pai held of himself.

Did Allie recall Pai now in this moment, too? Her hair smelled oily and bore a heavy trace of cigarette smoke, and he felt how loose her body had become, how unnervingly soft, as if he could tighten his arms and move them right through her, as though she were nothing more than a cloud.

"It's all right, Allie," he said. "You can pray or not pray. I suppose Mae prayed enough for everybody."

SARAFINO SAT IN THE PARLOR CHAIR. HE HAD BEEN LOOKING OUT THE front window when Alzaida and the priest came back into the rectory. He was still dressed in the sweats from the early morning. "The time is now," Sarafino said. "Now is the time."

"We thought you were resting," said Furtado.

"I rested. Now is the time for my ride. I feel like Ruth among the alien corn."

"You had a rough night."

"Not rough. But She is a power, Manny. A force. I can tell you that. I need to go out."

"It doesn't seem wise to me," the priest said. They had gone through this several times now; Furtado thought it had been dropped.

"Think about it," said Sarafino. "When is it going to get better?"

"You could be getting stronger," the priest said.

"Never con a con," Sarafino said. "It's that other stuff. The cops. Nobody will see me. I want one more look while I can. The old neighborhood. The West End."

"Take him," said Alzaida suddenly. "Just take him, Manny!"

"You didn't see Her last night, Manny. If you did, you'd know."

"We'll take him in your car," Alzaida said. "Please."

Sarafino turned and studied her for a minute. Her eyes were glassy again, teary and wide.

"You crying about me?" Sarafino asked.

"Oh, Sarafino," she said, "I swear I don't know what the hell I'm doing."

Furtado looked at the two of them and then relented. Or rather, he simply did not have the will at the moment to keep resisting. His hand moved absently to the back of his neck and he let it rest there a moment, felt the tenderness in the spaces between the knurled bones. He shrugged a few times, as though to throw off some unseen heaviness. He recalled then—more likely he inserted this when recounting the moment in the ledgers, written out sideways in the long margin—a fragment of Saint Mechtilde's *The Flowing Light of the Godhead*: *You must love nothingness, you must flee something, you must remain alone and go to nobody*. This from a woman whose visions and ecstasies praised God's billowing love. But to love nothingness seemed impossible to him. It was difficult enough to love the particular beings in one's life, or the troublesome beauty of the world of matter. It was difficult enough to feel love, like the attenuated pull from some distant, invisible star. Difficult, but at least possible. So he pushed himself to that enormous, delicate work. "All right," he said. "We'll go."

The priest changed into slacks and a flannel shirt and windbreaker, and then went out to the surplus bags and retrieved some outdoor clothes for Sarafino. He helped him into some baggy Levi's and a black woolen sweater. Sarafino pulled on a lined cotton jacket, and when they were ready to leave the priest gave him a clean ball cap, which he settled down over his ears. Furtado and his sister walked out the back door to the Toyota and looked up and down the parking lot. Seeing that it was quiet, they got Sarafino and walked him to the car, and he buckled himself into the backseat.

They cruised slowly out of the church parking lot, heading east into the municipal lot. They rolled slowly, and Furtado looked out upon the old high school and the cement stairway that angled up the embankment to the elementary school's flattened hill. All three in the car would be able to remember dimly when the lots and the grade school were nothing but dune and woods, when the church abutted the outermost edge of town, off in its hollow, where the old Protestant Yankees, presumably, ceded a building site to the Portuguese Catholics, who would, in fifty years' time, all but completely displace them.

The sun had long passed its meridian and was in the southwest now, and it shone from behind them and lit the ochre brick of the high school building and silvered the granite on the west face of the Pilgrim's Tower, which rose in the sky higher than they could see completely in the restricted frame of the windshield. This was more or less the direction Furtado and Sarafino had taken on the night they had stolen the statue of the Virgin, but neither of them spoke of this.

They came to the Back Street exit and turned east, down the hill, toward the center of town. The street was empty and Furtado drove very slowly. The houses on either side of the street were beginning to cast long shadows upon one another, and the shadows stretched eastward. The grand cupola of the four-faced town clock gleamed green atop the town hall roof and then went out of sight above the car as they bottomed the hill. There the priest pulled over to the south side of the street, against the back end of the town hall. They were directly beneath the Pilgrim's Tower now, and they sat opposite it and opposite, too, the long stone and copper bas-relief below it that showed the Pilgrims signing the Mayflower Compact in the town's harbor.

"This is where we had the Portuguese Festival last year," Alzaida said, looking over the sprawl of brown lawn in front of the bas-relief. Bare oaks and maple and ash crowded the fenced hill that ran up behind it, making a small wood beneath the tower. Sarafino leaned to his left and gazed out and up. "There were tents and long tables and all kinds of cooking. We had dancing in the streets, like when we were growing up." She didn't say anything about the boat or the Blessing of the Fleet. "Manny was behind the whole thing."

"No," said the priest. "It was a lot of town people."

"Well, still," said Alzaida crossly.

The priest pulled back onto the street and drove east. When he looked at an angle into the rearview mirror, he saw Sarafino slouching in the backseat, deep in the oversize jacket, the absurd cap pulled down on his head. They drove between the narrow houses, and Furtado could not tell if Sarafino was watching or paying attention at all. He was quiet when they rolled past the East End playground, where they used to play basketball for hours in their street shoes and school clothes, even when they had to shovel snow off the irregular asphalt of the pitiful court, or when they had to hang a rag of fishnet from the rusted iron rim. But when they reached the end of town, where Front Street and Back Street veered finally out of parallel and met in an acute turn, Sarafino sat up and said, "Roza's Garage."

"Gone for years," Alzaida said.

Chico Roza used to let them hang out there at the filling station on weekends, trying to get an old Studebaker running. It was some wreck of his—Chico, in his greasy coveralls and ham-heavy arms. Older, but not so old as their parents. He said the boys could have the car if they could make it work. They tore the engine apart and never got it back together again. Now, in place of the old garage stood a sharp, blue-gray, Cape-styled building that spread left and right from a double doorway, a white-trimmed picture window on either side. The sign over one window read WEBBER REAL ESTATE, and the other read JAMES FARLEY, ATTORNEY AT LAW.

"The town has grown up," Furtado said.

"They will rebuild our ruined cities," Sarafino said.

Neither the priest nor Alzaida said anything.

"Amos 9:14," said Sarafino. "Which is my birthday. Nine-fourteen."

They all remained quiet then. They drove at a crawl up Front Street. At times it seemed the houses were leaning out to touch them. On their left they could glimpse the running shimmer of the harbor, between buildings or down driveways or paved footpaths to the inner beach. They drove into the sun now, and the weathered cedar of the shingles and the painted clapboard of the houses on the harbor side were darkened in a painterly way, and the window glass of the scattered storefronts on the north side of the street mirrored a pale blaze. The light—the town's famous light—was tangled in all the filigree and improvement, the signs for bed-and-breakfasts, guest rooms, apartments, inns. Property. Money. "All people from away now," Allie said. They paused for a moment when they came upon the old East End Cold Storage building, one of the places where Sarafino's father had worked off and on, now a nest of condominiums.

"People live in that?" said Sarafino.

"Nobody from here," said Alzaida. Furtado glanced at her. Something was working anxiously behind her eyes. When she said, "Let's go down the wharf," he understood. Some small part of her had risen to Sarafino's cause in order to serve her own disquiet. She had wanted to go through the town herself. She wanted to find some sign of Tommy.

They continued up Front Street. Some light traffic. A scattering of pedestrians on the little ribbon of sidewalk. Nobody they knew. On past the Wheelhouse Tap, where, through the front windows, the priest glanced a few late-afternoon townies drinking at the darkened bar. They turned into the town square and passed the chamber of commerce building, where in those years before they had departed on buses for their military inductions, and all three turned absently and looked at the porched-in wooden building. "I remember everything," Sarafino said. Then they cruised slowly down the narrow wharf. When they came to the single structure on the west side of the wharf, just before it ended in its T, Furtado stopped the car. A curve of cumuli lowered over the distant hills to the south, a half ring that stretched to the east and west, pearled and luminous against the swart blue of the sky. The tide was going out, and there was a small wind-ruff running off to the southeast, and black reaches on the water where the distant clouds were throwing pieces of their shadow. A narrow, sinuous streak, all but invisible, marked the progress of a slow current moving out toward the tip of Long Point.

The building next to them had once been the old de Melo packinghouse. Now there stood a refurbished building with a nautical shop and a fish-and-chips stand, both closed for the season. Sarafino's father had worked at de Melo's, too, boxing fish and loading the big pine crates onto a forklift, and running them out to the waiting bobtailed trucks. The priest realized that he did not know much about Sarafino's father, though he'd seen him all the time at the Pombas' house. He remembered him as a small, stooped, dark-skinned man with broad features, always with a workman's cap on, always in his work clothes, always smoking a cigarette. He grew a grizzled and stubby beard in winter, when most of the packinghouses either closed down or laid off all but a few of the laborers, and he sat in his overstuffed chair wearing leather suspenders over a quilted long-underwear top. He was mostly silent, except when he talked with Sarafino's mother, usually in Portuguese, mostly with some kind of complaint or command.

Pai Furtado would bring the Pombas fish in winter, as long as the *Ilha do Pico* was still going out. Sometimes there would be a bucket of flounder, sometimes a big haddock that Sarafino's mother would stuff and bake like a turkey, or else simmer in a *moule de tomate*. On days when it was too windy or cold or stormy for Pai to take the boat out around the Point, he would now and then show up at the Pombas' with a six-pack of Narragansett beer, and the two men would sit in the bare little parlor and listen to weather reports on the old shortwave radio.

Whatever difficulties may have passed between these two men, whatever Sarafino meant about Pai's treatment of his father, Furtado never saw it in how they acted around each other—not like pals, not like Pai's cronies in the bars, but not like equals, either. And perhaps that was it: There was something patronizing there, of course, but also something like benevolence, a crumpled generosity, and power, a finger in someone else's life. Complicated things Furtado wouldn't have fully recognized as a boy. Well, and was old Pomba incompetent on the water? Bad luck? It wasn't just Pai, after all, who refused to take him on. No, Furtado had never known that Old Pomba wanted to crew on the *Ilha*, but why wouldn't he have wanted to? Why wouldn't his wife have urged him to and scolded him about it?

Sarafino's mother, heavy and gray-haired, kept to the kitchen. When she wasn't doing something at the stove or countertop, she sat in a straight-backed chair underneath a pinned-up and curling picture of the Sacred Heart of Jesus, which she had taken from a calendar. The only things on the walls of Sarafino's house were religious images—Our Lady of Fatima, of course. The priest remembered Fatima. And a little plastic holy-water font nailed to the parlor doorframe. A big wooden crucifix, too, with the previous year's Palm Sunday palm tucked behind it, brown and desiccated. Furtado's mother kept a palm all year like this as well, and on Shrove Tuesdays she would bake pieces of it to cinders in the oven, then crush them with her thumb and mark him and Allie with the black dust early on the morning of Ash Wednesday, so they could go to school with the dark smudge of the cross on their foreheads.

FURTADO ROLLED THE LITTLE TOYOTA FORWARD AGAIN, MADE HIS TURN at the end of the wharf, and headed back toward the shore. When he came alongside the east packinghouse, he braked and pointed out the wheelhouse and mast of the *Ilha do Pico*, visible behind two other boats tied off there. "There's the old boat," he said.

"Yep," said Sarafino, but he did not turn his head.

Allie took a slow look at the empty space where the white truck might have been. Furtado saw her face darken and then tighten. "Let's just go," she said.

Back up the wharf and down Front Street, heading for the West End, and Furtado was seized with a sense of his own recklessness. Sarafino in the back coughing dryly, the heavy sound of his breathing filling the silences,

Allie's leg beginning to pump nervously. There was something dreamlike to it all. Unreal. The metallic hum returned to Furtado's ear. The front of town hall, Parson's Pharmacy, rows of shops, the old movie house—at present a cluster of little seasonal stores, boarded up—Pires's Garage, now a mall and food court, also closed for the season. The bank, gone. The barber shop, gone. Now hundreds of yards of counter space for showing the tourists silver bracelets, T-shirts, beach gear, incense, candles, pottery. The priest wanted to speak over the noise in his head, but he was angry at himself now for coming on this foolish errand, and he did not want to say the wrong thing. He lamented how small was the charity in his heart. His heart thumped now in his shoulder. A modest reminder. When they came down the small hill that began the West End proper, Allie broke the silence and said to Sarafino, "Check out Juney's Tap. Our Papa's second home." It was where Pai had been sitting when he'd had his stroke, but Allie did not offer this. It was a proper restaurant now, the Café Balzac, cloth on the tabletops, expensive wine. "Yuppie gay," said Allie.

They turned left at the bottom of the hill, the narrow four corners where Front Street angled sharply to follow the shoreline, and the priest rolled to a full stop against the curb. "The Carvalhos are gone," said the priest, indicating the house on the south corner. "The West End Cold Storage, they tore down for that new wharf. Coast Guard now."

"She used to the see the saints," Sarafino said. "The old Carvalho lady."

"That guy Joachim is in the Azores now. That strange kid," said Allie. "He was older than us. He's got a real useful job. He studies Portagees for a living."

"He works for a university," Furtado said, annoyed. "He is doing all sorts of research. I am in touch with him. He needed some church records a while ago." He turned to Sarafino to say this, but Sarafino was already looking the other way, at the house across the street.

On their right stood the house where Old Man Coelho had lived with all his beagle hounds. The house had not been built up, as so many others in the West End had, but it was nicely kept, with new gray paint, bright blue shutters, and a white picket fence, where a winter-pruned rose tree grew. The dog pens were gone and a small gazebo squatted in their place. The three of them looked down the walk for a moment. "Remember not the sins of my youth, nor my transgressions," said Sarafino.

"Could you please stop talking like that?" Allie said.

A car came around the corner then, moving at a crawl, and squeezed past the stopped Toyota. It might have appeared to the man behind the wheel that they were admiring the house, or waiting for someone to emerge from the paneled front door. Furtado let him pass and then nudged the accelerator. His sister was staring furiously ahead. "Here's Frankie Boia's house," said the priest to Sarafino. "He still lives here."

"It's not his house," Alzaida said. "It's his mother's."

They drove around the bend in the street past the Boia house, and Allie looked around for the white truck. It could only have been parked across the street by the beach access, where Tom and Frankie always left it, but she had seen from down the street that it was not there.

The car went quiet. Furtado rolled on a little more. Houses shouldered against the narrow street. Hedges. Fences. The sidewalk, where even two could not walk abreast. Finally they came to the corner where a hilly lane left the street and ran northward, away from the harbor, the little corner where they'd all grown up. The priest pulled over to the side, hard against the sidewalk, to leave room for a passing car to get around them if one should come. "Here we are," he said as cheerfully as he could, though it sounded forced now. His old home, the Furtado house, stood on the water side of the street with a deck running along the upper floor. Many large windows had been installed on the upper level, and the house, once both roof and wall shingled with weather-darkened cedar, was now white clapboard with green trim. A white picket fence had replaced the privet hedge, and the long gear shed that had sat at the western edge of the yard had been torn down. It only barely resembled the old captain's house that they'd been raised in. It had been bought and sold once or twice—the priest wasn't sure—since Allie and Tom had sold it.

One house beyond, on the other side of the street, was where Sarafino had grown up. It had not been owned by his parents. They had rented the upstairs from a couple named Freitas, both of them buried now out in the Catholic cemetery. The house long sold. It, too, had been rebuilt, remodeled. "Sarafino," the priest said, "this must all seem very strange to you."

"I am a stranger in a strange land," Sarafino said.

"Will you just quit that for a while?" Allie said. "Quit that talk." Then she added, "Please."

"We used to look out your window, Allie," Sarafino said, drawing a series of rapid breaths. "Remember how we used to watch out for your old man coming around the Point in his boat? Those were good days." He was staring at the Furtado house now, taking it all in. "Your eyes are doves behind your veil," he said. "You are stately as a palm tree."

"Sarafino, shut up," Allie said. "Just stop. I can't stand it. You disappear and never come back—you let everybody think you're dead, for God's sake, and then you come back. Look at you. Look at what you did to yourself!" She shook her head. So much woe now in that soft face. "God, the two of you. One doesn't say anything and the other one talks crazy." She caught herself. She put her hand to her eyes, closing them, as if that might erase everything. "See what I mean?" she said. "Oh, I'm over my head here. Let me out!"

She said this as if someone were holding her back, or as though the car were still moving and she were demanding that her brother stop and pull over. But then she grabbed the handle and flung the door open. "I'm sorry," she said. "This is just too strange. I need to get out and walk for a while." She slammed the car door and began marching up the lane's small hill, a sorrowful figure in her denim coat, her stocking cap pulled down over her spill-away hair.

"That was on me," Sarafino said after a moment. "I can have that effect." He was stricken. Miserable. "I got confused about something."

"No," said Furtado, turning to speak to him now over his shoulder. Awkward. Painful. "No, Allie and Tom had some kind of disagreement. She's upset over it. It happens."

"I feel sick, Manny."

"I'll go back. Do you need a bathroom?"

"I'm all dizzy. I'm crashing. The mountain was burning with fire. The Lord was in the midst."

"We're going," said the priest. "Just settle back." Furtado wheeled the car up the next side lane and turned back toward the church. He fully expected to see Allie trudging along, but she must have walked another path, and he was glad, for the moment, not to see her.

Mariah Grey was working at the rectory when they returned. Furtado explained the ride to her, how it had not gone so well. She listened gravely and together they settled Sarafino in his room and hooked him up to his oxygen. She brought him some juice in a glass with a straw, and fixed the pillows so that he was propped up to help with his breathing. He was silent through their ministrations, and they sat and watched with him until he began drifting into a state of rest. The priest spread a light comforter over him, and they walked silently from the room. When they reached the kitchen, Mariah turned to the priest. "Something's come up, Manny," she said quietly. "I need to show you something." She was standing in heavy woolen boot socks, and he saw now that her knee-high rubber boots sat over by the coat pegs inside the door. She went to the boots and pulled them on. Her face was unreadable, but her movements were swift and deliberate. The priest followed her out the back door and across the small parking lot and around the back of the parish hall, where she had parked her truck out of sight on the small strip of gravel there. Dusk was not far off, and the light behind the building softened and scattered as though it were a fine dust and just the movement of their bodies could send it rolling in the crisp air.

Mariah walked Furtado around to the truck bed and threw back a heavy woolen blanket that lay over some piece of junk there. It took him a while to understand what he was seeing. There in the truck lay a dolly, or the remains of one—the steel frame black with rust, pieces rotted away, the rubber tires gone but the wheels there, shriveled and crusted. Flecks of dirt and flakes of the decomposed tarp. "You dug this up in the woods?" he asked. He tried to calculate something in his mind, but it skated away.

"Yes," she said. "Where Sarafino said it would be."

"This is it, then. The one we used."

"Is it?"

"I believe it could be."

"It was right there, in that spot."

The priest leaned over the side of the truck bed and brought his face close to the relic. He smelled its decomposed metal and its recent earth. He moved his eyes over it. Then he straightened himself. There was only one thing he could say. "Where is the statue of the Virgin?"

Mariah looked at him and then looked at the ruined metal frame in the truck. She hesitated for a moment and then shook her head. "Gone," she said.

eleven

"How?" asked the priest. He stared at the corroded metal frame in the back of the truck. It lay like the skeleton of some dead thing.

"He got through to me," Mariah Grey said. Her words in that hushed recess behind the parish hall sounded oddly, pleasantly bell-like. Her eyes shone. "He was so clear about it. And he took me into his confidence. I knew I would find it. And you knew of the place, too, so it seemed right. I've walked that pond before. I've paddled it in my little kayak, too. I was never in your spot, exactly, but right by it. And anyway, you could have stood right on it and never had the smallest idea that there was anything buried there. He wanted a sign from the Holy Mother, and I thought I'd bring the statue back to him. I know it seems like there's something a little off in his head, and that he talks strange sometimes, but he remembered those landmarks, didn't he? He remembered the kinds of features that wouldn't have changed much over time.

"When we were at the beach with Darwin this morning, Winslow had her metal detector with her. So I was keeping an eye on the dog and watching her with that machine. You know what it's like—you swing it back and forth, and the plate on the bottom of the wand has some kind of electromagnetic field in it, and it buzzes when you're over something. She was just playing around with it, but I had Sarafino's tale in my head, and then I put two and two together. So when I left the rectory this morning, after you fell asleep and your sister showed up, I got Winslow and her machine and a couple of entrenching tools, and we went off to the woods. We left the truck out in one of the park's parking lots and walked in from there. We found your old campsite, all right. Only it wasn't a clearing. We had to wade through the shallows of the two ponds and then go through some places on our hands and knees. We had to drag our stuff. But we found a place that had to be it. It was the only ground for it. Locked in with woods and brush. We had to knock back some of that brush, but we lit off Winslow's detector and circled around with it until it buzzed. I don't think we had to look for more than five minutes. There was no question when the machine went off. That dolly is a big hunk of metal. It was between some pine trees, and there was a really thick bed of needles on the ground. We cleared them away and dug. The earth is soft there. Sand under the humus. That's right where it was—maybe three, three and a half feet down. He had such a clear picture in his mind. It was right there."

The priest listened to her, then turned to the rusted dolly again and touched it. Damp. Cold. Black with corruption. Very real. He became absorbed with it, looking at it, tapping it with his fingers.

When he did not speak, Mariah said nervously, "Oh. Oh dear. Maybe you think I meddled, Father Manny. Maybe this was none of my business."

"No," said Furtado. "No, it's good to have this come to light after so long." But he wasn't sure if he meant it. He tapped along the rusted frame again but did not put his hands around it.

"The Virgin, though," said Mariah. "It isn't here."

"And you looked," he said. "I mean, I assume you looked more, with the metal detector. There was steel in the bottom of the statue. I remember. It was heavy."

"There was nothing else there," she said.

He just shook his head.

"We hauled the dolly out to the edge of a path and scooted in with the truck and picked it up. What should I do with it?" she asked.

"We can't not show it to him," Furtado said. "Tomorrow. Tomorrow we'll show it to him."

The light was flattening now, and the clouds off to the west above the bare trees had become radiant and purple. A chill settled in from the ocean. Mariah pulled up the collar of her vest. "I'll keep it in the truck, and I'll bring it back when I come tomorrow," she said.

The priest watched her drive off and then walked back to the rectory. He checked on Sarafino, then went into the office. It was dark out by the time Alzaida came tapping at the door. "I'm sorry," she said, easing herself in quietly. "How is he?"

"Resting," said the priest. He did not move from the chair behind the big desk, but he closed the file he had been reading and looked up at his sister.

"I'm sorry about all that in the car," she said.

"You were upset," he offered.

"I still am, in a way. All this stuff. I've been walking all over. I went out to the donut shop and had a coffee and sat for a while, here and there." She looked around. A rose blush sat on her cheeks now, but the color did not seem to belong there. "Can I use the phone in the kitchen? I'll be quiet." She walked away softly.

"Well, I don't know where Tommy is," she said when she returned a few minutes later. She still wore her coat, but it was unbuttoned now and the flush lingered in her face. "I called Old Lady Boia. She told me they were there a while today. She doesn't know where they are now, but she said they talked about going out fishing in the morning. I called Brabo Pereira down at the Wheelhouse. They were in there earlier today, too, but not now. Not that Brabo would tell me, anyway. I'm not calling any more bars, and I can tell you this much: I'm not making supper tonight. I'm not going to go home and sit around and wait, either. I ran into Cookie Cruz at the donut shop, and we're going to the Topsail for supper. They've got the *vinha d'alhos* catfish tonight. That and a glass of *vinho* for me. I'm going to unwind. I'll bring you some take-home on my way back."

"I'm fine," Furtado said.

"I really am sorry," Allie said. "About all this. I'll come back and sit with Sarafino tonight."

"Tonight I'm fine with him, but I'm going to need you to help me," he said.

"I will," she said. "I will. I mean it."

"I know you mean it," he said. He couldn't read her clearly. Anger. Remorse. Despair. He could guess, but it didn't matter to name anything. There was nothing he could do. He thought a moment. He decided not to say anything about Mariah or the old handcart coming up out of the ground. "I want you to come in the morning. Early. That's what I need—for you to stay with Sarafino for a few hours. I can't ask Mariah again. Can you do that?"

The priest watched her face as she reckoned. Tommy was still the missing factor. Still, he had a right to ask her. "I'll do it," she said.

"I'll give you a wake-up call."

"Oh, Manny," she said, starting to protest. Then she said, "All right."

THE FIRST VISIONS AT FATIMA CAME TO LUCIA DOS SANTOS IN THE spring of 1916. At first, Lucia saw only white clouds or vague shinings in the sky above the pastures and over the village. She was nine years old.

Furtado gathered such facts at first from his own memory of the stories—there was no end to them—and began writing them in the ledger that night in the form of lists. He drew boxes around them, double- and triple-lined in dark ink. At some point he went to other sources—there were several differing accounts of the Virgin's words and Lucia's testimonies in the bookshelf. He culled what he wanted from those versions, some skeptical, some credulous, and then he drifted into his own embellishments. The ledger pages here became crowded with small notes, some written sideways in the margins, some lined out. He veered off unsteadily into his own narratives. The pills and the gin lifted the aches of the day once again from his body, and the sounds of the old building fell away, and the floating of both mind and body was exactly what he desired to lay down his facts and his refutations.

Several months passed for Lucia before the shining clouds coalesced into the figure of an angel who appeared to her and her younger cousins, Francisco and Jacinta Marto. He appeared three times, several months apart, in the Cova da Iria, the pastures lying between some small hills where the children tended their sheep. The angel gave the children prayers to recite. He was shining and transparent and very beautiful. He told them that a greater revelation was coming.

That spring, on Sunday, May 13, the Blessed Virgin Mary appeared to the three children in the Cova da Iria. She was to appear six times in total. She spoke with the children and gave them messages concerning the fate of the world on each occasion. According to Lucia, who was by then ten, she tried to keep her younger cousins quiet about the visions. But after the third visit, when the three shepherd children were gifted with a vision of hell—shrieks and flames and the souls of the eternally damned burning like hot coals—word leaked out and crowds began to gather. Newspapers ran harshly skeptical stories. Europe was at war. Portugal was in a political lockdown. The Catholic Church was being openly persecuted by the new revolutionary government. Records claimed that well over ten thousand priests, nuns, and monks were systematically murdered during those years.

By the apparition's fourth appearance, in August, the children were kept away from the Cova in an effort to contain what authorities feared could become a dangerous resurgence of religious demonstrations. The children were famously kidnapped by town officials, who allegedly threatened to boil them in oil. But they stuck to their stories.

Some witnesses estimated there were at least ten thousand people at the site on that August day, despite the absence of Lucia and her cousins. But without Lucia's presence, the apparition was somewhat vague. There was a clap of thunder. The tree where the Virgin had previously appeared became colorful—so said some. One woman testified to smelling a lovely perfume emanating from the little oak.

Keeping the children from the Cova and threatening them with harm seemed to increase public interest. By September, newspapers reported up to twenty-five thousand people arriving at Fatima on foot and in horse and donkey carts, and some even by automobile. Lucia began to talk about "secrets" from Our Lady. The Virgin was asked to heal the sick. She promised a huge miracle in October.

The final appearance, on Friday, October 13, 1917, was the event that would establish Fatima as the greatest modern miracle in Christianity. By that time, the news of the children and of the apparitions had spread sufficiently that an enormous throng crowded the little valley and hillsides. The major newspapers had sent reporters to the scene. The crowds were so large and had traveled from such distances that the government did not think it was prudent to interfere with them. To be accurate about the number of people who were there is impossible; one hundred thousand was the most common estimate, but some accounts said sixty- or seventy-five thousand. A large number, at any rate, and a strain on the countryside, to say nothing of creature comforts and sanitary conditions.

By then, the little tree above which the Virgin appeared had been picked apart by souvenir hunters and vandalized by skeptics. Some say it was dynamited by local government functionaries. There was almost nothing left of it. And a cold rain greeted the pilgrims. The roads and trails had become quagmires from the rain and the traffic. There was little shelter. Some of the pilgrims huddled under umbrellas, but most merely stood, soaking, holding jackets and shawls over their heads.

Here Father Furtado stopped and considered. He attempted to sketch wobbly figures, perhaps to orient himself to the positions of the crowd. He made diagrams. Here is where it came to him: Father Braga was somewhere in this shivering throng. Half dream, half thought. Half gliding, half concentrating—those slow circling-back thoughts and images, working their way into some elusive heart of a thing that was all uncertain. At first Furtado could not picture the other priest. His youth—for Teofilo Braga would have been a young man then—was the problem. Shapes and countenances kept falling, melting, from him. For what could that fierce martinet have looked like as a boy-man, huddled in that nasty gray rain? Would he have come alone, or, more likely, with a group of men from the seminary . . . if he were still at seminary then? The tales of his heavy-handed—often mean-spirited—judgments here in the town stood in the way of a clear image, and Furtado let that be, let the shapes shift and slide. It was fine.

Some contours emerged as stable. He let the old priest now be a skinny youth, black hair plastered down on his long head. He let the eyes be strong and fierce, but they hovered on the edge of terror and rage. Sometimes he seemed miserably afraid, rabbitlike, mouselike. Then a darkness would flow from him. He would be standing far back from the children. The scant shelter from the sparse trees would have been taken already by others. He would hold himself, soaked and cold, with his own arms.

By this time, the children were seeing the vision. Lucia conveyed what she saw: not only the Virgin, who gave her messages, but Saint Joseph and the Infant Jesus, too, all in the sky above whatever remained of the blasted tree. Maybe it was the weather or the extravagance of the vision, but the performance did not go over well with the crowd, who huddled in discomfort. Slowly, hisses and boos moved through the assembly. A multitude of shouts swelled from the cold and wet pilgrims, who neither saw nor heard a thing. Fakery! A hoax! A wave of fury swept through the thousands.

Furtado watched the young Father Braga of his own vision. What of him? Did he shout, too? Was he disgusted with the foolish children and his own credulity? Did he curse himself for making this wretched journey? Again, the shapes and scenario shifted for the priest. He sipped his gin. He pressed his lips together, felt their numbness, then the gentle waves of pleasure and abeyance in his soft flesh. Let Braga be one of the shouters, then, one of the disgusted. Let him, at first disillusioned and then in ire, call out, "*Fraude*!" Let him shout into the growing furor of the crowd, "*Uma vergonha*!"

There might have been violence then. Such was the sentiment among that throng of seekers. But this was not the day for Lucia to be bested. Aware of what was going on behind her—or perhaps not—she pointed at the sky and exclaimed, "Look!" There are newspaper photographs in grainy black-and-white, filled to their frames with hundreds of faces turned upward, watching something in the sky. This was when the sun began to come out from behind the clouds and appeared to dance and plummet toward Earth, only to return to its appointed place again. This was when there were colors in the sky. This was the great miracle. But there was not a single photograph of anything in that sky—just those faces turned upward after Lucia's shout.

Braga didn't see it. The truth was that Braga was not alone in his disappointment. Well over half of the people there saw nothing. There would never be a consensus that anything at all happened at Fatima besides the sun's coming out after a hard rain and shining through the scattering clouds. Perhaps a partial rainbow. Many of those interviewed attested that nothing occurred. Thousands and thousands claimed they did not see a thing. Only the children, spoken for by Lucia, claimed to see the heavenly presences. Of course, many of the faithful agreed, proclaimed even, that something marvelous had happened. A great show in the sky put on by the Mother of God. Many fell to their knees. Many prayed for forgiveness and mercy, for they thought that the end of the world was at hand.

But there could have been no miracle. Not as far as Furtado was concerned. Not on the order to which the events at Fatima would be inflated.

For there was Lucia dos Santos.

A darkness of his own came forward here, something he might have stoppered if it were not for the pills and the gin, but he left it alone, a small pleasure to discover this dislike of that young girl. A tiny pleasure to indulge it. Because she made the whole thing up.

Lucia's mother—not unlike so many of the town women he had either known or known about while growing up, not, perhaps, so unlike his own mother—was deeply religious in the Old World manner—devout and superstitious. She could read a little, and she kept a few books in the house: accounts of saints and visions, stories of piety. She had read these to Lucia when Lucia was very young. And Lucia was a different sort of country girl. She was flighty and dreamy. She had fantasies. She was not obedient. Her mother punished her, whipped her, for making up stories about seeing angels and visions years before the events in the Cova. She craved attention and would capture village children with such wild tales. She told her little girlfriends that she wanted to be a saint when she grew up. Much of the imagery of her visions at Fatima was couched in the images and language of the stories her mother had read to her.

And Lucia continued to refine and rephrase Our Lady's messages over the years. Her poor little cousins—Furtado could not help feeling a great sorrow for them, how they were simply pulled into something completely beyond themselves. Francisco was never sure he ever saw or heard anything during the apparitions, and Jacinta, flustered when questioned, would simply say, "You'd better ask Lucia—she's the one who knows." The cousins both died in the great flu epidemic of 1918. Francisco was the first to go. Jacinta died months later after enormous suffering and finally a surgery—without anesthesia—to remove some of her rib cage. How to imagine the state of medicine in Portugal at that time? Furtado could not separate himself then from the terrors and pain of the little girl, who, it was said, died alone in a hospital, far from her family and anyone who knew her. But Lucia. Lucia was whisked away to a convent. She was never to leave. She was kept. It was easy to surmise that she was not right in the mind, that she had to be sheltered from the world.

Yet she continued to be the seer of Fatima. Sequestered in the convent, she wrote a memoir in 1942. Much of what the world knows of the miracle came from this document and subsequent commentary from Lucia. She claimed that the Virgin predicted World War II during Her apparitions of 1917, but certainly by now Lucia was looking back and making good. Her memoir gave greatly different versions of the messages and apparitions than she originally recounted in 1917. There was more material, more detail, more historical concordance as she used her knowledge of lived history to square things with the events of the previous twenty-five years. And, brilliantly, the Church held back the famous "third secret" of Fatima, creating a mystery that focused the Catholic world on the divine visions and spun hundreds of dire, eschatological guesses as to what the Virgin had said. It didn't matter that the secret turned out to be gibberish written down by what Furtado saw as a very mindful, disturbed person—Fatima was established.

And look at the town and Father Braga, what the miracle had done for him, though he had seen nothing, by his own admission to his family. He spent a life atoning for this lack, this unworthiness. Furtado entered these ideas in the ledger. He finished the tumbler of gin. His head worked far away now, deeply, as if from the bottom of a mine shaft or a safe bunker, while the gin and the pills laid their sinuous sweetness on the landscape above. Where milk and honey ran. He put it down that way.

And then he nodded into a dream. In it he drifted down to a place of wonder, where a small ancient road seemed to come to an end, the blacktop cracking and splitting and covered here and there by sifting dunes or wandering prairies of beach grass, and there was no town nearby, and whatever dim lights he had been following, whether true or otherwise, had vanished into a seamless gray sea that rolled on before him. Opiate and lush, the long nod filled him with comfort, and when he rose partially from it to a place where thoughts did not immediately transform into such recondite phantasms, he remembered a phrase, though not its source: *To long for God is to be with God.* And then he wrote: *The nature of everything is struggle*, for he heard at that moment Sarafino's voice coming from downstairs, and he bound himself to the earth again.

He descended the creaking staircase, the numbness still in his lips, a pinging in his ear, like some tiny black hammer falling repeatedly on a delicate piece of jewelry. When he reached the bottom of the stair, he kept his hand to the wall, as much to assure himself of its presence as to hold himself steady. In that darkness that was broken only by the light spilling from his study and from the small nightlight in the sickroom, he found his way to Sarafino's bedside. "I heard you," he said. "I'm right here."

"I miss that candle," Sarafino said. His form seemed larger and closer in the dim grayish glow. He gestured toward the little plastic shell of the nightlight as if to indict it.

"There's no answer for it," said the priest. "The oxygen. You have to breathe."

"All right," Sarafino said. "But flick the lights up, will you? My head is on fire."

Furtado turned on the table lamp, and Sarafino's dark eyes blazed for a second in that abrupt flare. "Let us cast off the works of darkness and put on the armor of light," he said. He pulled himself up on the pillows and adjusted the oxygen loops over his ears. "I could have done all that myself, Manny. But I saw your light on upstairs. It was bouncing around in the hallway. You work late. I never knew about how priests work. I didn't want to climb up there again. You know."

"I'm through working now," Furtado said, still not entirely done with the dreaming. He could nod again if he were alone. Nod into that underland. *Down. Down.* Instead he said, "What can I do?"

"If you could sit awhile."

"Yes."

"I'm a little parched."

The priest walked out into the hall and into the kitchen. He fetched some juice, moving slowly and with concentration, and he took down a tumbler and filled it with ice by the light of the open refrigerator, all the light anyone needed. He walked deliberately back to Sarafino's side and passed him the tall glass and straw. Sarafino took it in both hands and sipped delicately. "My mind gets all wired up sometimes," he said.

"Yes," said Furtado, "I know." He slid the straight-backed chair over toward the bed and sat down in it.

"Allie went off."

"Yes. She came back here, though. You were sleeping."

"I don't remember sleep."

"It's all right."

"That whole thing was on me."

"No. It's complicated."

"That is the one true word," Sarafino said. He leaned over and placed the glass on the nightstand. He tucked himself up some more. The priest glanced over and saw that a few inches of the juice were gone. Good. He leaned back into the chair.

"Don't think I don't appreciate everything, Manny," Sarafino said. "You took me in. It's a big deal. I always loved you the best."

"You're here, and it's all right," said the priest. The little hammer in his head went *ting-ting*. For a moment it sounded like it was coming from somewhere in the room. "You don't have to say anything like that, Sarafino. You will be fine here."

"It's not a con," Sarafino said.

"What is it, then?" the priest asked. "Tell me. What is it all?"

"Don't think I never took the time to figure." Sarafino reached for the tumbler and sipped again from the straw. He was burning from within. That was the energy that moved him—erratic and arbitrary. A tremor passed through his hand while he replaced the glass on the nightstand. The ice rattled. "Something happens, and then you do something, and then something else happens. You make up your mind that things are going to be different, but your mind isn't able. Some people's minds don't make things happen in the world." He took several breaths. The priest watched him, his flesh tingling and heavy now. "Your ma and my ma. All those old ladies. It was always *fado* this and *fado* that. Well, you see *fado* when you look backwards, so you think that fate runs forwards, too. But that's a con. You think of something and you do it, but the thing you do, it just cuts loose from you and goes on doing. That thing you did goes on down the road. Bodies pile up. Things catch fire. Whatever you thought, that gets left behind. It doesn't make a difference what you thought. You look back and you see this big connection to everything, but it's random, really. You can't stop it. That's the con, see? That's what the con is." Sarafino raised his hand, as if to halt something. "Don't get me wrong," he said. "I'm not bitter."

"And that's the con?"

"I would say so. But maybe you are thinking about something else."

Furtado listened briefly to the *lub* and *dub* of his heart—more probably a vessel in his head. Steady. Insistent. "I have been thinking about Our Lady of Fatima," he said.

"It's all the one Lady, no matter," said Sarafino. "Now, that is not the con. Once She's in your life, it doesn't matter what adds up or what doesn't. That's the way around everything, you might say. You would know more about that, I guess. That's why I'm not bitter, but I'm not saying I never was."

The priest looked at Sarafino and did not like the light of the big lamp shining in the room. He did not like the edges of things in such relief, not the dresser nor the right angles of the bed. And it colored the air wrong. It denied any distance. He considered the hour and realized he did not know exactly what it was, and so he went ahead without much decision. "I have some news," he said. Then he told Sarafino about Mariah and her visit to the woods, about the dolly and the missing statue.

Sarafino didn't say anything. He sat against the pillows and looked off into the yellow air at the foot of his bed. After a while he reached around in the bedcovers and picked out the glass rosary, and began to roll a big blue bead between his thumb and forefinger. A quick, small motion. Over and over. It seemed that was all he was going to do, but then he took a few sharp breaths and said, "Something here is not right."

"Why is that, Sarafino?"

"I don't know why you are asking me that."

"Is it because you are not telling me something? Are you keeping some things to yourself?"

Sarafino continued working the single rosary bead between his fingers, and Furtado watched him carefully. He watched the motion of his hand, and he watched his face. "Nobody came along and found Her," Sarafino said finally. "You would have heard plenty about that if someone had."

"This all happened so long ago," said the priest. "You were cranked up. Are you sure you put Her there?"

Sarafino gave the priest a hard look. "I laid Her there. Still bound up to that handcart."

"Mariah is going to come tomorrow and bring the dolly so you can look at it, make sure it's right."

"You said you saw it, right? You should know."

"It looked right to me, but l all that was a long time ago. And what other dolly could it be? I don't think the statue just moldered away. It was all lacquered and wrapped up, and anyway there was that steel rod and that steel plate on the bottom. It was heavy. Something would have been left."

Sarafino worked the rosary bead, and Furtado could see his mind working. "There's some things you can't explain," Sarafino said after a while. "You can't explain everything in the world."

"That night," said the priest, "I went home. You went all the way out there by yourself? Just you? Are you clear on everything? Are we looking at the same thing when we look back on all that? Maybe between us we have it all confused."

"And what about you?" Sarafino said. "You sure you stayed home? I know you never came down to the bus to see me go. I know that. Or maybe you went and got it after I left town. That whole damn business was your idea. You would have known where to look."

It took a moment for the priest to digest this. His mind was moving slowly; Sarafino was the one who seemed sharp now. Furtado thought carefully before he spoke. "No," he said. "I remember looking around the place where we dropped it. This was after you were gone. I looked all around that part of the woods. I'm sure of that. I remember that. I can see it. Anyway, I never thought you would have come back that same night and moved it all the way out by that pond. I can tell you that never occurred to me."

"It was the crank. The crank will make you do things."

"Yes."

They sat in silence for a while, Sarafino working the rosary bead and gazing off inside himself, and the priest sensing the usual changes in his own body drifting down slowly, like a leaf, a pressure in his head, the pulse still in his ears. When Sarafino spoke again, he said, "I should have come back and taken Her out of the ground. I don't know. But what is, is what is. I see that it's the sign. I get it now. But I don't know what it all means. *Thy will be done.* Isn't that right?" Then he turned to Furtado. "Manny, I have this other thing to beg from you. That is the place for me, right there. Put me in that hole out there. That's my grave."

The priest did not try to sum up everything all at once. There was a neatness to all this, and he didn't trust it, the missing statue and now Sarafino asking to be buried in that spot. He didn't say anything. He moved to the window and pushed the shade aside. The sky was dark, visible from this vantage only as an indistinct gloom behind the scatter of the streetlamp. The lamp's core itself shone dimly in a nimbus of hazy light. He pressed his brow against the cold glass of the windowpane and looked past the church grounds at the narrow lane squeezing between its huddled houses. He calculated that the dawn was not so far off, but he was already thinking of that one place he would visit in the morning.

twelve

THE AIR WAS DAMP AND COLD, THOUGH THE MIST OF THE NIGHT hours had resolved itself, and morning stars now shone, huge and gilded in the paling iron of the sky. Betelgeuse and Bellatrix and Pollux and Castor in the southwest, along with other stars that he couldn't name, and in the east, in strange relief against the graying blackness, Regulus and the rest of the sickle of Leo in its wide tilt over the quiet Earth.

The priest walked eastward across the broad and deserted municipal parking lot and mounted the concrete stairways that cut up the tall embankment to the elementary school and its asphalt yard that gave way onto Cemetery Road. The road sloped down easily to the north and he walked on its shoulder, in as much shadow as it afforded, but he could have walked down its center unseen and undisturbed at that hour. He headed for the Vets' bar and the state road. The cemetery itself lay on his right, silent and empty. The flagstaff on the top of its hill was uplit by a pair of spotlights that had shone the night long, and in this scattered illumination he could see the shadows of the gravestones as they rolled away along the contour of the land, their shapes and sizes blending into a low skyline.

Two dogs and then a third loped from a narrow yard into the road, and when Furtado could see their outlines clearly by the distant streetlamp he saw that they were not dogs at all but coyotes, swaybacked to the ground in their feral gait. Their eyes gleamed orange. They hunched and slunk, watching him, and then broke into a trot and disappeared among the gravestones. Coyotes had migrated even to this farthest end of the land, as they now were counted in every state in the country, but they had come here long after he'd left for the first time, and he had not grown used to them. On certain nights, when the ocean damp lay over the hills and dunes, the wild sound of their packs would drift faintly back into the town, and they would yip and shout as if in answer to the foghorns out in the far sand reaches. He watched for them to double back now or show up again farther down the road, but he reached the state highway and crossed into the woods without seeing them again or seeing a single car or any other human.

He had phoned Alzaida at four-thirty. When she answered, she said she was already up, but he could tell that she had been sleeping and that he had woken her. "Are you all right?" he asked. "Can you make it?"

"Yes," she said. "I'm on my way. Fifteen minutes."

"You're okay?"

"Yes," she said, the sleep fading from her voice. "It's just that Tommy was here while I was out last night. I know they're going out fishing because all the gear is gone from the garage. They must have sailed already. I think he waited until I wasn't around. Things are not so good."

"It doesn't sound so good," he said. "We're going to have a good talk about all this when I get back." He knew she was scheduled to be at the bakery at ten. There was no Mass that morning, and he would be back easily before then.

He had been eager to leave the rectory. He was already dressed in jeans and his high-top winter boots and was set to go when he heard Alzaida turn her key in the kitchen door. He had prepared a thermos of hot coffee sweetened with sugar and evaporated milk, and he had wrapped a large piece of *massa sovada* in aluminum foil and put them in the ample pockets of his parka. Allie was puffy-eyed and drawn and wanted company, he could tell, but he did not linger with her.

"I'll be back as soon as I can," he said. "It's just a visit I have to make. Everything's fine here. Just sit with him. Maybe get him to eat something when he wakes. I put all his pills in one cup on the table. You might want to see if he's up to showering himself."

"I know what to do," she said. She didn't ask him where he was going. She took off her heavy coat and laid it over the kitchen chair and began pouring herself some coffee from what was left in the pot on the counter. "Go," she said. "Go."

THE WOODS WHEN HE REACHED THEM WERE SILENT AND DARK. He walked a broad, soft path, lit from skyglow in enough relief so that he could follow it easily between the darker brush and clumped trees that bordered it. He followed this trail east to where it forked, one way leading back to town and the other deeper into the woods and eventually to the true wilderness of the sand dunes if he kept to it, though he would veer from it before that. When he reached the fork in the path, he turned away from the town. This land had come under National Park jurisdiction since he and Sarafino had roamed it. The sky was a lighter black now, a wash of indigo in it, and the brightest of the stars still shone. He felt the bracing pleasure of chill air pinching his face. Distances had become unfamiliar here in this world, where he had not walked in such a long time, and once, before he came to the first pond that would mark his way, he stopped and tried to think if he had already passed it, or if he had forked from the correct trail.

But then he reached it, its water strangely luminous and deeply black, and he stopped and listened and looked into its blackness and took in its dank vegetable air. He raised the hood of his parka against the damp.

Nothing moved. He had fished here for largemouth bass and shot ducks along the farther bank, which could be reached only by picking a trail through the deep briar and alder and scrub oak. In the winter the ponds became thick tectonics of gray ice, and he remembered walking upon them as though they were courtyards or plazas. This was how they'd discovered the deeper places that were too difficult to reach through the forbidding tangles of summer, when the horseflies and ticks and clouds of mosquitoes would light to feed on any open skin. They had made their hidden camp in a deep cove there and found that they could leave the heavy canvas pup tent pitched there, along with their sleeping bags and fishing gear. No one would ever idly wander to that place, and they didn't have to carry heavy packs back and forth when they went to the woods. When the ponds were thawed, they had been careful to always wade in along the water's edge or scramble in through different directions so as not to wear even the smallest path.

He stepped into the water now, as softly as he could so he would not trample the low brush or the winter reeds, lifting his feet only a few inches off the soft bottom as the water glided over his boot tops and seeped inside. The cold was bracing, but his double pair of wool socks would soon warm with his body heat; there was a kind of pleasure in this act, a rawness to it and a gentleness, too, that reminded him of some remote and distinct freedom—a world before the Fall, in the smallest and most personal terms. He had not thought this way in a long time.

He made his way slowly along the eastern curve of the bank, disturbing nothing, neither splashing nor faltering. When he reached the north end of the pond he found a space between some dark bushes where he could walk up the bank and into a boggy wood. Here there was a narrow strip of land, thick with stunted pine, that separated this pond from its sister behind it. No trail or path ran near this other, hidden pond; it was crowded on all sides by dense growth. He felt his way across the isthmus, waded into the smaller pond, and walked its shallows in the same way as he had the first, curving up the eastern edge, moving carefully until the bank curved again. Then he found purchase and pulled himself up from the water and up still further over an incline, and then, creeping under limbs and switches, found his way in. This was it, the old camp, ringed with tall pines and water and underbrush, deep and dark, invisible to the world. This was the place where the Virgin had lain.

What it yielded to him was simple: a hole, the narrow trench that Mariah had excavated with Winslow, just as she'd described it. The sky was bluing at the zenith, and as the light made its way down through the thick pine boughs, he looked at the shallow grave. A mound of dark new earth ran along it from the digging, and looking into it he could make out the strata of the weak soil, black at the top, and pale sand at the bottom where the humus and mulch of all the years had not reached. Sand—what the town was, ultimately and essentially. There was nothing telling in the hole. It was not going to answer any questions. He did not understand fully what the questions would have been.

The priest went back to his knees and ran his hand along the inside of the trench. He felt the earth there. There were some odd fragments, flakes, that must have been the remnants of the tarp, still scattered there, and a long gash in the forest carpet where Mariah and Winslow had wrestled the dolly up into the light. The site was otherwise undisturbed. The floor was deep with pine needles, a thick cushion. In small clumps at the roots of the trees, silky leaves of wintergreen hugged the ground.

He rose to his feet. The sodden wool in his boots was beginning to warm, but cold yet seeped into him. The air was wet and sharp. He took inventory: the hole, some trees, the hidden pond, a rusted dolly. The history of anything either was or was not in the thing. What would any relic mean without its story? Guesses and generalities. He had more than those, at least. That was something. He could watch his thoughts in an odd way now: One would begin and he would follow it, trying to race to its conclusion, but then he would lose his starting point, a disturbing kind of forgetting, and when he turned back to find where he had begun, he would drop the entire moment. Then there was a blankness and only the vague sense of having been pursuing something. He tried to think if his mind had always been like this. It could terrify him if he let it, this possibility that some slow process of erasure was already in place, already working itself out. It would be his own fault if that were the case. He wouldn't argue with that. He was lost like this in some internal fugue when a branch popped or snapped. This was off behind him, away from the pond, duneward, opposite from the way he had come in.

He had been silent and invisible, and there was no wind to have carried his scent. He might have stalked a deer. He turned slowly so as not to startle it and peered through the heavy growth that fell away in that direction. But there was no deer. What he saw was nothing at first, and then, scarcely breathing, he adjusted his gaze. There was a figure standing—standing as still as he was, partially hidden among the trees and the predawn light. He couldn't judge how long the two of them stood in that aspect, neither moving, neither wanting to make a sound. His heart raced. And then he saw, not by her features so much, which were obscured in that uncertain distance, but by her body shape, her stance, her green vest, her ball cap.

It was Mariah Grey.

It came to him that his hood was up over his head and that she might not recognize him, that she might have thought he was a hunter or a park ranger, as unlikely as that might be in this obscure cove. He pulled the hood back from his face and raised his hand in a greeting. He watched as she hesitated, then raised her own hand and began picking her way through the trees and tangled brush toward where he stood. He watched her stepping carefully, not breaking a branch, not marring the terrain. "Jesus, Mary, and Joseph, Father. You scared me to death. My heart is banging. I didn't know what I was looking at." Her face was flushed and a little tail of steam followed her words.

"You gave me a start, too," he said. "At first I thought you were a deer." They both spoke in hushed tones that did not violate the silence of the woods. She carried the entrenching tool in her hand, short handled with a metal helve and a beveled blade that could pivot and lock into different positions. Spade, hoe, mattock. When she saw him looking at it, she said, "Winslow and I made a mess here. We were in a hurry. I came out to clean it up. We didn't have time yesterday."

"It's remarkable you found this." Furtado gestured to the dug-out trench.

"Only with Sarafino's directions and the metal detector."

She stood with her hands in her vest pockets, her collar up. He looked at her and then past her and saw how she must have approached. "You came the back way," he said. "You must have skirted the bottom of the dune beyond that stretch of pinewood. I came by the pond. I don't know how Sarafino could have come in here with that load."

"It's hard to get here. I see what you meant about being off the trail, though. It's beautiful here. You kids camped here. He told me that."

"Yes. Camped. Fished. Hunted. Hid out. Everything."

"Huckleberry Finn and Tom Sawyer."

"I know you don't think that." He saw how she hunched her shoulders, and he watched her breath streaming. "Are you cold?" he asked. "I have some coffee in a thermos. And some sweet bread." He pulled the long silver bottle out of the side flap of the parka and took out the foil-wrapped bread.

"All right," she said. "Here. I always hike with one of these," and she pulled a small green square of plastic out of her vest pocket and shook it to length. It was a garbage bag. "Raincoat, groundcloth, shelter, and so on," she said. She spread it at the base of a pine trunk and sat down on one end of it. The priest sat next to her and they leaned against the tree. He poured coffee out in the screw-top cup for her and broke the heavy yellow bread in half. "It's so strange to see you here," she said. She took a swallow of the coffee, which steamed lightly from the cup in her hand. "I mean, in the woods. This place meant a lot to you, I know."

"Yes," he said. "It did." He sipped some coffee from the mouth of the thermos. It was hot and strong and sweet, and it warmed him going down. The hole where Sarafino had buried the Virgin lay at their feet a few yards away. They were sitting close now, sharing the narrow pine's trunk at their backs, and their shoulders touched. He was too close to her to turn and look directly at her when they spoke, so when he answered her he kept his gaze on the furrow in the earth and the great tangles of bracken beyond it, the deep green of the pine boughs rising above it.

"When I came back from the war," he said, "I was a little banged up. I stayed out West." He spoke very quietly. "I went to college there and then seminary. It took years for me to get back to this side of the country." He sensed he might talk too much, so he stopped himself. "Anyway, I never came back here again—to this pond, this spot, I mean. It seems hard to believe now."

"You were hurt in the war," she said. "You were shot down? I heard that. I've been tempted to ask."

"Oh, that," he said. "You must know by now how the town has its stories upon stories for everything. No, I was in an accident. That's all."

"A plane crash. A thing we have in common," Mariah said.

"Well, I wasn't driving," the priest said. He told her about how her own storied arrival in the town had attracted his attention, and they both laughed a little. "You came out all right," he said.

"I lost some teeth in the back," she said. "I'm all fixed up, though."

"Me, too," said Furtado. "Mostly, anyway."

"So we both fell out of the sky," Mariah said. Then, "Oh, I hope no one else . . ."

"No," Furtado said quickly. "There were four of us. All okay."

They were quiet for a while.

"And so you became a priest," she said.

"Yes. Well, by the time I was in college I knew I wasn't going to marry and raise a family." He had meant that lightly, but it fell too heavily in the hush of the trees. "I was called. I believe I was called."

"Because of the war?"

"Well, it wasn't just one thing. A call isn't just one thing. But that, too, and the accident with the plane. We went down into the sea. We weren't shot at. It just happened. It was the first time I ever called out to God—I mean, with my whole being. With some part of myself I didn't even know was there. The force of hitting the water was terrific. Like the end of the whole world. I never had an idea of God as terror before. I was stripped, you know, of everything I thought I was. In that split second. Bang. It woke me up. But then the sense of being called . . . you look back at certain points over your life and everything all of a sudden seems lined up. So then it seems that the call was always there."

When Mariah didn't speak to this, he continued, "God sets us to war with our own selves." It was a thought he never would have uttered, but it just came out, spirited out of him like the thin cloud of his breath. Parts of him were still numb.

"*Everything* is at war," she said, surprising him. Rescuing him, maybe, for his remark. "Everything eats everything else. Everything competes. Even these trees. For the light. I agree with you, Manny. Maybe it *is* how God thinks. It might be the only way He could do what He did here. Struggle. I think that's why I ended up doing science. Like I might try to find out something about Him. About how He works, anyway."

"Good luck to you," said the priest, and there was a short silence before he glanced sideways and gestured to the bread and coffee in her hands. "So, does it warm you up?"

"I believe it does."

"I would always bring sweet bread and coffee with me when I walked in the woods in the wintertime. Cigarettes, too. We thought they warmed us up when it was cold out and we smoked them."

She laughed. That little pop of steam. "Yes. I remember that, too. Thinking that, too. We'd huddle in doorways and smoke to get warm."

"Yes?" he asked. "Kids? Smoking in doorways?" And then, "How about you? How did you come back to the Church?"

"I was never out of the Church. I was born into it."

"Tell me," he said, "you told me once about your family being involved with the Catholic Workers, Dorothy Day. Did you truly never leave it? Even for a while?"

"Others do. Gay women do. All the time. And men. There are other places to go and be taken in and feel a community."

"Not you, though."

"Well, maybe I did leave, in a way. I went through a lot of the same things you'd expect. What you hear about—the teenage years, and then college. Coming into myself. Coming out. I was wild a little, too, you know. And I was always looking for something. I won't go into my personal life. You already have the idea that I wasn't too successful there. I was very confused. *Needy* is what they say now, like it's bad behavior. Like you're morally inferior if you're needful or confused. But I always looked up to Dorothy Day. I still wish I were more like her. I've done things just from being weak when I could have been strong. But I'm different now. And Winslow is part of that. Now I can make things happen, too. Love is so strange. It changes how you think. It changes what you do." She shook her head, as if to pull herself back on track. "Anyway, so I never really moved far from the Church. I never renounced it or anything like that, and then there was the Rainbow Scarf Movement, things like that—some parishes seemed to be opening up, things seemed to be changing. I suppose I was still a little nuts."

"This was still in Minnesota?" He appreciated the hush of the woods, the very quiet voices that they spoke in. Something was restored to him now that he was no longer speaking about himself, and he saw that there was a great deal he did not know about her. And why should he? They were not intimate friends, really. She seemed like a bird herself, all her flying around, but Furtado sensed there was embellishment behind all that. It seemed she could never have been quite at the exaggerated loose ends that she liked to hint at. After all, there had been enough gravity at the university to hold her through the protracted drudgery of a doctorate. Maybe it was a spiritual roving she was trying to get across, and that wandering for love. Yes, the wandering for love—he'd have to take that into account. He understood what Winslow saw in her: the quick mind, the robust body—she'd flown an airplane with only her dog! Yet he didn't fully trust *love* as a term for it. Must not his own mother's heart have burst for his father once, if only that once? Must not his father's knees have weakened and his breath caught? Hard to imagine, but possible. And then what? All that joy just a wave breaking. Beautifully formed, wild, dazzling. But moving. Breaking. As if breaking were its whole point.

He knew, vaguely, that Winslow had lived with another woman some time before Mariah had arrived in town, but beyond that he knew little about her personal life. It was none of his business, at any rate, though he was sure he could hear about it quickly if he asked around. Which he wouldn't. Mariah professed their happiness, and nothing he ever saw spoke to the contrary. So why this shadow? It was, he decided, simply his own. She was speaking again. He turned his attention to her softened voice.

"Yes. Minnesota. Wisconsin first. Well, the way I began to see it, it was my Church, too. I had as much entitlement as anyone. Why should *I* be the one to be cast out? And I had been reading, too, all that stuff about Day and Peter Maurin, and I thought, *Well, they were socialists.* Talk about outcasts! In that day! And it didn't stop them from making their claim on the Church, and transforming it."

"And that was your thinking."

"It still is. I love God, Manny. I love the world, and I love Winslow. And I need the Church. I don't just need it—I want the Church to feel me in it. I want the world to feel me in it."

"You want your footsteps to be heard walking in the garden?"

"Yes," she said. "Yes, why not? I believe in intervention. Moral agency. I'm a small person in a big world, Manny. I'm not trying to make myself out to be more than I am. But I will be active. Isn't virtue always action?"

He stared vacantly down at her feet, which were stretched out before her on the forest carpet. She was wearing boots with black rubber bottoms and leather uppers. He was listening to her now, but he was also thinking. Several tracks running. He was present and not present. "So all this despite Saint Paul."

"Oh, *Romans*. A very cranky old man who liked the idea of burning books. He's wasn't Jesus, now was he? But your church here—Fatima is a Church that leaves no one out, Father. You never say much about that, but it's the truth. I know you are trying to knit all the factions together. And I'm here to help you. I mean *help* you. I'll do anything. I want you to know that. Everything I do, it'll be to help you, Manny."

It soothed him somehow that she praised his parish. He might have guarded himself against that kind of easy tribute if she were someone else, but with her he simply didn't care to. Whatever she had to gain by flattering him or serving him, she could have, freely. He shifted his gaze to the hole in the earth. They had talked around it enough. He pointed vaguely with his hand still holding the thermos. "What we have to deal with. I told him all about what you found. He thinks it's a sign, the empty tomb."

"Why wouldn't it be?" she said softly. "Why *couldn't* it be? It might mean everything to him."

"Well, She didn't rise in some suspension of natural law, I can tell you that."

"No. But are you saying a sign has to be miraculous?"

"No," he said. "It's true. There are just signs." He stood up and took a few steps toward the hole. "We aren't going to fill it up," he said.

"What?"

"We aren't going to fill it up."

She rose, too, and moved to his side. Her step was silent on the carpet of pine needles. He turned and took the thermos cup from her and screwed it back onto the metal bottle. "Oh," she said.

"It keeps everything in play. This is what he wants now. What he thinks he wants. To go into the earth here. I'll bury him here. He asked me to, as crazy as that sounds. And I knew that I would. I hated the idea. I was angry, I suppose, that he would say such a thing to me. But I knew I would do it. Why not? It's merely illegal. It was working in me all the while I walked out here, but I didn't know that I knew it. I was trying on answers for why I shouldn't do what he wants. I don't have any answers why. I don't want those kinds of answers."

"You still care very much for him."

"He infuriates me," said Furtado. The words spat from him visibly, a cuff of steam into the cold. He said more mildly, "I barely know who he is anymore. But I will bury him."

She didn't hesitate. He saw how she didn't need to digest what he said or gather herself. She simply said, "We should camouflage it, Father. At least."

Then he said, "Yes. That's right. Let's cover your work here."

He began gathering boughs and dried fallen limbs—years' worth of wrack—and tossing them into the shallow trench, and she with her mattock leveled some of the mound of excavated earth. Then together they heaped armsful of the dead brown pine needles over everything and spread them and raked them with another bough. What they left was a gentle mound and a gentle depression, both blending in with the needle-thick ground. Nothing looked like it had been touched in an age. She refolded her plastic bag and tucked it into the pocket of her parka. "Well," she said.

"Get your feet wet," he said to her. "Come through the ponds with me."

"All right," she said. "I parked my truck over on the east edge of the woods. If you want to hike out that way, I'll give you a lift back to the church."

He walked ahead of her, slowly and carefully. The sky was full blue above them now, pale, and to the east, where the sun had come up, a fine mist rose, shell-colored and diaphanous. Furtado crept down the bank toward the dark shine of the water. He parted a small footway by grasping each branch before him and holding it until Mariah took it herself and then turned and set it, unbroken, back into place. They made their way to the pond in this fashion, and he was about to enter the water when a great whistling broke the air. It sounded like a riot there in the silent woods and it came fast, a beating of wings just over the treetops. It was a flock of mallards, dense, enormous, and they were passing too quickly and too low for him to get a sense of just how many there were, but the priest understood that they had been coming down to light in this hidden pond and he and Mariah had spooked them, and now they shied up and off to the south, climbing over the dark trees. Their wing feathers made the air hiss, and their underbodies flashed, and when they wheeled across the pond and up, the priest could see the yellow beaks and green satin heads of the males, and the darker gray-brown speckling on the females. The wings beat and blazed white on their undersides, and in a moment the tumult passed and the flock was gone.

"Good Lord," Mariah said. In the light now her face shone, ruddy underneath her ball cap, and she kept her head turned in the direction the ducks had approached from. The priest said nothing. His mind was moving, too, over the obsidian shine of the water and the bristling, silent pines. They walked Indian file, gently, the cold water lapping about their calves, not making a wake, skirting the shallows of the pond, up through the bordering strip of pines, and then skirted the next pond and made their way up onto the trail. When they stood on dry ground again, he turned and spoke to her, almost in a whisper.

"Time," he said. "Think of it. Sarafino didn't come out here and bury a dolly. He put the Virgin into the ground. He was high, sure, but he had some sort of plan. And by the time he, or whoever else might have helped him, took Her out again, the dolly was already no good. Too much time. It had already rusted and disintegrated. It was a burden. It was covered up and left because it had become useless." He was thinking aloud now. He had entered into that space where it seemed quite natural for him to do so. "Or winter," he said, the idea suddenly coming to him. "Yes, pull it over the ice. The statue would have been as light as paper if you'd slid it over the ice. So She wouldn't have lain there that long at all. It could have been a few months. He could have come back after basic training. And the dolly would not have helped. It would have been left. But then why cover it back up? How long could a steel dolly last in the ground? What would he have done with the Virgin?"

"Oh, Manny," Mariah said. She looked at him, her head lifted at just a small incline so that her eyes met his briefly, then darted, scanning his face. His impulse was to step back sharply from her, but he held himself in his place. He didn't know what she was searching for. "All of this troubles you," she said.

"No," he said. "No. All this was a long time ago. But Sarafino is holding something back from me. I don't know what it is, and I don't know why. I was with him. This craziness was all my idea. He never got over it, though. I have to take care of him now."

"But I'm going to help you, Father Manny. I know there are a lot of things piling on you. I know how that other priest comes. I know I was in the middle of all that"—she hesitated—"*trouble*. I'm not naive. It wasn't just Mrs. Horta. I instigated it, in a way. You think I didn't want her job? I know I pushed. I insinuated my way in. I knew what I was doing. I just never thought anything so bad would come from it. I wounded her very deeply. How is a person to ever know?"

"Everyone has something running in his head," said the priest. "A story. A narrative. Don't you? Doesn't everything fit into some scheme that's always running? Hers was just . . . way off in left field. It doesn't matter, the whys and whats. I chose you," the priest said.

"Well, I'm keeping things off you," said Mariah. "Just know that. I will take care of Sarafino, too. I feel for him in my heart, even though I don't have the history you have with him. But I will keep the weight off you. I'm not going to put you in the middle of anything again. You'll see."

"He stole that thing because of me," the priest said quietly, but he had already stepped away from her and turned to the path, and she might not have heard him. He was beginning to ache, and now a vague dread passed through him. Then he was saddened to find himself thinking so precisely about his study, the order of things there, the desk, the vials of pills lined up in their long, even rows in the narrow wooden drawer. Their comfort. It *was* comfort.

She did not answer him, and the two of them hiked quietly along the trail. Some crows sounded way in the distance, and as he and Mariah tracked to the east, they rousted a few cottontails, but other than that the woods remained silent, and the two of them fell into an easy cadence in their walking.

MARIAH DROVE THE LITTLE TRUCK INTO TOWN, STAYING ON BACK STREET and driving up Bradford hill. The side streets were empty. The town looked almost deserted, in fact. The houses stood serene in the early morning light, the surface of the street dark, as though some pigment of the night had soaked into it and hadn't returned to the air yet. The day promised to be rinsed and empty. They had the heater turned up, and the hot air warmed their wet boots and pants legs, but Furtado felt drowsy from it as well. He almost did not recognize the feeling. Mariah pulled off the back street at the top of the hill and drove into the municipal parking lot. She turned her head slightly toward him, about to say something, but before she could speak, the priest threw up a hand and yelled, "Stop the car!"

"Holy Jesus," she said. She braked, and though they had been traveling very slowly, the cab rocked slightly from the force. They both looked out the priest's window at the figure off to their right, sitting on the concrete steps that gave way from the parking lot up to the side entrance of the high school. It was Sarafino Pomba, holding his head in his hands, dressed still in the sweat suit he had gone to bed in. Mariah wheeled the truck around, cut across the lot, and pulled to a stop in front of the steps. They each got out of the truck and came to him.

"Sarafino," the priest said when he reached him, "what are you doing here? Where's Allie?" Already in his head he was upbraiding her. How could she have left him to wander like this?

Mariah crossed her arms and held herself and bent toward him. The engine of her truck was still running, its doors open like the spread wings of an insect. "Sarafino," she said in a voice that was calmer than the priest's. A quiet voice. Steady. The priest didn't say anything. "Sarafino, why are you out here? It's so chilly."

"I'm helping to look for that Frankie Boia guy," he said. "Allie ran off."

"Make sense," said the priest. He took a breath. "We can't understand you unless you tell us exactly what happened."

He looked up at Furtado and squinted in the morning sunlight. "You're Manny," he said. "I got tired." He was concentrating hard on his breathing. "It's not Alzaida's fault. She told me to stay put. Then she ran off. They called her up on the telephone. They can't find that Frankie Boia guy. I was trying to help, but I can see that I made a mistake. They are all looking for that Frankie Boia guy. Something happened. This is a mistake here."

thirteen

THE *ILHA DO PICO* CAUGHT FIRE AND SANK SHORTLY AFTER DAWN that morning. The sea had been flat calm and shimmering like quicksilver under the graying sky when the *Ilha* motored out of the harbor. The old dragger was steering for the channel southeast of Long Point when Dickie Avellar, in the wheelhouse of the *Minha Prada*, saw the flash and then heard the bang. The *Prada* was about a half mile aft of Tom's boat and was following his course, heading out for the fishing grounds. Pauley Gonsalves had been up forward on the deck of the *Prada*, flaking a length of hemp line, and he said that he saw a ball of fire mixed with black smoke just before the bang, and then fast on top of that a thick cloud started rising up from the fo'c'sle of the *Ilha*. He was sure the smoke was coming from up forward of the other trawler because the *Ilha* had not yet rounded the Point and her target angle had changed just enough for him to see more of her hull than if she were stern-to. What was weird, everyone said, was how fast the *Ilha do Pico* disappeared. The *Prada* would have been alongside in no time, but the *Ilha do Pico* plowed ahead for about half a minute after the explosion. The smoke rose straight up until it hit a small current of air and then started blowing off to the east, but the men on the *Prada* could not see through it to get a clear view of exactly what was happening on the old boat's deck. But they all agreed that it sank in minutes. They all saw the bow go down first, like it had diving planes on it. It was still motoring, they all said, because the engine seemed to push the bow under farther and then the stern came up and they could see the rudder and the top of the propeller, and the propeller was still churning, and then the whole thing went down like a rock. "I never seen anything go down so fast," Pauley told the Coast Guard. "Like, in a minute."

Dickie Avellar gunned the *Prada* and closed on the wreck site. Tom was in the water when they reversed the engine and halted, and Antone Nunes, who had come up from below when he heard the blast, threw out a line and a buoy, and he and Pauley tried to get Tom to take hold, but Tom would not stop beating his arms and legs over the water. He swam wild. He thrashed and screamed at the men up on the high deck and then plunged his head under the water. He did this over and over. He was screaming to the crew of the *Prada* for them to spot Frankie. "We couldn't get him to take a line" was how Dickie Avellar told it.

Tom would not leave the water, though it was frigid. He would not let them pull him up to the deck until they found Frankie, and Tom kept thrashing and thrusting his head under as if he might spot something by doing that. But the cold water exhausted him quickly, and when Dickie and his men saw that Tom himself might slip under, Dickie, thrusting the engine gently, sidled the big boat over to him, and Pauley and Antone clamped the aluminum boarding ladder over the side, and Antone held fast to Pauley while Pauley stretched overboard and pulled Tom up on deck. He was purple and shivering. Some of his woolen shirt had been burned away, and the sleeves lay upon his forearms, blackened and sodden. "We were worried about hypothermia right away, and we could tell he was hurt," said Dickie, "but he wouldn't let us take him below and get him into a bag or some dry clothes. You know how Tom is. You can't tell him anything. He was crazy for finding Frankie, and he stayed up in the wheelhouse with me. We finally got a blanket around him, but he didn't look so hot."

Dickie Avellar had radioed the Coast Guard and then radioed two boats that were already about a mile or more ahead of them. These were the *Sao Paulo* and the *Deolinda*, which both turned back, pulled close aboard, and cut their engines and joined the search. None of the men aboard any of the boats could attest to seeing any sign of Frankie. He might never have hit the water. If he had been below decks, it was likely that he never made it topside. Tom by this time had slumped to the deck in the wheelhouse of the *Prada*. Antone Nunes got him out of his freezing clothes and wrapped him in one of the polyfill sleeping bags, and the Coast Guard, which arrived in great speed, called for a small boat and took Tom to shore. Antone Nunes said that he was not conscious by then, but Dickie Avellar remembered that he was awake, just not making sense. They treated Tom there in town and then took him up the Cape to the hospital.

The priest had gathered all this information, over the rest of the morning, in bits and pieces. He and Mariah Grey had taken Sarafino off the parking lot's stairway and gotten him into Mariah's truck, then settled him quickly into the rectory. Mariah had tended to Sarafino while Furtado made a flurry of phone calls and came in on the scattered details of the story in its early stages. When he learned of the accident, he called the hospital and inquired about Tom, but he learned only that he was being treated in the emergency room. The woman he spoke with asked him to call back later, and when he told her he was a priest and Tom's brother-in-law and asked for particulars, she would say only that she knew that he was not listed as critical.

He left the rectory shortly before noon and drove down to the center of town. He saw that the wharf was crowded with several vans and trucks, and so he parked in the seaward lot to the west of the wharf and looked out over the harbor where he could make out the *Prada* and the other boats still laying to out beyond the tip of the Point. He watched for a time but could determine nothing, and so he drove out along Pond Road to the police station, where he talked with Cookie Cruz, the town's dispatcher, and she told him all that she knew.

It was already late morning by then, and Alzaida had driven the fifty miles up to the hospital to be with Tom, and so the priest came back to the rectory and called the hospital again, and this time he was told to leave his number and that he would be called back. When the return call came, it was after four in the afternoon, and it was Allie who spoke to him. "It's not real bad," she said. "The cold water got to him, but the doctors said it also helped make the burns not so bad. He's in a room, finally. They are going to keep him until tomorrow." Her voice cracked. He could hear the strain in it. "What about Frankie?" she asked.

"Nothing yet," he said. "They're still looking."

"Oh, God. What a mess."

"Yes," he said. Then there was a silence on the line between them, and he thought that he might have let some wrong note sound in that last word. Neither spoke, until finally he said, "I'm glad that Tom is all right."

"I'm going to stay up here for a while," she said.

"Yes," he said. "Call me again later, and maybe I'll have some more news." He didn't say anything about finding Sarafino in the parking lot.

By early afternoon the Coast Guard had put two divers over the side, and most expected that they would find Frankie in the hull of the *Ilha* somewhere. The divers said that the trawler was lying on her side in about seventy feet of water. One of them entered the hull and searched with a light, but they did not find Frankie's body. They reported a strong current moving at about two to three knots along the bottom, down below fifty feet, flowing westerly. They said the visibility was very poor at that depth. They did not have an estimate of the damage, but they verified a long hole torn in the hull, below the waterline, just aft of the bow. All the boats stayed out until nightfall, and the Coast Guard searched in expanding circles based on a center that moved in the calculated direction and speed of the underwater current, though everyone said the surface of the ocean remained moderate and calm for the rest of the day.

The priest's own chronicle in the ledgers would be more familiar and exact. Mariah had sat down with Sarafino on the parlor sofa and eaten with him. She had steamed some carrots and broccoli together, and warmed some chicken and rice. She ate as lightly as Sarafino did. They had finished their small plates by the time the priest finished talking to Allie, and he joined them in the parlor. The afternoon light was already dying. The deep shadows outside had overcome the little street entirely, and the long, low gloaming of the season settled a velvet darkness on the windows. Against this dusk the floor lamp filled the parlor with a warm, buttery light, and Furtado was seized momentarily with how calm and benign the room looked, the woman and the man sitting together in an order of complete domesticity, as though nothing tragic or menacing lay anywhere about them, neither inside the room nor in the night that was fast falling out of doors. Mariah had put a bright afghan around Sarafino's shoulders, and he sat hunched under it with his feet up on the edge of the coffee table. "I never knew that boy," Sarafino said. "I think I might have run with his brother, though, up in Boston. You ever been to Boston?"

He was talking to Mariah, but Furtado put in, "Sarafino, Frankie doesn't have a brother. You never knew him in Boston."

"I know a lot of people you don't know nothing about," Sarafino said. "I don't care that much about your old man's boat, you know."

"It's Tom da Costa's boat," the priest said. He spoke patiently to Sarafino, for he knew that the commotion of the day had flustered him, and no one had been good about keeping him on the oxygen.

"He thinks he's married to Alzaida," said Sarafino.

"He *is* married to Alzaida," said Furtado.

"You think you have the story on everything," he said.

"Sarafino, are you feeling confused?"

"Yes, I am, Manny. Some things are going on, and I can't get ahold of them. Where is Alzaida?"

Furtado told him again.

"You ought to go looking for that Frankie Boia. They can't find him. I couldn't find him either."

"You should always stay here," Mariah said. "Even if there's no one here or someone has to leave for a minute, you should stay here, in the rectory."

"Well, I know that," Sarafino said.

"I want you to lie down again and take some oxygen," Mariah said. "It will make the confusion go away."

"You seem pretty sure of yourself," Sarafino said.

"Will you do that for me?" Mariah asked.

"What's your end?"

"I'll say a Rosary with you. I want to say a Rosary. Come on." She stood up, and the two of them walked with Sarafino and got him into the bed and got the oxygen running.

"It's dark," Furtado said to Mariah when they were done getting Sarafino settled. He spoke quietly and looked to the window.

"I know," she said. "Mrs. Boia."

"Yes," he said. "It's a lot to ask. Can you stay here another hour?"

"It's all right. I'm going to stay with Sarafino and pray a Rosary. We'll pray to find Frank Boia."

Sarafino's eyes moved from Mariah to the priest and back again, but he did not say anything. He just breathed small, snuffy breaths and readied his beads.

"Winslow?" Furtado asked.

"She's fine," Mariah said. "I talked to her. I'll see her soon enough. Go ahead."

It took only minutes for the priest to drive to the West End. He rounded the curve on Front Street and parked against the sidewalk just around the corner from Mrs. Boia's house. He walked back around the corner, and stopped and looked out at the Coast Guard station as he reached her gate, and he could see all the way out to the end of its wharf, where some lights showed that a boat was alongside, but the activity out there told him nothing. He opened the wooden gate and walked around to the side entry and knocked, and he watched through the glass of the storm door as Catalina Pires walked down the stairs and let him in.

"Ah, Father Manny," she said. "*Boa noite. Entre!*" Her dark skin seemed even darker in the poor lighting of the stairway, and her gray hair was pulled back along the sides of her head with a pair of blue plastic combs. She wore a shapeless, earth-colored housedress, and she stepped to one side so the priest could walk up the stairs before her. "*Vá adiante, por favor, Father Manny. Vá p'ra cima. Matti Roderiques está aqui também. Há alguma notícia do seu filho?*"

He spoke over his shoulder as he walked up the stairs, self-conscious about his Portuguese, which was bookish and did not sound like the old speech of the *velhas*. "*Não, ainda não.*"

"*Esta é uma coisa terrível.*"

"*Sim.*" He stepped aside at the top of the stairs, and she led him into the parlor. Mrs. Boia sat on the faded burgundy sofa, her shoulders slouched, a gray cardigan sweater over her shoulders. She put her hands to her face and wailed when she saw the priest, and he realized she was looking at him as though he were death itself violating the redoubt of her rooms.

"I don't bring any news," he said quickly. "I came to sit with you awhile. They are still looking." A number of votive candles were burning on the table before her, and a fat, shiny porcelain lamp glowed brightly on each end table, but these lamps were surrounded by votive candles also, and so were various shelves lined with candles. She, or someone, had placed a plaster statue of Saint Jude, patron of lost causes, on one of the shelves, and a candle also burned at his feet. The room was close and hot, and the smell of paraffin wax made the air thick. Matti Roderiques had been sitting there in a Morris chair next to the couch, and when the priest entered she stood up to offer him her seat. "*Não, por favor, Matti*," Furtado said, and remained standing until Catalina came in and sat next to Mrs. Boia on the couch.

"I'm sorry that you have to go through this, Hortensia," he said to Mrs. Boia. Then he said, "God is here in the room with us." He sat in a small chair and faced the three old women and thought of what he might say that he really believed, but nothing came to him that would be comforting, and he sat there for a moment and took in the smells of the house that lay under the strident and comfortable smell of the burning candles. He found the deep and deeply pervasive odors of decades of cooking, the baking and long-simmered soups and the always-present sweet smell of fish, this last so light and vague it was almost like an idea, not a thing of the world. There was the other smell, too, and he recognized it as simple age, human age—Hortensia Boia herself—not uncleanliness, but the scent a body begins to exude after it starts its final shrinking and slowing.

Mrs. Boia had always been a small, thin woman, but she now looked deflated and reduced sitting there on the high-backed couch next to Catalina Pires, who was big-boned and fleshy. They were all three grim and frightened, but some other thing hung in the room, too. He understood what it was when Hortensia Boia fixed him with an iron look. Her eyes were dark-rimmed and baggy in her thin face, but they lanced him. "They are not going to find my Frankie," she said. "That Tommy, he got out of the water all right."

"Yes," said the priest. "He did. He's up at the hospital. My sister is there."

"My Frankie never got out of the water."

"No one knows that for sure right now," said Furtado.

She flared. "I lived in this town all my life," she said. "I moved into this house right after I married, and I lived right here almost sixty years. You see that *janela* there?" She pointed over her shoulder to the window behind her. It faced the ocean, but it was dark now, and nothing could be seen through it. A pair of 7x50 marine glasses sat on a small wooden bench by the window, next to a compact shortwave set. "You know how many times I sat in that window and watched for the boats to come home around the Point when my Biggy was captain? And I would listen in on the radio to them talking on the water? You are a nice boy, Manny, and you have been called to God, but don't you come in here and offer me hope when you know there isn't any, and you know that I know that, too. I have known every boat that went down for your whole life and more than that. So don't bring hope into this room. That is what will kill me." She held a wad of Kleenex in her hand and she gave a low, wild sound and rocked and pressed the tissues into her face.

"*Hortensia, o padre está aqui agora e nos devemos rezar com ele*," said Matti.

"Pray?" said Hortensia. "Pray? Is that what I'm going to do now?"

"Hortensia!" Catalina Pires spoke as if to an erring child.

"I'll never see him again," Hortensia said. "They will never find him." She spoke to no one in the room and not to herself, either. She stared into something incomprehensible. She was addressing the whirlwind or the farthest star. "*Que vou fazer de mim?*"

"Pray with me now," said Furtado. "Pray to Our Lady." In some world other than this one, he would create a place beyond caring and suffering and grief, he thought, but he knew he could not trust his thoughts nor his senses in this moment, and his old pains crept up on him. He took out his black wooden beads, and the women all produced their rosaries. He began with the prayer as a call, and they came back with the response, and together they filled the room, and the drone of human voices stirred something in his own breast, and he ached fully now. He watched Hortensia Boia in her fierce woe and her keen self-absorption. Her body like a dry shell. Her hair like a puffed weed that might blow in the wind. A living soul yet.

THEY FOUND FRANKIE BOIA THE VERY NEXT DAY. A COAST GUARD helicopter spotted some flotsam about three or four miles out in the ocean from where the *Ilha do Pico* had gone under. A fuel slick had come up and spread like a listless tendril, a thready shadow on the surface of the water, marking, in its snaking fashion, the tide and current. There was a life ring, some Styrofoam, a fender buoy, and some planking that had come from the *Ilha*'s fo'c'sle, all scattering in a rough line out to sea. Frankie's body, a dark shade floating, just breaking the surface, was among the strewn remains.

The priest was at his desk in the downstairs office when the phone call came. It was Cookie Cruz from the police station who gave him the news first, although the phone continued to ring into the afternoon. He called Hortensia Boia right away, but Catalina Pires was with her and Jesse Cabral from the funeral home was already there. Hortensia's voice was soft and flat; she spoke but a few words to him and got off the phone quickly. In between calls, the priest made notes on a yellow legal pad. It was never a small or ordinary thing when a boat went down, and there would be much to do.

He didn't wait for Mariah Grey—he went ahead and made his own calls and canceled all his pending meetings. He left a message for John Sweet and called off their session for the week. He made a note to call Jesse Cabral and coordinate a schedule for the funeral Mass. He would get the details of the burial arrangements from him, rather than Hortensia. There was no question about whether there would be a viewing of the body—after more than a day in the sea, it was fit for a closed casket only.

Alzaida had stayed all night up in the hospital with Tom. His doctor had said he might be released that day, but when she called Furtado, she could not find the doctor and no one in the hospital had seen him yet that day, though he was scheduled for rounds. Mariah Grey was home, getting some sleep. She and Furtado had agreed that they would split their time watching Sarafino until Alzaida could come and be of some help. The priest did not want to leave Sarafino by himself, even though he was taking the oxygen. For stretches of time he would lie in bed with his rosary, not moving much, as though he would never rise or speak again. As though anything that was vital in him had oozed out of him and left him empty and helpless, staring at the silent television, its blue light jumping erratically as scenes changed.

Other times, he would brace up with that strange second wind. Then he would rise and shuffle out and sit at the kitchen table, and he and the priest would take tea and talk about old times and sometimes the war. Furtado would make him a plate of baked cod or finely diced chicken and fruit and vegetables, or broth, or talk him into nursing a bottle of supplement drink as though it were a beer. And a second wind would come to Furtado as well. He felt it not as a physical lifting but as a swirl in his head, as though all the discord and energy of a storm had come into him, and his mind blew dark and erratic and whistled in circuits. He thought of Frankie Boia's death as a thing to roll over him, as something for him at the same time to roll under. To rise up from it and keep on going. And then he would look at Sarafino sitting there at the kitchen's little table, and he would see his death, too, an image of it and not a rounded thought. Nothing he could hold on to or see through to its end, whatever end that might be. There would be the business of burying Frankie Boia, but Sarafino lived.

And Furtado ached. And he prayed. He prayed with Sarafino, and then, when things quieted down and the phone stopped ringing, they settled on the sofa and he read to him. Sarafino wanted the Gospel of John, but Furtado could not bear it, so they agreed on Acts.

"You ought to read about when the ship sinks," Sarafino said. "You know what I mean?" Furtado thumbed the Testament until he found Chapter 27, and he read aloud and Sarafino leaned back and closed his eyes and sometimes nodded, as if in agreement with what Furtado was reading.

"I like that part about the snake," Sarafino said when the priest paused. "That Paul was something else. You couldn't mess with him."

"Well," said the priest, "he is the hero of the story. Maybe, though, the snake wasn't poisonous like those islanders thought."

"You figure, Manny, this guy comes through the shipwreck and then he gets bit by the snake and nothing happens, you figure he's got the power. Those guys on the island thought so. They even said they thought he was a god."

"Maybe they thought a lot of people were gods."

"Who wrote all that, I wonder?"

"Nobody knows for sure. But a lot of people think Luke did."

"Paul there, he knew the boat was going to go down. He told that soldier so."

"So it says."

"I'm sorry about your old man's boat going down like that, Manny. I say evil things sometimes. But that was a bad deal all around. I know it."

"Yes, a bad deal," Furtado said.

"Sometimes mean things just come out of me," Sarafino said. "I don't have anything against you or your old man."

"Who can tell what's inside of us?" Furtado said. "Sometimes we just don't know."

"I do," said Sarafino. "I know what's inside of me."

"What is that, Sarafino?"

"I have got this empty space with nothing in it. Like a iron box."

"Like a safe? Like, to lock things in?"

"No. A space. That's why Our Lady can come and visit me. I got all this room."

"In your heart? That would be a comfort, then."

"You think so? You think it's a comfort to have your heart like a big iron box with nothing in it?"

"I'm just trying to figure things out," Furtado said. "I'm just trying to follow what you say."

"Well you have God in your heart because you're a priest, so I don't see what your big fuss is. I think it's a damn shame that young boy drowned."

"Not so young. His name was Boia. That's what you're thinking. You think he was a boy because of Boia."

"I know Boia. Biggy. Old Man Boia. He used to drink up at Juney's. He had that boat."

"The *Graciosa.*"

"The *Graciosa.* That's the one. My father tried to get on with them, too. Nothing happened, though."

"Biggy was Frankie's father. He died a long time ago."

"He drown?"

"No. He had diabetes, I believe. His boat went down, too, though. I mean, after he sold it. To the Sousa brothers, down to the East End. They stove it in with their own drag door somehow. Bad seas. Nobody hurt."

"There was a mighty tempest in the sea, so that ship was like to be broken. I'm glad I'm not going back to the joint, Manny. Know what we used to call it on the inside? We used to call it the bucket. I don't have any idea why that is. I miss Allie, though."

"You're starting to skip around. Maybe you should lie down for a while," said the priest. "Get some of that oxygen."

"I don't want to be by myself."

"I'll come in there with you. I'll read some more."

Furtado walked with him into the room and got him hooked up to the oxygen. Sarafino was hot to the touch, and he lay back on the pillows without his blanket or quilt over him. The priest went to the kitchen and came back with a cold bottle of Gatorade and a straw and set it on the night table by the bed.

"I thought I'd be seeing more of Allie, to tell you the truth," Sarafino said. He pulled himself up and sipped some Gatorade, then wet his lips with his tongue.

"Remember, she's with Tom, up at the hospital."

"I get it," Sarafino said. "But here's what puzzles me, Manny: the Virgin Mary. I thought that because she rose up from where I put her in the ground, that was the sign. I don't know what to make of it. But this boat sinking, your old man's boat . . . you see what I mean?"

"No, Sarafino, I don't. I don't see any connections."

"Well, between you and me, Manny, we were connected the whole time. You and me and Allie. You see what I mean?"

"Why Allie?"

"Not Allie. That was a mistake." Sarafino closed his eyes and breathed in and out with concentration. Furtado watched his motion and then understood it. The way Sarafino used the air, filling his lungs with short breaths, saving up the oxygen in his muscles, was the way they would dive deep as kids, slipping under the water with easy, slow movements so as not to use up the stored air. They would dive deep on certain wrecks off the back beach, or in the channel cuts along the breakwater, or on the shoals in the elbow of the Point, where they could pluck the big, succulent, brown sea clams from the sandy bottom. They would lie naked on the warm sand then, the clams in wet burlap to be taken back to town and ground into pie or stuffed with *linguiça* sausage, the sun warming their wiry bodies, soaking deep into their bones. Yes, Sarafino moved in the world now like

a diver under the sea. Suddenly, Furtado thought of Frankie Boia, drifting like a weed along the icy currents of the Atlantic, and then he shook all such thoughts from his mind.

In that moment, Sarafino gathered himself. His eyes burned with a dark fire. He set the bottle of Gatorade down on the bedstand, again that slow liquid motion, nothing wasted. "There was this guy once, Manny," he said. "Maybe you heard of him. I was in prison with him for a while. His name was Vinny Castellano. Italian guy."

"No, Sarafino. Why would I have heard of him?"

"Killer. Killed his mother and his mother's boyfriend in an argument over a car. Something about a car. Or a truck. He stabbed them both. Right in their own kitchen. I thought that was famous. It was up in Boston someplace."

"I never heard about it."

"Well," Sarafino said. He paused for a breath, then slipped back into his slow, uneven speech. "He was in the bucket when I was there. He was an ordinary guy. He liked to talk a lot. He wasn't big or bad, nothing like that. But you gave him room. He had a way of walking, like he was saying, *I don't bother no one, but if you make the mistake of fucking with me, it will be your bitter end.* Like that. He used to talk about Winky Jee all the time. That's what he called Jesus. Winky Jee. He said if Jesus was all what he was supposed to be, he would have stopped him from killing his mother and the boyfriend like that. He never meant to, he said, but they pushed him into it. They were unreasonable, he said. He said they yelled at him. He said they made a bad mistake about who he was. He tried to tell them. He admits he was very cranked when this all happened. He had done a few spoons of meth. 'You don't know what you're doing here,' he kept saying to them. 'You don't know how this is going to turn out.'

"And when he started cutting them up—stabbing them, I guess he slashed them—they couldn't believe it that they were being killed right in front of their own eyes. He said it was then he realized that you can do anything you want. Anything. No matter what it is. Nothing is out of bounds. No one is going to stop you unless it's someone bigger and stronger or crazier. He said he felt like Jesus was just winking at him all the while he was stabbing those two relatives of his. I think it was a Ford pickup truck. Something like that. It was an argument.

"So when something went down in the bucket, when somebody started pushing someone around or things were going bad for somebody, Vinny would just say, 'Hey, give Winky Jee a call. See what he can do for you. See what good he can do right here.' And he would just watch you. This is the thing, Manny. He wasn't being a wiseass or anything. It was all serious. He'd get this real serious look all over him, like he was trying to figure out where Winky Jee was. Why he was just winking and going along with things, instead of taking care of somebody's troubles like everybody says he does."

Sarafino had to stop for air. He closed his eyes, but his faced glowed under the pallor.

Furtado studied that face in the yellow light of the room. "Well," said the priest, "we accept that Jesus doesn't intervene in ways you can see. You know that's not how it works." He didn't say anything else. There was nothing else he wanted to say.

Sarafino opened his eyes again and groaned or sighed, pushed himself over onto his side, and rolled his shoulder into the pillows, seeking a position of some relative comfort. He took a few more breaths and went on. "Well this is what Vinny said. He said, 'Winky Jee comes to take the sins of the world away. What about it, Fino'—which was my name in the bucket—'you think he took my sins away? You think he gave a shit that I cut those two people up? If he did all that stuff he was supposed to, wouldn't nobody be cutting nobody.'

"So Manny, I remember when these two guys come up on this punk in the metal shop one afternoon. I was working there because it was a job where you went if they could trust you not to make a shiv or do anything crazy. But these two guys had a beef with this other guy for something, and they came in and piped him. That means they beat him with a pipe, which we had in the shop. They piped his shins, which is how that goes, and then when he went down they piped his arms and ribs pretty good. He was howling and trying to bug himself up on the deck there. I stayed out of the way. I didn't see a thing, if you know what I mean, but then I looked over at the door, and everybody knows what's going down, and there's Vinny Castellano standing there, just watching this, like he's studying something. He's concentrating, looking for the hidden particulars. I don't know how a guy like Vinny gets near the metal shop, because everybody knows he's in for shivving two people, but he had that ability. You might call it suave. He was very respected. So then, when those two cons beat feet outta there, Vinny comes over and looks at the guy, and the guy is all groaning and sobbing. They whacked him pretty good. Vinny never had nothing to do with it. But he bends over the guy and just looks him up and down. He looks at him like he's trying to get into his head. Deeper. Deeper. Like, to the deepest place. Then he looks over at me. 'Fino, my man,' he says, 'Winky was winking the whole time. You could have done more good than him. Wink, wink.' He doesn't smile or anything. He's very serious. Then he walks off, that slow, cool walk of his.

"Here's what I know, Manny: You can't tell about this Vinny guy. He was nuts. That was for sure. He even told me more than once that even if he hadn't been cranked, he probably would have killed those people. Sometimes you just let go of everything that sits on your true feelings, he told me, and then this pure thing comes over you. For him it was murder, and nothing about that felt bad. He thought about what he did, and what he thought is that it felt pretty good. He only felt bad about being in the bucket. Now, what do you think of that? Winky was supposed to stop all that. What the hell is everybody talking about?

"I will tell you, Manny: All that about Jesus scared me because it was the truth. He never came through on his end. What I could think of there in the bucket at night, this one thing: Our Lady, She comes through. She helps sinners like me, and She is there at the hour of your death. Amen. So I would say, 'Hail Holy Queen, Mother of Mercy.' That was the only part of that prayer that I could think of, so I just said that over and over. Maybe a million times. You get so low-down. Then I thought how stupid I was for not knowing the whole thing by heart. That's when I started memorizing. Because if you have it in your head, you have it. Sometimes when my head is not working right, all those words I put there are still there. They don't go away, for some reason. But Our Lady, She is in me, Manny. Not just my head. I see Her. She has sent me signs. That is the God's honest truth."

"Sarafino," said the priest, "I can follow your story, but tell me the truth about this one thing: Do you think the statue of the Virgin really rose somehow in order to send you a sign?"

"What are you trying to say, Manny? You always talked two or three ways to the wind."

"How much of that night do you really remember? It was so long ago."

"I am sorry for that night, Manny. I'm sorry I went along with it. Poor Mr. Coelho didn't do any harm to anyone." Sarafino shook his head. "But then, that's how Our Lady came into me. You can't figure these things."

"What I can't remember, Sarafino, is where Allie was. Did you see her?"

Sarafino was quiet for a minute. He closed his eyes, like he might fall asleep. The priest said nothing, but waited and watched him. Sarafino didn't open his eyes. He didn't move. He said, "I was with you, Manny."

"After?"

"I took the Virgin into the woods."

"What about this, Sarafino? What about this scenario: You took the statue into the woods, but you came back to town at some point in your life. You must have. And when you did, you went back and dug her up and did something with her."

"You're saying She never rose?"

"I'm thinking of other ways to explain it."

"Why?"

The priest said nothing here. He could not put an answer into words for Sarafino. Manny was chagrined at his silence, but he couldn't find a thing to say. Finally Sarafino rolled to his back and settled himself into the bed again. "Your life is pretty easy, isn't it?" he said.

"I think it is, compared to what yours has been," said Furtado.

"You get paid for this? How much does a priest get paid these days?"

Furtado sighed. "It's an allowance. It's not a salary. It's about $13,000 a year."

"You get the place here. You get the house here."

"The rectory. Yes."

"Well," Sarafino said. "Well. That's easy living." He stopped and breathed again as though he were going to take another dive beneath the surface. As though he, too, were about to disappear under the ocean. "Manny, I don't see what difference it makes how the Virgin came out of the ground. You're hung up on that. I don't know why. If my head was working right, maybe I'd know. Maybe there is something I can't get my head around. But there's not any con about it."

Sarafino trembled a little then. He became agitated. He shuffled and jerked under the quilt. His chest rose and fell in small spasms, the darkness smoldering in his dark eyes. "And think about this, why don't you: If She didn't rise up by Herself, which I am not saying I agree with you on that, then maybe it was you! Maybe *your* memory is not so good." He snuffed at the oxygen. "Maybe you have some black spots, too. It was your idea to go and steal Her. Maybe it was *you* who came back and got Her, Manny."

fourteen

THE DAY OF FRANKIE BOIA'S FUNERAL BEGAN WITHOUT A SUNRISE. A cold, pelting rain with drops the size of human thumbs had blown in off the ocean the night before, during the Vigil for the Deceased, which was held in the large parlor of Jesse Cabral's Funeral Home, in the presence of the body, as was mandated and as was possible now that Frankie Boia's remains had been retrieved from the cold, long currents of the Atlantic. Hortensia Boia was there, and so were a number of town women—mostly women, as Furtado had known would be the case, though Allie was not there and Mariah Grey was back at the rectory with Sarafino. Father Furtado began the vigil ritual as prescribed, with the greeting and the opening prayer and then the first reading, from Paul's Second Corinthians: *We know that if our earthly body, a tent, should be destroyed we have a building from God . . .* And then a reading from the Gospel of Luke and then the homily and the Prayer of Intercession, and the Lord's Prayer and the blessing. When Furtado concluded the order of the vigil, there was a time for the eulogy, but no one had prepared one or wished to say one. But the women wanted a Rosary, and so he led the prayers, and the room, with its clean angles and elaborate moldings and ornate light sconces, swelled warmly with antiphons, and the sound of praying voices muted the pounding of the weather against the clapboards of the rambling Gothic building.

The storm had dragged a cold gloom into the late morning, and the rain was still blowing down from the sky when the funeral Mass began, but despite the weather, the Church of Our Lady of Fatima could not hold all those who came. The overflow mourners huddled together in the foyer at the back of the building, the main doors open to accommodate them, and the hindmost stood at the top of the outer brick steps, holding a wall of black umbrellas behind them as they crowded the double doors, looking in. It was like something from the old days, the priest would reflect later in the ledgers, something he had memories of from a time he could no longer exactly place, the church alive, a packed and living thing. But now, on this day, in the transept, a dead man in a long, narrow, mahogany-colored casket overlaid with draping white pall, and with a paschal candle set burning before it, the building itself not only was redolent of its usual essences—oiled wood and incense and the whispered combustion of hundreds of votive candles in their iron racks—but also brimmed with the odors of wetness, the cotton and wool of the rainflecked clothing, the faint tell of damp human hair, the breath and heat and closeness of bodies pressed together on the creaking wooden pews.

The priest moved through the order of the Mass as though he were in a trance. Something in him shrank from this, and something else in him forced him not to shrink but to rise up and embrace this thing that he had to do. He was not saddened by the death, nor was he joyful for this soul's rise to eternal life. He thought briefly that the possibility of such joy and sadness had left him somehow, and had been replaced by this racing in his mind and this inability to quiet the continuous racket of so many troubling considerations.

What he desired most was to stand and watch the people who had come to the church for Frankie, and when he was able to capture these moments in the long, ruled pages of his nightly chronicles, this was what he would give emphasis to, not his performance of the ritual of Mass itself. He would repeat himself, coming at the funeral and the gathering from various angles.

As he prayed through the order of the Mass, he took account of the many faces of the men and women, the fishermen and laborers and shopkeepers and newcomers, the young kids, and the *velhos* and *velhas* from both ends of town. There were faces that he had not seen in the church in all the years he had been back, and there were faces that he had never seen before in his life. Hortensia Boia sat at the front of the church, to the right of the coffin, and Catalina Pires and Matti Roderiques sat flanking her. Hortensia never lifted her eyes and never moved either to kneel or to stand. She looked gray as stone and insignificant, and her grief was impossible to read as the priest looked at her and looked again and again and saw the blunt and concussed set of her face and the way her eyes looked utterly blind, staring into the nothingness of the short distance before her.

And he found Tom and Allie, too, when he lifted his own eyes and swept over the rows of faces. He wanted to rest his gaze on them, but of course he could not. They sat together in the farthest pew on the outside aisle. Allie seemed crouched and crumpled to him, and Tom sat rigid, looking into his lap, his head of curls glistening wet even in the pale light of the hanging lanterns. He had chosen not to sit with the other pallbearers, and after he had marched in with them—Brabo Perriera from the Wheelhouse and George Campos from the bank, and Dickie Avellar and Pauley Gonsalves and Antone Nunes, all of them dressed purposely in the heavy fishermen's work clothes of the season, with checked-wool and flannel shirts on top, all, even George Campos—he'd left them at the front of the church and found his way back up the side aisle to sit far from the casket, with Allie.

Tom had been hurt, but not badly, though he was still marked and bruised. But he was shaken. The town had talked about nothing but the sinking since the first hours of that morning when the *Ilha do Pico* had gone down. Every aspect of the disaster, every theory, had been discussed and parsed and then reevaluated when any new piece of information came forth, and all the descriptions and particulars were compared with the histories of all the other sinkings in memory, and when the talk would turn from the old boat and from Frankie—everything from his father and mother and First Communion and high school to where he drank and with whom and how skilled he was with the nets, which was what all the men on the water knew well—the talk would go round to Tom and how this had really gotten to him in a way that no one remembered seeing since all those years ago when he and Allie had lost the baby.

Now the priest's head pulsed and surged with too many thoughts. A bit of panic passed through him, and he willed himself to stay with the liturgy even as he pictured himself losing his grip and simply wandering away—physically stepping from the chancel and walking, his white funereal garments flowing, out one of the side doors and into the blast and gloom of the hard weather. But he kept to the Mass. Yes, it was a physical strain that drew his flesh tight and pressed a deep pain across his shoulders. The casket, looming large before him; his father's boat, gone finally from the light of day; his sister; Sarafino—Sarafino hanging from his heart like a stone. A carillon of small bells sounded in his ears. He looked over at his altar servers, Joey and Freddy, Katherine Avellar, Gerald. The sounds were only in his head. The homily, reflecting on the risen Christ, nearly refused to come forth from his throat.

The wind and the rain remained fierce throughout the service, and when the Mass ended, the casket was carried into the long white hearse, which had backed up to the rear doors of the church, and then shuttled the few hundred yards around the edge of the grounds and up to the parish hall.

Hortensia Boia and Jesse Cabral and the priest had agreed beforehand that the committal would be performed there if the weather made it impossible to hold the rite in the cemetery. Hortensia had made it clear that waiting was not an option. Furtado moved through the rite with this smaller group but noted almost nothing about it in the ledgers. Yet he was oddly seized by something about the day and its weather just as soon as he walked out into the downpour and ran to the breezeway of the church.

He stood in the breezeway's opening and watched the men and women and kids hunching in a half run to their trucks and cars, and he watched as they pulled away from the church and disappeared, with their shining taillights and slapping windshield wipers, eastward across the parking lot or westerly out the bottom of the hill. Then there was only the noise of the heavy rain battering the buildings and the grounds. He stood just inches inside the open doorway and witnessed the way the wind drove the raindrops into their brassy tattoo and how the downspouts sputtered and gurgled. He watched the roil and spatter of the black puddles, the runoffs, the sudden rills, and in that moment he heard clearly how each separate thing registered its own report when struck by the drops—clapboard and shingle and car hood and bare tree and green tree, the asphalt and cement and brick, the tympani of the window glass. All at once. And there was in him a recognition of what peace—true peace—might possibly feel like. Just that recognition. Nothing more. That small thing stayed with him for the moments it took for Jesse Cabral and his assistant, Arthur Lopes, to drive off in the hearse with the body. He didn't move until that long white-and-chrome machine slid away like a yacht in the slanting rain.

"Everybody liked that boy," Sarafino said. "You can tell from the crowd. I would call it a multitude." He and Mariah Grey were sitting in the parlor window when the priest walked back into the rectory. The priest's hair was damp and flattened against his head. The lamplight in the room shined warm and serene, and the rain seemed to beat on the window glass all the more darkly and coldly for it. The heating elements along the baseboard ticked, and the gauzy curtains moved slightly with the heat, but Mariah and Sarafino were nevertheless huddled in coats in the straight-backed chairs that Mariah had pulled in from the kitchen for the sole purpose of watching the mourners come and go from the church. "We watched them all trying to get in the door," Sarafino said, and coughed and sighed. "It's too bad about this rain."

"Sarafino wanted to go into the church, but then he decided it wasn't such a good idea," Mariah said.

"She pointed out that I am a known fugitive," Sarafino said. "I should be down at the Wheelhouse with all that gang. I would go, too, if I was feeling better."

"And what about that other little problem, dear?" Mariah said.

"There's the law, and then there's the law," Sarafino said. Then he coughed and said, "I'm only talking here."

"I know it," said Mariah.

Sarafino, without leaving his chair, seemed to slump away from them now. Mariah and the priest looked at each other quickly and in so doing told each other that they saw the illness there in all its gravity. Sarafino rubbed the back of his hand across his lips and stared out the window, but he didn't say anything else, either.

THERE WAS A SMALL GATHERING AT HORTENSIA BOIA'S HOUSE. IT WAS not a wake. But her friends had come to be with her, some scattered neighbors who were still left from the old days, a few of the other mothers of fishermen, some of the *velhas* of the West End, and two or three of the younger wives and girlfriends stopping by on their way to the Wheelhouse. Umbrellas lay in the bathroom tub, and wet parkas and raincoats were draped over the backs of chairs. The rain drummed behind the women's voices. Platters of food were set out on the kitchen table; smaller dishes sat here and there in the parlor. A Crock-Pot of kale soup sat on the counter next to the stove, along with a black-speckled roasting pan full of *carne de molho*, and there were *favas* in peppers and garlic, and boiled *castenhas*, *queijo malasadas* and *bolos de folha*, a great porcelain bowl of *pudim d'arroz doce*, slices of *massa sovada*, and an urn of dark coffee. Because Frankie's body had been in the ocean for a day, nothing that came from the sea was served, nor would any of the townspeople eat any fish until a week had passed, though nothing was said about this.

Someone had lugged a two-foot plaster statue of Saint Peter, patron of fishermen, up the stairs. He stood on Mrs. Boia's scarred coffee table in a brown painted robe, with a ruddy cast to his face and the plaster-filigreed curls of his beard painted henna red. Save for a single votive at the foot of the statue, no candles burned; the house smelled of the food and the coffee and the strong, tinny floral perfumes of the women. Furtado talked with Hortensia. He told her that Frankie was with God now, and Hortensia said, "Well, Manny, wasn't he supposed to be with God when he was alive and here with me, too?" The priest told her that help with practical things would come soon, but he did not linger. Catalina Pires, wearing now a sober black waistless dress but still with the blue combs holding her hair back, offered him a plate of food, but Furtado was not hungry. He excused himself, went to Hortensia and clasped her hands, and told her he had more business about the funeral waiting for him; then he slipped through the rooms and down the stairs and out into the weather.

The Wheelhouse, by the time he got there, was packed and loud, the way it usually was on a Saturday night in summer or back in the old days when the fishermen would crowd in for beers on their way home from the wharves. Everyone was holding a drink or a bottle of beer. People at the bar or the long plank tables sat with plates of food in front of them. Furtado did not make his way through the crowd but kept to the front of the bar, near the door. He shook some hands, he smiled, he said hellos, but any kind of talk was impossible because of the noise of people shouting above Brabo Perreira's famous jukebox, which was banging out rock and roll, all of Frankie's favorites. A huge pickle jar sat on the end of the bar with a white paper sign taped to it: FRANKIE'S MOTHER. It was stuffed with bills—tens, twenties, ones. The priest didn't stay much longer than fifteen minutes, and he didn't have a drink, even though Brabo, serious and moon-faced, pushed a long-necked Budweiser across the bar at him.

There were more phone messages when he got back to the rectory, and a few little notes from Mariah stuck to his desk, most of them responses to his own earlier calls. He glanced at them, but he didn't touch them. He saw that John Sweet had called and left a message asking for him to call back, but he wasn't about to do that anytime soon. He listened to Emeril Cordeiro's voice on the speakerphone saying something about salvage, saying he couldn't reach Tommy at home. There had been some talk about raising the boat, but no one took it seriously. Tom had made it clear there was no reason to. It was finished. And under eighty feet of water. Well, it wasn't worth it, not even for the hardware, and Furtado had nothing to do with any of that anyway. The Coast Guard had talked to Tom and to the men on the *Minha Prada* about the explosion and fire, and the best explanation they could come up with was fumes in the bilge. Frankie had gone below to light the propane stove for hot coffee. That's when it had happened. Not unheard of, fumes traveling along the bilge. Of course, they had been doing a lot of repairs here and there. That old boat. Something might have not gone right. It didn't matter much now—it was indeed over. They were left with the facts: The *Ilha do Pico* lay on the ocean floor, and Frankie had died.

Night had somehow fallen, though the priest hadn't noticed when. Mariah had checked Sarafino before she went off—to go by Mrs. Boia's, she said, and then home to Winslow. The rain had not relented. It pounded against the roof and shingles, at times building to a pitch that seemed wild enough to beat the ancient rectory to pieces. Furtado kept the parlor lights shining, as though he himself were in some kind of ship, and he crowded the baseboard heaters to take the dampness and ache from his joints.

When he first looked in on Sarafino, he was still resting as Mariah had left him: perhaps sleeping, on his side, propped crabwise upon the pillows, the oxygen running, the rosary in his clasped hands, which lay atop the quilt that covered him. But when Furtado checked on him again, he was awake. The priest went to his bedside and touched his forehead and got him to take his medications and a little food. "I'm all in, Manny," he said. Furtado could see that—and feel it. Sarafino's head was warm with fever, though he huddled under the bedclothes.

"Do you ache?" Furtado asked.

"Yes. Way inside, too."

"Those pills will make you feel better. The doctor is going to come again. He will make you more comfortable."

"Okay.

"It's cold out. It's a real blow."

Sarafino didn't seem to hear him. He shuddered. "Oh, Manny," he said. "Don't leave me alone."

"I won't," said the priest. "That medicine will kick in soon. It will be better."

Sarafino's eyes shone wet, and the stain in them seemed darker for it. He didn't answer the priest except for a small sound he made, a sigh or a groan from down in his chest. Furtado lay gently on the bed beside him, on his back, with the whole long side of him touching the length of Sarafino's covered body, and he began to talk softly to him, telling him stories, jumping randomly from here to there. He did not talk about Frankie Boia. He did not bring up the risen Statue of the Virgin. It came to him, while he murmured various indiscriminate things—names and myths of the constellations that he could remember, the twelve Caesars and scraps of their lurid stories from his reading the Latin, cartoons they'd watched together as kids on winter Saturday mornings, the big, boxy black-and-white TV in the Furtado house, orange soda and cheese crackers—that underneath that droning for the comfort of Sarafino, this sickness would continue to get worse, and Furtado might not be able to hold anything together. Everything might collapse, and Furtado himself might fall to pieces, and with him everything would tumble down.

Yes, he felt himself falling apart, and he felt himself remaining intact only through some exercise of will. But what he held together did not seem to be a self, exactly. It was just a something. It was just a something that stood for something else, and the person who had ever been underneath all that had become lost in a jumble.

He tried to recall that pure moment in the rain, so few hours before, when he'd felt the possibility of every burden lifting from him, but he only remembered that something of that order had happened. To enter the feeling again was somehow forbidden by an unknowable and complex set of laws. Who wouldn't live in bliss continually if it were simply a matter of summoning it? The priest talked softly into the empty air above the bed, passing maybe an hour like that, and then he fell quiet and heard that Sarafino's breathing had changed and understood that he had fallen asleep.

Then Furtado made his way up the stairs with his tumbler of ice—ice even in that wintry, rainy night—and set it on the desk and then knelt at the *prie-deux*. The rain peppered the shingles above his head, a sharper, more distinct sound up there in the study, and a dampness crept in, an ambient chill, even though tufts of heat ascended from the downstairs registers. He would be silent about the nature of his prayer that night, but when the ache in his neck and shoulder became more than he was willing to bear, he went to the desk and swallowed several of the pills along with the cold gin, and he wrote in the ledger—wrote here in odd blocky letters, something that took time, drawing them, almost, each one bold and decorated with the broad lines of the pen. From Augustine again: *Is not the fact simply this, that I deceive myself and in your presence fail to be truthful in heart and tongue? Put this madness far from me, Lord, lest my own mouth be to me the sinner's oil to make fat my head.*

When he began to write after that, the words streamed out of him, a long, meandering account of the day, some of it illegible, but with the usual minute detail, a heavy hand leaning forward, rolling ahead. The pain in his joints had waned and his body had already begun its gentle illusion of hovering when he heard the rapping on the wall. It was a rapping, not the rain—he was clear on this. It was different—not something wild and arbitrary out of the sky, but Sarafino rapping, signaling what?

What now?

The priest made his way down the stairs and looked into Sarafino's room. The small nightlight cast something weaker than a candle's glow but sufficient to show Sarafino in bed under the quilts. He lay peacefully enough. He breathed in his insistent, shallow rhythm.

But then the knock came again. The priest turned toward it, and his body seemed to drift on a warm current of air. Warmer here downstairs. There was a pleasure in it, the heaters making their whisper under the storm, and all his flesh and bones alight. But something was wrong. The sound came from the kitchen, from the back door. He looked at the clock as he passed toward the door. It was one-forty in the morning. He turned on the outside light and peered through the heavy glass. Tommy da Silva stood there, soaking wet, hunched in the rain.

Furtado pulled him inside. "Is something wrong?" he asked. His head swam a little. That bell again. Or beep. "Is it Allie? Is anything wrong with Allie?" But why should something be wrong with Allie? He felt the hum of his liquor and tablets—a tilt to it all now. Tom in the middle of the night.

The Earth spinning a little differently. He put a hand out and touched the kitchen counter. The counter was steady and firm. "What is it?"

"I saw your light upstairs. I don't know what." Tom was hatless and his curls were plastered to his head, and little tears of rainwater glistened in the kitchen's light and made their sinuous way down his forehead and temples.

The priest took him into the kitchen and sat him at the table. He was aware that he moved with too much deliberation. He commanded himself to be present. The numbness in his lips. A pill too many, perhaps. He regarded Tom. Tom had been drinking. There was a flush in his face, something deeper than chill from the wind and rain, and his skin sagged. A chemical weariness in the vessels and cells.

"You must have been down at the Wheelhouse this whole time," Furtado said.

"A long time. Yes and no. I been out walking."

It took Furtado a moment to respond, to pull himself into the room. For it was almost two in the morning and Tommy da Silva was in the rectory kitchen, come in out of the night and the rain. Furtado had no idea of where this was going. "I want you to have some hot coffee," he said finally. "You are cold. I want you to drink some coffee."

"All right."

"Give me your parka. You're dripping. You're wet." Furtado took Tom's jacket and hung it on a peg by the door, then took a canister down from the shelf over the counter and spooned grounds into the paper filter of the coffeemaker and filled it with water. He concentrated on his motions, and everything seemed to take a very long time, but he could not help this. "We have to speak quietly," he said.

"Right," said Tom. "Sarafino Pomba. I know."

Furtado studied him. "It's bad about Frankie," he said. "I think maybe that's why you're here."

"It's bad," Tom said.

The priest backed himself against the counter, just to feel it again. He leaned his back into its edge. *This is what an anchor is like*, he thought. *Like an anchor for a little boat when the wind is blowing.* The coffeemaker hissed and burbled, and Furtado poured out two big mugs. Steam curled up from them as he brought them carefully to the table and set them down, and thickened the coffee with evaporated milk and sugar. Furtado sat down, and they held their mugs and blew the steam and sipped. Neither man spoke. The rain continued to pound. Tommy reached up and with the heel of his hand wiped away the streams of water that trickled from his hair. The priest tried to see into him, to read something about him. "Did Alzaida throw you out again?" he asked finally, coming up with nothing else.

"It's not like that," Tom said.

"I needed to ask," said the priest. "It's Frankie, then. Except for his mother, there was nobody closer to Frankie than you."

"It was that boat, Manny. It's bad. Very bad."

The kitchen's ceiling light glared down on them. Little floaters, little fragments of darkness, roamed the priest's eyes. But Furtado knew what to say. "The boat was hard. You tried to keep it going. You had a lot of pressure on you. Nobody can deny that. But you know enough not to blame yourself for anything. You survived and Frankie did not. That is hard."

"You don't know the half of it, Manny."

"Frankie is at peace," Furtado said. "You haven't done anything wrong. You stayed in the water, and you would have saved him if you could. You were a good friend." He hesitated. "You are a brave man."

"You don't know the half of it," Tom repeated.

Furtado closed his eyes for a moment, and the room took a pleasant turn in the darkness inside his head. He half expected Tom to look clearer to him when he opened his eyes, but when he did Tom was the same, crumpled, something out of focus about him, as though Furtado were looking at him through a steamed glass. He couldn't remember exactly how many of the tablets he had taken, but knew he had finished the tumbler of gin, and there was no pain anywhere in his body. He pressed his lips together and felt the pleasure of their numbness. He took care to speak clearly. "You walked up here out of that storm, Tommy, so I think you want to tell me something. But you've had some drinks."

"I saw the light up in your window. I wouldn't have come to the door if I didn't see the light up there," Tom said. "What I have to tell you, some other time I might not say it."

"All right."

Tom cradled the mug in both hands, as if to warm them. The priest saw the waxy marks of his burns, reddish white, little pools of smooth skin running back along the tops of his wrists and disappearing under his shirt cuffs.

"I am just explaining something here," said Tom, "so you can get where it all came from."

The priest nodded and waited.

"It's not like when your old man had the boat. Now everybody comes here from someplace else, and then they start telling us what to do. What you can do and what you can't. Who the hell do they think they are? If there's a house or a wharf or something, it's because somebody busted their ass fishing and made it. All the way back. And now you can't turn around anymore. You can't say 'boo.' I got to call up and ask permission to fish. Then they tell me where I can go. They tell me how much I can keep. Who are these people?"

The priest had heard all this before, but he kept quiet and nodded again.

"These people from away, don't kid yourself, Manny—they hate us. They would put us in ovens just to get rid of us, because, you see, we're dirty to them. And we are just in their way. We are like the ignorant savages. They love the town we built because it looks like a picture in a magazine or something. That's what they say, but they hate us. They laugh at us. And then they say we are the ones that hate them. You see? I know you don't like to listen to this."

"This isn't why you came up here, though, Tom. This isn't what you want to tell me."

"It gets there, Manny. It is and it isn't. I took over that boat, Manny, and it's not like the old days when your old man had it and he was the big dog. I busted my ass, and I don't have nothing to show for it. The whale-hugger boats make a better living. But Allie." Tom held up his hands. "I don't mean any disrespect to her. But she doesn't get it. It's all like, oh, we never should have sold the house, and then we have to keep her papa's boat going. But it was always on me. That boat—no disrespect—that boat was falling apart."

"Nobody blames you, Tommy," Furtado said. He no longer wanted him there at his table. He never did. It was an interruption. An imposition. And now he was weary of it. But he got up and poured some more coffee for Tommy and then sat down to listen some more.

"Words were spoken, Manny. Things were said. Allie and me. We had the worst fight I ever had in my life. This guy Sarafino comes into it. The boat comes into it. Allie was saying that we were going to take this guy into our house because he is sick with the AIDS and the cops are after him. I couldn't see it. But things got out of hand. Things were said, Manny. Things were said."

"Do you want to tell me what you said?"

"What I said, I don't care. What she said, no I don't. But that's when we got all crazy. I got loaded after that. Me and Frankie both. We went on a run. Drinking and other things. In my mind I kept getting more pissed. About everything. I kept getting crazy. Do you see? Do you follow me?"

"I do," said the priest. "I do, Tommy. I can see that you were mad and loaded and you went out fishing, and you think maybe you were careless and you caused the accident."

"There was pressure, Manny. It was all built up."

"I get it."

"No," Tom said. "No, you don't." He shook his head slowly. His eyes glassed over and tears welled in them.

"What, then?"

"What I came to say, Manny: It *wasn't* an accident. It's all on me. I wasn't thinking straight. I killed Frankie."

fifteen

THE HEATING REGISTER TICKED FAINTLY UNDER THE BANGING OF the rain. The priest turned slowly in its direction to make sure that was what he was hearing. Then he turned back and looked at Tom. "You must be cold," he said. "You must be freezing." He got Tom a small, thick towel, and Tom ran it over his face and head and laid it on the table beside his elbow. Furtado filled Tom's mug yet again with hot coffee. Then he sat back down at the table himself, folded his hands in front of him, and said, "You'd better go ahead and tell me now."

"He was supposed to light the galley stove," Tommy said. "I came up with the idea. We were doing some coke and drinking. A lot, I mean. I'm not laying it off to that, you understand. My head was all black inside. I was too pissed off for my own good. It was my fault. On me. Pissed for years, if you want to know. Allie tells me that, and I give her that. She's right.

"You see, I came up with this idea to scuttle the boat. It seemed like such a good idea. Once I got hold of it, I could feel it. I could feel that boat gone from off my back. Like everything would go with it. He was supposed to light the galley stove, Frankie. Then he was supposed to open one of those small propane tanks and haul ass up to the wheelhouse. This was my plan, you see. When the propane filled up the galley and hit the lit stove, it was supposed to blow and catch fire. We would have been aft, in the wheelhouse, then. The idea being, Manny, that we would just step off her while she burned and went down slow. You see, I knew we'd have a line of boats going out. We would have got picked up. Right like that."

"And something happened," the priest said when Tom paused. "You didn't intend it, but something happened."

"I don't know what happened, Manny. I swear to God, I don't know. Except that Frankie blew himself up. I just wanted to scuttle the boat. I never should have let that idea take over my head. But it did. It felt so good to think it. I never imagined anything could go bad like that."

"Tommy, this is *very* bad." The priest leaned toward him. He could smell the florid alcohol, the cigarettes, the coffee on Tom's breath, and it satisfied something in him. "In your defense, though, you did not murder Frankie," he said. "You didn't harm him on purpose. With malice. That's right, isn't it?"

Tom shook his head. "Don't."

"I'm not saying it's not bad."

"You have to ask yourself. I could have gone down and done the stove. I put that off on Frankie. I told him to go below and rig it up."

"I don't know the law, Tommy, but this is serious. They have names for things like this."

"There wasn't insurance. It wasn't like that. We weren't going to get anything out of it."

"You were sailing without insurance?"

Tom shook his head. "I can't get into all that, Manny. It's Frankie I have to talk about here. I don't know what to do."

They fell silent for a while. The wind outside slammed the walls with uneven gusts, and the heavy rain fell against the rectory in waves. The silence between the men extended, and after a while it was as though they might be on a bus or train traveling somewhere, two strangers, talked out after exchanging some usual pleasantries. But the priest was absorbed. He let Tom's story circle and circle in his mind. Then he said, "Tommy, there's something about all that you said. All that about fishing and the town changing. That's not why you did this. That's all fog and wind."

"What are you saying, Manny?"

"What happened between you and Allie. All that other stuff is bullshit. You wanted to get back at Allie. You were striking at Allie."

"What difference does it make?"

"All that other stuff, maybe that's really true for you. But you have to look at this thing square. The boat. Allie. You won't get better unless you do."

"Get better? This is not going away."

"No," said Furtado. He was the priest now. "But you have to claim yourself back from it."

"If you tried to give me forgiveness—I mean, official . . . I don't think that would work."

"No. It won't."

"I don't know what to do."

Furtado grew quiet again, and Tom watched him now, eyes flicking over the priest, looking for some clue in his face. But Furtado said only, "It's late, and I've been up working. Neither one of us is at our best here. I will think about this in the light of day. We are going to come up with something."

"I'm not going to the Coast Guard or the police," Tom said. "I'm not going that route. It doesn't solve anything."

The rain kept up its drumming. The two men sat at the table, nailed together. The rain was likely why neither of them heard Sarafino Pomba shuffling down the hall in his stocking feet and sweat clothes. He leaned the shambles of his body through the doorway and slid ghostlike into the kitchen. "You should have stove that hull in with a maul or a fire ax. That's how I would have done it—just let it leak slow. It's too bad about that boy. I never knew him, really."

Tom stiffened in his chair. He took Sarafino in. He looked him up and down. His eyes hardened. Something dreadful and violent, a coldness, came into them. The priest could see it. Then it passed. Then it was misery again.

"You don't know shit," Tom said.

"You been in the bucket?" Sarafino asked.

"What are you saying?"

"Jail."

"No. Not really."

"Well, what's the tattoos on your knuckles? They don't look store-bought."

Tom looked over at the priest.

"Sarafino, you shouldn't be up wandering around," Furtado said.

"Cain would be a wanderer on the earth," he said. He started to say something more, but then he began coughing. First a shallow, dry cough up in his throat, but then from someplace deeper. Suddenly he was in spasms, wracked by them. The priest jumped to his feet and moved to his side to hold him, for he would have toppled otherwise, while he heaved and wheezed. After some time, Sarafino got his breath back. He leaned against the priest. Furtado took his weight and walked him over to the table and sat him down.

"Yeah, well, that don't sound so good," Tom said flatly. He looked at Sarafino as though he were looking at a dead bird. He was studying him.

"It does smart," Sarafino said. He spoke in the same tone in which Tom did: declaring a fact.

"You were Manny's friend. I never really knew you," said Tom.

"I would've sunk that boat a whole different way. I can tell you that."

"You sound out of your head to me," Tom said. "None of this would have happened without you here."

"It's all just too bad," said Sarafino.

"You've got all that AIDS in your brain," Tom said. "That's what's too bad."

"Enough," said Furtado. "This is over. All this conversation is over now. Sarafino, I want to get you your medicine and get you back with the oxygen." He looked at Tom. "Tommy, you come tomorrow. We aren't done yet. Do you agree?"

"I do, Manny."

"Can you drive?"

"The truck, I left it down by the bar. I'll walk there. I'm good."

"No hard feelings," Sarafino said.

Tom took his parka down from the peg and pulled it on. He did not look at Sarafino. "I'll call you in the morning, Manny," he said, and opened the glass storm door and walked back out into the rain.

sixteen

AFTERMATH. FIRST DAWNING. THE CLOUD COVER BREAKING UP and a fresh wind, strident from the northeast, blowing the remnants of the front away. The earth, the streets, the sodden trees, the buildings all shone with an unusual glister and clarity. Father Furtado paced the grounds and assayed what the storm had left to clean up. Mostly branches down, and leaves. One shutter on the rectory hung lopsided. Nothing much amiss with the old structures, but when things dried out there would be sweeping and shoveling to do in the parking lot, where runoff from the north embankment had fanned yards of sand across the asphalt, and where deep puddles of standing water still gleamed, cold and black. By the time Tom showed up, later in the morning, Furtado had already mapped out a plan for him.

They sat in the downstairs office, the priest behind the now cluttered mahogany desk and Tom in a straight chair before him. Furtado began to explain confession. How in the beginning, in the early Church, confession was rare and public. And how communion was something that happened after a long period of public work and penance. He talked about how the misery Tom felt was sorrow for Frankie and his mother, but also grief for himself. Communion would be literal, as it was in the primitive Church. It would be to rejoin the community—to come back into common goodness. To not be separated by his transgression. Mass, sacraments, would be up to Tom himself. But he would be at the church every day. He would work there. He would sit quietly in the church for a part of each day. He could pray if he wished, but he had to spend that time sitting before the altar in the hush and stillness of the building. He had to follow his thoughts, wherever they might take him. Also, he would visit Frankie's mother. He would take care of her needs, run her errands, sit and talk with her, do her odd jobs. Eventually he would find his way to healing. They would decide together when his communion was complete. Tom sat in silence. His eyes were tired and glazed, and the priest did not let himself carry on. Furtado did not mention anything about Tom's going to the authorities. He let that option simply hover as a force behind the one he presented.

There was the money, too, he told Tom, which Tom and Allie would need through the winter. No one would look askance at Tom's helping at the church now. Of course, Tom's working at the church was same proposal that Furtado had offered to him when the priest had gone down to the boat. That this whole plan was reckless and self-serving occurred to the priest only once, for an instant. He dismissed the thought. He needed Tom. Lines had been crossed. All the territories before him were new now.

It was a Tuesday, on the Feast of Saint Clement, when Furtado next saw Father John Sweet. He had managed to keep Sweet away for what seemed like an age, marked by the great divide of the disaster of the *Ilha do Pico*, but it had actually been only a little more than two weeks.

By then, Tom had fallen into a routine of steady, competent work. Furtado had not known what to expect, but thus far Tom seemed to transfer the attention he had paid to the old boat to the church and its grounds. He spent the days there—not the half days of Mr. Horta, as Tom and Furtado had agreed, but whole, long days—cleaning and patching and painting. He attended to detail. He oil-soaped the old hardwood pews and then oiled and buffed them smooth with a fleece disk attached to an electric drill. He rooted leaves from the downspouts and anchored the shutters with heavy screws. He replaced blown-out shingles. He showed up one day with a contraption in the back of his white pickup—something that he had borrowed from someplace in town, a lawnmower- or snowblower-looking thing with a big, stiff roller brush in the front. It was noisy and efficient, and Tom swept the washed-down sand off the parking lot's aged blacktop in a matter of hours. He got things done. In just those two weeks, Furtado saw how much Mr. Horta had left unfinished.

And every day Tom lit a votive candle in the church and sat in the front pew in outward silence, staring at the altar, bearing up impassively under whatever thoughts may have drifted or stormed through his head. The priest did not abjure him to pray, nor did he tell him what manner of things he should or should not hold in his head, but when Furtado looked in on him furtively from time to time, he saw at least that Tom—active, kinetic, unreflective—was quiet, still, inward-looking . . . perhaps. Furtado fancied that God would come to him somehow, for he believed there was in Tom, despite his crimes, a kind of innocence that had left the priest's own soul long ago. He fancied that God might even insinuate Himself into Tom's consciousness with a greater stridency than was available to Furtado, and he watched Tom sometimes with an intimation approaching envy.

On the day before Sweet was to come, Tom crawled up into the rectory attic, something that the priest had put on his list of deferred maintenance—the drooping insulation, the old squirrel nests, the needed patching of the eave screens. But when Tom climbed down from the stepladder, he had other news. "Manny," he said, "the wiring, it's all chewed up. You've got exposed conduit up there, and it's old. They don't even make stuff like that anymore. That's got to come out quick. It's only a matter of time before something catches." The next day, he showed up with several tight spools of new, thickly insulated electrical wire, took the power down, and started pulling out the old, frayed conduit.

"Look here," he said. He showed Furtado a length of the stuff, dirty, stiff, and black. "Chewed. I don't know why you don't have little bodies up there all zapped. We've gotta cut the squirrels back, too. They'll get in again sooner or later."

"Where did you get the wire?"

"Joey Alves," Tom said. "He was working on those condos down the West End—the ones they put up in the old blueberry woods. The really ugly ones. This was just some leftover stuff he let me have."

"As long as it was leftover," said the priest.

"I won't have the power down for more than two or three hours," Tom said. "I'm running the storm generator for the downstairs—for the kitchen circuit and your office and Sarafino's room, but it's all shut off upstairs."

Mariah Grey was working in the office when John Sweet arrived, and Allie was cooking up a soup at the kitchen stove. Tom was thumping loudly in the attic, tools lay about in the downstairs hallway, and wire trailed up the stairway. A series of drop cloths, like stepping-stones, gathered the gritty and dusty footprints from the hall stairs to the back door. There was not truly a great amount of commotion, but the priest took the busyness as an opportunity to get Sweet away from the rectory and away from Sarafino, who was lying, quietly for the moment, among all the tubes and medicines behind the closed door of his little room. "We'll go over to the hall," Furtado said to Sweet.

By then the sky was a burnished deep-blue. A breeze blew lightly from the west and a chill rode in it, something good to breathe in deeply and to feel against the skin. The light was achingly bright at first, and when the two priests walked around to the back of the parish hall and entered the kitchen, Furtado saw that the relative gloom of that space would not be helpful. It was Sweet, though, who suggested a walk. In spite of himself, Furtado glanced down at the orthopedic shoe. John Sweet caught his look. His face widened into an unkindly grin, and he stamped his foot against the floor. Then he laughed.

Furtado darted back into the rectory and changed into some walking clothes. Soon they were headed up the state road at a wandering pace, Sweet rolling mildly as he walked, in a practiced movement: easeful, yet with something mechanical in it. He wore a stiff, high-crowned ball cap and big teardrop sunglasses. If his round eyes rolled, Furtado could not see them behind their shine.

They were silent for some minutes before Sweet brought up the boat. They talked about the sinking and Frankie Boia's death, and Furtado explained to him the magnitude of such a thing. In the old days, when the crews were larger, such disasters had been even more tragic, and each one had left a mark on the town. There were always deaths and sickness, but a boat going down took on a special significance. Furtado tried to be precise, but he felt the explanations slipping from him. Sweet paid him a peculiar and oddly rapt attention, though. He could feel it, and he did not like it.

"I'm making a study of the town," Sweet interrupted suddenly. "It's a unique place. It's a place all unto itself. I intend to understand it better."

"Really, John? You're sure you're not just investigating me some more?"

Furtado waited for Sweet to speak again, but when he didn't, he said, "It is becoming less unique, the town. Can you use words that way? Less of what it was, I mean. Now it's becoming much like everything else in the modern world."

"Surely you don't believe that," Sweet said.

"I half believe it, then," Furtado said, annoyed. He tried to change tack. "You like coming here," he said. "That's why you wanted to walk."

They were heading now to the state beach, walking up the slow rise of the road, keeping to the soft shoulder, which gave onto a berm of russet earth and dense, small pines to the north. To the south, between low hills and bracken, they would catch glimpses of the long, black-shining fens that stretched west of Caldeira's pond. Furtado kept them walking. They wouldn't halt or turn back now. Soon they would be at the ocean. Without breaking their progress, Sweet pulled back and regarded Furtado. "You look fit, Manny," he said. He waited a beat. "But . . . tired."

"I'm all right," Furtado said. "I've been all right. I'm happy that you're here to check in and carry that news of my fitness back to Calumet," he said dryly.

"I work for God, Manny," Sweet said. He stopped now and motioned with his hand. The gesture swept across the road and the enclosing woodlands, the lower reaches of the sky. "Look at this. Splendid. To think—this is part of your life forever. If something were to happen, you would never lose it. It would be inside of you. I understand these things. No matter what, you would really have all this forever. It can't be taken from you. This isn't the truth for everyone."

Furtado said nothing. He turned and looked briefly into the woods. What could John Sweet see in them? He could not see the hidden ponds, the erstwhile burial place of Our Lady of Fatima. The two of them could never look at anything here and see the same thing. Sweet seemed completely alien to him now, but there was safety in that.

The Virgin and Sarafino waited, but he pushed them from his mind now. There was a pleasant low note sounding in his ear, underneath the fresh resonance of the day, the wind, their soft footfalls on the sand shoulder of the road. He put his hands in his pockets and continued walking. Just ahead, some broken glass dazzled in the sun, a splay of crystal among the brown shreds of winter grass.

"You are my work, Manny," John Sweet said. "I don't forget that. You shouldn't either."

"I made mistakes," Furtado said, "and my housekeeper—well, old Mrs. Horta just had too much on her shoulders. It was an unfortunate misunderstanding. That's the best interpretation I can put on it." He felt himself flare, but he held back and said, as mildly as he could, "I know you have obligations, John, and I accept my part in them. We've covered all that ground, have we not?" Such effort it took, this agony with Father Sweet. It was nearly a ravishment, this strain to be present.

"Your medication, Manny, this medical condition you have . . . how does that go?"

"The old injury? It's fine. I use a little something from time to time. Not often. I have exercises."

"You're saying no problems there?"

"No," said Furtado. "None."

Sweet nodded and was quiet for a moment. A small alarm then for Furtado. A tiny warning light flickering. Maybe imagined. What could Sweet know? It flicked out of view when Sweet went on. "Not a drink, Manny? Doing well?"

"I have to say, John, a little nightcap sometimes."

"Dangerous," said Sweet.

"Worse the other way," said Furtado. "It becomes too large in my mind. I pray. I work. I work within my limits. I'm very well."

"You're a good walker," said Sweet.

That vague panic just brushed Furtado again. He passed it off. Too much. Too much on his plate. He wanted Sweet to go away, but he saw that it would not be up to him. No answer for that in the world yet. But now the breeze was sugared with pine pitch and bayberry, and behind that the rich salt of the ocean. The needles on the scrub pines flashed green and black and blue in the clean sunlight. He took solace from these things. A car rolled past them as they walked along the shoulder, an old green Ford, some kind of four-wheeler, with two town men in it. He knew them by sight, but neither attended church and no one waved.

Sweet pushed ahead in the conversation. Furtado recognized he was following an agenda, ticking items off a list. He brought up the proposal. He'd had an ear in Chancery matters lately, he was saying. He knew some of the men there. Things would go well with Fatima's debt. "Only you could pull it together the way you did, Manny," he said. "The native son."

They were coming to the road's end now, a few more yards into the terminus of the beach parking lot. The lot was empty, and the ticket booth at its entrance was boarded up for the season. Furtado kept walking, choosing the direction, Sweet at his side. The two priests veered right, onto the small road that fronted the beach, where they stepped off the asphalt and down onto the coarse sand. Furtado's legs sang out quietly from the walking and his sinking heels, but the ocean was shining like foil and heaving with a lazy swell that collapsed against the beach in long curls. A cadence. *Crush. Crush.* The breeze came more boldly here and the light fell in sharp pangs, magnifying itself as it came off the water and heightening the relief of the land, the long shore curving gently away from them.

They walked to the water's edge. A ribbon of polished stones rolled and gleamed and clacked in the wash of the waves: quartz, porphyry, granite, shale, and other speckled minerals whose names he had forgotten or never known. Perhaps because Sweet had brought up the injury, perhaps for no reason at all, Furtado bent and picked up a small flat stone and sidearmed it out into the water. It skipped across the surface four or five times before it sank.

"Now you, Sweet," he said. The younger priest bent stiffly and picked a stone and threw. It plopped into the water with a sharp *clunk*.

"Like this," Furtado said, and skipped another, though he felt a tiny wire of pain in a bone somewhere. Sweet tried again. The stone sailed out and disappeared into a wave. "Hours," said Furtado. "Hours and hours as little boys. It's one of the things we did here in those days."

Sweet held another stone in his hand, hesitated, and then tossed it pointedly, backhanding it into the water. "What are you trying to say to me?" he asked, with an unsettling timbre of emotion in his voice that came through to Furtado even over the slap of the waves. He was not sure how to respond, so he said nothing, but then he was quiet for too long and realized that he was simply staring. Sweet stood out like a cardboard photograph against that background of color and light.

"What is it, Manny? In your heart, what is trying to come out of you?" John Sweet asked. "Why have you brought me here? And what am I to make of you? When you look into me, what do you see?"

Still, Furtado would not respond.

"I don't care about saving you," said Sweet. "Don't worry too much about that. You can't imagine the wrecks I dive into. I've told you before, Manny, you are not the worst of it. You are right, maybe, to evade me. You are remote. You are shielded. Perhaps you think you don't belong with me, that I am something foisted on you by a malice—that was your word for it. That woman's telephone calls let loose a malice on the world, something that couldn't be taken back, and I am the result of that. Maybe you feel like a victim and that you must protect yourself. But you are not all right, Manny. I don't mean that you are shattered or broken, not like many I've seen. You don't have a true agony in your soul. I don't think so. But you know what's there, Manny. God knows what's there. And it has to come out into the light."

"You aren't failing," Furtado said. He didn't know what else to say. He looked at Sweet. The formidable Father John Sweet. He was a boy, really. The wind seemed to whistle through him.

"It's not a question of failing," he said. "I'll tell you something, Manny: Everything grows outward from the darkness of our hearts. There is not some evil spirit afoot in the world. There is no adversary. Buildings tumble. Children are run down crossing the street. Lives are smashed. But it all starts here and no place else." He pounded his chest with the flat of his hand. "And then there are pieces to sweep up. There is damage. And things can go so awfully wrong with priests. We are always in jeopardy. It's part of what makes us different. These forces are what call us to God. Can you see this? That's my job. If a parish is failing, that's always what's at the bottom of it. I see it, Manny. I'm not saying that for your benefit. Your church is challenged, but it's coming along. I respect that you do that with everything else you must contend with. But I am going to admit something to you: I am tired. I am weary, too. When you talked to me about how one time you contemplated leaving the Church, I was silent about something—I was silent about myself. I have thought about it, too, Manny: I don't know how long I can bear this cross."

Sweet stopped. Something traversed his mind. He visibly gathered himself. He raised his palms. A surrender. "I'm sorry," he said.

"Please," said Furtado. "If I am making things difficult for you . . ."

"I thought I would be building a school by now," Sweet said. "That I'd have a parish and I would coach soccer." He looked down at his corrective shoe and scuffed it in the damp sand. "I would be good at that." He shook his head. "I haven't lost sight of God in all this. The Holy Ghost lays out our travails, and we choose among them. I could have done other things—I am here by choice. But then there's always that yearning. And it's not a darkness—that yearning is a light, a call. And no matter how many devastated lives I look into and touch, that yearning is still there. I mean it. You can love God and still do horrible things."

It was neither love nor anything else like it, Furtado thought. God was too much of a mystery. His presence, the hint of it, was what devastated. Maybe that was what Sweet was getting at: That mystery, that vastness—it wasn't enough comfort. People needed something more. Furtado was tempted to say this, but he held back. He did not want to fuel Sweet any more than he already had, and anyway, he did not trust himself.

There was a wildness there on the beach. The combers were growing long and crashing like barrels now, and the wind was beginning to sting. There were no walls to hold people in here, and they would have to speak with great breath—almost shout—to be heard above the wind and the ocean. An exchange here could lead anywhere; there was no telling. Furtado could feel his own blood rising. What would he shout once he let himself go? He zipped his parka and pushed his hands deep into its pockets. "I could go to meetings," he said, "if that would help you. I could go up the Cape to those meetings you mentioned."

Sweet looked at him. Impossible to tell what was in those eyes behind the black shine of the sunglasses. But he settled back to earth. "You don't need to do that, Manny."

"I'm doing the journaling nightly after prayer," Furtado said, turning from the water, Sweet at his side, and together they started back. The sense that things had not gone well seemed to hold them paired and tethered. Furtado kept his mouth shut.

The walk back along the highway went more swiftly. The wind blew at their backs, and the sun was now casting its long afternoon shadows. Chickadees flitted in the pine boughs of the trees along the road, and a pair of cock pheasants exploded in a flush of burgundy and green and beat low over the bracken and off toward the ponds. A few cars passed them as they walked. Furtado heard them coming in a whoosh of air, but when they rolled past and up the road, they did not seem to belong there, with all their metal and shine.

When they began walking up the side road toward the church, Sweet said, "I have a good deal of paperwork to turn in."

"I would imagine," Furtado said.

"I'd like to be able to say some things."

"What is it, John?"

Sweet waved his hand. "Nothing, really. It's the proposal. I'd like to attest that I've been of some help with it."

"You've read it. You've talked about it, as you say, at the Chancery."

"All very unofficial," Sweet said, again waving the hand. Then he turned suddenly. "How is that work with the homeless man coming, by the way?"

Furtado halted. Thunder in his head. He rounded on Sweet but managed to keep silent.

Sweet went on, "Oh, things come to me, Manny. Don't worry, I'm not spying on you. It's all right. I admire your charity and your impulses. I know it's irregular. I understand why you felt you couldn't tell me: so much coming at you. I'm here as a friend, Manny. Think of me that way. I'm here to help."

Furtado composed himself. It was impossible that Sweet could really know much. He was furious at how he consistently underestimated this fixer priest. He pushed a pawn. "It's worked out," he said. "A breakthrough. Great progress. We've located some family up in Boston. He'll be taken in up there in a day or two."

"Wonderful," said Sweet, dismissing it all, walking again. His mind was elsewhere now, which Furtado took as a good sign. "Anyway, about this other thing. I'd like to think that perhaps my sessions with you were also helpful in your completing all that parish work, with the stress and so forth, if I could say that. Would that be fair to say? I'll be plain: It could be helpful to me."

"By all means, then, John." Furtado said.

"It will come out all right."

"Then all will be well."

"God willing," said John Sweet.

seventeen

FURTADO MET WITH THE PARISH FINANCE COMMITTEE SHORTLY after Thanksgiving. That particular day had ended peacefully, with the evening growing brilliantly dark and clear and cold, and as he walked over to the parish hall for the meeting, he stopped and looked up at the Pilgrim's Tower, which was now festooned with long strings of colored lights. They hung from the observation landing of the tower's ornate cap and cascaded down in graceful catenary arcs some two hundred feet to the ground, signifying the conical shape of a Christmas tree. Although the sky was cloudless and blazing with winter stars, the sea air made little globes of haze around the lights and softened them, even at this small distance. Furtado thought briefly of Frankie Boia, who had always helped with the hanging of the lights, and he thought of how Tom had gone to Arthur Santos, who was in charge of the yearly lighting of the tower, and had spoken up about taking Frankie's place.

The ache in the priest's neck and shoulder had been quiet most of the day but had begun a dull advance during confessions that afternoon, and now the night breeze pressed through the light nylon windbreaker he had hastily thrown on; as the chill settled into him, he felt the soreness spread within him like a small hand opening. He had taken two of the pain pills before he left the rectory, but they had not yet begun to work.

He lingered a few minutes in the early night. He hunched and folded his arms and took in the stars and the lights, looked over the cars parked against the side of the hall, and blew out long breaths of faint steam that curled away from his lips before disappearing. The season had turned in earnest now. He did not wish to think about it in any terms whatsoever, but it came to him anyway as he stood by himself in the dark: It was almost full winter, and Sarafino was still with him.

They were waiting for him—all except Bobby Dutra, the committee's attorney, who was working late, and who had already reviewed the plan and given it his vote of approval. The hall's corner meeting room was warm, and they all sat at the oblong table. There was a porcelain urn of coffee on the table, with cups and sugar and milk, and a plate of *doces* from Braga's bakery. Mariah Grey had distributed copies of the proposal to all the council members earlier in the week, and they had all had a chance to study it. They all sat with their copies in front of them now, in thin black binders. The priest greeted them and thanked them for coming, and he took the empty chair between Mariah Grey and Arthur Santos.

"I was admiring your work," Furtado said to Arthur. "The Tower."

"It wasn't much work," Arthur said. "We had a nice calm day. No wind blowing those lines around. We miss Frankie." Then he added, "That Tom is a worker, though."

Arthur was a bald, dark-skinned, barrel-shaped man, a stonemason who had learned his trade from his father and run his own business in town for as long as Furtado could remember. Liliana Mendes sat next to Arthur. She had been a town selectwoman off and on for a number of years and ran a small motel at the easternmost edge of town. Graying at her temples now, she wore reading glasses that she often let hang from her neck on a black lanyard. She had graduated high school a few years before Furtado, and he remembered her as one of the town's beauties, popular and standoffish. "I feel like we should stand up and applaud you, Manny," she said. "You and Mariah."

"I guess we've started," he said, and he smiled and looked around the table.

"There's probably not a whole lot to talk about, Manny," Dickie Avellar said. He had worn a wine-colored knit sweater over a collared shirt for the meeting. "We've all talked amongst ourselves more or less these past few days."

"And Mariah has kept us onboard the whole way with all the copies and drafts," said Liliana.

"Don't look at me, anybody," said Joe Zora, who had not spoken yet. Joe and his brother, Urbano, owned the town's heating-oil service. "I just came for the pastries." They all laughed. They were in good spirits. They were happy with what Furtado and Mariah had done. They wandered through the pages and brought up little details, pointed out one figure or another, spoke of how it would be impossible to turn Fatima down at this point, given all the work that had been done and all the other sorts of work that was needed. And they all officially voted their approval and signed off on the documents.

"It goes to Calumet on Monday, then," Furtado said. He felt liked and admired, but the feeling did not go into him very deeply. They sat and chatted awhile and drank coffee and ate the sweets, and he stayed behind in the hall after everyone left, listening to the rush of the big heater and the welcome quiet underneath it in the empty room. After a while, the pills he had taken began to lift the ache from his bones and muscles, and he got up and took the dishes into the kitchen and ran the dishwasher. Then he turned off the lights and the heat, locked up, went out to the parking lot, and stared up at the sky and the lighted tower until the cold once again settled under his windbreaker, and then he walked back into the rectory.

He let himself in the side door. The office was dark but the parlor lights were on, and when he didn't see Allie he moved toward Sarafino's room, but he stopped when he heard the murmur of their voices, a cough, something that might have been a bark of laughter. He didn't move closer to the little bedroom but instead stood quietly. He could not make out words, but the soft back-and-forth came to him in warm tones, the sound of his sister's voice taking on a sweetness, even though he could not tell what she was saying. And Sarafino, barely audible at all—short clips of speech, small groups of syllables, lacunae when he would stop to catch his breath. The moment seemed intimate, something easy between them, and the light from the room breaking into the darkness of the narrow hallway was like a hedge around them, and the priest could not make himself walk in on them and change any of that. He backed away and eased himself into the office and gently closed the door that gave onto the parlor. He sat there among the charts and papers with the small tensor lamp throwing a saucer of white light onto the desktop in front of him. He was sitting there an hour later when Allie tapped softly on the door.

"He's asleep," she said. "I didn't hear you come in. Why are you in the dark?"

"It's enough," he said. He tapped the gooseneck on the little lamp, and the light jiggled in a pattern on the desktop.

"He's sleeping better with that new stuff that Peter is giving him," she said.

The alkaloid savor of his own medicine had settled on the back of the priest's tongue, and over it the sugared taste of Lucy Braga's *doces* and sweet coffee still lingered. His lips were not numb, but they drifted in that direction. And his eyes felt heavy. "That's a good thing," he said, speaking softly.

"You sound tired."

"No. But the proposal is all done."

"It'll be good. Tommy talks about all the stuff that needs to get done around here. There's stuff he won't get to for months."

"We'll have contractors for big jobs," said the priest.

"I don't guess Tommy could do this forever," she said. "We need something steady. It's good to have for now, though."

"There'll be other things."

She closed the door behind her and sat down. She was serious now. "I guess I wore Sarafino out. He was ready to go wandering, but I steered him back into the house. He's so weak, Manny. I don't think he'd get three steps."

"Peter said it was beginning—the last part, I mean. He is beginning to fail."

"It's so good of him. Peter. He's a good guy. What's going to happen? I keep a candle going for Sarafino in the church all the time. One of the $5 ones."

"Peter says we can finish it out here. It would be unthinkable to put him anyplace else now. And we will help him pass, and then I will bury him in a private place. Like he asked."

"And no one will know? Really?"

"It sounds crazy. It's criminal. But that's what he wants. Why shouldn't I give it to him?"

"And you're sure you won't get into trouble?"

"It will be fine," said the priest. How far he'd come. Then, how far from what? He let it go. He was with his sister, and they were talking now. He could feel his heartbeat all throughout his body. Not banging—easy, gentle.

"It's so sad, all this. It's so confusing."

"All will be well," he said.

Alzaida fidgeted. She looked over her shoulder. She scooted her chair closer to the desk. "Manny, there's a couple things. More things."

He shrugged against the soft humming in his bones and waited for her news.

"There was a guy that came to the house yesterday."

Furtado straightened himself in the chair. "What guy?" he said.

"It's about Sarafino," she said. "It's okay," she said quickly. "It's nothing, but I just had to tell you."

"Tell me, then," said the priest.

"He was looking for a death certificate for Sarafino. He was some kind of insurance investigator. He's not a cop or anything. He came down from Boston. He tells me he was looking into the death of Sarafino Pomba, but there's no certificate anywhere. No death certificate, no burial certificate. I told him I sure didn't have one. I told him anybody around here that knew anything at all knows that he died a few years ago. Nobody really knows him here anymore, and it's all just like what somebody heard. He says, *in* Boston? Like, in the city? And I said well, I don't know. That's what most people mean when they say *Boston*, but there's nobody that knows anything about him, really. It's just something somebody heard a while back. He didn't seem too hot to know a whole lot more. It was just like he was going though the motions on something."

The priest was quiet for a while. He found himself rapping his fingers on the desk, and Allie watched his hand intently and did not look at his face. "But he came to your house? Out in the Village?"

She drew a breath. "Manny, I wrote Sarafino a letter a while back. A long time ago. It was an answer, really, to a letter he wrote to me. He got ahold of me and I wrote back to him. I mean, I asked this guy questions. I wanted to find out what was going on. He told me he had seen the letter there, along with some other old letters and stuff of Sarafino's that he had found someplace. The guy said he was just following up on everything. That he worked for some insurance company."

"Oh, Alzaida."

"Manny, don't. Please. I know it was horrible that I didn't tell you everything. But listen to me. I was going to."

"Tell me now," the priest said. "Don't leave anything out."

She put her hand to her lips, and tears rolled from her eyes. She trembled for a moment and would not raise her face to him. "It was me who got Sarafino into the Church. And unlocked the window to make it look like he got in that way, and then I locked the doors with him inside. I used the other keys, which I still have. He did pay some guy to drive him down here, but then I met them at the beach parking lot and took him here. We had set it up. You were going to find him here, but it was always that he was going to stay out in the Village with me. But that didn't work out, and after that fight with Tommy, I sure couldn't tell you.

"Don't you get it, Manny? I told Tommy about all that. About being in touch with Sarafino and getting him here and everything. That's why the fight got so bad. That's what made him blow it so bad. I threw that all in his face. It just got so crazy when he heard that. And then we both went nuts and all. I couldn't tell you after all that. But now I promised Tommy I would tell you. I promised him when he came to you about Frankie and the boat. I told him I would wait for the right time. And then the guy came, and I thought, well, I better stop waiting and just tell you. It wasn't fair if I didn't."

"Does this man have a name? What insurance company?"

"He gave me a card, but I threw it away. I didn't want the damn thing in my house. His name was something like Morris. Morrissey, maybe. Why does it matter?"

"Sarafino should have told me all this," Furtado said.

"Don't, Manny. Please don't. He's afraid of you. He's afraid you'll turn him loose. Look, Sarafino had an insurance policy. It was from some labor union he worked in, in California. He had a $60,000 life insurance policy, and I guess he got to keep it after a certain amount of time. But I guess you can sell those policies, too. That's what he did once he knew he had the AIDS: He sold it for $15,000 to some couple up in Boston. They bought a lot of these, is what this Morrissey guy told me. People do that. They would come around to the clinics and talk to people. You can have papers drawn up. I guess how it works is, you sign them as beneficiaries or whatever. It was quick money, and Sarafino was never going to see anything out of it any other way. He had no one behind him to give the benefit to."

"It's a viatical contract," said the priest.

"That's it. Yes, that's what it is."

The priest tapped his fingers on the desk. He thought for a minute. Easy, rolling thoughts. "You knew about this beforehand," he said. "You knew about this before this Morrissey ever showed up."

"No, I swear, Manny. Not the insurance thing. But Sarafino did tell me he had some money and that he would pay it out to me and Tommy for taking care of him."

"But . . ." said Furtado.

"But it was all gone by the time he got here. He doesn't have anything."

"You lost out on your deal."

"No, Manny. No. It was never the idea of the money. It was for Sarafino. I swear."

"You needed money, though. Tom said something about the boat's insurance lapsing."

"Yes," she said dismally. "We screwed that. We were going to pay it."

"So there were problems again with money? But you have a new truck. You guys went to Disney World last winter."

Alzaida shut her eyes and took a breath. "It's got to come out now. I didn't know how much he told you. They took a line of credit out on the house. On Frankie's mother's house. Tom and Frankie were paying the monthlies. Some out of the boat's share, too. She just signed the papers. She didn't have any idea."

"So Hortensia is stuck with the debt?"

"Tommy's giving her most of the money from working here. We'll get by on the bakery money till summer."

"That will cover the payments?"

"I guess so. I don't know all the facts and figures of it, Manny."

"You just thought you'd pick up some cash from boarding Sarafino."

"No, Manny. I loved him once. Just like you."

"Maybe it was all a con. Maybe he never intended to pay you anything," Furtado said. "That money could have been gone for years."

"He came back to see me," Allie said.

"He told me he came back to see me, too," Furtado said. "That *I* was the reason. I don't know how much that means."

"It means a lot. You and Sarafino were like shadows for each other when we were kids, but you never understood him. You never understood him and me. Didn't you ever notice? Didn't you ever see anything? Think anything? No, you wouldn't have. That's not you, Manny. And when it came to Sarafino, you thought you had something special with him. Don't deny it. People used to talk, even. You couldn't see around your own self."

"You're not talking sense, Alzaida."

"Manny, Sarafino and I were together that whole last year. He didn't want you to know, and neither one of us wanted Papa to know, God help us. It was a secret. We were crazy for each other. I don't know how it started. It was like we were the same person, almost. That's how close we felt. People say *soul mates*—that's what I mean. I felt like we had the same heart. We grew up together. He was funny. I could say anything to him. And he always told me how much he loved me. It was all sex, too. All the time. Whenever. We used to do it all the time in Papa's house. You never had a clue? We would do it up in the window, with him behind me, and watch Papa's boat come around the Point. I thought he was going to come right out and say that when we drove by the house that time. That's why I got so mad and got out of the car.

"Don't you see? We were kids, Manny, but I loved him. And I'll tell you this. You might think I'm stupid, you might think I'm a fuckup, but I know one thing: I never felt like that again. I would have done anything for him. I love Tommy, but it's different. It's all like work. Maybe you have to be a kid to feel the way I'm talking about, but I had it, Manny. I really don't think you ever did. I really don't think you even know what I mean. People might think it's because you're a priest, all deep into yourself and bottled up and far away, but you were always like that.

"And when Sarafino left for the Army, he was supposed to come back. He was supposed to come back and be with me, Manny. But he wouldn't come back after that shit you guys pulled breaking into the church. His head got all screwed up in that war, and he thought he couldn't ever come back. All that crazy stuff about Old Man Coelho. He was nuts, I could tell. I never heard from him after those couple of times. And when his parents moved out, I knew I wouldn't see him again. It was like he *was* dead. And then Tommy started coming around. I don't regret that, Manny. Not Tommy. But Sarafino and I were so close. And he knew after all these years that if he needed me, I'd take him in. And now it's all crazy."

The priest sat silently and thought a while longer. He was seeing so many things all at once. All the while Allie was talking to him, he was watching things unfold. He let his fingertips tap softly against the desktop. Its solidity was a comfort.

"No," he said finally. "That isn't everything. That doesn't work, Allie. It doesn't add up. You are still keeping things from me."

"That's all you want to know, Manny. Believe me."

"No, Allie. It *is* unfair. It's unfair to start something like this and then not tell me everything. You might think it's just you in the middle of this. But from where I sit, I'm in the middle. Think about Tommy, too."

She trembled again. Her face went bright with tears. Furtado remembered the box of tissues in his bottom drawer, and he grabbed a handful and passed them to her across the big desk. She took them and swiped at her wet cheeks. "God, Manny. Tommy knows. That awful fight. It came out finally." She looked at him. "You have an idea," she said.

"The last time Sarafino was here."

"Well, yes, Manny. Of course, you would be right," she said bitterly. "He was here. He came back. Years ago. I don't know, it was during that time when Tommy was running the boat and we got mixed up in all that cocaine stuff. It was a bad time. Horrible. It wasn't just us. Everybody. It's still around, you know. Meth, too. It's not all just drinking at the Wheelhouse, you know." She paused. "Anyway, he was here for about a week, maybe. He was wacked out. He was here and then he split. No one knew. He was nuts. I was nuts."

"Is this around the time little Jaime died?"

She had not been looking at him while she spoke, but now she lifted her head and studied his face. "It was when I got pregnant with Jaime," she said. She waited for something from Furtado, but he didn't speak. He didn't move.

"It was Sarafino's baby," she said, as if explaining to someone very slow, someone frankly stupid. "And please don't ask me if I'm sure. I'm sure. At first not. But after the accident with Jaime, Tom and I never got pregnant. It took a while, but I knew—I don't know when I knew. It's Tommy. Tommy can't have kids, for some reason. At first I thought, *Oh, God is punishing us. God won't let me have any more kids because of what happened to Jaime*. But then I figured it out. And then I knew it was

Sarafino. That's what I yelled at Tommy when we were fighting that night. After all that time, it came out. That's what made Tommy so crazy. Why he got all drunk and coked up. I screamed all that right in his face."

"You and Sarafino. All these secrets."

"It sounds bad when you say that, Manny."

"It *is* bad," he said.

"Are you saying that because now you have to have the secrets, too? I don't know what you want. What do you want me to do? What do you want me to say?"

"Sarafino. What else do you know? You must know more. I need to know. That's what I want," said the priest. "I want to know all the little things in all the cracks and corners. I have to. Look at me."

"I *am* looking at you, Manny. Sarafino doesn't know about his baby. He doesn't know anything about that. That can't be spoken to him."

"I don't intend to say anything," the priest said. "It's a bit late for that."

"There was never a time for it," Alzaida said.

"His miracle, then," the priest said. "That's when he went back and dug up the statue."

"I don't know anything about that. He was with me a lot. Tommy was out fishing or running dope or whatever. It wasn't more than a week. We were wrecked the whole time. It was such a terrible time."

"You saw him the night he left for the Army? How did he get all that done? I don't remember you that night. Were you home? I don't remember anything about where you were."

"You guys ran off. I was mad that you did. But he came back and got me. He came right into the house and got me right while Papa was sleeping. I don't know where you were. Maybe you were home. We sneaked right out. We went back to his house, on his couch. He had to be at the bus early. He had a little paper bag with his toothbrush in it. Some little things.

We went down to the bus together when the sun came up. He was so high. He was buzzing. We got bread at Braga's. You never came. That's how I remember it, anyway. That's how it is in my mind when I think back on it. I always suspected you had something to do with breaking into the church. I'm pretty sure Mae did, too. She suffered after you left for the service. It wasn't all because of Papa, all that sadness of hers. But then after a while, everybody thought it had to be somebody from away."

"No," said the priest. "No, I think he told you, though. Maybe *you* went and got the statue. Maybe you did something with it. Or you tried and couldn't get it the whole way back and left it someplace in the woods. Maybe you left it floating in the pond and it just rotted away."

Alzaida looked at him hard. "Manny, you sound crazy. Are you all right?"

"I'm not sure," he said.

"It's me," she said. "I've laid too much on you."

"No," he said. "No."

"Because you're not making sense. I say all this to you—*all this*—and that's what I get back? Some fucking statue?"

"Papa's statue. My statue. Sarafino stole it with me because I talked him into it. I stole it to get at Pai, and it all landed on Sarafino."

"You're obsessed. *Get at Papa*? That doesn't make sense, either."

"It did then. And that whole risen-statue business—it's not a miracle," Furtado said. "Sarafino's behind it somehow. He's come back to get me. Some idea of payback. Something. I will figure it out."

"Stop it, Manny. You're really making me nervous here. I'm opening all my guts to you. It's what you asked me for. Who cares about all that other crazy shit?"

"This idea about the miracle . . ." the priest said. But he knew she was right. He had stumbled and lost his way somehow. His face burned. His head spun. The chimes sounded in his ear and rose into a whistle before they trailed away. "I'm sorry," he said. He fell silent. He drummed his fingers on the desk again, and Alzaida sat up in the chair and stared at him.

"Do you want to pray with me now, Allie?" he said finally.

"No, I do not," she said.

So the priest prayed by himself later that night, as he did every night, at the *prie-deux* in the study under the roof, and he thought of all that Alzaida had told him. He prayed in order to make some meaning out of it, and he prayed as a release from whatever it was that was driving him forward like this, whatever this thing was that had him in its grip. When he finished praying, he took several more pain pills and drank from the iced gin, sharp and palliative. His entry in the ledger that night showed that it had been a Saturday, the Feast of Saint Andrew, and he copied out a piece of the first reading prescribed for that day, a passage from Paul's epistle to the Romans: *But how can they call on Him in whom they have not believed?* Then he answered the Apostle: *They can call because they* can *call.* He put down many clear details of the day; sometimes he addressed his sister, and sometimes he wrote to Sarafino or John Sweet.

He filled many pages, and when he was done he closed the ledger and turned out the lamp, and carried the empty gin glass down the darkened hall stairs. He passed through the kitchen—it felt like gliding now, a suffusion of well-being despite all he had heard tonight. To go forward now without such a powerful commixture of chemicals was unthinkable. This surcease of pain and this taste of an enduring bodily bliss *did* reveal something about God, he told himself: a revision in the story of Christ's need to suffer. A rebuke, even, of God's inadequacies, His unfinished work, and the unfinished work He left for us lesser beings. And still, what the delicious, bitter white tablets said to God: *We love You. In the face of all this, we love You.*

Furtado moved with an unnatural ease and silence through the kitchen's back door and out again into the parking lot to where he had an unobstructed view of the Pilgrim's Tower and its wreath of hanging lights. The colors murmured to him in the faint wind. He savored this as all his senses lifted wearily, as though he were being drawn up into the sky and the cold stars. He remembered then exactly how Alzaida had looked crying, her shoulders heaving and her face crumpled and her skin aglow with the slippery tears. He could not remember the last time he had cried. At this moment, he could not remember ever crying in his adult life, though this seemed incorrect to him. *Behold your suffering servant*, he said silently, but it was not spoken now as a prayer.

When the chill finally drove him inside again, he walked softly to the small bedroom and steadied himself in the doorway. He watched for a while as Sarafino drank in the oxygen with his short, rapid breaths, and then he slipped off his shoes and, being careful not to wake Sarafino, lay down once more beside him on the bed.

eighteen

THE MONDAY AFTER THE FOURTH SUNDAY OF ADVENT—FOUR days before Christmas—grew gray and cold, but not cold enough yet to snow, and ever since noon or so, a light drizzle had been drifting down over the town, darkening the surfaces of the streets and houses and bringing a pervasive dampness into the rectory's small rooms. Mariah Grey had turned up the thermostats, just a modest increase, mindful of the price of heating oil, and had placed a small electric heater on a tile on the floor of Sarafino's room, though he claimed not to need it. Tom had come in from his private hour in the church and had been sitting with Sarafino in the bedroom, telling him stories about working the old boat and talking about some of the hell he had raised back in the glory days, when he'd chanced to see that one of the Havahart traps out on the grounds had something in it.

The priest had gone off on parish visits, intending especially to spend some time with Mrs. Boia, but Mariah was working in the rectory office. Tom told Sarafino he would back shortly, then stuck his head in the office door to tell Mariah he was going outside for a while and to ask if she could keep an eye on Sarafino for just a minute. When he told her, "We got another creature," she looked up at him and said, "Tom, you are the only creature around here."

Through their continuous company with each other working in the church and rectory, and through all they shared in watching over Sarafino, Tom and Mariah had in the most improbable way come to like each other. They were easy and relaxed in each other's company. Furtado could not imagine what they might discuss openly, but for his part, he said nothing to Mariah about Tom and Allie's private matters. Nothing about scuttling the boat or about Sarafino's having been with Allie. Nothing about the baby—her story about the baby—tragic, absurd, true, foolish. How worthless, all the words. Nothing could ever be a clear sign for the heart. Not a word, not a million words.

Furtado knew, once again, that there were grave and serious reasons he should leave the Church, but he also knew that there were reasons why he should stay. Chaos all around, but you couldn't tame it. No, you navigated your way through it. You sailed. By light of day, he knew he was not doing well. By light of day it seemed that he might still find himself a purchase, some sort of choice or choices that might issue from his own will—but even then he felt the pull, as silent and inexorable as gravity itself. And again, the odd illusion that it had always been there, this peculiar drift toward descent.

But he would console himself in small ways. Practical matters were improving, at least: the debt forgiveness, the restructuring. Mariah and Tom were efficient and helpful at what they did. Tom was especially good at working with the building and grounds volunteers. He simply ran things like a boat captain, and the crew got things done and felt good about it. In his ledgers from time to time, Furtado noted how the parish business was running smoothly, and how the church itself had not looked better in years.

Tom had so far removed eight gray squirrels from the churchyard. The Havahart was simply a wire cage with a handle at the top and a bait trip at the back. The trip snapped the cage door shut, and the squirrel remained inside until it was released. Tom or Mariah would lift the cage like a suitcase, put it in the back of one of the trucks, and let the squirrel out at the far edge of the woods. All of Allie's feeders had been taken down, so the baited traps worked easily.

On that day, another gray had been trapped, a large one, and Tom bent to inspect it. The squirrel was frightened; it clawed frantically at the wire siding of the cage and then pressed itself against the back and shivered there, its eyes wide and glassy, its fur wet. The drizzle floated down and settled along the brown grass and dampened Tom's hair and shirt as he bent over the trap, and he decided then to run the trap out to the woods quickly, rather than keep the wet animal in the cage any longer.

He put the cage on the truck's passenger seat and draped a towel over it to calm the squirrel. Then he drove out to the state highway and along the pine woods. He stopped once, ready to unload the trap, when he saw a small, young coyote, ears up, fur wet and matted, body poised against a raft of briar. He got back into the truck and drove a little farther along the scrub pines, until they began giving way to sand dunes. He pulled over, walked the trap into a small clump of trees, and opened it and let the squirrel go, far enough out here so that it would not make its way back to the church, far enough from the predator to give the little thing a chance.

When he returned to the rectory no more than half an hour later, Mariah was still at the desk. He stood in the office doorway. She had been creating a flowchart on the computer and was getting ready to post it on the website that she had created. She was absorbed in what she was doing and did not notice Tom immediately.

"Hey," he said.

"Hey," she said. She typed a few more words before she looked up at him. "You must have run your friend out to the woods."

"Yep. How's our other friend?"

"Quiet," she said.

"He goes like that," Tom said. "Quiet, and then he gets on a tear about something. You never know what's going to come out of him."

"Sometimes beautiful things," she said.

"I don't get that so much," Tom said.

"I just think there's something special about him."

"I wouldn't know about that," Tom said.

"Sometimes we'll be saying a Rosary or talking, and I'll see something come over him. Then he'll just ask me to leave. He'll just throw me out so he can be alone. The Virgin Mary is so much in his life."

"Well," Tom said, "he never throws me out. He likes me better than you. I'll look in on him. Maybe we all three can have coffee or tea or something if he's in the mood. I'll warm some bread."

"Why not?" she said.

But Sarafino was not in his room. The oxygen tube lay on his pillow. His sneakers were gone and his sleeping sweats lay on the floor in a pile. When Tom saw this, he went upstairs and looked in the little study, then came back down and checked Furtado's bedroom, the bathroom, the closets, and the unused empty room that was simply called the empty room. When he had looked everywhere in the rectory, including checking the kitchen door, which was closed but not locked, he ran back to the office.

"Sarafino's gone," he told Mariah. "He's not here. I looked in all the rooms. He's off somewhere. We have to get him."

"Oh, God," she said. "This is my fault. I just thought he was asleep."

"I'm going to look around all the grounds in back. Around the hall and everything," said Tom. "You look along the street in front."

They both rushed out, and after about five minutes, Mariah came back and called Hortensia Boia's house. The priest had just arrived there. "You have to come back here, Manny. Sarafino's gone missing," she said into the phone. The priest said nothing. He simply hung up. He was at the rectory in minutes. By then Tom had come back, and together they told him what had happened, how it had happened.

"Call Alzaida at the bakery," Furtado said to Tom. "Tell her to come up here and stay here in case he comes back. Tell her not to tell Lucy Braga anything, but to come up here. Tommy, you go in your truck and cruise up and down Front Street, Back Street, side streets—just grab him up if he's anywhere. Mariah, you go out the pond road, out toward the highway. Go slow and look in yards, whatever. I'm going over by the schools. If we don't see him anywhere in a half hour, we'll all come back and think some more."

Tom was already headed for the door when Mariah said, "I think he's wearing a green cap and a green parka." She pointed to the empty peg on the kitchen wall where she had hung her clothes. "Mine."

The priest drove the little Toyota slowly, the windshield wipers flapping away the film of light rain as he peered ahead. Sarafino had to be close by. Furtado was angry, but his anger seemed like a dream. Maybe even someone else's dream, for, in fairness, there was no one to be angry with, but the feeling hung about him. He could not clear his head. He tried to go over what Tom and Mariah had told him, both blurting, apologizing, when he had rushed into the rectory. No one's fault, but they each blamed themselves. He calculated that Sarafino had been outside anywhere from a half hour to a little over an hour. He couldn't have gotten far in his condition in this rain. Furtado thought that he might have had one of his fits and wandered just far away enough to collapse or hole up someplace. He might have knocked on someone's door or just walked into a house or shop. He might even have entered the high school building.

The priest pulled up to the cement steps, the same ones where he and Mariah had found Sarafino sitting those weeks past. He parked and walked around to the side door of the school and let himself in. The hall before him seemed both compressed and cavernous at the same time, the green tiled floor, the rows of skinny lockers. Classes were in session. He walked quickly and quietly. He entered the girls' bathroom and scanned it. He walked to the other end of the hall and did the same with the boys'. He went up to the second floor and checked the bathrooms there, and then went down the stairs and followed the hallway out to the gymnasium but stopped when he heard a gym class in session, muffled shouts, basketballs banging the hardwood. If Sarafino had shown himself anywhere, there would have been some flurry, some disruption. But things here seemed normal. There would be no point in looking further, no point in peering in classrooms.

Using the same thinking, he decided not to search the elementary school just up the hill. He drove out of the parking lot and around to the street that ran up past the entrance to the Pilgrim's Tower, but he did not take the turn-in. He kept going past the front of the schools and out toward the graveyards. He was not aware of deliberating, exactly, but it seemed right to him to follow this direction. It came to him that maybe Sarafino had been heading someplace else back when the priest and Mariah had found him on the school steps, for he would not have had any reason to go into the schools or up to the tower. Could he have gone farther? Could he have the breath, the strength? Furtado drove out to the cemetery, pulled onto the gravel road that ran to the utility shed, and parked the car.

It was an unlikely place to search. It was too far. It was raining. But now the priest was drawn forward by his own momentum, and maybe, as he would reflect later, by the fact that he could think of nowhere else to look. And when he walked along the lane up over the hill, the way they had come with the Virgin bound in tarp and twine so many years ago—when he came to the gravesite just under the hill's crest where they had once startled the drunken Senhor Coelho—he found Sarafino kneeling and crumpled, wearing Mariah's parka, dark with rain on his skinny frame, the hood pulled up, and his head nested in his arms on the wet brown earth.

The priest ran to him and called his name, but Sarafino did not move or answer. But when he knelt next to him and put his hands on him, Sarafino spoke: "*Salve Regina, Salve Regina, Mater misericordiae, vita dulcedo et spes nostra, salve.*"

"You are wet," said the priest, "and freezing. I'm bringing the car up here."

Sarafino began repeating the prayer again while the priest ran to the car, eased it up the narrow lane between the gravestones, and gathered the shivering Sarafino into the front seat.

When they reached the rectory, Sarafino could not stand on his legs, and so Furtado leaned into the car, bent his knees and put an arm beneath Sarafino's thighs and the other around his back, and lifted him gingerly, and then carried him like a child to the kitchen door. He banged at it with his foot, and Allie appeared and let them in. The priest carried Sarafino to the bathroom immediately, where he took him out of his cold, wet clothes, sat him on the stool in the shower, and ran warm, then warmer, water over his body.

When the room began to fill with steam, Furtado shut the water off and toweled Sarafino from head to foot—Sarafino's body, white as a skinned fish, and its bruises and sores and angular bones showing through—and called for Allie to bring dry clothes, and Furtado dressed him and carried him to his room. Allie had made the bed with new sheets and blankets and extra quilts and had turned back the bedclothes neatly. She pulled them back further when the priest carried Sarafino in and laid him in the bed, and then she folded them back over him, a mound of the old hand-sewn quilts, thick and warm. They fastened the oxygen tubes over his ears and into his nostrils, and they sat with him quietly until Mariah Grey and Tom returned. Mariah called Peter Khyber immediately, but he was not in and she had to leave a message.

They all took turns sitting with Sarafino until he pulled himself over on his side, still under the layers of quilts, and tossed himself into a shaky state of rest. Then the little house flashed with the weary tensions among them all. It was dark by then, and the four of them gathered in the parlor and spoke in low tones.

"God, he's so sick," Allie said.

"Peter will come," Mariah said. "He will get us through this."

"He could have got caught. They could take him away," Allie said.

"It's all right," said the priest.

"How many now?" Allie said. "There's the four of us and Peter . . ."

"Winslow," said Mariah Grey.

"The insurance guy," said Allie.

The priest started to say John Sweet, but he didn't. Instead he said, "No one saw him. No one knows who he is. It won't go any further. We just have to be with him. We have to watch him. And at this point, what could anyone do to him?"

"They could take him *away*," Allie said. Tom and Mariah both turned and looked at her, their faces strained and dark, and Allie looked back, but there was little energy left anywhere in the room, and then no one said anything for a long time.

THE PAIN WAS WORSE AFTER HAVING LIFTED AND CARRIED SARAFINO. Something in Furtado slipped—the shoulder raged, the base of his neck raged—but the priest kept to the *prie-deux*, the weight of his bowed head dragging down the length of every muscle, every sinew, in his whole body. He prayed long, bitter extemporaneous prayers to his mysterious and infuriating and terrifying God who lay hidden off in the black reaches behind and beyond the God of Lamentations, the God of Isaiah, the God of Genesis, the God behind the God who wrestled with Jacob, the God behind the God, behind the God. He asked for nothing in these prayers. He disdained asking. He would not ask. But he labored, perhaps in madness, at some kind of penetration, at some kind of schematic that would include Alzaida and her disruptive powers, and Sarafino and his illness, and Tom and his rage, and Mariah and her vigor, and the gravity of the Earth and stars, and the rains coming off the Atlantic, and the fish in the sea, and the soul of Frankie Boia, and the meaning of *soul*, and his father's boat lying on its side, finally, deep in the cold eternal eddies. And if there were a grand algorithm, it would have to be the world itself, for only the world could contain or signify the world. And then he was back to God again, and God and the world led him, with humiliation, to his own pitiful cares, his own pathetic ache.

When he could bear it no longer, he rose from the kneeler and drew himself upright. The pain lessened but did not lift. The hour was late. He walked down the stairs and stood for a while in Sarafino's room, watching him in the shadowy light. Sarafino had slept fitfully since they'd tucked him into the bed that afternoon, but now he seemed to rest with more ease—the medication such a help now—though there was that small motor running underneath his breathing, that thing that was so labored and mechanical.

Furtado satisfied himself that there was nothing Sarafino needed now, and then he padded up the stairs again, put several pain pills in his mouth, and crushed them with his teeth, holding them on his tongue, feeling them soften, and then washed them down with a mouthful of the gin that had sat among the melting ice cubes in the tumbler on the desk, waiting for him all the while he had prayed.

His ledger entries were gestating into something more like raw thought than like text; at this point, whether another's eyes might chance to see them was not something he ever considered. This shift seemed to coincide with an increase in his entries about the pills and the gin, always couched in positive, deeply affectionate terms. Some of the ledger pages now were covered in sketches or diagrams of things familiar and things unknown, sometimes with labels, sometimes without. There were maps of the town's streets with buildings drawn and named the way they had been seventy-five years earlier. There were drawings of his father's boat that resembled blueprints, cutaways, various aspects showing dimensions, weights, engine specifications. Some pages were purely columns of figures or lists. Others were prayers, epistles, quotes, paraphrases. At one point he'd taken up the scale and features of the Pilgrim's Tower, a long, arcane dissertation in numerals based on the number 252—its exact height in feet—that ran for pages and recurred between bits of other, more comprehensible writing.

Despite the precarious spiral Furtado seemed to be in, the ledgers showed and described times of sharp clarity and concentration, too. That feature was also part of their puzzling nature. For he always returned to protracted narratives of meticulous phenomenology—what happened and to whom, what happened next, feelings, judgments, scrutinies, self-deceptions, truths—as if details were a secret text that would eventually yield something up to him. And there was never the slightest gesture toward dissembling.

Furtado began that night by predicting that Sarafino would wake soon, so he wrote in short bursts: phrases set off by dashes. Fragments. Simple sentences. As though he might have to put down the pen at any moment and attend to Sarafino. Even so, when the distant rhythms reached Furtado, like the mutterings of his own heart, he did not immediately take notice of them or identify them. In fact, he could not tell how long he had been hearing the sounds before he became conscious of them. But when he did, they slowly became clear: the syllables of his name, murmured in a kind of insistent chant, barely audible. *Manny, Manny, Manny, Manny*.

"I'm right here," the priest said. He was standing in the bedroom now, but he did not remember how he'd gotten there. His voice sounded oddly sweet and unfamiliar to him.

"Manny," said Sarafino, "I need . . . some water."

"Yes," Furtado said. Then he said yes again, but it seemed like a long time before he moved. But at last he got a glass of juice and a can of supplement from the kitchen, and helped Sarafino to sit up against the pillows, and when he passed him the tumbler of iced juice, he splashed some of it on the quilt. He regarded the wet splotch for a moment and decided that attempting to clean or blot it would very, very difficult. He sat then in the chair, which he slowly pulled up against the bed.

"I had to go," Sarafino said.

"It was a bad idea," Furtado said, pleased with how easy talking seemed to be, now that he was sitting.

"I thought it was the hour of my death."

"I don't know how you managed to get out there."

"The Virgin Mary," said Sarafino.

"Are you saying she helped you?" The priest realized he was listening to intricate, marvelous sounds in his ear. A kind of symphony of hums and chimes. Not unlike cellos and glockenspiels. No melody. But some order beyond melody. Alone, he would have paid attention to it and tried to understand why it seemed so beautiful. But he let it ring away, and he attended Sarafino. "You can't ever do that again," he said. "Talk to one of us first if you ever think you are going to do something like that."

"I thought it was . . . the hour of my death," Sarafino said again. Weak now. In a long, slow curve of motion, the priest rose and checked the gauge on the oxygen device. He made an adjustment. Then he looked away from what he had done, and then looked back again to check his work.

"She was there, Manny. Real. She came. And spoke to me."

"You had a vision."

"I did. That's what I'm telling you."

"All right," said the priest.

"It's not a con."

"All right," Furtado said again.

"I know you don't buy it," Sarafino said. His hand shook on the glass of juice as he drew from it in two or three heavy swallows, and then he reached unsteadily and set the tumbler down on the nightstand. "I am just . . . saying the actual truth of what is, Manny."

"You went to the graveyard and saw the Virgin Mary."

"She was beautiful."

"Did She tell you to go there? Is that why you went off?"

"I buried Her, Manny. But I never dug Her up."

"All right," the priest said. He felt the languor in his voice.

"When I saw the Coelho name there on the stone, all wet, I thought, *Oh, She wants me . . . to pray for him.*"

"And you did?"

"That's when She came. I couldn't move. There She was. All of a sudden. Standing there. Right on the graves. A blue robe and gold crown. She was beautiful. Shining. Bright. All around me and all through me. Everything smelled like flowers. She had that crown on her head. It was bright. Like the sun, only it was still raining all around me. She talked to me. I felt so good, Manny."

"Are you cold now, Sarafino? You are shivering." Sarafino pulled at the quilt and tucked it up by his chin.

"She talked, Manny. She said so many things. I don't remember what She said. That's the problem, Manny—I fucked it all up. It was important things, and I was supposed to remember. My head is all wrong inside. I was ready to go with Her. I was okay to die there, but you came and got me."

Sarafino trembled harder now. His eyes flicked around the room. The bed shook. "Everything hurts," he said.

The priest floated up and stood over him and, making a great effort to move slowly and gently, touched his face and felt the fever. Sarafino was burning up. Sarafino was on fire.

nineteen

PETER KHYBER BROUGHT WITH HIM SEVERAL KITS, SOME VIALS of medicine, a small pack of hypodermic needles that were already filled with a clear liquid, various instruments, his stethoscope, a blood-pressure cuff, and a number of sealed plastic bags containing tubing, plastic fasteners, and bottles. He laid these supplies out on the dresser, and then he asked Tom and Mariah to go to his Jeep and bring in the collapsible IV pole and the machine, an oxygen generator, which would be more efficient now for Sarafino. He measured Sarafino's fever at 102, which was what both Furtado and Mariah Grey had found over the night and throughout that morning. Sarafino seemed to be laboring for each breath now, and he did not speak or move much, except to occasionally try to shift his position in the narrow bed. Peter's face was sober as he leaned down and spoke in a loud voice: "Hello, Sarafino."

Sarafino let out a feral sound, like a growl, but then the priest recognized that he had spoken two words: "Go away."

Peter stepped away from the bed. He pressed his lips together and nodded, and then he turned to Furtado. The priest left the room, closed the door behind him, and joined Mariah and Tom in the parlor. They had both been with the priest since early morning, and had sat with Sarafino when Furtado had gone to morning Mass. They were quiet and gloomy.

Peter emerged from the sickroom after about half an hour. He explained to them what was happening and what they must do. "Everything now is palliative care," he said. "He knows that." Peter was serious and matter-of-fact with them. Furtado had told him about letting Sarafino wander off, but Peter did not comment on that beyond saying, "I don't think he'll be capable of that again. He's actively failing now." He told them what he wanted them to do, and Mariah wrote down notes, and they all looked over the additional medications. Then he showed Mariah how he wanted the IV pole to be set up and how to work the controls. Peter showed her where he had inserted the IV valve into Sarafino's forearm and told her everything about how to tend to it. Tom set up the oxygen machine in the empty room and ran the tubing down the hall and into Sarafino's room. Peter showed them the generator's controls, and Mariah wrote more notes. Tom regarded the clear plastic tubing snaking down the hall, then left the rectory and returned with a large power drill and, in a single loud minute, drilled a baseboard hole between the two rooms and reran the tubing through it.

Furtado had been struggling with his own fatigue. The coming of Christmas, the preparations of Advent, the Purple and the Rose, had all been touched with the gloom of Sarafino's sickness, and now there was no question that this was a final turn. The priest took several pain pills early in the morning, and they had braced him somewhat. Now he was thankful for Peter's coming. The three of them buzzed now from his presence and his crisp, easy instructions as they bustled and made the adjustments. The priest sensed his own small renewal. The mood lifted. "I'll be checking in," said Peter as he left. "And I'm always right at the other end of the telephone."

THEY TOOK TURNS, THE FOUR OF THEM. IF THEY WEREN'T SITTING directly with him in the room, they were close by and checked on him regularly. Sarafino's fever hung on and he ate little, taking only small sips of liquid. The IV kept him hydrated. They helped with his medicines, which allowed him comfort and helped him sleep. When pain broke through, they droppered morphine onto the back of his tongue. They laved his forehead with cool towels. When he hadn't changed his position in the bed by himself, they rolled him easily or propped him. They rubbed his skin tenderly with soft squares of flannel. They prayed the Rosary by his bedside.

Through it all, Sarafino said little. He sank away from them daily. Once he grabbed the priest's arm and said, "We're leaving in the morning. I heard it from the lieutenant. They're lifting us in. On the shithooks." Another time he said, "Where are the guards? How come there's not guards? They must have all run off. With that Jesus guy."

"Sarafino," said the priest, "you are here in town. You are with Manny and Alzaida. You are staying here, in the rectory of the church. I'm Manny. Alzaida is sitting there in that chair." It seemed impossible that a week before, Sarafino had walked half a mile in the rain. And looking back at himself, it seemed impossible that Furtado had navigated the parish through the Christmas devotions and celebrations, the midnight high Mass, the open house at the parish hall, the visits with gifts to the needy families. All that seemed an age ago. He noted little about it. His concern was with Sarafino.

"You remember us," Allie said.

"I remember Allie. And Manny. You are too old to . . . be them. I don't know what ever . . . happened to Manny. And Alzaida."

"We all grew up," Allie said.

Yet he would rally again. Again, with Furtado and Alzaida sitting with him. Sarafino lucid and distant. Tinier than ever. "Have you done the last rites? Extreme unction?" Sarafino asked. "I can't remember."

"I'll do them right now," the priest said. "The Anointing of the Sick. Is that what you want?"

"Yes," he said. So small in the bed's vast wilderness of quilts and pillows. The cannula. The IV. "That's what I want."

The priest went to Mariah, who was filing collection slips in the office, and he told her what he was doing and asked her to call in Tom, who was working somewhere out on the grounds. Then he went to the sacristy and took down the decanter of blessed oil from the ambry, and a vial of holy water, and decanted a little of each of them into cruets and brought them back into the rectory. He laid these on the kitchen table and then thought for a moment, and when Tom came in the back door with Mariah, he told them that he would anoint Sarafino in the old manner, because when Sarafino had asked for the sacrament, he had used its old name, what it had been called before Vatican reforms: extreme unction. He believed that Sarafino had this in mind and that it would please him, and the priest himself wanted to do this, but his own reasons were out of reach to him, or perhaps he did not care to know them. He had not been using the gin during the day, but he was using the pain pills, and other pills—muscle relaxers, anti-inflammatories, even sleepers—steadily now, day and night. Yet he felt, if anything, that his judgment was cleared by this. He felt his energy increase. He sat at the wheel of command. He would hold the old rite, and he would hold it in the Latin, the way he and Sarafino had known their prayers as boys.

He had Tom and Mariah bring a small end table from the parlor, and they placed it in Sarafino's room near the foot of the bed. The priest went back to the sacristy and returned with a piece of dried palm from the Palm Sunday palms that were saved in plastic wrap in a drawer, and brought it into the rectory, along with two blessed candles and two small rectangles of linen. Mariah set the table with a white cloth from the kitchen, which she folded to size, and together they set upon it a crucifix, the small, heavy, freestanding, gold-plated cross that had belonged to Furtado's mother and that he kept in one of his dresser drawers.

They placed the candles in brass holders on either side of the cross, and put down a small bowl of water, the cruets of blessed oil and holy water, and a saucer with several cotton balls on it. The priest had Alzaida cut a tiny slice of Portuguese bread and place it on a saucer, and then he said that he'd like her and Mariah to cover their heads. Mariah went to the kitchen and came back with their ball caps, but Allie told her to wait a minute, and she went out to the hall closet and her sewing basket and after a moment came back with two rough squares of blue cloth, which she folded neatly into triangles, and she and Mariah wore them as kerchiefs, tied under their chins and draping down their backs between their shoulders.

Then the priest laid one of the pieces of linen over Sarafino's breast, and he asked Tom to switch the oxygen synthesizer to standby mode, shutting off the flow. When Tom returned, Furtado lit the candles. "I'm going to begin," he said. "Who will read the responses for me?"

"Mariah," said Allie. Tom nodded, and Mariah took the copy of the rite and held it before her like a hymnal.

"Sarafino, we're ready."

Sarafino looked at him and slowly closed his eyes and opened them again.

"Will you speak? I turned off the machine for just a few minutes because of the candles."

"Yes," Sarafino said. "I'm okay." He gestured with his hand. The priest caught the hand in the moment it fluttered up, backlit in the muslined rectangle of the window. A thin hand, still graceful in its way, narrow and long-fingered. Beautiful decades ago, he recalled. Beautiful still, because it lived and moved. Furtado lifted the crucifix from the table and touched it to Sarafino's lips for the ritual kiss, and then he turned and looked at the room: Tom and Allie and Mariah and Sarafino, what they had become. Himself, too. Bound together.

He replaced the cross and sprinkled the room with holy water. "*Pax hic domui*," he said. And Mariah read, "*Et omnibus habitantibus in ea.*"

Together they moved through the rite in Latin. When the priest reached the moment for confession, he leaned over Sarafino and asked, "Do you confess your sins?" "I did it all," he said.

"Is there something you want to confess that you have not spoken of?"

"Nothing."

"And the appearances of Our Lady?"

"True."

"What about Her rising?" The priest saw Alzaida's flash when he asked this, and she looked at him balefully but did not interrupt.

"True."

And Furtado granted absolution.

Then he blessed the piece of bread from Lucy Braga's bakery—bread baked there in the town in the same way in which it had been made in the old Portugal and the far islands of their grandmothers and grandfathers, and of Furtado's father. He blessed the bread and gave it as the viaticum, the soul's food for the journey into death. He pinched some crumbs from it and placed them between Sarafino's lips, and Sarafino licked his lips and took and ate the crumbs.

The four of them stood around the bed, breathing together in the little room. They moved through the prayers, Furtado's voice and Mariah's back and forth in the hypnotic Latin, until they came to the time for anointing, when Furtado asked Tom to lift the linen cloth from the bed and pull back the bedcover. The priest took the oil and the cotton, and in the manner of the old rite recited, "*Per istam sanctam unctionem.*" He anointed Sarafino's eyelids and ears, his nostrils, his lips, and his hands and feet. When he finished, Tom pulled the cover back over Sarafino. The priest wiped his hands on the remains of the slice of bread and then washed them in the bowl and wiped them on the linen cloth. He recited the Kyrie Eleison, with Mariah responding, and they moved through the remaining prayers of the ritual and ended with the *benedictat*.

The priest snuffed the candles and immediately replaced the oxygen cannula under Sarafino's chin and over his ears, and had Tom switch the machine back on. Allie began to clear the little table of the implements, and Furtado pointed to the bread and the cotton and the bowl of water. "I've touched them with the oil," he said. "They have to be buried in the earth."

Allie looked at Tom. "All right," Tom said.

Sarafino snuffed the oxygen. Tom took away the material to be buried, and Mariah cleared the room of the table and then left the rectory when Winslow picked her up. Tom went home to the Village to take care of some things at the house, and Furtado and Allie sat by themselves in Sarafino's room, watching the cold light in the window and watching Sarafino, and talking with each other and to Sarafino, though he didn't answer. But just as it was growing dark, just before either the priest or his sister thought to turn on a light in the room, Sarafino spoke to Furtado. His voice rattled, but his words were clear. "Manny," he said, "I know there's something important . . . I am supposed to tell you. About Our Lady. I can't remember. I'm sorry . . . Manny . . . I can't . . . get it."

"Is it about the statue?" the priest asked. He slid his chair over by the bed.

"Who is the other one?"

"Sarafino," said the priest. "Your miracle. Tell me what you did with the statue. Maybe that's it. You need to tell me."

"Is that the one that's gone?"

"You did something with it. I need to know," said the priest.

Sarafino's head shook back and forth on the pillow. Then his eyes traveled the circuit of the room, as though he might find what he was looking for sitting somewhere on the bureau or up in a corner of the ceiling. He snuffed hard at the oxygen. "I don't get . . . any of this," he said. "I don't understand . . . what is happening . . . to me."

"Your miracle with the Virgin," said Furtado.

Suddenly Alzaida jumped up in a rage, knocking her chair over. She stood over her brother. "For God's sake, Manny, stop it!" she said. "None of this is about *you*. You leave him the hell alone!"

twenty

"THE APPARITIONS OF MARY," SAID JOHN SWEET. "WHY, THEY ARE everywhere! They occur daily: Florida, Pennsylvania, New York, Los Angeles, all over the Midwest. Who knows in what nameless towns, in what wheatfields and cornfields?"

Furtado suddenly could not remember how the subject had come up. He feared that at worst he'd slipped and said something about Sarafino's visions. He was not at his best. Sweet was restless; strain showed on his face, a play of nerves under the tight skin. His leg jiggled in his gabardine trousers. "But Fatima. You want my opinion? Look! We are sitting in the rectory at the parish of Our Lady of Fatima. And I have thought about this. Because your parish is Fatima, it's my work to think about this. You know as well as I do that the Church does not insist on anyone's belief in such a miracle." He raised his hand in a broad gesture. "*But*. But if you want my judgment on it, I see it as a miracle in practical terms. Before the Virgin Mary appeared to the children at Cova da Iria, the Church there was threatened and the people of Portugal were oppressed. But after Fatima appeared, the Church came back. It rose up. It took hold again in a way that could never be pressed down. Religion emerged from the shadows and the fear, and this spread into the world at large. You see? Very practical terms, regardless of what you want to say about those kids. But I don't see what my opinion could mean to you on this."

They sat in the parlor, Sweet on the sofa and Furtado in the stuffed easy chair. Furtado had set out black coffee in the rectory's good china, delicate white cups with fluted white saucers, maybe as old as the building itself, and Sweet had set a black, accordion-style briefcase on the floor beside the darkly polished end table. Furtado had not seen the briefcase before. The rectory was quiet. Furtado caught a flash of Tom as he moved past one of the windows—his padded barn jacket, his woolen watch cap pulled down over his ears. The weather had snapped. Arctic air was coming down from Canada. A blessing. Tom was working on an extensive list of things to get done. It would be a long day. He would not interrupt the priest's visit.

The sky had dawned clear, and the morning had been dazzling in its winter brightness, a shine like opal, but now there came a murky reef of stratospheric cloud riding out of the north with the freezing air, changing the light and making the small street and the church grounds look melancholy, as though all the lives in the small houses on the lane were dreary and hopeless. Furtado had purposely kept the thermostats very low but had turned on all the electric lights, which soured and leached Sweet's complexion. Furtado suspected he himself looked as bad.

He had put off seeing Sweet for the better part of two weeks, but when the other priest had called suddenly that morning and told Furtado he was on his way down to the town with something that could not be postponed, Furtado—despite the situation with Sarafino—could not offer up any excuse that Sweet would allow to deflect him. And now, when there was so much to do, they sat together, and Furtado, weary and on edge, willed himself to get through it.

John Sweet waved his hand again. "Your church. Your lovely parish. All named for an apparition." He smiled, dismissing the subject, but the smile was forced and frightening. Furtado told himself to remember: *Always caution, always a moment of thought before speech.* He couldn't divine yet what was in the wind.

"A strange place, a complex place, this town," Sweet said, his eyes wide. Bulging. Rolling. Not unattractive eyes. Not ordinary eyes. "I appreciate the pressures on you. Your roots here. Your family. All the changes. I'm not oblivious."

"John, I'm sober; I'm in charge." Furtado was unsure if he was keeping his irritation out of his voice. He tried to speak evenly, affably. "I'm doing the work of the parish, and I'm doing the work you subscribed me to. I have been working hard. I'm tired sometimes. But soon I will attend those meetings. Up the Cape. I have thought that through."

Sweet drank from his coffee cup and placed it back on its saucer with a little *click*. A glow came into those eyes now. His face shone suddenly in the parlor light. "Evil can beget evil," he said abruptly. "Good can beget evil. And what looks like evil can beget good." He smiled. "You see? I contradict Aquinas! You are not the only heretic here."

"Sometimes," Furtado said carefully, "I just can't follow you, John."

"You are forgiven!" said the fixer.

Furtado studied him, thinking. He said nothing.

Sweet bent and reached for the black leather briefcase. "You are forgiven," he said. "Fatima is. The parish. The debt!" He opened the case and took out a document. It was spiral-bound, with clear plastic covers, about as thick as a magazine. "It's all here. I am the first to tell you. I asked Rego to let me bring the news. He is very pleased. We talked quite a bit. He wants to talk with you, too, of course, but he's aware of our work, yours and mine. It's done. Your second option."

"The second option."

"Everything you wanted in the second option, it's all here—your documents and theirs. From the Chancery. Now Fatima is on the road to solvency. Renewal."

"I'm glad to hear it, John," said the priest after a moment. His gaze fell to the window again. The empty churchyard, the sad light. He wished he could be out working with Tom now. There were so many things to do. As for the proposal, he had never doubted that he'd get what he wanted, but it was fulsome of Sweet to be so theatrical about it.

"Read it at your leisure," Sweet said when Furtado not did reach over to take the report. "I believe I have been of some help. But it had to be done by you, finished by you. Your place in the town, your relationships with the people, are valuable. George Rego understood."

Furtado tried to remember the help Sweet was talking about.

"I don't think you're sober, Manny," Sweet said into the awkwardness. "I have a feel for these things. I have a great intuition about them. This isn't pride speaking."

"I can't think of what to tell you, John," Furtado said. He took a cautious sip of coffee.

"You can tell me what's in your heart," said Sweet. He wore a navy wool sweater above the black slacks. Heavy wool. He had begun to sweat, even in the chilly parlor. Little beads of perspiration flecked his forehead. His cheeks flushed.

"I don't like your being here," Furtado said. He pushed ahead with care. "I suppose I resent it all the way back to my housekeeper and her foolishness. People like that should be kept away from the evening news. She called my superiors and accused me of pederasty, for God's sake."

"Ah," said Sweet. "You see, I sensed that, Manny. It's natural, you know, these intrusions and investigations. But even your old housekeeper and her . . . I think we called it malice . . . that might be the Holy Ghost! What is balm for one may be fire for another."

"It really should be over," said Furtado.

"It nearly is, Manny." Sweet let out a deep sigh and drank more of the coffee. "I've spoken to her again, you know."

"To Idalina Horta?"

"Yes, your housekeeper."

Furtado said nothing.

"You don't inquire about her?"

"I don't," said Furtado.

"She suffers."

"I can't help that," said Furtado. "I suffer."

"She needs to be forgiven. From your lips."

"Not until I can do it sincerely. I'm thinking of my own damage. Which no one else seems to consider." Furtado thought for a moment. "So you say you spoke to her again?"

"Yes."

"But your visit—I presume it was you who visited her?"

"Yes."

"Yes. But your visit wasn't about forgiveness, exactly, was it? You went back to her to check. To verify. To make sure she still stood by her recanting. After all this, John! You went back to see if her story had changed again."

Sweet shook his head slowly. "It's simply a protocol I must go through. I answer to the archdiocese. It all works in your favor. The assault the Church is under now, you have only the smallest idea of its proportions. There are powerful enemies into whose hands this all plays. Believe me, I am your greatest friend and ally in these matters. I care for you. God loves you. Just a few more things."

"What are these things? Am I going to be placed under the obligation of forgiving *you* for something, too? Is that what all that little homily was really about?"

"I've upset you. You're angry. I understand that. But you must understand, too. It's all so . . . complicated now. The fact that children were brought up. The lawsuits. The public attention. We have to document so much. So much care has to be taken. It's the times, Manny. But you have nothing to worry about. All will be well."

"I'm glad to hear it," said Furtado. He struggled to recover his caution. He mollified his tone. "I am very glad to hear it. And in fairness, John, I thank you for how you handled everything. The parish council, the boys' families, the old woman . . . you were very good. You made not a single wave. You didn't allow anything to spread, and in a town like this, that's"—he smiled purposefully—"that's a miracle."

Sweet paused. "Sometimes I'm not well myself," he said.

"I don't understand," said Furtado.

"I'm not well sometimes."

Furtado just watched him.

Now Sweet smiled. He leaned forward and clasped his hands. "This job." He shook his long head. "Sometimes I'm not well."

"Would you like to go out?" Furtado asked, seizing the opportunity to get Sweet away from the rectory. "These rooms are close and formal. Let me take you out someplace for something to eat."

Sweet looked around the room, as if his own thoughts might be written on one of the walls. Then he looked back at Furtado. "Yes," he said. "That's a wonderful idea. I don't believe I've had breakfast or lunch."

"Neither have I. It puts a tension on things. That's what we're feeling. There's not much open, but I know a place."

"Yes. This is a lovely room, Manny," Sweet said. "You are very lucky." He looked around again. "The parish runs well," he said, as he got up from the sofa and affected a casual tone. "That fisherman's mother? She is well? I take an interest in your work, Manny. I take it that homeless man has been taken care of?"

"Oh. Yes, yes," said Furtado. He had taken a pill, merely one pill. The welcome bitterness in his mouth, his lips prickly with it. "My assistant has been spending a lot of time with Mrs. Boia. One of the old ones. And yes, we got the confused gentleman taken care of. He's gone back to his family. We are busy here, but things go well. It's good to be into the new year, weather and all. Just sit back down a minute and let me get a change of clothes on." He took the coffee cups to the kitchen and changed from his cassock into slacks and a heavy jacket. Then they left the rectory, where Mariah Grey had been sitting the whole time behind the locked door of the sickroom with the dead, shrouded body of Sarafino Pomba.

Sarafino had died the day before, at about one thirty in the morning. The priest had put down just a few details in the ledger. If the Blessed Mother was there at the final hour, She was there for Sarafino alone, in some other realm or dimension; there were no outward signs of her. Sarafino died with his rosary wrapped around his right hand and with Tom and Allie and Mariah and Furtado at his bedside. They had called Peter, but he had not arrived from up the Cape until after the death.

Furtado had droppered some morphine on the back of Sarafino's tongue before the agonistic breathing started, and he'd prayed over him in a way that Sarafino would hear, if he was hearing at all. Sarafino had not spoken a single word in days, and he died silently, save for the muted rattle of his last breaths. Allie had wept. Furtado, after ensuring that no life remained, had rearranged the body flat on the bed in a posture of peace and repose, though Sarafino had died lying on his left side with his legs drawn up at the knees and his arms bent, his hands in fists below his chin, like a weary prizefighter.

The four of them had planned days in advance what they would do and who would do it. Mariah had already brought cotton sheets to the rectory, and she'd helped as Alzaida cut and sewed them into the shroud, saving strips that she sewed in double thickness to wind the shroud and tie Sarafino's jaw and limbs. Furtado had washed the body with soap and water and a linen cloth, and he'd asked Alzaida to wrap Sarafino with him, but when she refused, Mariah had helped and together they had bound Sarafino's body in the white shroud and let it lie on the bare bed.

They would bury him tonight in the place where the Virgin had once lain. This was what Tom was preparing for: gathering the tools that they would take with them late, after the bars had closed and the town was asleep. The cold snap would work in their favor. Tom had already determined that the ponds were frozen. This was the business that occupied Furtado when John Sweet burst upon him with the news from the diocese, and it continued to occupy his mind all through the strained lunch.

The Topsail was still open, one of the few town restaurants to keep winter hours during the week. They sat in a booth near the back and were waited on by Adelaide Lema, a parishioner, the daughter of an old school friend of Allie's. Her mother still worked at the Topsail, too, but only during the busy summers. "Hello, Father Manny," she said. She was beginning to look like her mother. Furtado could see the weight settling on her hips and thighs. She smiled brightly. Dark eyes. Dark skin. "And hello to you, too, Father. It's good to see you again."

Sweet returned her smile through tight lips, but his eyes rolled and settled warmly on the girl. "It's very good to see you again, too," he said.

"You've eaten here," said Furtado.

"Oh, yes," said Sweet.

"How often do you actually come to town?" Furtado asked. He felt himself color.

"When I can," said Sweet. "It's not all business. It's restful here, in a way. Any priest would envy this parish. Anyone would envy you." A thought seemed to move across his face. He dabbed at his lips with his paper napkin. "You see, Manny, I don't always come to annoy you. Sometimes I just drive down on my own."

"There's fresh *vinha d'ahlos* pork chops," said Adelaide Lema. "And the *lula* is really good for a cold day."

"*Lula* for me," said Furtado.

"That would be calamari stew," said Sweet. "I'm studying Portuguese, Manny." He tapped his open menu with the back of his hand. "What do you think of that?"

"We call it squid," said Furtado.

"I will try some," said Sweet. "I will try everything eventually. It's all wonderful. I will go to sea on a fishing boat. I will go out and follow the whales."

"You come here and check up on me," said Furtado, when Adelaide had left for the kitchen. "You don't have to be coy."

"Manny, I love the people here. I love the little town. I sit. I talk. I get to know things. You must put yourself at ease. I'm not always working."

We must put Sarafino in the ground, thought the priest. *I must endure this*. His shoulder ached, and he reached and rubbed it absently. He had taken two more tablets, only two, when he had changed clothes in the rectory. He felt nothing from them. He looked at the wall clock over the kitchen door. He knew that Sweet was down only for the day, and that soon he would have to begin the drive back up to Calumet. He calculated the hours. He smiled at Sweet. Sweet's complexion had returned to its usual pallor. His eyes no longer shone with that unsettling gaze. The Topsail's dining room was empty save for them, and it was dimly lit and warm. "I will put myself at ease then, John," Furtado said. It was strain to speak in such an even tone. "And I am very happy about the proposal." He raised his water glass in a toast, and then Adelaide Lema brought their *lula*, blackish red and steaming in the bowls, and plates of hot, thick-crusted bread, and Furtado watched how Sweet concentrated and examined it as he ate it.

THE PRIEST SAID MASS FOR SARAFINO AT MIDNIGHT. TOM AND ALLIE and Mariah sat close together in the front pew of the church. The church was locked, cold, and empty. They'd kept it dark, except they'd lit the statue of the Virgin and the altar lights. The priest chose to abbreviate the Mass, and he moved through it quickly. After Mass they all attended to a few last-minute things, and at about one forty-five they assembled in the rectory kitchen. They all wore dark clothing now, full of purpose, and the priest was embarrassed at how they looked, like bank robbers or terrorists.

Tom had walked out across the ponds to the gravesite once already, and had found the ice solid and complete. The most dangerous part of the night would be driving Sarafino's body out along the trails to a place where they could then carry it in to the gravesite. Furtado reasoned that once they were on the pond and into the heavy thickets, they would be invisible. It was unlikely, in any event, that a park ranger would be out in the woods at that hour on such a winter's night, but the priest insisted on details. He and Tom and Allie would be dropped off at the edge of the woods and would walk in. Winslow and Mariah would wait long enough for them to arrive at the point in the road where they would begin the walk into the ponds, and then they would drive into the woods with Sarafino, covered with a tarp, in the truck bed. Darwin would be with them in the cab. If they were stopped for any reason, the cover would be that the dog had run off earlier that night, and that they had just found him and were returning home. No one would look under the tarp. And when they met and unloaded the body, Mariah would join the other three and take Sarafino to his resting place. Winslow would drive the truck out of the woods. Same story if someone stumbled upon her: Lost Darwin. Found Darwin.

They conferred once more on the plans, and then Tom and the priest brought out the shrouded Sarafino, carrying him in a gray woolen blanket as if on a litter, each holding an end by the corners. They placed him in the truck bed, tucked the tarp around him, and distributed some other random articles as blinds: a few cement blocks, a length of two-by-four, a bag of road salt. When they had settled the body in the truck, Winslow took the priest's car and drove the others to the woods while Mariah waited at the rectory.

The priest and Tom and Alzaida walked the paths single file. The woods were profoundly black. There was not even starlight to show the paths against the trees. They all carried small flashlights, but only the priest shone his, only from time to time, to get a bearing on the path, and he swung it low, along the path's edges. He had covered the lens with a piece of red balloon that he'd salvaged from the parish hall's party supplies. The red light oozing from the flashlight was hard to see from a distance, and, more importantly, it did not decrease their night vision as white light would. It was how all the boats and ships were lit below decks at night, but there in the woods, it was hard to see by.

The walking warmed them slightly, but when they reached the bend in the path where they had agreed to meet, they sat huddled against one another in the darkness and shivered, thankful that at least there was no wind. After a time, they all heard the muffled sound of the engine at once, then saw the stab of the lights—only the parking lights—and then the truck, crawling so as not to raise the engine noise.

They worked quickly and spoke little. Mariah joined them as they slid Sarafino out of the truck bed. Immediately, Winslow and the dog drove on, slowly again, and the woods seemed to swallow them completely in the cold and the dark as the truck's muted lights passed around the bend and disappeared.

It was hard to see. Even though they wore heavy gloves, the cold made their hands numb and unresponsive. The priest had taken another tablet before the Mass and carried two more in his pocket, but he would not let himself take those until they'd buried the body. His ear played a sweet electronic tune, soft and calming, and the frigid air lifted his mind to a strange and dreamlike clarity. He could see everything they needed to do, all at once.

They finally got Sarafino centered in the blanket. Each took a corner, and they stepped out onto the first pond. The ice was slick beneath their feet, and walking was awkward. "You say 'down' whenever it's time to rest," the priest told the others. "Then I'll say 'up,' after a minute or so. Other than that, no talking." The priest held the blanket corner with one hand and the flashlight with the other. He flicked it on and off, sweeping the ice in front of them. They hugged the contour of the shore, just to be safe. The ice held. It was far better than crashing blindly through the brush. They fell into a rhythm, sliding their feet along, Sarafino swaying lightly between them in the bellied blanket. It occurred to Furtado that they could simply slide him on the blanket, but he rejected the idea. Sarafino was light. He was nothing. He was like carrying the wind. They had to stop and put him down only twice before they reached the second pond. Here, Furtado had Allie and Mariah walk and crouch carefully ahead as they picked their way through the dense pines and growth, shining the lights steadily now that they were so far from any paths, and he and Tom carried the blanket in narrow file through the darkness until they reached the hidden pond's ice. They traversed this in the same manner as they had the first, staying with the curve of the shore.

When they reached the point where they would enter the deep thicket, they realized that they would have to proceed on their knees. Again, Allie went ahead with a light, but this time Mariah stayed behind and shined her light toward Tom and the priest so they could better pick their way through the growth. All of them crawled, and Furtado and Tom managed the body in a series of small forward lifts. Each lift was a fine wire of pain for the priest, but he said nothing; though he ached, he could put the ache aside. His mind rolled over and back, over and back, across all that had to be done, and the rolling was a kind of comfort, as if such thinking made their journey less brazen and absurd.

They were able to stand again when they reached the cove. Mariah and Tom pulled battery lanterns from their parka pockets. The white light seemed brilliant among the imposing pines and bracken, and they each hung their lantern from a low branch so that it shined on the grave. When Tom had come out earlier in the day, he had carried a backpack with two folding shovels and other materials, as well as his .410 rabbit gun. He'd worn his hunting license on his parka as a blind, but he had met no one on the wooded paths as he walked the edges of the ponds and ducked into the deep woods, where he had finished digging the grave. He had pulled out all the branches and needles that the priest and Mariah had filled the indentation with, and dug the shallow trench deeper. He must have worked for hours, though he'd said nothing about it when he returned, except that it was done. The grave now lay about five feet deep, well down into the sand. Tom had removed the earth carefully and mounded it neatly. He had thought about details. Everything would have to be put back in place so that their disturbance would be camouflaged again.

Perhaps they were exaggerating their caution, for it was unlikely that anyone would traverse that thicket, and even if someone did, after a winter and a spring any traces they might leave would be obliterated. And who would ever think to look for a grave, anyway?

The cold seemed to pool into that spot like water. Furtado watched the vapor plume from their mouths. They stood looking at the grave, recovering for a moment from the exertion of having brought Sarafino's body along through the bracken. Furtado thought then of the times he and Sarafino had made camp here—even in such cold as this, but with a tent and heavy sleeping bags and a fire.

Sarafino lay on the blanket in his white shroud, a small, thin package. "Good," Furtado said. "Good, Tom. All right, then. We shouldn't wait."

Tom uncoiled a clothesline, pulled a glove from his hand with his teeth, and cut the line in half with his rigging knife. Mariah and Allie slid Sarafino's body over to the foot of the hole, and Tom passed the two lengths of line under the body. When they had positioned the line just right, they each took one of the four ends and carefully walked the body over the mouth of the grave. They stopped when the body was centered, and then they lowered it. When Sarafino was settled down in the pale sand, they pulled the ropes out from under the shroud and up out of the hole, and Tom quickly coiled them back together. There was no wind in the thicket, but the long, exhaling *shush* of a light breeze moved constantly in the high boughs of the pines all around the ponds, and from beyond that sound came the faint and ghostly squall of a band of coyotes, so distant that the priest thought he was imagining it, but he watched the others and saw their heads move slightly, as his did, an animal gesture, the senses gone quick.

Then the moment passed. The silent humans remained in place, two on each side of the grave. No one spoke until the priest said, "Mariah, the candle?" She pulled a votive in a glass from somewhere in her nest of pockets, set it in the mounded fresh earth, and lit it after several tries with her ungloved hands and a book of paper matches. The flame shrank to a tiny bead, then elongated on the wick and bounced for a moment before settling into a pallid glow.

Furtado uttered an incantation in Latin, and then he committed Sarafino Pomba into the earth, into the mysterious eternal night. Into the mind of God. He ended with "*Requesiat in pacem*," and the others, cued by Mariah, said, "Amen."

Alzaida said, "I can't watch the shoveling. I'm sorry, but I can't." No one answered right away. Furtado knew they must move on. They had made a plan, and now they would stick to it. He reached down and threw a handful of dirt into the grave. "Now you," he said to Alzaida. "Just do it."

"I know," she said. "I brought him here. I know." She squatted and picked up a double handful of the dug-out sand and tossed it into the hole. "That's it for me," she said.

Mariah and Tom threw dirt into the grave as well, and then Tom took up one of the shovels. Because Manny had to be back at the church, they'd decided that Tom and Mariah would stay and bury Sarafino, fix the grave, and cover their return tracks after daylight.

It would take a few long, cold hours, but the work would warm them, and Tom had brought a small thermos of strong hot coffee in his parka. Mariah lifted the candle from the loose earth and set it in the shelter of the base of a tree, and shifted the battery lanterns slightly so that they shone more onto the piled sand and not into the mouth of the grave, and then she picked up the other shovel.

"You should go," she said. "Winslow will be looking for you out on the road pretty soon." Alzaida was crying softly. Furtado laid his gloved hand on her shoulder and turned her toward the black tangle of growth that they would have to crawl out through.

The sound of the shoveling behind them faded almost immediately as they made their way down to the pond with their tiny lights. Once they reached the ice, the priest turned and looked back. The blackness swallowed everything. No noise or light escaped from the thicket. The thing was as good as finished, but while his heart ratcheted in his chest and his legs quivered, he felt no real elation, no sense of closure, no happiness in keeping his promise. It was in that moment that he sensed the enormity of all that had happened and all that he had done. Just as suddenly, his utter fall from grace and from all things adduced to ideas of goodness seemed abject and complete. He could not even cry out in this strange, abrupt sorrow.

He turned again and looked toward the path. He could see Allie only as a different darkness in the enormous night that surrounded them. They carefully followed the contour of the pond back to the narrow isthmus of pine woods, crossed it to reach the next pond, and, walking hunched against the cold, made their way together through the profound obscurity of the woods. If Alzaida still cried, she cried silently, for Furtado could not hear her and could not see her face. And all the while, this new and unfamiliar pain bloomed, and he knew it to be some breakage of the spirit and nothing of the body. Nonetheless, he slipped his two tablets into his mouth and chewed and swallowed them, but they did not spread any comfort along this raw distress, and each step he took was a separate misery.

twenty-one

THE HOUR WAS STILL DARK. SLEEP WAS OUT OF THE QUESTION FOR the priest. His reserves were gone, but he was beyond the need for them. Far beyond. Now he went where his body led him. He walked into the church and lit the altar and stared at it for some time. The heat was on very low and the building was cold, but the altar seemed beautiful to him now, the sanctuary candle burning and the statues in their inhuman perfection glowing with a humanlike grace. He could not pray or kneel. He simply stood and looked for a long time, before he shut off the lights and locked up and walked back to the rectory.

There he began to set things in order in Sarafino's sick room, which was now to go back to being just a room. He stripped the remaining linens from the mattress and threw them in a pile in the hall. He removed the plaster statues from the bureau and redistributed them to their original places in other rooms. He gathered up all of Sarafino's clothes and bagged these items for the dump. The linens he placed in the washer, along with towels from the bathroom, but then he had a change of mind and pulled them out again and put those in dump bags also. He removed the extra chairs and the lamp that had been brought in, and took a bucket of water and Spic And Span and washed down the room with a thick sponge. He rubbed lemon oil into the table and the bureau and opened the curtain and lifted the shade. He made up the bed again with fresh sheets and a white bedspread. He arranged everything so that it became a guest room again.

When he stepped back and looked at the room, he was pleased. It looked spare and empty and quiet, and it gave no hint of the dramas that had played out in it. It looked like a room in which nothing could ever happen, and it was comforting to think that such places could exist in the world, even if they were not real.

His hands shook as he prepared coffee in the kitchen. He ate nothing, but he swallowed more of the white pills and drank several cups of the hot coffee. It was daylight now, and the thermometer in the window showed that the temperature had risen into the high twenties. He went into the bathroom and washed his face with cold water, and he shaved and brushed his teeth and put on a fresh woolen shirt and sweater, and then he donned his parka and watch cap and went out the back door to the car.

The drive to Tom and Alzaida's seemed like a great journey. The sky was ribbed with some high clouds but mostly clear and blue, the watery sun, still low in the east, shining orange and brass on the undersides of the clouds. He did not see another car, and it felt like the highway was rolling toward him and then under his wheels and that the car stood still, though the speedometer read 50. He turned off at Village Road; a pickup truck and a long white sedan were parked in front of DeMelo's store, but otherwise the small road was empty of traffic. He rolled on up the hill and onto the dirt road that led to Alzaida's. Lined with dense green in summer, the road now curved up through brown dead grasses and bare trees. On the left a boat—a good twenty-plus-footer—sat trailered and tarped for the winter, and behind it were stacks of lobster pots, both wire and wooden, all heavily weathered, and behind them a dark-shingled shambling house. He drove on past it to the turnaround, the last site on the road, and stopped in front of the rail fence there and got out of the car and walked up onto the deck of Alzaida's gray-and-white Cape. The white truck and Alzaida's old Rodeo were parked outside, in front of the garage, which could not be used for the cars because it was always filled with gear from the *Ilha*. The yard here simply stretched away from the house and off to the hill and more trees, scrub oak and some pine and alder, and there was no boundary where the yard ended and the Village woods began. The nearby trees were hung with feeders and suet balls, but the priest saw no squirrels or birds, and the yard and the woods, lit by the early winter sun, were deeply quiet. He stepped across the broad deck to the side door and tapped. He could see Alzaida sitting at the kitchen table behind the window.

His sister came to the door and opened it and sat back down. He closed the door behind him quietly and followed her over to the table. "There's coffee," she said. "And some cinnamon buns, but they're a little old." He went to the counter and poured some coffee. There was still a tremor in his hand, so he took one of the crusty buns, thinking that it might cut the caffeine somehow. One of Alzaida's cats sat on the counter by the package of buns and flicked his tail and watched him.

"Tommy just got in from the woods. He's crashed out," Allie said when he sat down. "He can do that. It's from fishing. He could sleep on an atomic bomb."

"You haven't slept," Furtado said. Her face was severely shadowed, and she wore a heavy quilted robe, matted down and tied at the waist.

"What do you think?"

He drew on the coffee, which was oily and bitter. "I think it's about me."

She looked at him. It was a raw, wild look. "What?" she asked. "What is?"

"Everything. All this."

"You don't sound right, Manny."

"You said. You said it wasn't about me. Do you remember you said that? But it *is* about me. The whole thing."

"I'm tired, Manny. Can you see that? I'm breaking into little pieces, if you want to know. What would you do if I was somebody else, somebody from church? Wouldn't you try to help? Or wouldn't you just leave them alone? Because I'll tell you: When I saw you at the door, I thought for just this little tiny minute, I thought, *Oh, Manny is here and he wants to see if I'm okay. Manny has come around to see me*. Then I saw your face. Nothing changes."

The priest was on a steep downhill now, coasting, reeling forward. There was no stopping. "You said it wasn't about me. Do you know why?" Another of her cats, a lean white-and-orange female, jumped up onto the table and walked around. Alzaida made no move to shoo it off. The table was cluttered with old newspapers and mail, some dishes, an ashtray half full. A mug of cold coffee sat at the other end of it, and the cat stuck its head into it and began to lap from it.

"We just got through burying Sarafino." Alzaida said. She spoke with her arms crossed over her breasts, and she looked out the window, not at him.

"You can say it's not about me because you know." This was what had come to him. This was what he was certain of now. "You know—you *think*—you *think* it's about you. Because you did bring Sarafino back here. Because you think you were in love with him when you were a kid. You were a kid, for heaven's sake. But never mind about that. And I won't even talk about the money you thought you'd get from the viatical contract. No. You think that it's not about me because it's you he gave that statue to. I don't know. I don't know how or why or what, but he didn't want me to have it. He could have told you where it was. You went and got it. Something like that."

"Manny, I shouldn't even be talking to you about this. You're wound up. You're over the top. You should get some rest."

"No. My mind is clear."

"If you thought about what you are saying, you could see it makes no sense. And who would care about this anyway? Nobody thinks it was a miracle."

"Me. Don't you see? He would think that *I* would."

"Manny."

"I am the reason for all of this. I dragged Sarafino into it, and it harmed him. He came back. He took his revenge on me. I only did it to get back at Pai. Sarafino didn't like him either. Pai was so mean to us, and he had this big act outside the house. And he crippled you. Look—you never left town, you never had a life because of him."

"Just leave my life out of it, Manny. And, say what you will, Papa worked hard. He put food on the table. He was who he was. He did his best. Maybe you just knew you couldn't live up to him."

"Yes, yes. I know all that. But you know I'm right, too."

"I think you hide out, to tell you the truth. The Church, it's like this big glass bubble around you. Shit never comes down on *you*. And everybody called Papa Pai. And now here you are, and what do they call you? Father. I'm not stupid."

The priest stared out the window. He saw dark spots, like hands, darting swiftly at the corners of his eyes, and then he realized they were birds swooping down toward the feeders. Starlings, maybe. The cat jumped from the table. His paws made an enormous *thud* on the hardwood floor.

"It would be so simple if you would just tell me," he said. "Because the Virgin did not rise from that hole in the ground. She was never there. Not for long, anyway. Sarafino came back because of *me*. Not because he loved me, not because of our friendship as kids. He wanted to torture me for what I did to him. He showed me the work of my hands. He wanted to bring a plague on me. And he's doing it. Maybe you are, too."

"Manny, you are scaring me." Allie turned and looked him full in the face. He saw the fear in her eyes.

"Why is that?" he asked.

"Because you're losing it. You've gone way around the bend. You're going to have a heart attack or something. Remember Papa; it's in your genes. You need to go rest. There has been a big strain on you. Not just Sarafino but Mrs. Horta, too, and all that crazy shit. Now you're talking about Sarafino's revenge? Rest your mind. Please, Manny. And let me rest."

"You don't have it here, do you?"

"Manny, you are acting very, very crazy."

"No, I can see now that you don't have it. It's okay. I am sorry, Allie." He rose from the chair and carried his cup and paper napkin back to the counter. He filled the cup with tap water and set it in the stainless steel sink. "You are absolutely right. I'm going to get some rest now. I'm very sorry. Tell Tom I thank him for staying behind last night. I thank him for all his hard work." He stepped toward the door. "I thank you, too," he said, before walking out into the bright air.

The road back to town passed quickly. Minutes. There were other cars now, one or two, and a delivery truck of some kind. He came into the town by Front Street and drove slowly with no cars behind him, and he watched the light ricochet off the harbor between the shoreward buildings. He could see the dark ridges of shadow out upon the water, waves kicking up from a freshening breeze, the tide on the way in. He passed the center of town and glanced down at the wharf. A few masts at the end. The street looked clean and washed, but the sun, in its low winter track, cast an ashen light over the sidewalks and storefronts. He rolled slowly. He would make one more stop. It was still early, but not so early that it would be uncivil. He followed Front Street into the West End and curved with it around the old Carvalho house, past the old Coelho house and Mrs. Boia's, and when he came to his own former home, he pulled to a stop.

The house had looked empty weeks ago, when he and Sarafino and Allie had stopped in front of it, but now there was a big car in the driveway, an SUV with Rhode Island plates. He called it a driveway, but it was really just a narrow slot between the side of the house and the hedge that bordered it on the west side. It was where his father's gear shed had once stood. There was just enough room for him to squeeze the Toyota in behind the SUV.

He rapped on the front door. He regretted that he was not dressed in his collar and black shirt. He waited a moment and rapped again. He didn't look at his watch. He could tell from the light that it was not too early. It was not inappropriate. He rapped again, not hard. He was mindful. He was not here to cause trouble, after all. The street was quiet. He could hear the faint *churf, churf* of small waves on the sand behind the house. And then he heard footsteps coming. They gladdened him. He set his wits. There was always something comforting about a house and then footsteps coming to the door.

A slender man appeared in the doorway. He was in his fifties or sixties, bald and youthful. He wore wire-rimmed glasses and a blue cardigan over a flannel shirt. "Yes," he said. "Hello." He did not smile, but his voice was friendly.

"I am Father Furtado," the priest said. "I'm the pastor here, at Our Lady of Fatima. I don't mean to bother you." He glanced at his Toyota behind the SUV. It was a Land Rover. He saw that now. He wished he had said something else. He started differently. "I used to live in this house as a boy. It was my family's house. My father's. He came here from the Azores. Portugal. He was a fisherman."

A small dog yapped somewhere back in the house. Then another man appeared. He was dressed like the first man, wearing the same kind of glasses, but he was heavier. He wore a camel-colored turtleneck that mounded over his midsection. "Barry," said the first man over his shoulder, "this is a priest who used to live here when he was a boy."

"Here in the town?" asked the second man, who introduced himself as Smith. Just Smith.

"No. In this house."

"Invite him in," said Smith. "You're letting all the heat out of doors."

"I hope I am not being a nuisance," said Furtado.

"Not at all," said Barry. "We're just having coffee."

The priest walked into his old home for the first time since before Tom and Alzaida had sold it. These men were not the original buyers. He remembered Allie telling him something about the sale. He had not considered that: how many times the house might have changed hands. He'd never paid attention.

He looked around as they walked back toward the kitchen. An alien place, and yet utterly familiar. It was hard to take in. The priest sat at a small round table with the men. Barry brought a plate of sliced bagels. There was jelly and cream cheese in little porcelain pots. Smith poured Furtado aromatic coffee from a china carafe. He could not relax, but he told the men stories about the house. He showed them where things used to be, way back before. He showed them the part of the kitchen wall that had been a walk-in pantry, where his mother had lined up scores of Mason jars filled with piccalilli made from the garden, and with beach-plum jam, each jar sealed with a disc of paraffin wax. He told about how the women would come together to make the jam, a huge gathering, steaming pots in the hot summer kitchen, the mothers with their hair tied up in cloths. He told them about the same sort of gathering in winter and spring when they baked tubs of *massa sovada,* the sweet bread. He told them about the fish stews and the baked haddock. He could not stop himself from talking, even though he thought it might be working against him.

Yet Smith and Barry seemed to enjoy his visit. They showed him things they had done to the house. He asked them. No, they had not bought from his family, but they were the second owners after. They pointed out the big picture window looking out at the harbor. They showed him the refurbished planking on the floor. Crown molding. Many colors on the walls and doors.

"I have actually come to ask a favor," the priest said finally. He told them about his father, that his father might have left something in the house. Something from the Old Country. "Oh, I'm not sure what it is. Something large, I think. My sister told me something might be in the cellar or under the shed." He looked out the side window at the Land Rover. "Of course, the shed is gone." He felt something tighten in his head. Veins knotting. His neck and shoulder began to thrum.

"We haven't seen anything in the cellar," Smith said. "We don't use it much."

"The round cellar. Under this floor," said the priest.

"Yes, I know. The little cellar," said Barry. He glanced at Smith. "You are getting me curious. Your father, the fisherman. This is a mystery."

"It's likely a thing of no value," said the priest. "But it's a family matter. It would be something of enormous worth to the memory of my father. It might mean . . . it might mean everything." Furtado did not quite trust that he was saying things correctly. He felt the first hinges of a new kind of panic swinging open. He remembered what Allie had just said to him. He thought he might sound mad. He tried not to betray his agitation. "It would have to do with the Old Country," he said, as indifferently as he could.

"From Portugal, you mean."

"Yes," said the priest, taking a breath. "I believe that could be right."

"Well then," said Barry.

The priest looked over at the woolen throw rug in front of the window. The planked floor was an even gray, a deck gray but with a sheen, just right for the house. The rug was a design of blue and blood red. Under the rug was the trapdoor. He could hear his heart hammering deep in his body. "Same place," he said, indicating the rug.

"Down we go," said Barry. "You *really* have me curious now."

They pulled back the rug and opened the trap door. Furtado remembered the little cellar as a kind of cistern, musty and full of cobwebs, unlit. Sometimes his father would inspect it with a candle or a flashlight. It could have been a root cellar once. The ladder leading down into it had been lopsided and rough cut. But now there was a stair, bright with the same deep red as some of the doors. Smith flipped a switch on the kitchen wall and flooded the pit with light. The three of them stacked their way down the ladder. The diameter of the cellar was eight or perhaps ten feet. The floor now was smooth concrete where it had been earthen, and the walls were carefully mortared cinder block with some shelves attached on one side. A few corrugated moving cartons were stacked there. And there was a folding footstool, a yellow battery lantern, a box of candles, folded blankets—army blankets. Furtado took it all in.

"It's our storm stuff. You can see this was all redone," Smith said. "We are the ones who had the cellar done. Nothing under the floor, either, as far as we know. The workers went down a ways to anchor that new wall."

But between the top of the wall and the subflooring, there opened all around a gap of about eighteen inches, giving way to the crawl space under the house. Furtado stared at the opening, and Barry caught his look. "This was all reinforced and repiped," Barry said. "If there was anything found down here, we don't know about it. But please, here—step up and look around." He opened the folding stool and clicked on the battery lantern, which he called a hurricane light. "You never know," he said.

Furtado stepped up onto the stool and shined the light into the crawl space. He felt a wave of nausea. The pills. The coffee and bagels. The horrible cinnamon rolls at Allie's. The light faded into the dark far corners of the foundations. Pipes, joists, cement, sand. It was impossible. He had made another error. A terrible error. His heart jumped crazily in his breast. Maybe Allie was right. Maybe he would die. He got down from the stool slowly and carefully. He was aware of the sweat running along his scalp. His whole body was prickly. "My sister must have been mistaken," he said, steadying himself. "You have been very kind to put up with all this. I'm very sorry."

"Please don't be," said Smith. "Your stories about the old house were wonderful."

"Would you come to dinner sometime?" Barry asked. "Can we reach you at the church?"

"That would be very nice," Furtado managed to say. But he needed air. He made his way to the door, thanking them all the way.

But the air, cold and fresh as it was, did not help. He got into his car, lowered the windows, turned on the ignition, and just sat there for a while, not moving. He listened to the quiet vibration of the engine. When he felt he could safely do so, he backed the car out of the narrow space and drove slowly westward, to the turnaround by the West End breakwater's fence, where he parked the car to see if he could get his heart to stop banging. He kept the engine running and he looked out over the water, out to the last reaches of the land. The sun was full up, and the clouds were strangely violet and thunder-blue and shone with a metallic luster that seemed to come from deep within them. They boiled high into the thinnest atmosphere. Shafts of light fell through them like pillars of fire. He caught his breath as best he could and he drove again, turning eastward, back to the church, but he did not go far before he pulled over on the shoulder of the road and opened the door and leaned out over the ground and was sick.

twenty-two

Then it snowed profusely for a night and a morning and all into the afternoon and night again. The priest slept for fourteen hours, waking only to medicate himself against the pain that interrupted his dreams, which came as raw kaleidoscopic fusions without narrative or any discernible meaning. When he finally rose from the bed, it was to gray afternoon light coming in through the window in long slabs, and when he pressed himself closer, he saw the snow. Snow falling and snow on the ground. Small drifts. Mounds. Everything flocked and softened and the big flakes sallying down from the leaden sky, thick and fast. He realized it was late in the day and the winter dusk was not far off. He felt a small comfort in his breast. Snow would cover Sarafino's secret grave.

He turned the thermostat up a few degrees and showered and shaved and dressed in heavy corduroy pants and a flannel shirt. He went into the office and saw that Mariah Grey had been there and had left him some notes. He looked at the yellow Post-it stickers in their even row across the lip of the desk. John Sweet had called to cancel their meeting for the week, something he had never done before. Alzaida had called. Joe Zora had called to see if the parish council would meet later in the week. There was a call from a pharmacy up the Cape about a prescription. He would have to make a trip soon—he would not go without the painkillers, though he had laid away many vials in safekeeping. Mariah had posted a cancellation of the day's Rosary and called the usual attendees to save them the trip up to the church. She had put a list of the names she had called on the desk above the Post-it notes. There were some other things. Some bills. Mariah had everything stacked and ordered.

He went into the kitchen and took several pills, chewing them, thinking only of their taste and how that taste was a promise that blissful changes would surge through his blood in a few minutes. He was sitting, waiting, drinking black coffee and eating some buttered bread, when the telephone rang. He let the machine pick it up, but he sat very still and listened to the grainy voice coming from the office. It was Mariah Grey. He picked up the extension. "Father Manny, I hope I waited long enough. You were resting."

"I am up," he said. "I don't know what came over me."

"I talked to Alzaida earlier. She said you were very tired."

"She said tired?"

"A little something has come up, Manny."

"Something's wrong?"

"No, Manny. No. Nothing dire. But there are a couple of things to talk about. Mrs. Boia, for one. Winslow and I have been talking about a business arrangement with her. We're going to see her in about an hour. At five, at her house. Can you come?"

"Is she all right?"

"Yes. She's fine. It's about the debt Frankie left her with. We're taking her down some supper."

"All right," he said. "I seem to have fallen from the earth." He could not tell if his head was clear. He was not sure of what to use as a reference point. "Is she all right?" he asked, and then realized he had already asked that.

"I can come by and pick you up," Mariah said.

"No need. No. I'll see you there." He hung up the phone, glad for the call. He did not want to be in the rectory now. He did not want to ruminate on the past two days, and he knew that he would do so. He knew he would go up under the roof to the ledgers, of course, but that would come later. Now he sat on the bed and pulled on woolen socks and his L.L.Bean leather-and-rubber snow boots. He took out a woolen scarf and crossed it over the throat of his shirt and put on his parka and gloves. He left the parlor lights on and turned the thermostat down, then went out the back door.

The new snow squeaked beneath his feet. He did not walk to the Toyota, which sat now like some soft domesticated animal, a hunch of snow in its little parking spot. Instead he walked around to the east, along the municipal lot. He watched the snow come down, striking brilliance in the globes of light thrown by the streetlamps. The plows had been out, and piled-up snow already lay in long, low berms along the edges of Back Street. A car came by. The cones of its headlights carved bright tunnels in the falling white. The motor was resonant and quietly deep, muffled by the storm, and the car moved quickly out of sight, spinning a welter of snowflakes in its wake, and then the town sank into a hush, with only the squeaking of his boots on the dry cold snow.

He headed east, away from Hortensia Boia's house. A little walk. It would get his blood going. He walked down Back Street, behind the town hall and then to Center Street and down onto Front Street, where he walked farther east for a few minutes, watching the snow, watching another car or two motor by, none he recognized, which was the usual thing now, what with all the new people. The deep chill of the previous days had abated with the snowstorm, and the walking was easy. He did not allow himself to think about anything except the buildings and the street, but when the soft, halcyon warmth of the pills began to come forth, he found himself drifting among memories and associations, nostalgia, *saudades*. He was solitary for these moments. No cars or people. Then the town seemed his alone, his own creation, all its history, all its people new or old, all his, as though they spilled from his own existence. As though they depended on him for their very being. He stopped and stepped into the center of the street. He turned in a circle and looked up and down, east and west. Something both wonderful and terrible could burst in him. He wanted it to, whatever it was. Then he considered how no one could bring you to God. And how no one could bring God to you. Yet there He was. And there He was not. It was all the same.

As the pills continued to warm him, he walked west at an easy pace, a bit of the float with him, royal, holy—he used whatever words came to him, for the words were like the snow. Every so often the breeze would freshen and the snow would blow into new and different forms, and he felt he could walk forever, his pains quieted, his mind lifting just clear of the woe and disorder of the world, whatever the world might be. The one world. The one true world.

He came to the gate of the Boia house. The sky was black now, the yawning lush black of winter, and the snow fell steadily aslant from it, piling in corners, deep above his ankles. Soon the plows would be out again. He walked to the back and rapped on the door. Mariah Grey came down the stairs and let him in. She was wearing a heavy, loose red sweater and jeans, the cuffs of her jeans tucked into her thick wool socks, gray with two narrow red bands at the top. Her boots were on the floor at the top of the landing, and another pair of boots sat beside them, so when he looked into Hortensia Boia's parlor, he was not surprised to see Winslow there.

Winslow stood up. "Hello, Manuel," she said. She wore an open flannel shirt over a sweatshirt and large, baggy carpenter's dungarees, with many pockets and a hammer strap on one side. The room felt warm to him. Hortensia sat in the wing chair with a sweater over her shoulders. There was a sharpness to her features that seemed new to the priest, as though it might be some consequence of her son's death, but he couldn't be sure. She might have always looked that way.

"*Boa noite*," he said. "You look well, Hortensia."

"*Isso é uma mentira*!" she said. She hardly moved a muscle. "These ladies have brought supper, and it's ready for the table."

"It is," said Mariah.

Winslow looked to Mrs. Boia. "Shall we go into the kitchen now?"

The priest shed his boots and outer clothing and followed them. The rectangular table had been set, and on the gas range sat a pot of beans and an aluminum-foil pan with a baked ham in it. There were sweet potatoes in another such pan, and on the table were a bottle of sparkling cider and a bottle of Portuguese wine. They sat without much ceremony, and the priest said a brief grace. He watched Hortensia in the overhead light of the kitchen as they passed the plates around, Mariah serving up the food. He could see that Hortensia was enjoying their presence, their attention.

"Oh," said Winslow. "The buns." She got up and pulled a cookie sheet of biscuits out of the oven. They were the kind that came in a can that you had to unzip, Furtado could tell, but they filled the room with a warm, yeasty smell. Winslow put them on a plate and they passed them around the table.

"You need to turn the oven off," said Mrs. Boia.

"Oh," said Winslow. "Yes." She got up and turned the dial and sat at the table again.

"I don't think your friend cooks much," said Hortensia, looking at Mariah.

"You are making fun of me," said Winslow.

"Oh, yes," said Hortensia. "Isn't this nice, though." They all ate a bit, making little conversation, and the sound of the knives and forks seemed to go on too long. "They are going to buy my house," Hortensia said finally.

The priest looked at Mariah.

"It's a plan," said Mariah. "It's an intervention. We have been talking about it with Hortensia for a while. I felt you had to know. It wouldn't be right if you didn't."

"And I am here to see that nothing is untoward?" Furtado turned. "Hortensia, is this what you want? You know that Bobby Dutra can look at any papers for you. You should talk it over with him."

Hortensia Boia reached for the wine bottle and poured some wine into her glass. It was *vino verde*. It looked like kerosene or some other volatile liquid in the cut glass. Furtado had never imagined Hortensia as someone who would take a drink. It was his own failure to see her. He looked now at the wrist and hand that had reached out to take hold of the bottle. That now held the glass. The hand was pale and thin, but if there was anything weak about it, it was a factor of age and nothing intrinsic. He saw bone and sinew. Gristle. She raised the glass and drank. Mariah and Winslow drank also. He looked at his empty glass and realized that the sparkling cider had been placed there for him.

"I don't blame Frankie for taking that money out of the house," Hortensia said. "I signed those papers. I didn't bother to read them. What difference would it have made? Do you think I would have said no? I didn't care what I was signing. I didn't want to have the knowledge of what I was signing. I don't want that stuff in my head. It was better to just sign and let him go. Him and Tommy. My God, those two. I used to chase them around down there on the beach." She nodded her head slightly and indicated with her glass that she was talking about the beach behind the old Cold Storage building, now the Coast Guard station. "All us mothers used to go there. We would scream and holler at those kids. We'd swear at them in Portuguese and they wouldn't know what we were saying. We kept that old language for ourselves when we had to talk about our secrets."

She swept Mariah and Winslow with her eyes, which were bright now, and she drew herself up. "And there were plenty of secrets," she said, but she did not look in the priest's direction saying it. "That was old Father Braga, you know," she said when she turned to Furtado. "He was the one who forbade us all from passing the Portuguese on. He didn't want it spoken in the home. He told us it was time to be American. He was a terror, that one. And you should have heard him speak English. You couldn't tell it from the Latin." She sipped her wine. "Tommy and Frankie, running around the beach in their underdrawers when they were too small for a bathing suit. And we'd see my Biggy coming around the Point in his boat, and I'd pick up Frankie in my arms and I'd show him. "That's Papa, I'd say. Here comes Papa."

No one said anything, and the old woman went on. "I'm not going to cry, don't worry. I'm all cried out for now. Frankie never planned to die. He never planned to leave me like this. I figured that whatever they were up to, I would die before Frankie, and he would maybe take care of things. He always tried to. Nobody young plans to die. Who knows how God thinks? He takes everything away if you live long enough, so maybe that is a kind of reward for living. I don't know what that could possibly mean, though. *Fado*. I don't know."

"He seems like he was a good son," Mariah said. "I knew him to say hello. We never really talked, I don't think."

Hortensia looked at her. She was about to say something, but she merely pursed her lips.

"The whole town liked him," said Furtado.

"Well," said Hortensia, "It's not the *whole* town anymore. But that's neither here nor there. No, he would never have left me that debt. And Tommy, God bless him, he gives me that little bit every week, and I know it's not easy. Tommy was loyal to Frankie, and the other way around. That's how it worked. They never saw a line between them. If one of them had a dollar, they both had fifty cents. Of course, if one of them lied, the other would swear to it, too. They raised some hell around here. But I tell you what: I plan to die. Not yet, but I plan to. I am getting ready for it. That's what this is all about, Manny."

"But where will you go?" the priest asked. He gave both of the women a dark look. "What's this plan?"

"Hortensia stays here. It's her home."

"I'll *die* here. That goes in writing."

"Well, the plan is that we'll buy the house." said Mariah. "We've always wanted to get down by the harbor, and this is perfect."

"They wanted the upstairs," said Hortensia, "but I've lived up here all my life. I'm not moving."

"That's clear," said Mariah. "Winslow and I move in downstairs. We buy. Hortensia rents back from us, and she has an enormous nest egg."

"Plus," said Winslow, "we are right here downstairs if she ever needs anything."

"It's all going into writing," said Hortensia.

The priest reached for the sparkling cider and poured some into his glass. He tried to remember something, then lost it. "So then," he said, "this is a satisfactory thing for everyone?"

"There's no one for the house to go to," Hortensia said. "It can work for me now."

"It's a way of intervening," Mariah said. "It's a way of stepping in for Hortensia. And it's helpful to us, too."

"I would make them bring me up dinner every night," said Hortensia, "but I have a feeling I'd get pretty weary of that."

"You're making fun of us again," said Winslow.

They finished eating, and by then Mrs. Boia looked tired—perhaps she was just tired of the company. Mariah and Winslow cleaned up in the kitchen and wrapped things in plastic and foil and put everything away in the refrigerator. They washed the dishes in the sink and set them to dry in the wire dish stand on the counter, and then they joined the priest and Hortensia in the parlor.

"When is all this supposed to happen?" Furtado asked.

The women waited for Hortensia to speak. "We have a date. I forget when. Next week."

"Two weeks. We are putting everything in a contract. We want you to look at it," Mariah said to the priest. "Before we go to the lawyer."

"I will," said Furtado. "I'd be happy to. But I would ask Bobby Dutra to look at it with me. What do you think? Everybody here knows him."

"That's Madeleine's boy," said Mrs. Boia. "The West End Dutras, not the East End family. He was always a good kid."

"We'll have him come then," said Mariah.

"Can we have a Rosary, Father Manny?" said Hortensia. "This would be a good time for a Rosary."

"All right," he said.

"I'm going to walk on back home," Winslow said to Mariah. "I'll see you when you come in."

"All right, dear," said Mariah.

No one said anything else until Winslow got her coat and boots on and let herself out downstairs. Then the three of them said a Rosary in the parlor, with the smell of biscuits still in the air and the snowflakes making the tiniest puffs of sound as they hit the window and slid randomly down the black panes.

It was strange back in the rectory. For however long Sarafino had been with the priest, there had been something of a family there. Not just the people trafficking through each day—Mariah and Allie and Tom and then the doctor—but the focus. The activity. The concern. The common purpose. Now the house seemed dark and empty, and the priest could not easily find the shape of his routines. He walked down the hall and looked in on the spare room. It was as he had arranged it. He looked into the other spare room, and he saw that the box of medical supplies and the oxygen generator were now gone. He hadn't looked earlier, but Mariah must have taken them. Or perhaps Peter Khyber had come by while Mariah was working in the office and Furtado was asleep. Just that quickly—the traces of Sarafino Pomba vanishing.

He went into the office and looked over Mariah's notes again. He made some notes of his own, phone calls to make, some things he needed Mariah to take care of. It might have been midnight when he ascended the stairs to the study, tumbler of gin in hand. He took two more pills. He knelt and prayed. It was an abject prayer, a ramble, something that had probably been hurled or whispered or whined to God a thousand-thousand times before. All the usual lamentations. As if his heart were not his own.

When he finally sat at the desk, he wrote at the top of a new page, "The Feast of Agatha, Martyr, Patron of Sicily." The cold air in the room felt good and smelled of the old wood of the house. Furtado wrote for hours, recalling all the details that had piled up, all that had gone past, until the ache began to return. Then he sat back in the oaken chair and let his hands fall to his sides. But his head raced ahead. And he knew. It all hung there for him in the air—a word, finally. A single word.

He watched the sun rise from the parlor window. First the graying of the sky, then its paling and yellowing. Then came a deep mineral blue, and the new snow blued under it until the sun rose high enough to illuminate the roofs and then the street, and then the whiteness became a dazzle. It was only seven thirty. He dressed and left the building, walking. He walked west, the snow not crusted yet but smooth in the street where the plows had graded it down, and slippery under the rubber soles of his boots. The sun at his back. A heat building under his watch cap and his parka. The town luminous, transfigured.

He turned up Pond Street and climbed up the hill past old houses and new condominiums, forking left and then right until he came to the condo where Mariah and Winslow lived. It was the first unit on the left on the ground floor of a long, motel-like structure, two stories high, a cedar-shingled building whose scar upon the land was not as abusive as that of some of the other new buildings that had gone in. The weathered gray of the unpainted shingles blended with bare winter bracken, and the roofline did not rise about the trees—those that still remained, surrounding parts of the pond. Nothing had been shoveled off here yet, and Furtado broke a trail of sorts to their door, stepping warily in the calf-deep snow.

He knocked once, and Mariah answered. She peered out at him through the glass of the storm door and squinted against the whiteness before she recognized him and opened the door. She stepped back to let him enter. She was wearing baggy sweatpants and a fleece top, and he could tell she had not been up long. He would not have cared if he had woken her. She looked at him uncertainly.

"Intervention," he said. "A moral agent."

Her eyes flicked. "Come in out of the cold, Father."

He kicked his boots against the doorjamb and stepped in. The doorway gave onto a tiny entry space and then opened to a small kitchen with a round table and four chairs. The table was piled with papers—newspapers, magazines, journals, sheaves of typewritten manuscript of one kind or another. He took it all in at a glance, and then he looked past the kitchen and into the living area. Sofa, chairs, bookcases, television. Photographs and paintings on the walls. Darwin had loped out from somewhere and stood lolling his tongue and sniffing, but he did not approach.

"When you used the word *intervention* last night," the priest said, removing his watch cap and opening his coat, "it rolled right over me. I didn't connect it. I was not myself, perhaps, at that moment. It wasn't until much later. Very late, in fact. Then it rang like a bell, that word. Out of nowhere. It's what you do, isn't it? Your footsteps in the world. You *intervene*. You must tell me where She is."

Mariah just stared at him.

"Acting in the world," the priest continued. "An active force. It is agency in a time when there is so little agency. You wanted a miracle."

She sighed. "*He* wanted a miracle. He so desperately wanted one. Oh, he needed one. His whole life was crying out for one."

"And what about me?"

"I protected you, Manny. I kept the weight of that off you. I said I would ease things for you, and that's what I did. It's what I thought I was doing. It would have been too much to ask of you to have you deceive him like that. But for me, I could do it and not involve you."

"You couldn't involve me. Ever. Because I would have said no. You knew that. You were protecting your own desires."

He watched Mariah stiffen at this. "How could I have even suggested it to you?" she said. "In what possible way could I have uttered such a thing? And with that Father Sweet coming around. That was all because of me, wasn't it? I put my foot in it with Mrs. Horta, the poor thing, and look what happened. How could I have asked you? How could I have involved you?"

"You tell me you weren't thinking of yourself?"

"I was thinking of him. I was thinking of you, too, but I thought wrong. I am so sorry, Manny. I didn't plan it. I didn't think of it until we had it in the truck and were driving back with it. Even when you were looking at the dolly in the truck bed, I thought of saying something. It was the way you looked at it. But then the moment passed, and once I hadn't said it, I couldn't go back. Then I knew it was for the best. And poor Sarafino. It meant something to him. It gave him something to lay his dark thoughts against."

"But I suffered," said the priest. "Didn't you see? It involved me anyway. Didn't that mean anything to you?"

"I saw your mind working, I admit. I thought it was just another puzzle for you. I didn't think you suffered. I didn't really get how much it meant to you, either. When you seemed stressed or distracted, I just supposed it was Father Sweet and whatever was still the fallout from the troubles. I've already said what I feel about all that. Alzaida, you know, told me just yesterday how you came to her house all wound up about the statue. She said what you were going through. It was on my mind last night at Hortensia's. I should have told you immediately after he died, Manny. I put it off. I didn't have the courage."

"That's not entirely true," said Winslow, stepping out of a side doorway—bedroom or bathroom, he could not tell. "Mariah did it because of me, too." Her voice, direct and clear, startled Furtado. She was dressed in a tan quilted robe that was frayed along the bottom where it touched the floor. It was tied at the waist with a dark green sash or scarf. Her hair was not in its usual braid but hung down over her shoulders in a thick, wild cascade. She crossed through the kitchen and stood next to Mariah. When she turned, just so, to face the priest, her eyes, gray and flecked, became magnified behind the shiny lenses of her heavy black glasses. "I have to take some of the blame."

"No. Please. That's not right," said Mariah.

"Come and sit down, Manuel. Take off your coat and sit with us," Winslow said.

Furtado looked around. He realized that he had been standing in their entryway the whole time, and he was suddenly embarrassed. He said nothing but walked behind them to the kitchen, where he laid his watch cap and parka over a chair, and followed them into the living space, where they sat, the women on the sofa and he in one of the soft chairs.

"Let me speak," Winslow said. "When the buzzer on the Garrett went off, I knew we had found something. And we dug. And there it was. I have dug so many things out of the ground and off the beach, Manuel, but I don't believe I have felt the kind of excitement I felt then. Not even with the big kedge out at the edge of the flats. And when I saw it, I told Mariah, I said, get me this. Talk to them. Ask Manuel. I must have this. Because I can do something with this. I can bring it back to life. It's true. Don't let Mariah tell you that's not what happened."

"I don't think so," Mariah said. "It's not that simple. He wanted something sacred in his life, Sarafino did, and I thought I could give it to him. His sign. But it was horrible. It was a dead thing. All the fine features, all the colors you talked about, were gone. There was all this rot and corruption. You could not have shown him *that*! It would have been inhuman."

"We could have said nothing," the priest said.

"I was foolish. I was arrogant."

"But you pleased me with it," said Winslow, "and we have been through all this." She turned to the priest. "Manuel, I am the reason for her not telling. At least, not telling you right when Sarafino died. It was my idea. I wanted it finished before anyone—before you—saw it. I've been working on it every day. It's a great challenge, but I'm doing it. I'm bringing her back, little by little. It was for my sake, really," she added quickly, "not yours—though I'm not proud of that, necessarily. We talked about this yesterday, Mariah and I."

"We quarreled," said Mariah. "This was after I talked to your sister. After I heard you were so upset."

"I just wanted to finish it before you saw it. It had to be right. But it was always yours. That has to be clear. Nobody here thought that it was anyone's but yours. It's almost there, Manuel, but you must please let me finish."

The priest looked at them, first one and then the other. Then he raised his palms, as if in a gesture of calming, as if he were anyone to conjure serenity. "I want to see Her. Now," he said. "Where is She?"

The women glanced at each other. "All right," said Mariah. "Come."

The Virgin lay on a door that had been placed upon two sawhorses to make a worktable. There were two more such tables in Winslow's studio, one piled with materials—pieces of wood of all sizes, a steamer trunk, an enormous jar of brown and green coins, pieces of plywood, bottles, and cans of paint whose sides were layered with drips of the bright pigments they held. A nicked and spattered workbench ran along the length of two walls, and this was littered with more paint cans, but there were tools also that the priest recognized. A drill press, vises, power saws, a lathe, sanders. One entire wall was a pegboard upon which hung hammers and handsaws of all sizes, and chisels and screwdrivers, and a vast menagerie of paintbrushes and spatulas.

The room was large—as large as a two-car garage. Winslow had converted it, he knew, from the adjacent unit, which she had purchased many years back. It had been a small single, a contiguous space for living and sleeping, but the kitchen area now had been reduced to a deep sink and storage cabinets. At the rear there was a small untidy bathroom whose door was missing. There were large windows along the north wall, and the snowy light of morning seemed bound by some inertia and did not press itself far into the space. The room was cool, nearly to the point of being chilly. Furtado looked around and then up at the ceiling and then at Winslow. Before he could speak, she said, "Hold on," and then she struck a wall switch and the rows of fluorescent tubes above him stuttered and then blazed alight. Everything in the room jumped into sharper relief, and the space itself seemed to open up and close down at the same time. The Virgin flashed white as chalk.

The priest approached the statue slowly. "Oh," he said. "Oh." He looked at the women.

"We're just going to go back next door for a minute," Mariah said, and they left through the heavy door that joined the two spaces. Then he was alone with Her.

But it was not Her. Not the Her that he remembered. Not the Her of Sarafino's visions and torments and absolutions. As he bent and peered at Her, he saw that She had been covered completely with a layer of some sort of thin white paint, flat and nearly transparent, so that he could see patches and fills in places, all dimly showing through. The smaller features of the face ghosted through the coating in various shades of darkness—wood and glue, he could tell, and also something else. They had been remolded. The crown upon her head was now merely a derbylike round of white-coated wood. He circled her. Under her feet was a metal baseplate, but clearly a new one, shiny stainless steel, held in place with a large, recessed bolt.

He noticed then that the table nearest to the Virgin was arrayed with photographs of Her: old photos, newspaper photos, photos from the church, which Mariah must have copied from the archives. Some had been enlarged to grainy, life-size approximations of photos, and some of these had been overlaid with transparent plastic on which grids had been printed. Sets of strange rulers and calipers lay along the table.

What was this thing now? A project? Art? A relic from the earth. And yet some essence of Her remained. For this image, Sarafino had suffered. And Old Man Coelho—was it fair or accurate to say he had died because of Her? And what about Furtado himself? This was the most troublesome. There was something like contempt in him for all this. For he was large and alive, and the Virgin was small and tainted with rot—or had been, until Winslow's ministrations. She was a hunk of wood. There was nothing grand about Her here, laid out on a plain door, under these lights, surrounded by these implements. What foolishness. But he was electrified nonetheless. He trembled, and his mind spun and prowled but gave him nothing. He leaned and laid a hand on Her form. The surface of the wood, with its sketchy coat of primer, had an odd feel to it. At first he wanted to draw his hand away from it, but then he rested it there, cupped to the curve of Her waist, and it felt comfortable. She wasn't much. She wasn't worth Sarafino's broken life.

He felt his hand shake. He was breaking down. He had been breaking down for a long time. Fuses had blown. He searched himself for a single appropriate feeling and found nothing he could rely on. He moved his hand. He brushed the white primer that lay over the contours of the body and felt the fine, unsanded grit of the surface. It was how he was still standing, touching Her like that, when Winslow and Mariah walked quietly back into the studio.

They seemed to wait for him to speak first, but when he did not, Winslow said, "Manuel, I understand that this was a huge transgression."

"It was his sign, though," Mariah insisted. "I don't regret that. If Sarafino had seen the thing we had pulled up from the ground, if he had seen that decay . . . It was really better to just . . . have her gone."

"Regardless of me or anyone else," said Furtado. "And not just gone, either. But . . . what? Raised? Glorified?"

"I did not gauge that right," Mariah said. "I am deeply sorry for that."

"I had thought that I might finish before he died," Winslow said. "Then it would have been a different discussion. We *would* have come to you. We were *going* to come to you. It might have been good for him to see it as it once was. But it has taken so long."

"And this will look like it once did?"

"I'm very close. Yes. It will. The core was in wonderful shape. What wood! A lot of the filigree and detail was gone, but I've built it back up with compound. I filled other places with wood and glue—you can see here and here," she pointed. "I have to do the trim on the crown yet. But I'm priming and sanding now, too, as you can see. That will go on for several more coats, and then the colors and then the clear coats."

"And you think you can get it right?"

"I do, yes."

"Did it ever occur to you that you might need the help of someone who had actually laid eyes on her?"

"That's a rebuke," Winslow said, but neither her eyes nor her voice carried any hint of emotion.

"But it's still a question," said the priest. His head thundered. "And you didn't answer."

"What do you want, Manuel?"

"I have more photographs than this. And I have memories. I'm going to come and make sure."

"You're going to watch me?"

"I won't stand over your shoulder. But yes."

"And suppose you do? And then what, when it's done?"

He thought, but not well. "I don't know yet."

Winslow drew up a breath, and her chest rose beneath the quilting of her robe. "All right," she said. "It won't be so long now."

The priest thought some more. "Good," he said. "Maybe by the time you're done, we will be able to see things more clearly. We will see things in a better light."

The three of them stood around the statue, looking soberly at one another. It seemed that despite the overhead lights and the tall windows—which were now graced with more of the bluish reflection from the decks of snow—a grainy whirl of some kind of particle looped around the women and Furtado, as though a wind blew in the room, as though they could lean into it and be gently lifted by it and then promenaded through the air, softly, around and around. *Like angels drifting*, he thought. Or like in Dante, like the shades of Paolo and Francesca, who had carried their desires with them into the afterlife.

After some time in silence, they went back next door, where they sat in the living room and drank coffee. They all made an effort at conversation.

The priest and Mariah brought up the work to be done at the church. They spoke quietly and flatly about the proposal to the diocese and all the changes it would bring. "I can ride you over to the rectory with me," Mariah said to him finally, "if you want to wait until I shower and change. It would only be a minute."

But the priest elected to leave. He thought fancifully that maybe he had been struck in the head with something—some heavy board leaning against the wall of Winslow's workspace, maybe. He understood he was not well. There had been something dreamlike to all this talk among the three of them, as though the words didn't follow one another correctly. He was afraid that for his part, he might have gotten some things wrong. Now, as he dressed to leave, he somehow forgot that it had snowed, and when he walked out the front door he was momentarily dazzled. He stood on the step and looked out at the sunlit carpet of white, the buildings, and the sparse woodland beyond them, and when he felt his legs steady under him again, he walked carefully along the gleaming streets and lanes back to the church.

twenty-three

DAYS PASSED. A STIFF BREEZE CAME AROUND FROM THE SOUTH, easing the temperatures again, and brought with it a light rain that lasted a morning, and under the rain the recent snow shrank and then disappeared, except for thin crusts and rinds that blackened with striations of dirt under the hedges or along the shaded sides of buildings and tree trunks. The priest walked every afternoon to Mariah's studio. On the first day he carried more pictures—snapshots from the albums that Alzaida had saved—ill framed, shiny, and curling, but in color. Mariah scanned them into a computer, and Winslow blew them up and studied the coloring. They talked about color. Furtado talked about the effects of the color, what the colors were supposed to do. "Old-fashioned," he said. "They were supposed to draw you in and lift you up. They were supposed to illustrate something."

"I get it," Winslow told him dryly. She worked in a sweater and coveralls, hair in its formidable braid, the heavy glasses sometimes on her face, sometimes hanging around her neck from a black lanyard. All of her movements were slow, deliberate, and athletic. She handed him fine sandpaper and told him how to rub—"light as a moth," she said. And she laid on more primer, brushing and sanding until the body seemed like a chrysalis, encased in the finally opaque, dull white shell. And then she began the coloring.

He did not comprehend all her mixing and fiddling—additives, oils, compounds, resins. She sometimes spoke to him as she worked. She told him of the remarkable shape the wood was in after so many years in the earth. She thought it was a combination of being down in the sand and the many coats of lacquer that had been applied over the pigments. "I don't know what was in those lacquers," she said. "Who knows? Maybe Old World secrets. I'm relying on modern chemistry, myself." Lost as Furtado was, he tried to guide her choices of the enamel, which she based on the photos but changed subtly: the blue that she seemed to darken, for instance; the white that she turned to cream.

She was generous, at times, about telling him what she was doing as she was doing it, but he could not concentrate. When Winslow herself concentrated, she fell silent. Or she would assign him some task—he could tell it was just to keep him out of her way—and then she would check on what he did, often redoing it herself.

Mariah stayed away from these studio afternoons, and the priest wondered if she ever came into the studio when Winslow was working. He didn't ask. Furtado could not stand the process: It went too quickly, or it went too slow; Winslow was too precious in her ministrations, or she was too blunt and heavy-handed; her vision was not right. She came at it from the wrong angle. She had not lived its context. And yet there was something about her bearing and her self-possession when she worked that made the priest believe she was judging him. He was not her equal here in this room. Still, he pushed himself to be present.

They argued about what he remembered. They argued about memory itself—all too familiar to him. He understood that much of memory was a creation. He conceded that to her. But he told her that whether he was recalling or creating, his sense of how She looked was superior because he had actually seen Her, and Winslow had not.

He was using the pills night and day now, mixing them with other medications, and they seemed like life support to him, as though he could not breathe or see light without this extra boost. It was like an engine that needed to be running in the background, feeding his motion, driving his thoughts. That his head jumped and jangled, spun and floated, did not matter. Without his various potions and powders, he feared there would be nothing there at all, like a television hissing static, stuck in the no-man's-land between legitimate channels. With Winslow's every stroke as she restored the image of the Virgin, Furtado knew himself to be delaminating physically, as if the layers of his corporal body were curling, peeling away.

Perhaps Winslow sensed this. He knew she was indulging him because of some inner imperative, some scruple she held because of her part in deceiving him. But he recognized that he was acting crazy. Moving behind her once, he stumbled, the meds singing like pond frogs in his inner ears, and he banged into one of the tables—the one holding the photographs and grids—and the door top slid from the sawhorses and crashed to the floor. She spun around on him then, startled, all animal, a fire in her face, and a sound came out of her—not a word but a fierce exhalation, as though she had been struck in the body by the heavy blow. She recovered immediately.

"Oh, Manuel," she said, "are you all right?"

The floor rocked harshly under his feet.

"Manuel!"

He looked around. He looked at the mess: the photos, the papers, the tools, the tipped sawhorse, and the fallen door. He knew then that he would have to go, and that he must not let her be the one to say so. He got to his knees and began gathering the photographs.

"I will give Her back to the church," he said, speaking to the floor but to Winslow, too. His hands felt clumsy. "When we are finished with the renovations to the building, the renewal, I will bring Her back into the church. It will be just what we need. I will credit you with everything. I will, of course, tell of all your efforts here."

"Manuel, please get up," Winslow said. "I'll take care of all this."

He stood uncertainly. "I understand that you need your solitude," he said. "I understand that."

"You are tired," she said. "You are grieving. It's all right."

"I'll stay out of your way."

"It's all right," she said.

But when he didn't return, she didn't send for him. She didn't ask him to come, even for a short visit, to see her progress.

FURTADO SAID NOTHING TO EITHER TOM OR ALLIE ABOUT THE STATUE. There was enough for them to keep hidden in themselves already, and the thought of further complicating their lives in any way was unbearable to him. As for Furtado, nothing seemed to ease his heart or mind except focusing on the fruits of the proposal, building the community back, and continuing to open up the church to new communicants. He thought about such things in images, mostly: a renewed building, a shining new roof, a full church, his greeting people on the back steps after Mass. The palpable goodwill of smiling, nodding parishioners.

But nights, he still could not get used to being alone in the rectory again. It was strange to him that he could not, for Sarafino had been with him hardly more than a hundred days. Sometimes he would go to the spare room where Sarafino had lain, and would lie there in the dark, on top of the white bedspread, clasping a pillow to him, and think of Sarafino and how his body, in its fevers and malaise, had felt next to Furtado's own. A paper thing. A heart stuttering. It came to him in these moments that

God's angels—His counselors and emissaries, His advocates—had pulled back from Furtado, just out of mutual reach, and he could nearly see them, standing off in a peripheral darkness, watching him with disinterested curiosity. He saw that it didn't matter that he did not believe in such beings, or, at least, he didn't believe in the hackneyed manner in which they seemed to adopt humanlike forms—which he could sense now. Their distance and their clinical observation of him explained his deepest tempers. He was unhitched now and had wandered beyond any familiar terrain. Perhaps these specters might soon begin wagering as to what would become of him.

The statue. The Virgin. What truth was there, then? For he was relieved not to be going to Winslow's. The great mystery had become her mere project, and now it was simply mundane labor over wood and paint. Would it ever be as significant again for anyone as it had once been for the town, or for Sarafino? For Furtado's father? His father the prick, as Sarafino had said. And yet hadn't there been something driving Pai—something underneath all there was about him—that had had in its essence a kind of goodness? He'd provided, as Allie was quick to say. He had striven.

The priest remembered that once on a winter day, as a kid, he had driven out to the parking lot at the state beach. It had been deserted, of course, and snowing, heavy flakes blowing down behind a stiff cold breeze coming out of the north, but the visibility had been decent. And in the heat of his father's car, Furtado had sat and watched the distant blue-and-white hull, the orange dory on the overhead of the wheelhouse—a lone, toylike boat expertly motoring with the tidal race behind it, easing its transit back toward the harbor. One boat. His father's. The *Ilha do Pico*. It must have been twenty degrees outside, not counting the windchill. It would have been groundfish then, flounder maybe, flukes. A few boxes. Hard to tell.

But that was where the old man's hardness counted for something—whatever else he was or did or did not do. Not easy for the priest to allow, even now, after all these years. What had all that strife been about, really? Still, he could now walk to the gentle eastern hill of the cemetery, making his way among the galleries of stones bearing the Portuguese names, and he could, on some days, kneel at his father's grave and—so strange—love him, and it seemed as if his love would travel through death itself to reach him.

What had been so important a hurt that Furtado had had to wait until Pai was gone from the earth before he could face this love, a love that was impossible to differentiate from sadness? He ached with despair: about Senhor Coelho. And his mother's sorrow. And Sarafino's life spinning into nothingness, his beauty destroyed, his possibilities annulled. Furtado reflected how he had never a notion of even one of Sarafino's dreams for himself. Maybe it was true that he had wanted nothing but the Virgin, the thing now on the flat door in Winslow's studio. Wood that had been purloined and buried and then purloined again. Such a history!

And watching Winslow work—bending to the Virgin's frame, applying this touch or that adjustment, he himself rubbing the body with the delicate abrasives, the daily job of Her as She shrank to pure material; there was hardly anything to Her. After all this travail, he had blurted madly that he would return this thing to the church, but now who would care? Those old days were gone forever, and no one dwelled on them. What was this, after all, but vanity, obsession, delusion? One could say *belief* and be saying the same thing. He was so very tired of it all.

He stopped eating almost entirely during this time; his only sustenance was his gin and his cocktail of various prescriptions. One night, keeping to his ritual of prayer and work up in the study, he became too tired to stay at the desk. Although he sat in the swivel chair, it was as though he staggered. Then he rose and did stagger. He groped and looped his way down to his bedroom and crawled beneath the bedclothes and sank into a black sleep that was punctuated by unquiet dreams. Among them was a dream of feeding on something cold and delicious beyond imagining. When he awoke in the morning, the sun was burning through the drawn window shade and the room was filled with a soft, filtered light. He walked to the kitchen and found dishes and a carving knife. An empty wine bottle. A scrap-laden platter that had sat in the refrigerator and contained the cold roast and potatoes Alzaida had left for him. At first he thought that someone had been in the rectory, had broken in and eaten his food and left the mess—for it *was* a mess, scattered and dirty across the kitchen counter, tiny leavings on the linoleum floor. But then he realized that it had been he himself, or at least his body, walking without knowledge or consciousness, save for the dream. The long, heavy-bladed knife disturbed him. It looked as deadly as a sword, lying there among the soiled saucers and forks.

When he ascended the stairs the next night, he found a piece of writing in the ledger that continued beyond where he remembered having left it. It was crazed and senseless: clots of badly formed letters that did not add up to anything; in some places Latin-like word parts that were obviously made up; little pictographs, hieroglyphs, bent and indecipherable; threads of repetitious spirals, deltas, blotted stars, and loops; strings of numerals with the number 3 circled every time it appeared. Monkeys could have ravaged his house and left this; or, in another time, it would have been called the work of demons. It was terrible. He had come back up those stairs after he'd eaten, and he'd sat and written, and he had no memory of it. Whatever had been in his brain—whatever he had thought was this insight or wisdom or important detail of the work of the day—was now nothing but the scratchings of madness.

He was desperate to pull himself back into the world. He went down to the office to busy himself with some parish work, something to put his feet on the ground. He took out a notepad and checked the answering machine. There was another message from John Sweet saying things at the chancery were temporarily held up, and that he'd be hearing news in a while. Nothing to worry about. It had been left on the machine while Furtado was saying the Thursday morning Mass; Sweet had known that Furtado would be celebrating Mass then, and Furtado understood that Sweet had chosen that time deliberately, to avoid a conversation. It suited Furtado as well, but then he received another call the next day. This one was from the chancery, a man named Cirelli. Furtado knew him vaguely.

"Has Sweet got with you yet?" Cirelli asked.

The priest told him about the message Sweet had left him.

"All right, then," said Cirelli. "We'll get this straightened out up here."

"What?" asked Furtado. "Get what straightened out?"

"It's Rego. We'll get this straightened out."

The priest let it pass. He called Liliana Mendes and told her that things were in a bit of flux, and that the council should wait before meeting again. That some new information might be coming in. He asked her to call the other members.

Up in his room, he copied from Teresa of Avila. He wrote that true humility walked happily along the road that God leads it to. But he was not humility. He was not a quality. He was at least certain of this. He was a being.

He found his way to Saint John of the Cross. He summarized a long section that discussed how spiritual consolation can lead to feelings of luxury in the spirit. That the forgiveness of a sin can lead to such pleasure that this pleasure can transfer itself to the sin proper. This seemed impossible to the priest. It was beyond anything he could imagine. Who had ever felt forgiven to such a degree? And wasn't sin its own pleasure? Wasn't that its secret power? He would destroy the notion of sin if he could. He would destroy the very idea of it. It would vanish as a concept.

He addressed letters to himself in other voices. He signed various names to these: Isaiah, Teilhard de Chardin, Father Braga, Simone Weil, Martin Luther and Martin Luther King, Mother Theresa, John Lennon, Joan of

Arc. Through them he admonished against his habits and proffered advice to himself, but nothing took. He puzzled over the troubles at the diocese—bureaucracy, after all his work. He railed. His rantings spilled over the lines and along the margins of the ledgers.

When he awoke on the morning of the Feast of the Chair of Saint Peter, he found himself fully clothed, down to his black dress shoes and over-the-calf socks. He arose from nothingness. He sat on the edge of the bed, keeping a quilt about his shoulders against the morning chill of the small room, and waited for the world to settle around him. It did so slowly and in pieces: first the familiar throw rug and then the even planks of the floor, and then the misty green of the walls and the parchment light pressing through the drawn shade. He had no idea what he was rising from or why he was dressed so, until the memory finally broke through: He had already arisen once and said morning Mass. The blackness that had been standing in place of this memory alarmed him, but he rose and shook it off.

He went to the kitchen and saw that coffee had been made. Tommy's truck was outside, and Mariah's was also parked there in the back. He listened. He could not hear anyone's presence inside the rectory. He poured coffee from the glass pot and walked with the steaming mug to the office. Mariah had been there—he could see from the stacks of files, the open day planner, the busy clutter of the desk—but she was elsewhere now. He walked the small rooms. He was not quite present. He waited some more to see if he would sharpen himself, but when he didn't, he changed into a pair of loose-fitting jeans and a flannel shirt. He put on his ball cap and stepped outside to feel the air, then stepped back in and pulled on a woolen overshirt. The sky was low and silver and heavy with incipient weather. He felt as though he might be dreaming. It was almost pleasant. He thought Tom might be over in the storage garages, but as he walked toward the hunched, weathered buildings, he was hailed from behind.

"Manny! I was just coming to get you." The priest turned, and in the hard, late-morning light, Tom and Mariah approached him, walking from around the back of the church, she with her hands in the pockets of her green vest and Tom dressed much like the priest himself, shirt over shirt, his thick curls loose upon his head.

"I fell back asleep after Mass," Furtado said when they stood together.

Tom and Mariah said nothing.

"It's not like me," the priest said.

"Are you feeling all right?" Mariah asked. Her own face sagged a bit, even in the silky, bracing air.

"I am tired," said the priest. "And the rectory is empty. It's an adjustment."

"It is," said Mariah. "So much."

"It's all God," said Furtado. "So complex."

"We've been in the church," said Mariah.

Tom took a pack of cigarettes from his outer shirt pocket and shook one out and lit it with a small butane lighter. "I wasn't thinking, Manny," he said. "You know the attic in the rectory?"

"Is something wrong up there?" Furtado said. "You fixed all that. Isn't that right?"

"Not there," Tommy said. "It's the church. "You see what I mean? I should have been thinking, *Hey, the squirrels have done a job up here under this roof; I'd better go check out up in the church, too*. But I never did. It never came into my head."

Furtado did not want this detail about the church at this moment. It brought the financial plan and the business with the chancery charging back to him, and all that lay beyond his reach right now. And it conjured that phone call from Sweet. He hadn't liked the sound of it. Something was up. He had tripped up somewhere. He couldn't put his finger on it. He didn't have enough information, not yet. But the church now, under the roof.

"Another mess?" he said at last.

"Oh, yeah," Tom said.

"It's something we can defer, though, I expect," the priest said. "We have the contractors coming. At some point, anyway."

"The squirrels and who knows what else been up there for years, Manny. Nests, all that. Like the rectory attic, only worse." Tom turned and squinted back at the church roof. "There's quite a bit of space up there, by the way. I never thought about it. You been up there lately?"

"No," said Furtado. "You know, Louis Horta used to take care of all that."

"Yeah." Tom drew on his cigarette and exhaled a long funnel of blue smoke. "Not so much, maybe."

"I can help Tom clean it out," Mariah said.

"The way I figure, Manny, I'm going to get that crap out of there. I'll get some light up there and take a good look. That way, when the surveyors come, they won't be looking at all that litter. I don't know if there's any real damage, but it's hard to tell with the way it's all junked up now. I figure it's got to get cleaned out no matter what. Better not to leave it like that. I can't get to it for a couple of days, though, because Joey Nunes looked at the problem I've been having with the heat over in the hall, and right now I'm going up the Cape to get some parts for him, and we're going to tackle that first. I have to do that on his time, which he's got tomorrow. The radio's giving snow, so I'm taking off right now."

"I'll take a look up in the church myself," Furtado said.

Tom shot a glance at Mariah, then narrowed his eyes and regarded the priest. "Let me know before you do," said Tom. "I'll take a minute and do it with you when I get back. Or tomorrow, when Joey and me are working in the hall. I left the big ladder up there. It's laying down on the floor of the choir. I figure it's okay."

"Yes," said the priest. "No one's going up there to bother it."

"I took some messages for you, Manny," Mariah put in. "I wrote stickums for you, but there's two I left on the machine. I'm not sure what they are, so I left them for you to hear. Medical stuff, I think."

"All right."

"Father Manny, I'll stay around if you need me. Are you sure you're okay?"

"I'll take another nap if I need one."

"Okay, then," she said. "I'm going to go down to the bank. Then I'll eat some lunch with Winslow. I can come back again this afternoon. I can bring you something to eat."

"No need today. We'll see what the diocese is sitting on. The deposits are counted?" He was not sure if he'd already asked this.

"They're already in the truck. I'm taking them with me." She smiled, but it did not carve her face deeply. It was a weary smile. Willed. She walked off toward her truck. Tom pitched his cigarette and walked to his own truck and pulled slowly across the parking lot, trailing Mariah down the hill, and the priest stood by himself again. He looked up at the roof of the church, at the belfry, at the old shingles, everything looking resolved and muscular in the cold, thickening air, the day settling down with a palpable weight all around the streets and houses and trees, and Furtado himself not quite earthbound, not quite present yet among it all.

Back in the rectory, he went to his bedroom and clicked on the little television, which Winslow had insisted he keep, and turned up the volume so he could listen for the weather. A general ache had settled in his muscles and joints, so he went to his repository and took several of the white tablets out of the amber vial. He went to the kitchen and drank them down with hot black coffee, to which he had added a few inches of gin. He carried this cup with him back into the bedroom and looked at the images on the small, grainy screen. A woman chattered and laughed. A man twice her age mugged for the camera. He could not understand a thing they were talking about. He turned the set off and dialed the all-weather forecasts on the radio in the kitchen. The authoritative drone of information, incessant and without the sieve of false personality, created a feeling of confidence in him. And the pills were working. This, then, was well-being. The familiar names: Newport, Block Island, Cape Hatteras, Cape Ann, Gay Head, Gloucester, Cape Cod. The snow that Tommy spoke of was being tracked as a heavy storm. It was nothing they were not ready for. It would storm and then it would not storm, and everything would endure as it always did.

His step was light and trancelike as he entered the office. He sat in the chair behind the desk and let a wave of the deepest comfort roll through his body. He shivered and let out a long breath, nearly a moan. When he closed his eyes, pleasant designs rose up, and he understood that these were his thoughts turned now into visual objects. He sank beneath them as he might sink into a cove of warm water, the wonders of the sea undulating around him. He nodded for a while and then raised himself from the reverie to drink from the bitter, laced coffee. He looked over Mariah's notes. He leafed through the bills. He looked at the spreadsheet with the weekly revenues. His mind rolled ahead over these things. He took in their significance, their general meaning. His thinking was such that the details didn't settle anywhere for him, but the drift of these things spoke to him, and it all seemed proper and in order. But then he moved to the phone and played the messages that Mariah had left for him.

The first was from a pharmacy in Brewster. "Father Furtado, please call us here when you get a chance. There are some problems that have come up with your prescriptions, and we need to get some information." The second was slightly different. It was from a pharmacy in Orleans. He replayed it several times to make sure he was hearing it right. He listened for nuances in tone. He concentrated on the words and played out their meanings. Each time he hit the play button was like opening a door and looking through it and hoping in an abject way that what had been standing on the other side a moment ago would somehow be different this time, or even gone altogether. "Father Furtado, a Doctor Sweet called. He asked us for information about your medications, but we didn't release anything without your consent. Give us a call, please, when you can. Thanks."

Doctor Sweet. Of course, he *was* a doctor of sorts. PhD. Psychology. Nothing to do with medicine. But it didn't matter. Furtado let the room spin ever so gradually and gently. A plank had broken—all the planks, all the scaffold. He understood: All the pharmacies would call sooner or later. This was not a flank he'd expected to receive an attack from. He had not, truth be told, expected an attack at all. He was astonished now that he had not seen this coming, for it had been obvious. He should have been more careful. He recalled Sweet's conversations and questions. Of course he had let Furtado push ahead with the debt restructuring—why not? Why step in the middle of that, working with town people he did not know? Now it was clear: Sweet had waited him out, and Furtado, the fool, had given him everything he needed.

He decided to call Sweet right away, but he was moving slowly, breathing slowly, and even then, in that state, he knew he had to wait until his wits were more at the ready. There might yet be something he could do; he thought eating might help him gather himself. But when he went to the kitchen, he found nothing appealing in the refrigerator, so he packed the coffee mug with ice and filled it with gin, settled into the swivel chair, and transcribed his memory of the phone calls in the ledger.

When he went back down to the kitchen, he sat at the table and rehearsed what he would say to Sweet. He stared out through the storm door's glass and watched the deepening of the day, and in such a state saw the first molecule of snow, next to invisible, a spit. Then nothing for the longest interval, and then another fleck. Then another. He realized that only he could see them. That it was a power he had, and that others would see nothing at all. He rose and walked outside. Colder now. Grayer and quieter. Here and there, another random particle of snow in wild trajectory, weightless, imperceptible to all but him. The air braced him. The cold seared through his shirt.

When he walked back inside the phone was ringing, and he understood at least this much about the workings of God: Even before he answered, he knew it had to be John Sweet himself calling. There could be no doubt. It was as easy as reading playing cards, and he moved to the telephone with a certain complacency, even as he understood nothing good would come of any further talk with Father Sweet.

The Fixer's voice was clear and sharp over the wires from Calumet, if indeed a voice carried over wires anymore. It was possible that there was no Father Sweet at all, just this reticulation of waves and electricity. But Sweet was there, all right.

"Manny, I won't be indirect with you. Things have become larger than they should have. It didn't have to be this way. I think by now you know what I'm talking about."

"Why don't you tell me?" Furtado said.

"It's all gone up to Rego now."

"What's gone?"

"Everything. It's all on the monsignor's desk now."

"I've received some calls, John. Some very disturbing calls."

"From him?"

"No. Nothing from him. No, I heard from the drugstores, John. Your name was mentioned."

"You need to come up to the diocese for a meeting with us. That's where this is now."

"The bishop, too?"

"And Rego and one or two others. Can you drive?"

"Now? No."

"I mean generally. It's going to snow. I've set something up for Wednesday afternoon. The roads will be cleared by then. I could send someone for you."

"I'll call you back," Furtado said. He hung up the phone. It began to ring again almost immediately. He reached over and turned the message machine off. The phone rang for a while longer and then stopped.

In the evening he sat alone and felt the chill settle over the rooms. He pulled an afghan around his shoulders and sat in a soft chair by the parlor window and looked out at the night. The storm had still not come fully to the town, but now a scant snow—visible to all—was flashing meteorlike in the quiet light of the streetlamps on Church Street. The phone had continued to ring into that afternoon, but finally the priest had shut off the ringer, and now there was quiet in the rectory. He had taken another handful of pills, and despite the cool temperature in the parlor, he sipped his gin from the tall glass filled with ice.

The parish of Fatima was lost to him. Sweet would take it over. Furtado saw it all now, tick by tick, move by move. It was all right. He floated with the rightness of it. He floated above something black and violent connected with it, too, but whatever it was, it wouldn't resolve itself. He was not quite in his body again—or was in it in such a way that he felt only composure and complacence.

He looked out over the street and remembered the first time he had seen snow through a window looking out on darkness. He had been sitting in his mother's lap as she rocked, and they had watched the night through the icy glass, and he'd seen the reflection of her eyeglasses moving against the sky with the motion of their rocking. "What's that?" he'd asked, and she'd answered without looking, without even knowing what he was seeing there in the window glass, "It's the angels coming to tell the shepherds about Christmas."

At some point the priest went up the stairs to his study with yet more gin and pills, and he kneeled and prayed, and he made small, disconnected notes about the pharmacy calls and about Sweet's move on the parish. He forgave Sweet. He accepted the blame himself. The last sentence he wrote that night, crooked and nearly illegible, was: *There are squirrels in my roof.*

WHEN THE PLANE WENT DOWN INTO THE GULF, IT WAS NIGHT, THE 0100-hours launch to relieve the earlier patrols out on station. The word was that the war had already been lost and that things ashore were crumbling, that even Saigon was coming apart, but still the aircraft went out on their regular missions around the clock. The ocean showed silky and black off the bows of the carrier, and Furtado walked as usual with his gear to the plane. The ship was already executing command Fox Corpen—powering into the wind for the launch—and the breeze that this generated came strongly down the deck and riffled his bloused flight suit as the ship rumbled.

There were four in the crew. Everything was normal. There were no unusual thoughts in Furtado's head. It was all routine. The aircraft was an S2F, a stoof, a surveillance plane with two turbo-prop engines, small, loaded with electronic equipment. The LC's name was Crowley; they called him Mad Dog because spittle formed around his mouth when he got excited. It was derisive at first, but Crowley caught on and turned out liking the name, and had it embroidered on his steamer cap. Sitting on the catapult, as Furtado sat strapped in the backseat and heard Crowley run the engines up, the little stoof shook and trembled—all just as usual, all according to drill. Then the airedale down on the deck whirled his torch and pointed, and the cat fired and everyone lurched and they were hurled into the black sky. They dipped—always that gut-punching initial drop when the plane cleared the deck—but then powered up and climbed, and everything was noise and vibration and the queasy feeling in the stomach from the g's, and all was just right until suddenly, immediately, there was fire somewhere. They could see it indirectly, the jumping orange, and they could feel it and smell it.

Then Mad Dog was on the radio with the controller back on the ship, and then he was banking to port and feathering the number-one engine and everyone was yelling at once. It was Furtado and Fatty Martin on the gear in the back and Lieutenant Ayler next to Mad Dog in the cockpit. That lieutenant, a baby-faced guy from Louisiana, kept trying to light off the fire suppressant, but it wasn't doing anything.

They heard the controller's voice from CATTC say the deck was clear. He gave them vectors and they banked around on fire, coming down for the hook, everybody with the control frequency in their ears, and they could hear it all, controller cool, no pressure in his voice, like, *No sweat, no worries, we've got you*, and in they came on one engine, dipping for the arresting wires, but Mad Dog came in too high and the hook missed them all. Then the controller barked, "2-7, up, up, up," and Mad Dog powered down the angle deck to get up in the air again, but the one engine wasn't enough—fire all over the place now—and they shot off the edge of the angle and tipped ninety degrees, wing down like a keel, and there was all fire and blackness, and then they hit the ocean like hitting the side of a mountain.

Which was where Furtado was again now. Except it was not right. It was all out of whack. He could feel the heat of the fire all over him, the worst on his face, and the smoke, but it was all confused. He was calling out to God to save him again, yet everything was wrong. Where were Mad Dog and the other guys? Where was Lieutenant Ayler grabbing Furtado by the collar and dragging him out because he could not move his arms, and the smashed stoof sinking, settling into the blackness, and everything upside down and sideways, the Gulf water surprisingly warm, and the feeling of breakage and blinding pain running all through him?

And then he saw the fire streaming up the angles of the roof, the rafters, and it finally came to him: This was not the plane. This was not the crash from that other life. His eyes burned and watered. He could not breathe. *He was up in the attic of the old church.*

He began crawling madly, looking for something: the trapdoor hatch in the floor, the ladder back down to the choir loft. Nothing made sense. But there was no time to think about why. The fire was dirty and orange and lit itself along the boards above in smudged lines, the rafters themselves alight, small hands of flame running their length up to the shallow peak of the roof, and parts of the roof skin itself burned, and little stars of fire drifted down upon him and all around him.

He could not gauge how long he had been up there. He batted at his clothing and scorched the palms of his hands. His hair was afire, and he swatted at it as if beating at insects. He scrambled without direction but then somehow found the hatch, but he found it headfirst and toppled through it, throwing his arms back in a last-moment reflex. He caught the rough edges of the wooden frame, but his hands could not hold his weight, and he tore loose immediately and fell, hitting the top of the big fiberglass stepladder below him. The cap of the ladder caught his midsection. It felt like the blow broke everything inside him, but he kept falling, the ladder tipping back out from under him, and he landed, somehow righting himself as far as his knees, on the floor of the choir loft.

The pain was stunning and pure, all through him, even with all the medications in him, but he managed to get his forearms up around his head and raked the burning flakes from it and batted more at his shirt and pants. And then there came a flashing—a great light pulsing up and then plunging into darkness and up into light again. He rolled to his back. Smoke drifted down from the hatch. All the lights in the church were surging and dying as the circuits burned. The building seemed to rock with it. He rolled off his back and rose to his elbows and tried to vomit. His insides were bitter and the smoke was like gravel in his throat and chest, and his mind circled around on the idea that something terrible had happened, that perhaps he had done something terrible. He did not know what it was or how he'd come to this—he knew only that the church was burning.

Something roared. Then the roaring died and came up again. Wind. The skin of the roof had somewhere burned through. The wind in the rafters blasting the fire. The roof snarled with it, and then a row of sprinklers in the ceiling began to hiss, but the wind and the flames squalled again and the lights surged and the sprinklers abruptly quit. The priest got his arms around a chair in the loft and pulled himself up onto it. Heavy smoke was wandering down in black tendrils now from fissures in the ceiling, and everywhere the overhead was bellying and buckling, and then, near the transept, the ceiling broached and a drizzle of fire drifted through and began to burn in the aisle and among the pews.

The priest twisted his body around and tried to make his way to the loft stairway, to get down to the back doors, but he found he could not walk through the pain in his knees. He pulled himself then along the floor of the loft, and when he reached the stairway he half slid, half pulled himself until he came to the landing at the back of the church. But there he met with the heavy, locked doors, and even when he stretched up and got his hands on the bar levers, they would not operate.

Now he crawled over beneath the belfry and found the bell rope. He pulled himself up on it and wrapped his forearms around the heavy hemp line and began to bob up and down upon it, until the bell began to toll. Its weight tore at his shoulder, and the pain thrilled through him. He moaned and heard his own moaning coming from deep within his chest and throat as the bell rang out and the wind blasted the fire up in the framework of the roof. But the swinging bell began to lift him up and let him down in its own rhythm, its inertia taking over, and he was able to hold on and keep the toll steady, a flattened clanging in his ears now, through the wind and the fire.

In the nothingness of his blackout, something horrific had happened. It was all the worse for his having no consciousness of what it could have been. But now the church was burning, and now he did not have a sense of anything but that, least of all of saving himself. But he called out to God—God nameless and formless and enormous and terrible—from all the confusion and cacophony of his mind, like a child declaring himself. Understanding one thing only: that he would never leave off tolling the alarm. And someone would hear the bell and then see the fire, and then help would come. He could not undo whatever had been done, but he could die here now. He could die saving his church.

twenty-four

OF THE BURNING OF THE CHURCH OF OUR LADY OF FATIMA, THERE were many accounts. Furtado recorded his own version in his ledgers, obviously pieced together from a number of sources. He began this writing in the rehab facility at Calumet, where he worked on curing his addictions and on his physical healing. He would spend a total of seventeen weeks in Calumet before being given a place at Mount Perousia, during which time the fevered writing, the wild leaps and digressions, gave way to calmer, more measured tones.

On the night of the fire, before the last of three walls had collapsed in the blowing snow, camera crews from as far away as Boston had managed their way through the storm, all the way to the town, and set up their vigil beside their white-and-blue vans just outside the perimeter of the fire trucks, three of which had been called from up the Cape when the town's firemen had realized that the blaze was beyond their control, and that the rectory and even the neighboring houses might be threatened.

All was chaos. Black smoke, lit eerily by the fire department's hastily rigged floodlights, roiled off in a hard angle behind the wind, and great ragged sheets of flame blew up into the sky. Whenever one incendiary spot was suppressed, another would erupt, and the heavy streams of water blew up in steam and spray and made a kind of fog that rose and disappeared into the smoke and slanting snow. Cinders flew in the air with the driving blizzard and rained back on the neighborhood in gusts of fire and ash, so that the rectory roof had to be sprayed continually with water for its own safety. Men scrambled and stumbled and held their ground, thigh-deep among the hindering snowdrifts in the frozen dark, and the overdriven pumps and generators throbbed against the storm and the blaze. When the wind blew hard, the heat from the fire pressed on the faces of the onlookers, townspeople who had come out from the houses along the adjacent streets or from farther off in the town, word of mouth traveling—something huge and terrible was happening.

When dawn finally came, the rubble of the church still smoked and smoldered, and the rectory roof was sheeted with rime and ringed with the long daggers of icicles. The heavy snow had abated by then, but the wind still blew and small flurries fell sporadically. The sky was low and dismally gray. The town lay covered in blankets and drifts, white and deceptively peaceful. But Church Street and the municipal parking lot were still busy with the fire engines and trucks, and the news vans, and clusters of men and women coming as close as they could to inspect the destruction.

By late morning the rubble had ceased smoldering, and in some places water from the hoses had frozen into fantastic shapes, and many photographs were taken of the ruins. But even these images, and the accounts on TV or in the newspapers, did not tell the whole story, because the story was not ever a single story but many stories, and not all of them agreed.

The priest had put down his own narrative, as much as he remembered. He had kept to the bell rope, but he'd swooned at some point and remembered being pulled by his legs—it was the stabbing pain that had brought him around. He'd been hoisted over someone's shoulder and carried by several men out into the riot of snow and noise, but also out into the air, frigid but breathable, and he'd hacked and vomited and wept caustic tears and been laid someplace—the back of a rescue truck—and given oxygen to breathe. He understood that it had been Tommy who'd pulled him from the back of the church, from that corner under the belfry where no one might have thought to look, except that Tom had heard someone say that the bell had been ringing before the alarm had been called in. Minutes later—very few or very many, there was no agreement—the belfry had given out and the great bell had come crashing down through the burning timbers and embedded itself in the floor where Furtado had lain.

Tom had run back into the church repeatedly, salvaging whatever he could grab, even while the firemen had shouted and struggled with him to stay out of the building, which at any moment, they knew, could send a burning beam or a whole section of wall down upon him. But he'd soon quit from the smoke and shortness of breath, and after that he'd watched, slumped against the warm hood of one of the engines, as the east wall crumbled and fell under plumes of greasy smoke and gouts of water from the powerful hoses.

And the priest. It was impossible to say what he had done or not done. He searched himself in agony and could remember nothing about his climbing up into the attic of the church. That the fire started in the roof was clear from the beginning, and clear from the priest's own telling of what he knew of that night, but when asked to give his official statement on the matter, he remembered only sitting up in the rectory's study—he admitted that he had taken a great deal of medication and had been drinking heavily—and he repeated again and again that he did not remember even leaving off from his work at the desk. Only that he'd come to himself amid the fire and the smoke up under the church's rafters.

One story that gathered some momentum was that Father Furtado, knowing he would lose the parish, had sworn that no one else would have

it and had set the fire out of spite. But this tale was quickly refuted by many parishioners, who had never witnessed anything like malice or anger in their priest. In fact, Father Furtado could be seen as the hero in this matter—he'd rung the bell until he almost died, and no one needed to have known about his movements in the church attic; he was the one who'd come forth in honesty.

He told all. All that he could remember. Yet another version had him drunk and medicated out of his mind and crawling under that roof, for whatever reason, with a lit candle from the altar to find his way. This story seemed ready to take hold, especially since the priest had admitted to the medication and alcohol, but Tommy da Silva was the one who put a different slant on everything. It was Tom who came forward about the trouble-light.

He explained how he'd intended to get some decent lighting up in the attic but had had several jobs going at once, and so he'd used a standard trouble-light with a hundred-foot extension cord. But he took the heavy wire bulb protector and shield off the light socket so he could change out the regular hundred-watt bulb and screw in a large, high-wattage flood. He knew the trouble-light wasn't made for that; he did it only that one time. But the priest must have found it there and bumped the bulb against something up there and broken its glass, and the filament must have flashed or fallen into some of the squirrel tinder.

During one of Tom and Allie's visits to Calumet, the priest asked Tom directly about all this. He had to know.

"Tom," he asked, "was there ever a light? And did you do that to it?"

"Absolutely, Manny," Tom told him. "It was my mistake leaving it lay up there like that. You would never be in this mess. It's all on me." Allie stood at the foot of the bed with her arms crossed over her breasts and said nothing.

It was, finally, on no one. There was certainly no foul play. Nothing was found one way or another, and no one could blame Tom, for regardless of what he'd done to modify the light, he had not used it that night and had not intended for anyone else to, and the priest had no recollection of anything except his own inexplicable presence up in the rafters.

But then there was the Virgin.

The hospital was a peculiar time for Furtado—a peculiar time coursing from other peculiar times. He underwent three separate surgeries under general anesthesia, and he spent about fifteen days on the morphine pump, which he operated on demand by pressing a button on the top of a small cylinder held in his right hand, which produced deep, timeless, mercurial dreams. Except for some minor medications during his beginning rehab later on, this would be his last taste of opiates of any kind.

One knee had to be repaired, and two cervical vertebrae were fused to correct the chronic pain in his neck and shoulder. An initial procedure had introduced a chest tube through a small incision between his ribs to inflate his collapsed lung. The broken ribs had been strapped, and he was required to lie in traction and trusses. He was very groggy during these early days with the lung, but Father John Sweet was among the first to visit him. Sweet prayed that Manny would heal, and he told him that all would be well, all would be worked out. He also told him that he would see to things at the parish, and for him not to worry about procedural matters and daily business. "I will tend the lambs," Sweet said, his soft round eyes rolling. "I will feed the sheep."

When Mariah and Winslow came, they offered Furtado their impressions of the ruined church. "Gone, Manuel," said Winslow. "A part of one wall standing, and a big hole where the basement was. It's full of brick and fallen timber, charred wood, ashes."

"It's all iced over, too," said Mariah. "They're going to have to get some heavy equipment. They're going to have a long cleanup."

"The ice is something," said Winslow. "A cathedral of ice. Walls and towers of ice."

"Sweet's going there," Furtado said. His voice sounded dreamy and tired in his head. He was aware of a great deal of pain coming from several places, but the morphine made it all feel like distant pressure. Like something he was hearing about on the news, something alarming that didn't concern him much. "Is it done?"

Winslow didn't hesitate over his meaning. "Yes."

"It's the right time," he said.

"With Sweet and all?" Winslow asked.

"Yes. Especially."

"All right, then," she said. She folded her arms and nodded, and her eyes narrowed as she looked at him lying there in the hospital bed.

The next day, Mariah and Winslow came again to Calumet to visit Furtado, and they persuaded Tom and Allie to drive up and meet them there. The women had paid for two rooms at the Best Western out by the highway exit. That way, they all could stay overnight and spend time with Furtado on two successive days, especially since he was due to have the chest tube pulled the following morning, when the results of his MRIs would be discussed further.

They all took turns sitting with him. Sometimes Allie would talk to him, and sometimes she and Tom would just talk between them while the priest dozed. Mariah even read to him, though Furtado might have been asleep or unconscious part of the time. They ran little errands for him, fetching ice chips or juice boxes, bothering the nurses' aides to check the fluid in the chest tube or bring balm for his cracked lips. The four of them together were in the room with him until early evening, when he was given his sleeping pill.

When they all left the hospital, they ate at a Sizzler Steak House near the motel. They settled into Tom and Allie's room and rented a movie, but about halfway through, Winslow grew tired and went back to her room to bed, where Mariah joined her after the movie. All four drove to the hospital again at about eight in the morning. They met the surgeon on his rounds. He told them a few things about Manny's condition, and they stayed at the hospital for a few hours. Mariah and Winslow left for town just before lunchtime. Tom and Allie stayed until later in the afternoon. Thus, all of them missed the great commotion in town that had started shortly after sunrise. Although Father Furtado would not be able to gather the details of this until much later, he would eventually enter the day of its discovery in his ledger: the Feast of the Holy Martyrs Perpetua and Felicity.

It was early, about six thirty, when Maureen Avellar took her dog out for their morning walk. She had been thinking about the fire and the loss, and she'd gotten it into her head to walk up to the church. She later admitted she was thinking of sneaking under the yellow safety tape and taking one of the fire-scarred bricks for herself, something from the ruins of the old building that had meant so much to her—to all the Portuguese Catholics born in the town. She thought she might keep the brick someplace in her house as a memento. She knew that the town crews would be bringing in the bulldozers and starting demolition and cleanup when the weather eased.

The air was cold and clear, and the sun had been up for about half an hour. Stormy, Maureen's dog, was dragging along on the leash as Maureen came down the slight incline of Church Street, and as soon as she drew close enough to make out any detail in the wreckage, she noticed something was there, in the hollow remains of the church. What was odd about it, she said, was the glint of color among all the char and ash. It looked like a person for a second, and then she realized that it was not. She thought for a moment that it was a trick of the early, flat light on some twisted column of ice.

Susan Vieira, writing in the *Cape End Light*, would quote her: "Then I thought, *Oh my God, I'm having some kind of vision*. You know, like the *velhas* used to talk about when we were kids. Because by then I was close enough to see that it was Our Lady. Even Stormy started acting weird. I said to myself, *Oh, man, I'm not ready for this*. I called Joanna, you know, on the cell phone. I called her right away and said, 'Get over here, meet me at the church, just put on something quick and get over here.'"

Joanna Nunes, Maureen's sister-in-law, lived not far from the church. She came quickly in her van with her daughter, Mary, who was getting ready for a special early-morning band practice at the high school. Mary was sullen and sleepy-faced, but when she stepped out of the van and looked up at the church, she knew right away something big was going on. They put Stormy in the van, and together the three women walked carefully over the frozen, slippery ground, under the yellow tape, and up to the edge of the destruction.

The sun had risen a few more degrees, and the sky to the east was brightening, a few very high clouds glowing like ginger on their undersides. "The light was weird, eerie," young Mary Nunes would say. And there Our Lady of Fatima stood complete—glorious, beautiful, and erect, on a small pedestal of brick in an elevated section of the debris. She shone blue and white and gold surrounded by the hard field of cinder and ash, among the gray and cheerless arabesques of dappled ice.

The story made the news. It was called a mystery. A number of news writers from Away tried to make something of it, but the story didn't seem to carry far, and it didn't last long. It was, after all, only a statue, and clearly persons unknown had deposited it there. It was not as if the Virgin Herself had appeared to someone. The town, however, did not get over it quickly. Too many people remembered the original Virgin and its disappearance. Much of the talk centered on whether this could be the same statue or simply another, a duplicate. Yet someone had harbored this for how long? And now had chosen to place it there among the devastation. It reached back, somehow, into the town's own history, which always came forth in an assortment of versions, secrets revealing secrets, until no one could stand on definite ground.

Theories and suspicions multiplied by the day. Names were put forth, motives discussed. That other morning of so many years ago was recalled by some of the older men and women. But nothing would ever come of trying to piece the puzzle together. No one had seen anything, and no one was coming forth about it. The priest did not devote much more space in the ledgers to this than he did to the commotion back in the town, though he set down a few fragments of conversation. Of course, Tom and Allie, Mariah and Winslow did not get back to town until well after the Virgin had been discovered, so they had nothing to offer in the way of any clues as to what might have happened on that night they were all up in Calumet, tending to Father Manny. By the time either party returned, the site of the fire had already been thronged with spectators, people with cameras and video recorders, kids just crunching around on ice at the edge of the yellow tape, everyone come for a look at the beautiful Lady.

Tom and Allie went back to the hospital the following day and talked with Furtado, who was still not entirely present.

"You were so crazy about that statue, Manny. Are you going to tell us anything about this?" Allie asked.

"No," said Furtado.

"So you're telling me you don't have any idea about it," said Tom. His voice was flat. It was a tone that left things where they were. It was a tone that said he wouldn't speak about it again, if that was how it was going to be.

The priest's head was heavy, and his thoughts all wanted to roll away like a slow river. "My ideas," said the priest, "would be worthless."

When Mariah came to see him a few days later, she sat close to him and told him everything she knew. The firemen had let the statue sit in the ruins where the women had found it until close to nightfall of the first day, and then Tom had gotten some men from the cleanup committee to move Her over to the parish hall, where She was locked up for safekeeping. Tom had slept on a cot there through the first night. No one wanted anything to happen to Her. The parish was buzzing. It was something marvelous that almost countermanded the fire itself. It was to be a beginning.

"Perhaps it's merely something awful," said Furtado.

"No, Manny," Mariah said. She leaned down to him, and he could feel her breath and smell the coffee she had drunk. Her clothes were vaguely smoky. "You've rescued something. You saved something out of all of this. For yourself and for the town. For Sarafino, too. That's how I see it. Nothing was in vain. You boys took Her and kept Her—you were saving Her, in a way, and you didn't even know it. Consider: If She had stayed in the church the whole time, if you boys had never taken Her, she would have perished in that fire. It's perfect. Now. Now was the time She was waiting for. The parish needs Her now more than ever, and now they have Her. Now we can rally around Her. So there is a miracle after all. We will rebuild." Her cheeks glowed. She was pretty, he thought, as if he were seeing that quality of her, expressed in just that word, for the first time.

"You must stop talking like that," said the priest. He meant to chide her for this facile optimism, for this disingenuousness, but there was a wooziness in his voice. The words issued from him without any potency. He thought he was going to say more, about Sarafino's ruin, about the devastation of the church—and about how she was justifying herself and Winslow, too, by *not* bringing it up. But he clicked the button on the morphine pump once more and allowed his lassitude to wash over him, and he closed his eyes and nodded into the warm, protective silence.

And still, there was so much more. His own dark shadows, his father, his mother, the town, and his people in all those years before Mariah ever knew them—and could know now only in casual stories, abbreviated, never an experience. What could this woman possibly comprehend about his parish? But. But. She looked forward. She believed in a future. Yes, she looked ahead. That was something. She had flown airplanes. She'd fallen from the sky into the arms of a woman she adored. That seemed to count, too.

And clearly, it was no longer to be his parish. Surely Mariah must see that. Sweet, no matter what he was or did, would have something to build around. Sweet would remain as Fatima's fixer. Let Mariah be right, then. And let Furtado be finished.

Then the thinking went away, and in its place a cascade of images filled his head, something green, something yellow, reeds bobbing in the wind by a pond, a deep stone well at whose bottom lay a bright silver shape that he had never seen in the world before. Then, as in a dream, every disconnected piece and fragment seemed to make sense—the kind of sense, he knew, that did not exist except in that twilit world of depths and shades.

Sweet had come to his bedside again after the Virgin had been discovered. He was manic, ecstatic, furious, jubilant all at once. "What a place, Manny. What a town. Think of it. Where else could such a thing have happened? It will be our lynchpin, you know. I have talked to everyone. Glorious, glorious. Such a thing! Somewhere in the town is the person who did this. Imagine it. Imagine that soul. A parish with that profound soul hidden in it. The depth! The richness! The darkness! It will be the making of something! Everyone is passionate about it. It was there all the time. Somewhere. Imagine."

Sweet was frightening, dressed now in a cassock, black, flapping like a crow, some wild thing of the imagination, a lunatic, a general. Of course, he was deep in his own triumphs. He came back several times as Furtado healed. He was looking for information. Sweet was gripped now, too, by the statue, because for him it seemed a link to the past of the town, and he wanted to penetrate that. A great opportunity, too, to be at the forefront of something—the rebuilding, the renewal.

But finally Furtado sent him away. He told his doctor and his counselor that Sweet disturbed him and would set him backwards. They agreed, and Furtado no longer saw the other priest. He was glad to be rid of him, but he admired something about Sweet. It was the dogged and relentless way in which he had pursued his ambitions—such small ambitions, after all: merely a parish of his own. Of course, he had been on watch for one for a long time. Even by his own admission, Sweet could not have continued being a fixer. It would have hollowed him out. It would have killed him. Furtado had misjudged him. He'd thought him either a bumpkin or a madman, certainly dangerous, but he had miscalculated his tenacity, his intelligence. He was not sure when Sweet had decided that Furtado's was the parish he would take. Perhaps from the beginning, when he'd begun to fall in love with it. Or perhaps at some point when he'd seen that Manny was incorrigible, never sober, full of duplicity.

Furtado thought of the specific moments when he could have crossed over and given Sweet what he needed, and how he'd restrained himself. Maybe there was contempt for him. Something. He thought back to their walk to the beach, Sweet buckling along on his bad foot and offering a gambit, which Furtado had refused. Was that the moment? The moment the church was set, inevitably, to burning? He recalled the story of Paris, first gazing upon Helen, and how the topless towers of Troy shuddered for the brief second on their foundations. It didn't matter. Sweet fixed things. Let him succeed, then. Let him fix everything for Rego and Mayhew. Let him undo the disasters. Let him raise the parish and renew the town. He had Mariah and Tom to help him. He had the Virgin. *Pace*.

There was one other thing for Furtado to do now before he changed his mind about it. He discussed it again with his doctors and his rehabilitation counselors, and it was set into motion, and on a frosty afternoon a shrunken and timidly bent Idalina Horta stepped into his room. She appeared gray and blurry to him. She and Louis were living in Taunton, Massachusetts, with one of their daughters. It was not a long drive to Calumet. Furtado invited her to sit, but she would not. She could not stay long, she said. Her daughter was waiting.

"Do you forgive me, Manny?" she asked.

"I do," he said. That was as much as he remembered of her visit, or at least as much as he put down in writing. But he reflected later. Though his powers of observation were dimmed at that time, he saw it in her face and in the way she turned and withdrew from him: She perceived this forgiveness as a simple victory, a little battle (or perhaps an enormous one in her head—who could tell?) that she had won for herself. A scrap of something she had now recovered. What other struggles raged there? He was too weary to be concerned. Let it go, then. *Pace. Pace.*

Coming off the alcohol and pain pills after the surgery was not so difficult for Furtado. He never admitted, at least not to himself, that he had been truly dependent, and saw only preference where others saw addiction. And since nothing harmful was available in the antiseptic environment of Calumet's rehabilitation facility, there was no temptation. There, he strengthened the repairs to his body with daily exercises and attentive manipulations by young physical therapists who pulled, stretched, kneaded, heated, and chilled his mending parts.

It was during this time, too, that he learned that the persistent tinnitus in his head was the ototoxic effect of the opiates, and that they had been slowly destroying his inner ears. Once he was off the pills, the whistles, beeps, hums, clicks, and tones simply and gradually vanished. He eventually found the long sessions of physical therapy and group discussions tedious and boring, however, and when Mount Perousia finally had an opening for him, he was more than ready to go. It was the best outcome. It was also the only option the diocese presented him with.

The priest continued his ledgers in the quiet and available solitude of the Mount. His little cottage there was tightly built and snug. It was simple within, and Furtado kept it neat. Against one wall was his single bed, a plain wooden crucifix at its head. The other walls were white and unadorned, except for a framed and glassed print of one of Giotto's Madonnas, the Holy Mother's face grim and resolved, and the infant Jesus looking like a wizened, shrunken old man. Adjacent to the print, two easy chairs faced a broad window that looked out upon the rolling pastureland. There was a small table between them, and the chairs were angled slightly to ease conversation with a visitor.

There was not a specific rule about visiting one another's cottages, though the custom of solitude after the evening meal was generally observed by all the men. Often Brother Guillermo would come during the afternoon and sit in the window and talk long and affably with Father Furtado. Brother Guillermo was a large man, balding in middle age, with a fringe of heavy black hair, like a tonsure, around his shiny head. He walked slowly, bearishly, and smiled quickly, a heavy-lipped and simple smile that never reached his eyes, which were deep-set, brown, and sad, and pleasing to look at. He seemed always filled with energy and goodwill. He sang opera and baked breads and pies. He could sing for hours, completely by heart. Father Robert might have been the administrative head of the community, but Brother Guillermo was the one who kept things going from day to day. He had grown up in San Diego. His father's parents had come from Veracruz, Mexico, and his father had worked in the San Diego tuna fleet back in its heyday in the postwar years.

The two men's obvious connections were made quickly. Furtado thought at first that Brother Guillermo was fulfilling some sort of professional duty by spending time with him, but he became disabused of that idea after a few weeks. The two of them enjoyed one another, and Furtado reflected on his loneliness over the years. He could not remember any time as an adult when he had ever had so much of a friendship as this. Sometimes the two of them would take over the kitchen and bake great batches of bread, and Furtado would listen to Brother Guillermo sing from Verde or even Mozart. He would explain the songs and the stories to Furtado as they poured flour and kneaded the great bowls of dough on the long, clean stainless-steel counters.

It was another winter now. Furtado had been clean and sober for twelve months, the last eight of them here at Mount Perousia. The hills were cold in a way his old town never became. Here there was no sea, only the rolling land with its stands of hardwood and pine and its broad outcroppings of gray primordial rock, and when the gelid air drove down from the wilds of Canada and over the northern outlands of New York and Vermont and on down among Perousia's ancient roads and stone walls, the cold settled in as if by gravity and thereafter seemed to rise from the land itself. The light was different, too, flat and matter-of-fact. There was nothing here like that phantasmagorical shimmer off the North Atlantic, off the bare silica dunes.

Mount Perousia had changed in some ways in the years since Furtado's last time there. The facility was larger now. Six new cottages had been added—squat, neat studios, white and green, edging upon some pastureland. The main house had been enlarged at the back, creating a bigger refectory area, a library/sitting room, and four new resident rooms. There'd been sixteen guests when Furtado was last here. Now, counting himself, there were twenty-six. Father Robert still presided, a bit grayer, his glasses thicker and heavier on his square face, but he looked lean yet, and agile. He was perhaps sixty. There had been six brothers here before, and even with the new lodgings, there were still only six now, though none of them from Furtado's first stay. Sometimes two or three brothers or another priest would drive up from Amherst for short stays, or for the day, depending on the activities.

Mount Perousia was about order and routine and contemplation, but it was not monastic. The men celebrated the Eucharist and observed liturgical hours, but it was not a place of penance, nor of works. It was, as its charter made clear, a place for love and healing, and, if healing were very difficult—even impossible—a place for the shattered to live in shelter and compassion. Everyone worked at small or large jobs that rotated and were selected by preference and ability, but the real work of maintenance was planned and supervised and carried out mostly by the brothers.

There were no priests here with serious sexual problems, nothing of the order of disturbances that had captured so much attention in recent years and done so much harm to the Church—and, in their indirect way, caused at least some of Furtado's complications. Such men were cared for and supervised very closely in a facility in another part of the state. Mount Perousia served a different kind of man. Several of the priests in residence were very old. Most had suffered from depression or alcoholism. Some had lost their vocation and come to Perousia to search for it again. The brothers of Saint Matthew of the Mount saw such despair not as a sin but as a kind of suffering, and the order recognized such suffering as a holy state and therefore redemptive.

The physical beauty of the place itself was a tonic. The parcel of land was large enough to have its own private gravel road winding into it, tucked away from the leaf-peeper hotels and bed-and-breakfasts that had proliferated in other parts of the countryside. At Perousia there was nothing but the rolling land, its orchards and stands of woods, its ancient pastures and stone walls. One felt cared for here. There was an inherent goodness in the place. Nurses and two physicians visited regularly, and one of the brothers, Brother Douglas, was himself a registered nurse-practitioner. At Mount Perousia the group discussions did not seem like counseling, and the meetings with sponsors—always brothers—did not seem like treatment or work, as they had back in Calumet. Prayer and meditation were central, but so was taking advantage of the gift of the land. There was always time to walk the fields and paths. And there was a brilliant, deep pond about a mile and a half into the property, wooded and sheltered, where ducks and Canada geese came to light, and herons lived along with bass and pickerel and frogs and turtles. In summer it was girded with white lilies and cradled in dense green. In winter it became a silent, waxy eye, surrounded by purple brush and the white-skinned trunks of birches.

Around the compound itself, there were renowned working parties, organized by Brother Guillermo, in which something might be painted or some brush might be cleared or some work might be done on a building. It was obvious to everyone that such tasks could be completed far more effectively if they were done by the brothers themselves, but they always turned into something more than work, the priests and brothers singing sometimes, and there was always laughter. Furtado was sure that many—even all—of the others had a similar experience to his own. Laughing. Laughing from deep in the belly sometimes, and the surprise of it, the surprise at how unfamiliar such a thing had become.

The life here, the life of the Mount, was a puzzle to him at first. Or rather, as he expressed it, his own feelings about that world puzzled him. His sense of the place was completely different than it had been on his first furlough here. Of course, his circumstances then had not been so dire. But now the place absorbed him, and as it did, he took it into himself as well. It was easy being here. His old world, the world of the town and the parish, he could not place in any of the familiar ways of talking about such things. Certainly, none of that was in front of him anymore. Yet neither was it behind him.

The best he could do was to lay it off at some remove, perhaps like a once-read book, covers closed but its insides intimately known, once lived but no longer lived. What he saw when he looked at it was a shape, sometimes a color, and that was all. He felt little inclination to open all that up again. But some news came out to him. Less and less now, for he never returned comments on anything specific to the church or to the life of the town as he'd once discerned it, and that seemed to discourage further dispatches.Allie wrote to him about once a month, telling him of the passing of her days, the cats, work at the bakery. Tom had sailed the summer on a whale hugger and was doing odd jobs now until the season came around again. He still helped with the church grounds. He never missed a day or a candle, as Allie put it, referring to his devotions, held now in the converted parish hall until the new church could ever be built. He would never quit it, she said—he was doing it for Frankie. They were still trying to figure a way to buy a boat of their own, to sail in the whale-watching or harbor-cruise trade. They kept on at their lives.

Mariah sent him cards about as frequently as Allie sent her letters. Big greeting cards with short messages scrawled in them, always bright and cheerful. Sometimes Winslow would sign underneath Mariah's hand in heavy blocky letters, the same way she signed her art pieces.

Furtado could not tell if the parish would pull itself together or if the town would survive with some of its essence intact. It was not up to him, at any rate. Sweet was pastor there now, and the rebuilding had begun. Mass was held in the parish hall. The statue was there, to the right of the altar. Each week a special collection was held in Her name, and Sweet had brought in an archdiocese consultant to map out the fundraising for the rebuilding, which would be an enormous project. Architects were already meeting, and the parish council was involved in the planning. Mariah Grey worked closely with them all. Allie let him know that people were not taking to the new priest quickly. Furtado wished them well, but none of that had an effect on him.

But he missed the sea sometimes. He missed something else, too, but if it was the town, it was a town that no longer claimed a place in this world. He thought about his father sometimes, and his mother, and the boat, and Sarafino, but all as if from a great distance, with a detachment that was itself a kind of welcome stillness of the heart.

He regarded such thinking as a skill. He practiced it. There were always people to help with such efforts at the Mount, this giving up of melancholy and regret. He settled into peace. Peace. This was what peace was finally like. This *was* peace, the thing itself. The quality, both inside him now and around him—like the changing light or the air. It didn't matter that his unwillingness to accede to the Church's orthodoxy had not changed; God was someplace—or everywhere. Mount Perousia made it easy to look for Him, if one needed to, and Furtado did. He still looked. It was what he had traded his life for. No one here tried to pull him back into those specific dogmas that he found so impossible to embrace. And he was young! Younger than ever, it seemed, now that he was knitted and fused and toned and limbered. And clearheaded! One could go on forever like this, swaddled like this, until the end of days.

Then came a particular day in February, the Feast of Saint Polycarp. There would be nothing unusual about such a day, though Furtado's ledgers would show that this saint's day came exactly three days after the feast day of Jacinta and Francisco Marto. The children received their own feast day because they were designated as *blessed* by the Church, not yet saints, perhaps never to be, but possibly someday, depending, really, on the politics at the Vatican and perhaps in Portugal. Jacinta and Francisco did not have time to grow and had no chance to contemplate the truth or untruth of their visions at Fatima.

The priest merely noted this in his ledger; he ascribed no significance to it. On Polycarp, he reflected briefly. He had been the Bishop of Smyrna and vastly influential in shaping the primitive Church in the second century. He was an outspoken apologist for Christianity during one of the major persecutions, and as these stories so often ran, he had to be silenced by the authorities of the empire, for the new religion was destroying the social order. The old man, at eighty-three years, was taken to the amphitheater by a squad of Roman soldiers, who set him afire. But he did not burn. His body would not burn in those Roman flames. And so the centurion in charge stabbed him to death with his dagger. Likely, Furtado speculated, the centurion had been moved by the old man's unspeakable agony as the fire began to consume him, and had dispatched him out of a soldier's mercy.

The priest made this entry in his ledger on the morning of that day, and he copied out a fragment of one of Polycarp's letters from a book on his life, one of the stack of books he had taken to his cottage from the main reading room: *Firm in the faith of the brotherhood, loving each other, united in truth . . .* He contemplated the effects of brotherhood at the Mount and wrote a few sentences more, emphasizing how he had missed so much of this in his earlier stay there, something he attributed to his own vanity, which he felt he had finally begun to put aside. He left off writing here just after dawn and before he left the cottage for morning prayer in the barn chapel. He would write one more entry later, and then he would put the ledgers aside and give up these daily exercises entirely.

FURTADO ATTENDED MORNING PRAYER AND BROKE FAST IN THE refectory at one of the long and heavy oaken tables. Each table held no more than six men, for the purpose of promoting fellowship at the meals. He and three other priests sat with Brother Guillermo and one of Brother Guillermo's lieutenants, Brother Alphonse, a young and bright-eyed man from Bronx, New York, who, although slight in build, always sounded tough and streetwise simply because of his accent. Brother Alphonse was skilled at carpentry and was usually seen around the compound wearing heavy workman's boots and a wide leather belt that drooped on one side from the weight of the many tools holstered there. Whenever even the smallest thing went right, a miter-joint fitting, or a hinge repaired, he would exclaim, "Praise God!"

That morning, he and Brother Guillermo talked about a project they were thinking of doing in a few months, when spring came. "We'll need all your help, you know," Brother Guillermo said, looking down the table. Furtado and the other priests nodded. Brother Guillermo and Brother

Alphonse wanted to build a kind of screened-in porch, a stand-alone meditation room, really, out by the pond. In winter there would be a small woodstove, and the screens would be replaced with long windows. In summer the screening would allow sitting in the evenings and nights, keeping the clouds of gnats and mosquitoes away. It would be a place of silence and observation. "I'm drawing it now," Brother Alphonse said. "It will be almost invisible, camouflaged. It will tuck right in. I have almost everything I need for it in the barn already."

"And there just might be some donations," said Brother Guillermo.

"Praise God," said Brother Alphonse.

Furtado pictured something like a duck blind. He thought of the ponds back in his town. He thought of his camp. He thought of camouflage. He thought of Sarafino's quiet grave.

The sun that morning had risen above the eastern hills and almost immediately vanished behind a light layer of clouds. To the north, heavier weather was darkening the sky with bands of gray, and the front showed as a clear line rising slowly as it advanced southward. Snow was coming again. By late morning, a kind of gauzy mist hung over everything and the temperature rose into the higher twenties. By noon the sky was dropping long feathers of snow. Furtado felt at ease with himself and with the change in the weather. After midday prayer he walked back to his cottage and did some perfunctory cleaning. There was never much to do, given the simplicity of the space, but he sponged down the shower and swept and emptied his wastebasket into a paper sack that he would carry up to one of the Dumpsters later. He read for a while, and when Brother Guillermo came tapping at his door, he opened to see that two or three inches of new, clean snow had already accumulated over the worn and crusted cover from previous storms.

Brother Guillermo came in, removed his rubber boots with the leather uppers, and sat in one of the chairs in the window while Furtado stood at the microwave, making tea and heating the apple turnovers that Brother Guillermo had made the day before.

Furtado mentioned the book he had been reading. Brother Guillermo was not much of a reader, and he liked Furtado to give him digests of all the books he read. He had been rummaging through *The Nicomachean Ethics*. He told Brother Guillermo about Aristotle's idea of the three-part soul, and how a test of true virtue, virtue completely divorced from any ideas of God, could be derived from it. "Maybe, you see, it's better that way. Then God can be God. Then we can have a clearer picture of Him without getting Him all confused with our problems and whether we're good or not."

Brother Guillermo listened and nodded. "As long as God loves me, it doesn't much matter. God knows we can't be virtuous." They both laughed. They sipped tea and watched the snow coming down in the pasture and ate the warm apple turnovers. Brother Guillermo began talking about apples, about what was left on the Perousia's land. Most of the trees had been untended for years, but there was still something of a harvest among the Astrakhan apple orchard, and here and there were remnants of other orchards or single trees that had grown from seeds scattered by birds or animals, what Brother Guillermo called volunteers.

Most commercial growers now produced only the most popular varieties: the Delicious, the McIntosh, the Pippin, and so forth. But at Mount Perousia, one could find red Astrakhans and Bethels and Tobias Blacks, varieties inching toward extinction. Not all the apples were usable. Some trees gave forth only crabbed, hard fruit. But others, particularly the ones Brother Guillermo and Brother Lawrence had begun tending, produced robust apples, and the picking parties had gone well this year; there were apples in bins in the kitchen and the barn.

Sometimes, while walking away from the paths or following one or another of the old stone walls, Furtado would come across some of the older trees, singly or in little groves, undergrown with scrub oak and poplar.

There were also the remains of a cider orchard, but it was far from the domiciles and almost subsumed in the forest, and the brothers had made no attempt to rehabilitate it. When the wild apples fell to the ground, the coyotes ate them, coming out from the deeper woods and the farther hills. As the weather grew colder, they ventured up into the Astrakhan trees and foraged for falls, the ones the brothers had left behind because they were too damaged to be used, and along with the splayed paw tracks in the old snow, they would see the coyote scats, thin and hard and lumped with appleseed.

Furtado had for some weeks been quietly walking out to the woods, to the edge of one of the farther ruined orchards, and dropping kitchen scraps over the snow for the coyotes. He would see their tracks in the snow and sometimes their scats, and once or twice caught glimpses of the animals themselves, single or in pairs, distant and wary. This was what he thought of now when Brother Guillermo was talking, and after his friend left the cottage, the priest changed into a pair of heavy corduroy pants and a turtleneck sweater and pulled on a pair of long, ribbed socks. He put on his high-top work boots and tucked the pants into the elastic of his nylon gaiters. He dressed in his down-filled parka and pulled his watch cap over his ears, took up his gloves, and set out for the kitchen.

The snow on the path had been trod on slightly, but in places it already reached to the tops of Furtado's gaiters. It was a heavy but powdery snow, and the big flakes were falling harder now and beginning to whirl in the slight wind that rose and fell across the compound. The buildings seemed to shrink and recede into the whiteness. He met no one on the path. There was no one in the kitchen, either, and he let himself in through the side door, pulled the yellow plastic swill bucket out from under the sink, and filled it more than halfway with peelings and trimmings, some heels of bread, and other scraps. He took the bucket by its handle and let himself out again. There was a clock on the wall of the kitchen. It was a white disc the size of a hubcap, with black hands and a black border around its edge—the kind of clock seen everywhere in public buildings. In the ledger, late that night, he would write that he could not remember the exact time, but he believed it was before three. Perhaps a quarter to.

He walked into the falling snow now, the wind, still soft, angling the thickening flakes down upon him. He still favored his left leg somewhat—it had been damaged more and hadn't healed as neatly as the other. He felt no discomfort. The snow was lush and quiet. He headed up a footpath that took him along the edge of one of the pastures, and then he followed the line of a stone wall in the direction of the old orchard—Bethels once, he thought Brother Guillermo had said—although the trees were in a wild state and no one did anything with them. There were bare, thin-trunked oaks all around, with lichen on their bark and snow cradling in the elbows and along the tops of their limbs. The snow narrowed and shortened his vision, but the woods were silent and beautiful with it.

He walked through the twisted old trees and trash growth of the orchard to its farther edge, where he saw one of the brothers—or perhaps a fellow priest—off at the very boundary of Furtado's sight, emerging from the dark trees beyond and walking slowly up the shallow rise toward him. Furtado stopped. The figure was small. He couldn't register who it might be. Then behind the man a coyote loped, crossing behind him, low and shadowy in the white scrim of the snow. Furtado watched the man come forward. Another coyote scuttled out of the tree line, and then another, and then the man stopped and looked around at the trees and the snow-covered brush. He stood there a few seconds, as if waiting, and then turned and walked toward Furtado again.

It was then Furtado saw that this was not a priest or a brother, but a young boy, and that there were now two more coyotes shadowing this figure, veiled by the falling snow but becoming distinct. Furtado, holding the bucket of scraps, took a few more steps. The powdery snow swirled away from his knees as he pushed ahead. When the two were no more than ten feet apart, he saw through the snowfall that the boy was in fact a young girl.

She was dressed in a long woolen skirt and a Levi's barn coat. Beneath that she had on a red hooded fleece sweatshirt, the hood sticking up through the collar of the jacket, covering her head. She kept her hands in the jacket pockets. Furtado set down the yellow bucket. It pressed itself lightly into the snow. The girl walked up to him and gave her head a quick shake, sending snow flying from the hood. Her skin flashed from the depths of the cloth. Her cheeks were touched ruddy with the weather, but beneath that flush they shone dark, milk tapped with coffee. Strands of her hair had blown loose from the edges of the hood, long and deeply black.

"Hello," she said. "You live off that way, with all the men. I came from the other side, beyond all those old orchards. Across the creek." She turned her head and shoulders, a gesture, the slightest twist, and when she did the coyotes came slinking out of the falling snow and stood around her and Furtado. There were eight, maybe ten, of them. They looked like wolves with their muzzles and fur whitened in the snow, and their eyes were dark and yellow, glinting and moving restlessly, but the animals were small—not wolves, certainly coyotes—and Furtado watched them. He took them in as they came about and circled, and the girl looked at them and then at the priest and said, "They won't bother you."

The girl made a small O with her lips and blew a puff of steamy breath into the snow, as though she were shooting at the snowflakes. "It always thrills me," she said. "The snow."

The priest looked at her small figure and at the track she had left, her deep footprints addled and crossed by the animals' tracks. The hem of her heavy skirt was rimed white where it had been trailing in the snow.

"You aren't wearing any shoes," he said.

The girl looked down at her bare feet, sunk in the soft snow. She shuffled them a little. "The cold comes right up through me," she said.

The priest looked past her again. Behind her. "You don't live around here. There are no houses over there."

"No, there aren't, really."

"You are not real," said the priest.

She reached down and picked up a handful of snow and tossed it at him. It fell over his face, and she laughed. He tried to lift his hands to brush the snow away, but he found he could not move them.

"Here," she said. She stepped to him and reached out and grazed his skin with her fingers, brushing some of the snow from him.

"Something is happening to me," he said. "My heart. Or my brain."

"I don't think so," the girl said, backing away from him.

"I'm not going to go through this," the priest said. "I'm a reasonable man."

The girl's face grew serious. Her eyes darkened. He would remember them as bright, black, profoundly beautiful. "Would you like to lie down in the snow now?"

"Lie down? No," said the priest. "I don't want to lie down."

"Can you see how comfortable it would be? Soft and cold. It would numb you. You would just go to sleep forever. Very peaceful. And the snow would cover you like a quilt." One of the coyotes came forward, shaking snow from its head. Its coat was flecked with white and grizzled. It circled and stood by the girl. She looked down at it. "My friends here wouldn't disturb you. They are dear to me, and they would never do anything I didn't want them to."

"No," said Furtado. "I don't want that."

"All right, then," she said. She lifted one foot up from the snow and then the other. They were delicate, narrow feet. "That just feels amazing," she said. "I love this world, don't you?" She looked at him. "Are you cold? Are you shivering? Your parka is very heavy."

"I don't think I can move," the priest said.

"I know. That happens sometimes. Sarafino was like that."

"I buried him," said the priest.

"Yes," she said. "I always liked him. You took care of him. You all did."

"I've walked out too far," the priest said. "I should not have come out here."

"But the animals want their food," said the girl. "It's difficult in winter, when all the fallen apples are gone. When all the squirrels and rabbits are under the snow."

"I don't care for any of this," the priest said. He tried to lift his arms again, but they did not respond.

Her eyes flashed, and his gaze was drawn to her face, her cheekbones, her skin. Young and smooth. "I was twelve when they came to me, Manny. Think about that." She traced a little semicircle with her toes, which were red and glistened where the snow had melted on them from the heat of her body. "I was spinning wool. Look," she said. She patted the heavy wool of her skirt against her thigh. "Angels came. I was sixteen when I first gave birth. I agreed. They put it to me as a question, but that was ridiculous. What was I supposed to do? Thy will be done—that's what I said. I was supposed to be a detail, you know, something to tidy up loose ends. I was a little girl in a story, that's all. They didn't reckon well.

"Now," she said, "now I'm the Queen of Heaven. Now I'm the Mother of God. Now do you think anyone can displace my own will with theirs? Do you think anyone can gainsay me? Do you think I can ever be made to go away?"

"Where is God?" asked Furtado. It took a great effort to speak now. He was pushing the words through stone. "You are not God."

"Be very glad I'm not," said the girl. Snow had gathered on the shoulders of her coat, like epaulets, and she brushed it off and shook her head and brushed the top of her hood. The snow kept falling, thick and soft, and the breeze, when it lifted the flakes aslant from time to time, made no sound in the bare tree limbs.

"Let me tell you," said the priest again, with considerable effort, "I don't believe in you. You look like some kid I'd see wandering around in a mall, listening to her headphones. This is some sort of hallucination. You have something to do with the chemicals of my brain. Something with neurons. And you are all wrong. Where is your crown? Your angels?"

The coyotes were growing restless, and the girl glanced at them and smiled. "These neurons, these chemicals in your head, they are very convenient. They are wonderfully efficient. Did you make them? Maybe you made them when you made all this." She swept her hand in a gesture that indicated the orchard, the hills rolling away out of sight.

"I'll make that offer again, Manny. Would you like to lie down in the snow? I would lie next to you and hold you for a while. Your death would be very peaceful and sweet."

"No. I am prospering here. My head is clear. You have no right to do this. I have come to myself finally. This place is what I have always needed."

"It's lovely here," she said. "But you won't stay. You are not going to bake bread and talk about apples for the rest of your life, Manny."

"What, then?"

"I'm interested to see what. You just never know. You could still just lie down if you'd rather."

"No," said Furtado. "This is not right. I'm doing this to myself somehow. I'm doing this to ravage my own peace. Why now? I'm beyond hope."

"Maybe you are finally raising your wager about what you believe and what you don't believe. Now that *I'm* here everything counts, one way or another."

"No," said the priest. "Right there. You just as good as admitted I'm talking to myself. This isn't ever going to work. I've read books. I've studied. I understand this sort of thing."

"You people and all your words," said the girl, shaking her head. "What a noise you make. Crying for truth, begging for mercy, trying to get clear of your little brains. Well, I don't blame you. But God lives beyond those words." She paused and shuddered. Her breath trailed white in the cold air. "*Way* beyond. What do *you* think is going to happen now, after this hallucination, as you like to call it?"

She waited, but when he did not answer, she said, "You know, I really like that artist—the one with the sandpaper and her iron chisels. What patience! She did a lovely job bringing my image back to life: the crown and the robes and all that. That woman doesn't know it yet, but she's in love with me. Like you are. Like Sarafino."

"If you are so real, tell me this much—tell me something I don't know. Did I burn the church?"

"I wonder."

"If you were real, you'd know," Furtado said.

"*You're* real, and *you* don't know." She smiled, pleased with herself.

"You are *not* real."

The girl wrapped her arms around herself and gave a bright laugh. It was like a small bell ringing in the orchard. "You're funny," she said. "All right, my friend, we both have things to do. It's cold, and you shouldn't be standing around out here. Do you remember the story of the man I kissed on the mouth, and he was struck dumb?"

"A myth."

"Oh, yes. Another story." She took a step toward him. Snow blew dizzily in the space between them. He would have stepped back from her, but his legs only trembled and did not move. The coyotes all snapped to their feet and swarmed nervously around her. Some of them sniffed the air.

Some of them shook the snow from their heads and backs and made small noises in the wells of their throats. The girl's face was alight with a smile. She took another step toward him, and he could feel the heat from her. She put her hand out and laid it on his cheek. Her palm was creamy and soft against his skin. Then she pulled her hand back and struck him. A slap. It sounded like a rifle shot, sharp yet flat and muffled in the flocked grove. The force of it would have knocked him over if he had not been frozen in his tracks.

"I'm going to go now," the girl said. "You go, too. Go back to your little house by the pasture and warm yourself."

"I understand the mind," he said, "how it can play tricks." But he stared at her and tried to memorize her. The girlish beauty. The eyes. The rough wool skirt. The way it fell over her small hips and legs. The dark brass buttons on the coat, and the red fleece of the sweatshirt hood. His face stung.

"Go back. Nothing will be the same now. You can trust me on that."

"This isn't right," he said.

"Go," she said, and gave another laugh and kicked snow at him with her bare foot.

With that, he found that he could move again. He looked at the yellow bucket sitting in the snow, beginning to fill with it, but he turned without picking it up and began walking back toward the ruined stone wall, which he could follow back to the paths that would lead to the cottage. He turned once after he had walked a few paces, and he saw the girl and her animals walking from the grove, away from him, off into the thickening snow and the dark woods that lay beyond.

When he reached the cottage, he removed his shoes, shook the snow from his clothes, and hung up his outergarments. Then he went directly to the bathroom and looked into the mirror on the medicine cabinet. On his left cheek was the print of the girl's hand, almost as if it had been traced there, a deep red, whitening at the edges. Dreams could be this sharp and clear. He touched it. It still stung. He went to the microwave and heated some water, and while it hummed he set a towel down on the linoleum inside the cottage door to take up the melting snow from his boots and parka. As the tea steeped, he scribbled hasty notes onto the little pad he kept by the refrigerator, then stood by the heat register and drank and warmed himself. When he finished, he checked his image in the mirror again. The mark of her hand was fading.

He dressed again swiftly, putting on dry pants and pulling his gaiters over his boots. He took the notepad and a pencil and put a small flashlight in his pocket and set out for the far orchard. There was perhaps an hour of daylight left. He walked as quickly as he could, sloughing his gaitered legs through the powdery snow, taking the path, shading the wall. The snow was falling steadily. When the wind blew, the big flakes danced and rose and fell crazily. He found his own tracks, half filled already with the new snow, and he followed them. He pushed himself along. He hurried.

He traced his way back to the orchard, to the grove of old, twisted trees, and he walked to the yellow bucket where he had left it, for he had left it purposely to mark the exact spot where he had spoken with the girl. He approached slowly and made himself observe everything. He noted the trees, the snow in them, the way there was still some light in the sky behind the snowfall, a gray like galvanized tin. He listened to the silence of the orchard.

His footprints were there by the bucket. The scraps in the bucket had not been touched, and it was nearly filled with new snow. So were his tracks. Hers and the animals' were there, too. And in that place where they had stood together when they spoke and she struck him, there were two sets of footprints, deep but filling in as the snow fell, their contours softening.

He stood and looked out over the small incline where she had walked, and he saw the tracks of her departure, muted but visible yet, both the girl's and the beasts'. They trailed out over the snowfield, beyond his sight and into the far trees, and even as he stared he could see them effacing slowly, so slowly that there was a kind of rapture to it. The cold meant nothing to him now, or perhaps he simply did not feel it. The wind began to quicken then, and the snow drifted and swept and gathered on his shoulders. His cheek stung and his eyes watered in the wind, and the tears blew back along his face. The night itself seemed to seep from the trees and reach out like a soft fog, the snowy twilight ever deepening.

There was no single moment when he could say her tracks had vanished—only that they filled slowly and then brimmed, becoming nothing but the slightest depressions in the snow, and then were gone to the eye altogether. And even then he didn't move. He stood until the night rose like a bar of iron, full and black, and even the closest trees became shadows, and then those shadows themselves dissolved into the greater blackness and there was only the sighing of the wind and the sound of his own blood pulsing in his ears, and under that, the soft *tick*, *tick* of the heavy snowflakes lighting upon him.

credits

Cover painting "The Catholic Church at Provincetown" by Nancy Maybin Ferguson, from the private collection of Reed Boland (photographed by James Zimmerman).

Photo of author courtesy of David A. Lipton.

about the author

Frank X. Gaspar was born and raised in the Portuguese-American community in Provincetown, Massachusetts. A graduate of the Writing Program at the University of California, Irvine, he has won numerous awards for his work, including the Morse Poetry Prize, the Anhinga Poetry Prize, the Brittingham prize in poetry, and a National Endowment Fellowship in Literature. His novel *Leaving Pico* received a Barnes & Noble Discover Award and a California Book Award for first fiction. He currently lives in California with his wife and son.